Ebonwilde

Ebonwilde

CRYSTAL SMITH

CLARION BOOKS

An Imprint of HarperCollins*Publishers*

ISBN 978-1-32-849632-4

Map art by Francesca Baerald
Typography by Cat San Juan

22 23 24 25 26 LSB 5 4 3 2 1

First Edition

To my parents,
John and Lillian Campbell,
for letting me read past midnight

13 YEARS AGO

Recite your virtues.

It was the last thing his stepmother told him before she and her red sleigh disappeared into the snowy distance. "Recite your virtues," she said. "It'll be over soon enough."

Dominic did as he was told, beginning the familiar litany as the last echoes of her sleigh bells tinkled eerily across the cold expanse. He'd been forced to memorize them as penance for being caught with a deck of playing cards when he was nine; his father made him stand on a small chair with no food or water until he could recite them all without pause or mistake. It had taken two full days.

"Humility," he intoned, taking one last look at the northern skyline before turning to face south. "Freedom from pride and arrogance."

The bleak Ebonwilde ahead of him, he lifted his lantern and moved one foot forward in the snow. "Abnegation," he said. "Surrender of worldly wants." Another step.

The air had been still the entire ride from Fort Castillion to the drop-off point, where silver shoots of frostlace flower were growing straight out of the snow, unfurling their pale, fringed petals toward the frigid sky. Frostlace only bloomed at Midwinter, on the longest, coldest night of the year. By dawn, they'd be gone . . . but then, so would he.

As Dominic passed the blooming flowers and edged closer to the woods, the wind began to kick up, battering him with snow crystals that bit into his skin like thousands of vicious, icy insects.

"Fortitude: the ability to bear pain and adversity with courage."

At this, Dominic's recitations paused. His stepmother's words, as she'd pulled him from his bed, came back to him. *Get up, boy. The time is at hand. Don't drag your feet, now. This is an honor. You have been chosen for a grand purpose. You're making your family proud.*

But the way she said it—with the tiniest hint of a sneer wrinkling her narrow features—made him wonder which part was the lie.

He considered it as he trudged through the calf-deep snow. *Is this an honor or a punishment? Am I here now because I am important? Or was I chosen for this because I am not?*

Not that the reason mattered much; he was to die tonight either way.

His mind wandered. Had it been this cold the last time this sacrifice was made? Had his great-great-uncle's bones ached as much as his did now? Was it better to die in one's youth, without the additional ties of progeny or community or household to tempt you from discharging your responsibility? Or was leaving everything behind easier at an old age, having gotten to experience those joys and pains to their fullest?

He used the repetition of the virtues to chase creeping, peripheral doubts back into the darkest corners of his mind. "Honesty," he muttered through thick, numb lips. "Forthrightness of conduct. Judgment: the ability to make wise and considered decisions and reach sensible conclusions."

That's when he saw the sigil carved into the black bark of a crooked, ancient tree. Ice was crusted into the scar, making each of the spider's seven legs gleam white in the moonlight. This was the marker for the beginning of the end; once he passed it, there would be no turning back.

He paused there, brushing away the hot tears that had begun to gather at the corners of his eyes. He wanted to fulfill his duty. He wanted to be the embodiment of fortitude, of self-sacrifice, of bravery. But, to his shame, he was afraid.

He didn't fear death; he knew death was coming. He feared that once this was done, once his sacrifice was made, it would be forgotten. That *he* would be forgotten.

He sniffed, wondering if they'd lay a grave empty, like they did when his father's body was lost in the collapse of the mine, or if his stepmother and young half brothers would bicker over their breakfast biscuits in the morning, completely oblivious to his absence at the other end of the table. To make it easier on them, he'd even laid out his own memorial candles by the altar in the Night Garden.

Twelve tapers, one for each year of his life. Shouldn't be too much to ask. When his father died, Stepmother kept all forty-six burning for a month. Dominic didn't want a month—he'd be happy with just a day.

Then he chided himself for his vanity. What did it matter to him, anyway? Funeral rites were for the comfort of the living, not the dead. It was no concern of his whether they lit his funerary candles, or placed a marker over an empty grave.

But he hoped they would, all the same.

It was then that he heard a crack; he looked around for the cause of the sound and saw a quick flash of ginger fur. An animal of some kind, scrounging for food in the desolate forest on a cold winter night. He shook off his apprehension, and took his first step past the spider marker.

The fog came up slowly, stealing into the basin like a ghost, and was now wafting in great white swaths all around him. The stars over-head were dimming, dimming, dimming, and soon the only light was the wisp of flame in his lantern, and its scattered sparkles across icy branches. The wind's bite grew sharper, and as Dominic approached the dark clearing that was his final destination, he thought he could hear voices within it. They whispered a canticle in a strange, foreign tongue, transforming the woods into an icy cathedral, buttressed by pine and spire-like spruce.

Welcome, said the winds in voices dry and scraping, like the scuttle of beetles over bone. *Welcome, son of Castillion.*

Across the clearing, a twisted and blackened old apple tree stood sentinel, its long-barren branches heavy with snow.

Dominic turned and turned again, suddenly aware of everything at once—the feel of frostbite gnawing at his toes within his too-thin boots, the rasp of icy leaves hitting against each other, and the impression of shadowy faces forming behind the nebulous mist.

Shakily, he bowed his head, trying not to look at the wraithlike figures circling him.

"I am here to face the Verecundai—the Shamefaced Seven," Dominic cried. "Show yourselves!"

We are creatures of the dark, whispered the discordant chorus of voices. *Put out the light and we will come.*

He opened the door of the lamp and the flame burned its image into his eyes, but he hesitated before he could draw the breath that would extinguish it. If it was light they feared, this little fire was the last bit of power he had over them until the ritual was complete.

The Verecundai had been men, once. Powerful mages, favored servants of the Empyrea. But when they plotted to betray her, to take a piece of her divinity for themselves, she punished them with a curse: They would not die, but neither would they live. They would exist as shadowy wraiths for all time.

It was said that Dominic's ancestor Marcellus Castillion had bound them to this lonely, barren glade of the Ebonwilde. Marcellus had been a blood mage, and proclaimed that once every hundred years on Midwinter, a son of his line would return to the spot and sacrifice himself to keep the wraiths imprisoned, securing prosperity and peace for another generation.

Recite your virtues. It was Dominic's own voice reminding him this time, in his own head. A familiar habit he could fall back upon; he was too sad, too scared, too astounded to do anything else. He'd gone from humility through abnegation, fortitude, honesty, and judgment. What was left on the list? He closed his eyes, feverishly scouring his memory to find them.

Obedience, he thought. *Submissive compliance to established authority.*

Remembering why he'd come, he put his fears aside and blew the lantern out.

The wraiths materialized slowly, knitting together from shadow and towering over Dominic, composed of ever-shifting mist that made their visages impossible to fully fathom. He only seemed to be able to snag glimpses—fingers that were too long, teeth that were too sharp, eyes that were too black—before the image would dissolve into vapor.

Does he see us now? the voices asked, as if to each other. *Does he know us?*

"I know you," Dominic said. "The heretics who betrayed the Empyrea. Who stole a piece of her divine light for themselves."

Ah. There was a ripple in the fog, and a low rumble, like they were conferring with one another. *But does he know himself? Does he know why he is here?*

"I'm Dominic Castillion, son of Bentham Castillion. I have come to sacrifice myself to keep you inside this prison for another generation, as so many of my line have done before me."

Sacrifice? they said. *This is not a sacrifice.*

"If not a sacrifice," he replied, "what is it?"

A test.

A test? His Castillion blood was needed to seal them away, so that they and their malice would remain in the confines of their forest prison. That's what all the lessons said. This same process had been completed dozens of times throughout the Castillion genealogy. None of those who had gone before him had ever returned—what part was a test?

"I don't understand," he said. "I came here to die."

The Verecundai asked, in their cold, death-tinged voices, *Do you wish to die?*

And despite all of his preparation for this moment of temptation, Dominic replied fiercely, "I don't want to die. I don't want to be forgotten. I want to *live*. Live and be remembered."

Put forth your hand, son of Castillion.

Dominic did as he was told, and the shadows congealed around his open palm, merging into the shape of a spider. It was glossy and silvery black, with seven spindly legs, sharp as knives. Its abdomen glowed from within, dimly, like a piece of the aurora had been trapped under a smoky glass. He trembled as the spider roved up under his sleeve, across his arm, and to his chest just over his heart.

He cried out when it stabbed him, and screamed as the poison racked his body. He contorted from the pain, praying to die before his body fell to pieces.

Endurance, he recited, clutching his arms to his stomach as he coughed and coughed, leaving a spray of blood on snow. *Withstanding difficulty and pain without giving way.* The blood coalesced into thin lines of glowing crimson that snaked under the icy crust of snow, shooting across the ground until they swirled up the trunk of the tree, into the twisting limbs down to the farthest point of the sharpest branch. One white blossom formed, unfurled, and wilted as fruit swelled beneath it.

When it was done, a single ruby-red apple hung from the tree's aged boughs. In a near trance, Dominic approached the tree, lifting his hand to pluck the fruit from its stem. It was perfectly symmetrical, round and ripe and the color of blood.

Eat, the voices said.

Dominic took a bite.

The fruit was sweet and strong and tasted slightly of salt and copper. As soon as he had swallowed it, his mind was flooded by strange thoughts and pictures. Voices of people he never knew commingled with images of places he'd never been. It was a kaleidoscope of color and sound as the earth seemed to spin backwards, stars streaking across the arc of the sky until they fell into a perfect circle of eight points with the moon at the center.

And then there were hands, dashing gold ink across a parchment map of the heavens, connecting the stars into the constellation of a spider. *Aranea,* they wrote next to it. *The Spider.*

He saw them trek across an untamed wilderness to collect the child who had been born beneath that strange cosmic configuration—a girl with hair as black as ebony, lips as red as a rose, and spirit as pure as white snow. Her name was Vieve.

You have been chosen by the Empyrea, the mages told her.

You will be her heir.

The first queen of a new and perfect world.

They brought her back to their grand observatory, where she was taught magic beneath the watchful eye of the endlessly starry sky, the passage of years marked by the shifting of gears in a giant overhead orrery, where brass planets rotated around a gleaming golden sun with the same dedicated devotion as the mages to their celestine Goddess.

The youngest of the mages was a boy named Adamus. He was drawn to the girl, and she to him. They grew into adulthood together like sapling trees, peerless in their power and youthful beauty, as enchanted with one another as they were enchanting, two halves of a single whole.

If I am to be a queen, she told him, *you must be my consort.*

Command me, my queen, he whispered back, *I will obey.*

When the day of Vieve's ascension arrived, Dominic watched as the mages dressed the girl in garments of finest silk and fastened them with a brooch in the shape of a spider, crowned her in a circlet of silver, and brought her to a forest glade under the same portentous alignment of stars that had accompanied her birth. The boy-mage she loved led her to the center before taking his place among his fellows, who formed a ring around her.

She began her spell as she had been taught, unpinning the brooch to draw a drop of blood from her fingertip, and then spinning the magic within it into a thread. Each of the eight mages did the same, and she pulled the magic from their blood in silvery strings, braiding their essences together, one with another.

Above, the stars began to shake and tremble as they, too, began to bleed in long, brutally bright streams of light that poured into the mages from above and then flowed from their fingertips into the threads of the spell. The girl was incandescent, as if made of starlight herself.

A cry sounded from the heavens, tearing through the fabric of the sky as a shape began to gather from the roiling viridian clouds of the firmament.

The Empyrea was coming.

Her wings stretched from one horizon to the other, each stamp of her hooves sending arcs of lightning across the crystal dome of sky. She lifted her equine-like head in a scream and Dominic trembled at the sound of it. He had been taught all his life that the Empyrea had touched the earth at its dawn, that humanity had sprung up in her footsteps. That it was from her love and light that mankind was created. But that could not be true; the closer the Empyrea came to the earth, the better Dominic could see the *hatred* simmering in pools of fire that were her eyes.

She was not descending to save, but to raze. Not to create, but to destroy.

Vieve stopped still, the threads of her magic drifting in the crackling air, the tapestry of her spell unfinished.

No! Dominic tried to scream a warning, but he was a voiceless observer, helpless to change this outcome. The young mage Adamus, however, opened his eyes as if he had heard it. He broke from the circle, springing forward to save her.

It was too late.

Seeing the truth of the Empyrea's intentions, the seven other mages had already drawn their swords.

It was over quickly. The Empyrea's wings dissolved into streaks of clouds, the lightning stopped, and the air went still as the tear in the sky mended itself, sealing the Goddess behind it.

And in the center of the glade, Vieve was dead. Killed by the mages who had raised her, who had loved her, who had taught her everything she knew, so that the Empyrea could not use her as a weapon with which to destroy mankind.

Adamus had crawled to the center of the circle and was cradling Vieve's broken body as her eyes stared sightlessly at the heavens. He took the spider brooch, still glowing softly with the embers of stolen starlight, and used it to prick his finger. Then he glared up at the other seven, and pronounced upon them a curse:

Even as you have taken from me, so will I take from you. You shall not die, but neither shall you live. You are cursed to walk this fallen earth until its end, when I and my love are born again and reunited, queen and consort, to reign in the Empyrea's perfect new world, free of pain and death.

Fidelity, Dominic thought as he watched the man mourn. *Unswerving faithfulness and devotion through all adversity.*

The seven mages shrieked as their bodies disintegrated, and swirled forward, right through Dominic as he watched, stealing his breath and his warmth and plunging him into impenetrable darkness.

The last thing he heard before losing consciousness were the whispered words: *The long wait is over. They have, at last, returned.*

When Dominic woke, he was lying in the snow, face turned up toward the moon. The wind was gone. The white wraiths were gone. All was still and silent.

Had he fallen asleep in the snow? It seemed a senseless thing to do—but how else could he explain any of it? The things that were swimming in his head defied logic. They were dreams, of course. Nightmares.

But in his hands was a red apple with one bite taken from it. Atop the crust of icy snow, the flame of his lantern was still burning brightly. Beside it sat a brooch in the shape of a spider, its center stone still glowing softly.

It was all real. He'd gone into the Ebonwilde woods, faced the shades hiding within it, and come out alive.

But changed.

The snow did not seem quite as cold, the air less bitter. And he thought, if he listened hard enough, he could still hear those dry, whispering voices in his ears.

In the sky the first soft streaks of dawn were beginning to show, and all around the edge of the glade were the shriveled petals of the spent frostlace flowers. The longest night of the year had passed. From here on out, the darkness would slowly abate.

It took him nearly a day to trudge through the woods back to Fort Castillion on his own, climbing the hidden switchbacks on the western side of the mountain and slipping into the fort through its back entrance, through the secret warren of tunnels and caves Dominic's ancestors had built their home upon. Inside, however, all was still. There were no dogs to greet him. No groomsmen in the stables. No guards at the door.

Everyone was gathered in the courtyard, coming somberly in and out of the glass cathedral that was the Night Garden. He was greeted by a guardsman. "There you are, Lord Dominic. Thank the stars you're here. When we found her ladyship like that, and you nowhere to be seen, we expected the worst." He paused, mouth falling open as

Dominic removed his hat. "What has happened to your hair? There's a streak there that is white as snow!"

"My hair?" he said distantly, hardly registering the comment. "Her ladyship?" he asked, confused.

The guardsman crouched next to him, speaking kindly. "Yes, my dear boy. I'm sorry to be the one to tell you this, but your stepmother died early this morning. We found her frozen to death in her sleigh, right outside the village."

Dominic ran to the greenhouse, pushing people aside to get to the front. The soldier hurried after him, concerned for the boy, coming into responsibility for his province at such a young age, and without any parental figure left to guide him.

His stepmother's body was laid out for mourning under the Night Garden's glass dome while around her, thirty-two candles burned, one for each year of her life.

The guardsman said gruffly, "She was never in very good health. Or humor." He shook his head. "Apologies, my boy. I should not be speaking ill of the dead." Then, "When you're ready to begin making decisions, we'll be ready to follow them."

"I'm ready now," Dominic said abruptly. And then he made his first decree. "Mourning is over," he said. "Remove her body."

"What should we do with it?" asked another of the watching men-at-arms.

"Find a pit," Dominic said, "toss it in." And then, one by one, he blew the candles out.

PART I

THE MIDNIGHT STRIKE

I

NOW

AURELIA

10 DAYS TO MIDWINTER
1621

My teeth were at his throat.

I could taste salt on his skin; just a hint, from a thin sheen of sweat. Beneath it, blood pulsed through the artery in his neck. I could hear it singing to me, calling to me, *begging* me to set it free. To break that fragile barrier of skin and let the magic flow hot against my lips, like a kiss. And I wanted to.

Oh—how I wanted to.

"Aurelia." The word was little more than a breathy exhalation, but it struck me oddly, like a discordant note from a mistuned string. I paused, poised on the brink of the killing strike, and remembered the name.

My name.

My eyes drifted down his neck, where a vial of blood hung from a cord, nestled against his chest. I knew it. Knew the sense of it, the smell of it.

My blood.

My clawlike grip on him went slack. I grabbed the vial and gave it a hard yank, until the cord snapped and came free. Then my eyes darted to the man who had been wearing it. Crimson velvet cape, white brocade overcoat, black lambskin gloves, dark brown eyes, and hair the color of ice.

Dominic Castillion.

The edges of my awareness suddenly sharpened. We were not alone here—wherever *here* was. Castillion and I were being watched by a circle of gathered people; some were dressed like statesmen, others like soldiers. All were wearing the Castillion livery. They were frozen, gaping at me, caught like insects in a spider's web, too stunned or scared to move.

"Be calm," Castillion said, though I wasn't sure if he was addressing me or the audience.

"Where is Zan?" I croaked, my voice brittle from disuse, grabbing fistfuls of his cloak. "Where *is* he?"

One of the men in the circle moved forward, hand on his sword.

"No," Castillion said. "Stay back. I've got this." Castillion gently pulled my hands down from his cloak. "Aurelia," he said slowly, "I know this is strange. I know you're scared. I know you have a lot of questions. I will answer them all, I promise. But first, I need you to let my guards leave the garden. Let us take the injured to the infirmary, and then you and I can talk as long as we need. Can you do that? Please? I know you don't want to hurt anyone else."

He tilted his head to the side, and I followed the line of the gesture with my eyes, turning to see three men on the ground behind me, moaning. One was clutching an arm to his chest, one had a cut in his head that was seeping blood into his eye. The last was holding a hand to his neck, where blood was spilling between his fingers.

"I didn't do that," I said frantically, whirling around. "I couldn't have done that." I tried to wipe my hands on my gown, only to have them come away bloodier than before. "This isn't right. It isn't real." But it *was* real, because there was my casket of luminous glass, lying open and askew on a funereal dais.

This was not the Assembly, where the sanctorium pews were populated with the remains of the mages Cael had killed upon his own emergence from that casket, but it wasn't hard to overlay the image of those prostrate skeletons across this violence and recognize the similarities between them. It was a horror. A display of depravity. And it was *mine.*

I felt a hand on my arm. "Aurelia . . ."

"Get back!" I cried, shrinking from Castillion's touch. "Get *away* from me!"

"But, wait—"

"*Go!*" I flung out my arm, but whether it was to attack or to scare him into retreat, even I didn't know. But the magic, drawn from the soldiers' unwilling blood, blasted like a gale-force wind, sending him flying into the scrambling group of watchers. When he was able to get back to his feet, his face finally registered a flicker of worry.

Then he nodded, turning to the man nearest to him. "Get them out," he ordered. "Don't let anyone see, and speak of this to no one. Understand me?"

When the watchers did not move, Castillion continued, "This is my responsibility. I'll take care of her. We just need space, all right? As much as we can get."

As the men and women filed out, I sank to my knees, despondent, bloody hands turned limply upward in my lap, the vial's cord tangled in my fingers.

"Aurelia," Castillion said, crouching beside me. "I'm going to see them out. I won't be gone long. You'll be safe here in the Night Garden until I return."

In mere seconds, the greenhouse—for that was what the Night Garden was: an enormous, elaborate greenhouse—was empty of all life. Except for me, but I barely qualified.

They bolted the door behind them.

As a garden, it was an unusual one, with copses of birch and silver-green fir and trimmed with flowers that flourished at night. Gardenia and evening primrose spilled from hanging baskets, while five-inch-wide moonflower blossoms twined up iron pillars that branched into buttresses. White candles burned in the branches, held upright in place by hardened wax rivulets. Overhead, purple wisteria blossoms became a dreamy canopy, and on each side of the dais, great urns were overflowing with the shimmering leaves and tightly closed buds of frostlace flower that would bloom on Midwinter Night, soft white veins visible through the diaphanous amethyst-colored petals, like delicate, snowy spiderwebs.

Judging from the blossoms, Midwinter was only a few weeks away.

The centerpiece of the garden was a statue of white marble, at least twelve feet tall, depicting a man and a woman locked in an intense embrace, each with a halo of stars crowning their lovely foreheads. I might have thought the piece was relaying a moment of carnal passion, were it not for the knife hilt protruding from her back. This was not a representation of love, but rather its cruel extinguishment.

At their feet, the sculptor had chiseled a single white apple. A streak of castoff blood bisected the fruit, as if the stone had worn away in that spot to reveal its true color underneath. Above, a dome sparkled, the night sky black behind it.

How funny, I thought dully, that I had emerged from one glass prison only to be barricaded inside another.

My memories of going into the casket were strange — two different perspectives overlaid into one. One version of me lying down inside, the other standing over, watching. Taking something from around my neck and placing it under my other self's hands. A ring. Zan's ring.

Where was it now?

I stooped over the casket and scraped my fingertips over every inch of its interior, then moved to the marble floor, streaking through the sticky splotches of blood. I was still scrabbling around in that mess when I heard the bolt of the greenhouse door slide open and a single set of heavy footsteps come up the path toward me.

I glared at Castillion over my shoulder. "Where is it?" I croaked. "Where is my ring?"

"If you had a ring, I did not know of it," he said. "Nor could one have been taken from you while you slept. The box was sealed when we removed it from the Assembly and remained so until the moment you came out of it. Here . . ."

He put out a hand as if to help me to my feet, but I flinched away from it with a snarl. "Stay *back*," I warned, remembering the men I'd hurt, whose blood still coated the floor.

"I'm not afraid of you," Castillion said quietly, as if reading my mind. "You were frightened. Confused. I harbor no judgment against you, Aurelia. Nor do any of the others who were here to see it."

I gave a guttural scoff. "You're lucky I didn't kill you in front of your friends," I said. "Because I wanted to. I wanted to kill you, like I killed your men."

"My men aren't dead," he said. "Gravely injured, yes, but they'll survive. And they'd do it again, every last one of them, without question."

I ignored his hand and awkwardly got to my feet on my own, glaring at him the whole time. At our last encounter I'd made a pact with him: I'd save him from a watery grave if he'd join Zan to raise me from mine. But with Zan nowhere to be seen, it remained a point of curiosity why Castillion hadn't just let me fester inside my coffin for the rest of eternity. He could have walked away. He *should* have walked away.

"Why?" I asked, finally.

"They trust me. And I told them that we can trust you."

"But you can't trust me," I said. "Because if I find out that you've harmed Zan in any way . . ."

"I have not touched Valentin. In fact, I have invited him here on multiple occasions, including this one, and he has declined every one." He cast a pitying glance at me and then added, "Your prince never came for you."

2

THEN

ZAN

MIDWINTER NIGHT, 1620

"My grandmother used to festoon the house in sage and rue to keep Midwinter spirits away—and here you are, spending the holiday in a tomb."

Jessamine's forceful voice sounded in the quiet dark of the crypt like a crack of a hammer against an anvil. Zan groaned and turned away from the throbbing light of her candle, his own having burned down to a nub hours ago. "Midwinter?" he asked, cringing.

"I suppose I shouldn't be surprised that you don't know what day it is," she said dryly. "Lorelai and Delphinia prepared some bread and smoked ham for you, and I left a bale of hay in the stable for Madrona. It isn't much, of course, but it's something." Bottles clinked at Jessamine's feet, and she frowned down at them. "There won't be any wine with the meal, however. Seems someone has cleaned out the Stella's wine stores."

"You said some were Aurelia's bottles." He lifted his arm to shield his eyes from both Jessamine's candle and the withering glare it illuminated. "I think she'd want me to have them."

"If by 'have them' you mean 'have them broken over your idiot head,' then yes. I do think she'd want you to have them." She peered past where he sat at the base of Aurelia's stone sarcophagus into the alcove concealing the rest of the long box. "By all the stars. Is this what you've been doing down here?"

The slab that concealed Aurelia's mortal remains was plain—not like the detailed visages carved into the older caskets radiating the center vestibule. He couldn't leave it that way; he was an artist, was he not? And while charcoal was his usual medium, he knew enough of painting technique to do her *some* justice at least.

He depicted her as she had looked on the Day of Shades, as she took her last breaths: dark hair waving around her temples, eyelashes fanning against her rose-tinted cheeks, a slight, serene smile on her lips. He'd elaborated from there: adding bloodleaf petals that swirled like snow around her crown, many-pronged stars caught in her hair, and trails of red-violet sombersweet bells that grew in tangles around her feet.

Midwinter, he thought as he gazed down at her visage. *Has it really been six weeks already?*

"What's that?" Jessamine asked, pointing to Aurelia's hands. "Is she holding . . . a spider?"

"It's supposed to be a flower," he said crossly. "And it's rough now.

It'll look better when I've finished it." He barely remembered paint-ing it. Truth was, it *did* look a little like a spider. Some of the priests' wines were more potent than others.

"I bet with some proper training, I could turn you into an *excellent* forger. Unfinished flower aside," Jessamine said, voice soft. "It looks just like her." Then she looked at Zan—disheveled and sallow, bags under his eyes and covered in intermingled streaks of dirt and paint —and gave an exasperated sigh. "Though I'm shocked you had the wherewithal to achieve it."

"I work better drunk," he said with a shrug.

"You need to get out of this place," Jessamine said. "Get washed. Get dressed. Eat."

"I'm not done," he said stubbornly. "I can't show Conrad until—"

"Conrad is already gone," Jessamine replied. "He and Kellan left for Syric weeks ago. I'm going back to the Canary tonight. After that, there will be no one here but you and the dead."

This gave Zan pause. "Weeks?" He grimaced. "They should have waited—"

"There was no time to wait. These are strange and troubling times in Renalt. Conrad is a king. And no matter his grief, he must set his feelings aside and *be* king."

"Are you attempting to compare me to an eight-year-old?" He picked up a tin can of black paint and sighed. Empty.

"I am attempting nothing. I am *absolutely* comparing you, and finding you wanting."

"My country doesn't need me; it has Dominic Castillion." He

picked up an unopened tin of paint and began to work a small knife beneath its lid, but his hands were unsteady.

Jessamine snatched the knife away from him. "This is ridiculous," she said. "If Aurelia could see you like this, she'd be—"

At the sound of her name, Zan's hand went instinctively to his chest, feeling the pointed vial through the fabric of his shirt. The last of Aurelia's mortal blood hung like a weight around his neck, a desperate want and a tormenting doubt wrapped up in one.

He could still hear her voice in his ear, a coy whisper.

Come and find me.

Hope was such a pernicious, perilous thing. A rope to promised safety that could lead instead to the brink of a chasm, with no quarter for retreat or net to catch your fall.

Aurelia was the miracle worker, not him. She was the one with the power and the self-possession required to wield it. Zan had no doubt that if it were *his* quicksilver body entombed at the Assembly, she would find a way to reach him and to raise him. She was dauntless, with will enough to break the universe and remake it to her own liking.

She had blazed into his life like a comet, bright and brilliant, setting his entire world aflame. He had thought that she had sparked something inside of him, too. For the first time in his life, he saw his own potential. With her beside him, he could actually imagine a version of himself brave enough to lead an army, to run a nation, to be a king.

He had mistaken her castoff glow as his own, and its absence left him in an even deeper darkness.

Still, her words haunted him. *Come and find me.*

No—Aurelia was dead. To believe otherwise was a torment. A trick. A lie dressed up as a possibility. And if he let it gain hold, he'd lose himself to it completely.

Just then, the clock in the Stella's tower began to chime the hour— it was midnight. The sound, delivered down the belfry stairs into the cavernous tomb, was amplified by the stone, and each toll sent pain shooting into his wine-muddled mind like an arrow through water. He put both hands against the stone wall and cried with all the force he could muster, "By all the bleeding stars, *be silent!*"

As if in response to his command, the bells went still mid-chime.

Jessamine had one eyebrow raised. "Are you done?" she asked after a long minute.

"I need more paint," he muttered.

"What you need," Jessamine said, "is to get your head out of your ass."

"I'm fine," Zan snapped.

Jessamine gave a deep, irritated sigh. "I'll leave the food in the priest's pantry. Don't let it spoil or Lorelai will never forgive you. And don't die down here, please, or Aurelia will never forgive me."

Zan turned his back on her, looking at his half-finished painting. *Too late,* he thought. *I'm as good as dead already.*

★

It was the light that woke him: the soft bobbing glow of a candle on the other side of the tomb. Zan blinked at it wearily, lifting his heavy, throbbing head from his numb arms, folded across the top of Aurelia's coffin. He'd fallen asleep again, but for how long? He remembered Jessamine coming down to scold him, but he couldn't recall when —or even *if*—she'd left. Was she back already?

"Jessamine," he said groggily, rubbing his eyes. "Fine. You win. I'll come up."

The light paused at the bottom of the belfry stair, but she said nothing in reply.

Zan struggled to his feet, his limbs stiff and sore, and had to catch the wall for balance after stumbling on some of his empty wine bottles. Swearing, he hurried after the waning light as the candle moved farther up the stair, as if warning him to follow quick or be forced to feel his way around the crypt in the dark.

"Jessamine," he said again. "I told you, I am *coming.* Feel free to slow down." When the light continued farther up the spiraling stairs, he began to mumble obscenities under his breath. The woman was a tyrant.

The Stella's chapel, when he stumbled into it from the belfry door, was impossibly still. He'd expected to find Jessamine waiting with folded arms, clicking her tongue in dismay of his dishevelment. "Jessamine?" he asked again, moving slowly through the pews, his voice a garish intrusion into the stillness of the steely blue semidarkness. The Empyrea stared coldly down at him, superiority personified in stained glass. How many times, during that long night in Arceneaux's cruel grip, had he begged for the Goddess's intervention? But it was Aurelia, not the Empyrea, who answered his prayers. Aurelia who had rescued him. Who held him. Healed him. And then died in his arms.

Suffused with sudden anger, Zan picked up one of the chairs in the choir behind the altar and hefted it into the Empyrea's mocking face.

The glass cracked apart and fell in a cacophonous wave, and after the dust settled, the only things left in the pointed-arch frame were the night sky and the Midwinter moon . . .

And a figure moving into the hedge, holding a bobbing candle-light.

It wasn't Jessamine, Zan was sure of that now—the person was too tall, too wide. Boots crunching broken glass, he scrambled through the window frame after them. "Wait!" Zan demanded. "Who are you? What are you doing here?"

After the fire in the manor and the Tribunal's massacre in the village, no one beside Zan was miserable enough to want to stay. Who, then, was now wandering the ruins in the middle of the night, on Midwinter no less?

Without its leaves, the hedge was little more than a thatch of tangled, spiny branches, and Zan could follow the light through it, quickening his pace to keep up. When he made it clear of the thicket, the first thing he saw was not the trespasser, but Aurelia's ill-tempered horse, Madrona. She was snuffling around a low cobble wall, searching for frostbitten remnants of the vegetable garden. She huffed as he approached, two columns of frosty air expelled from her muzzle. He patted her back. "How did you get out of the stable?"

She tried to bite him in response, but he was able to jump out of the way before her teeth connected with his skin. He was about to scold her when he saw the trespasser again at the edge of the garden, overlooking the empty village. A man, Zan determined. A big man, seemingly dressed in the robes of a monk, which probably meant that this person had been poking around in the Ursonian priests' few remaining belongings.

Zan swung himself over the wall and cried, "Hey!" The monks had been pivotal in helping Aurelia escape from the Tribunal those months ago; they were her friends. Besides the wine stores he'd liberally borrowed from, he'd treated the rest of their things with a respectful reverence. That someone had disturbed the relics of their life at the Stella Regina filled him with a hot, irrational anger. "Hey, you!" he said. "I'm talking to you!"

He clapped a hand on the man's shoulder and immediately recoiled, gasping, as a rush of bitter cold throbbed up his arm into his shoulder.

Slowly, the man turned, his round face catching the light like a waxing moon, and Zan stumbled back in stunned horror. The last time he'd seen that face, it had been staring at him upside down as its owner bled out on the Stella's altar.

Father Cesare.

The priest's robe was soaked in blood across the midsection, his guts bulging from a grotesque gash visible through the slices in the fabric. He reached toward Zan again, his thick fingers outstretched as if to place a blessing upon his head. Zan recoiled, and the fingers began to transform, stretching and slimming as they got closer to his face. Cesare's skin began to pale, and his face began to sink and sag, thinning until it wasn't Cesare anymore at all.

It was Isobel Arceneaux. Onyx-eyed and purple-lipped, with livid black veins worming under her pale skin, her once-glossy hair clumped together in dull hanks. Her jaw fell open as if to speak, but no sound came out.

His stomach heaving in revulsion, Zan scrambled backwards, jumping onto the low garden wall. The movement startled Madrona, who began to run alongside it. In desperation, he lunged for her, knocking the air out of his lungs as he landed crossways on her back.

She gave an outraged neigh, but he was able to right himself and wrap both hands around her neck before she could fling him off. When he ventured a look over his shoulder, Arceneaux was gone but the Stella Regina's clock shone brightly, both hands frozen at the number twelve.

3

THEN

KELLAN

MIDWINTER NIGHT, 1620

Kellan coughed and sputtered, and flecks of blood dotted the dirt-packed floor like constellations. His assailant was a man built like a bull, thick-muscled and mallet-fisted, with a blank red rage behind his eyes as he barreled toward Kellan, ready to finish the fight.

As the man moved in, Kellan rose again to his tired feet, grinning madly through the blood welling up from his busted lip and flooding his mouth with the taste of metal. The man lurched forward, swinging wide, but Kellan ducked and spun into a low kick that brought the man's feet out from under him. He toppled like a felled tree; it was the opening Kellan had been looking for the entire match, and before the man could right himself, Kellan had wound his right arm around his neck from behind.

He bucked and kicked as Kellan squeezed tighter and tighter, knowing that if he didn't end it here, he wouldn't get another chance. When the man's grip finally went slack, Kellan let go, and the limp man flopped heavily into the dirt as applause went up from the spectators in the stadium.

"And in round three," Malcolm, the fightmaster, called, "the Gryphon has defeated Mastiff! The Gryphon is tonight's winner!"

This was Kellan's favorite part. He stepped over the Mastiff's inert body and carefully removed his gloves before lifting both arms into the air in triumph.

There were several gasps and a moment of pregnant pause before the entire crowd broke into a raucous cheer.

He had not only felled the mightiest of the ring's combatants, he'd done it with only one hand.

He was turning from one side of the arena to the other, soaking in the adulation, when his eyes caught upon a flash of bright red hair as a cloaked figure spun and moved the wrong way through the crowd toward the door. His jubilation faded, and he let his arms flop back down to his sides as the weariness of both the fight and the six weeks preceding it caught up to him once again.

He collected his winnings from Malcolm and set out into the cold night, pulling down his hood and hunching his shoulders, becoming just another of the city's careworn inhabitants, moving dully along their ordered, unvarying paths like mindless ants. On the other side of the city, Syric's castle watched over the people with a detached imperiousness, too close to let the citizens forget who ruled them, too distant to make any real difference in the quality of their lives.

But while the castle was the same as ever, the rest of town had been vastly altered since the night he and Aurelia had left it. The Tribunal had locked it down after Queen Genevieve and Simon de Achlev had escaped, disallowing all but a chosen few to enter or exit. Isobel Arceneaux—after clawing her way to the top of the Tribunal hierarchy —had issued the decree herself, right before she'd set off for Conrad's coronation at Kellan's family seat in Greythorne.

After five centuries of terror, the Tribunal's decision to close the city walls proved to be their undoing. Cut off from trade and travel, the common folk of the city had taken the brunt of the suffering until they could stand it no longer. By the time news of Arceneaux's death had arrived here, most of her fellow magistrates were already dangling from their own beloved gallows.

Kellan wondered if the city could ever be washed clean of those centuries of murder, malevolence, and abuse. Even the fighting arena was once a Tribunal court, where the accused were hauled into an arena from squalid pens to be subjected to a barrage of inquiries from pious Tribunal judges that were more aimed to debase and humiliate than prove a witch's innocence or guilt. Anything could be hammered into proof if the inquisitors were creative and dedicated enough. And they were. They always were.

The Tribunal might be gone, but their presence would cling to every roof and window and wall of Syric forever, like stubborn, oily soot.

By the time he made it into the square, it had started to rain in a dismal drizzle. On any other year, Midwinter Night would have been marked with dancing and singing, with roasted goose and baked apples and candlelit windows and the clanging of a thousand joyful bells beneath the clock tower at midnight, marking the end of the longest night. There was a small crowd gathered in that spot, but from what Kellan could see, none were carrying candles or cowbells. Rather, they were all gathered around a man seated on a black horse as he preached.

Kellan couldn't hear what the man was saying, nor did he wish to. The Tribunal's absence had caused these small-time zealots to spring up like weeds, peddling some version of the Empyrean religion or another, and he had no use for any of it. He moved past the crowd as quickly as he could, ducking onto the doorstep of a tavern hung with a sign depicting a broken lyre. The Scheming Minstrel, it was called. It smelled of stale bread and old ale, but it was clean enough, and the keeper, Ivan, didn't ask very many questions. Kellan tossed him one of his new-won coins on his way past the bar and up the stairs.

When he got to his room, he found it already occupied.

She was waiting for him, looking out the lone window onto the city below, her shape illuminated by the moonlit face of the clock tower on the other side of the square. The space was filled with her scent, like wildwinds and woodfires and rich, damp earth.

"I knew it was you," Kellan said after a moment. "At the fight tonight."

Rosetta turned slowly, her yellow eyes flashing from beneath her hood. "I went to the castle looking for you first," she said. "They said they hadn't seen you for days."

"Well," Kellan said, removing his damp cloak one-handed and

placing it on the peg by the door to dry, "they told you wrong. It's been two weeks since I was there, at the *very* least."

"Kellan," Rosetta said sternly. "Don't you think Conrad needs someone like you nearby? You *owe* it to him to—"

"I owe him *nothing*," Kellan barked. "I owe that family *nothing*."

Rosetta's mouth twisted as if she were tasting something bitter, but she did not reply. She may not have been the one who brought the sword down upon his wrist, but she carried plenty of the blame for the circumstances that led to it, and she knew it.

They'd grown close during those long nights in Greythorne's dungeon, but his grief and her guilt had become a gulf between them.

After a long moment, she said, "Who is left to fight for him, if not you?"

"I do my own fighting now."

"I am *not* talking about letting yourself get kicked around for a few stupid coins in the sparring pen," she said sternly. "You're a soldier. A *protector*. And Conrad might be a king, but he's also a little boy, and—"

Kellan loudly pulled a chair from beneath the small table, where a cruse of spirits was already laid out on a tray alongside several pieces of cut gauze and a small, cloudy mirror. "Are you done?" he asked, reaching for the bottle. "I've got quite a headache from all that getting kicked around."

"Here," she said exasperatedly, after a moment of watching him fumble to wet the gauze one-handed. "Let me do it."

He hissed as she began to dab at the cut over his eyebrow. "I don't need your help," he said. "I was doing just fine on my own."

"Of course you were," she said, her fingers cool against his skin. When she thought he wouldn't notice, her eyes darted down to the unfinished end of his right arm, and then back up to his face.

After Aurelia had blasted them away in a torrent of magic pulled from his just-spilled blood, they'd ended up at the Quiet Canary, where Rosetta had worked through the night to stretch the ragged skin over the exposed bone and stitch it together at the end. Because of her efforts, he'd healed up nicely enough on the outside. It was the *other* wound that festered: the hazy, red-tinged trauma of the night he lost everything—his brother, his home, his hand, his life's purpose . . . and Aurelia herself.

In his mind's eye, he saw her again: ash-blond hair whipping in hot wind. A halo of crimson light. Embers drifting around her, bright against a black sky. The flash of a sword.

And then the words.

I'm sorry.

He must have stiffened, because Rosetta murmured, "It stings, I know. The cut is deep."

You have no idea, he thought.

After the abrasion over his eye was properly salved and stitched, she began to explore the bruises in various stages of healing with a too-gentle touch across his cheeks and chin, while the corners of her lips drooped. She felt bad for him, he could see it on her face.

Before she could make it to the split in his lower lip, he'd gotten abruptly to his feet. This was too much. Her snappishness could be unpleasant, but this saccharine pity was *intolerable.*

"Did I hurt you?" she asked, taking his sudden withdrawal as an indictment of her mending efforts. "I'm sorry, I—"

"Why are you here, Rosetta?" Kellan asked, pacing in front of the fireplace. It was harsher than he meant it to sound, but he was too tired to feign manners, and she wouldn't appreciate them anyway, having so few of her own.

She removed the satchel from her shoulder and flipped it open before carefully withdrawing something from inside. It was a new glove made of a delicate, loosely woven silver fabric. He recognized the material: quicksilver thread from her spelled spinning wheel. The glove looked light and flimsy, but the way she held it made it seem heavy.

"Couldn't let Midwinter pass without giving you a gift," she said, holding it out to him.

Never mind trying to hide his missing hand; this glove would make it impossible not to notice. It shimmered with every movement, light glancing from it in smooth silver ripples that revealed an underlying pattern of filigree twists and curling knots. It was beautiful. She had obviously spent a great deal of effort in its creation.

He stood by quietly as Rosetta approached, lifting his arm and fitting the silver glove over his lower arm. It was long, reaching all the way up to his elbow.

Rosetta's nimble fingers began to dance in patterns across his arm, each swoop and swirl sending tingles into his flesh, as if she were sewing it through his skin and bone with unseen threads of energy.

"What are you *doing?*" he asked, half in opposition, half in admiration.

"Shhh," she replied, her eyebrows knitted together in concentration. "You'll see soon enough."

As he watched her work, the individual threads began to melt together, swirling like molten silver over the contours of his forearm. One by one, each of the glove's limp fingers began to fill out and become solid.

He lifted his arm to watch the hand form, a fully metal replica of the one he had lost. He turned it around, again and again, his mouth parted in amazement. And while such a great amount of metal should have been heavy, the weight was negligible.

When her spell was complete, the glove shone like polished mirror.

Rosetta stepped back. "How does it feel?" she asked.

"Good," he said, lifting and lowering it. The hand had formed in a relaxed position, with the fingers close together. "Anything heavier might have caused some shoulder pain getting used to it, but this should be fine."

"No," she said. "How does it *feel?*" She reached out, placing her hand against the metal, fingertip to fingertip. "Can you feel that?" she asked.

"Should I?"

"Yes," she said. "It's made of quicksilver."

"And . . . ?"

"*I'm* made of quicksilver." And in an instant, she had re-formed herself into her second shape, a fox. She blinked at him with her yellow eyes for a moment, head tilted, before changing herself back.

"Quicksilver is never a single thing—it can become anything you wish it to be. And now that this is bound to you, you should be able to command it, to bend and transform it to your will. Hold it out and give it a try."

Kellan did as she directed, stretching his silver hand out in front of him and concentrating, bidding his fingers to flex. He stared hard, letting every other thought fall away, until sweat was beading on his forehead and the veins stood out in his neck.

Rosetta watched, her own frustration growing alongside his. "If you want your fingers to move," she snapped, "simply *tell* them to move."

Kellan's focus broke and with a roar, he slammed the unchanged arm against the post of his bed. It went right through, exploding the rest of the beam into a shower of splinters. Rosetta blinked at him, shock making her breath come fast, before crossing to him and kissing him with a ferocious, feral hunger.

He wanted to pull away, to maintain whatever scraps of dignity and composure he had left . . . but he couldn't resist. She was the spark to his parched tinder; he answered her kiss with equal intensity, and soon she had robbed him of his overcoat and undershirt, digging her fingernails into his shoulder blades as he brought her to his bed.

Afterward, they lay side by side beneath his sheets, untouching, as the clock tower in the city square began to chime the hour. Rosetta pulled on her shift and went to the window, parting the curtains to reveal the moonlit face of the clock.

"Midnight," she said, and he began to absently number the chimes. Eight. Nine. Ten. Eleven—

And then, nothing. The bells stopped sharply, silenced mid-note.

At the window, Rosetta stiffened.

"No," she whispered, her brows knitting together as if she were *willing* the hands to move again.

They never did.

4

THEN

CONRAD

MIDWINTER NIGHT
1620

Conrad had spent much of his earliest years following after his sister.

Most people, his mother included, were so busy preparing him to be a king, they forgot to let him be a child. But not Aurelia. She read silly stories to him, taught him rhymes, and told him secrets. She made up adventures for them to play, like the seek-and-find game with coded ribbons and ingenious little prizes. She'd laugh and race him up and down the halls when most others preferred that he sit still and quiet. He could never get enough of her company, following her like an eager puppy, tripping over his clumsy feet to please her. To earn her smile, her words of praise.

It was during one of these games that he'd first heard the whispers about her. He'd followed the ribbons and found the prize—a box of sugared figs—and tucked himself away under a hallway table to eat them when two gossiping chambermaids went past. "She's a danger to her brother," one said. "A witch is never content with what she's given. She wants the throne, and she'll take it. Not even the Tribunal frightens her anymore."

"I think she pays them to stay out of her hair," said the other. "Do you see how she looks at the little chap? Such envy. Such hatred. She'll use some kind of potion to do it, mark my words, sneak a poison into his food. Or plan an accident. Lure him out onto a ledge and then push him over it."

"Poor child," said the first, clucking her tongue, speaking as if he were already dead. "He'd make such a handsome king."

Feeling sick, he'd dropped the last fig and pushed the box away from him. Aurelia wanted to hurt him? *Kill* him?

How quickly his admiration was supplanted by suspicion. It shamed him now, how he'd pulled away from her.

But he had learned things from watching her during those early years: how to make yourself almost invisible by shrinking into the background, how to hide things in places no one would think to look, and—most importantly—how to get in and out of the castle without being noticed.

And so now, as he moved from shadow to shadow, down one lesser-used corridor and then another, he silently thanked her for the lessons, though it helped that Hector and Pomeroy—his new bodyguards—were not very good at their jobs.

Kellan would have *never* have overlooked such a thing, but Kellan no longer concerned himself with the travails of the Renaltan throne or the family that sat upon it. He'd seen Conrad back to the city safely, but once he had handed the king over to the court, he washed his hands of all of it. He didn't even say a proper goodbye, choosing instead to leave his captain's cloak neatly folded at the end of the bed in the chamber he'd never occupy.

It was probably for the best, Conrad decided. Kellan saw him more as a child than a king, and would have treated him that way, always coddling or scolding or questioning his decisions and undermining his authority. Conrad didn't need that. He was perfectly capable on his own.

When Conrad finally made it past the outside gate—the last hurdle—it was nearing dusk, and without the sun, the winter air was starting to carry a bite. He tugged his woolen scarf higher and pulled a black cap down over his too-bright curls, hunching his shoulders beneath his dark cloak. He wished, not for the first time, that he were taller; his age was his greatest vulnerability both in the castle and outside it. He was tense and wary walking down the first few streets, but as he inched close to the city center and there was more of a crowd to disappear into, he began to relax a little.

When, at last, he came into view of the quiet clock tower and saw the collection of people gathered beneath it, he let out a relieved breath.

Just as he'd hoped, the preacher was there once again.

Conrad had first encountered the man from his carriage upon his initial arrival to Syric, when passing the square on the way to the castle. He was riding his black horse then, too, dressed in a robe of purple velvet. He had a heavy medallion around his neck—silver, and shaped like a moon.

Halfway through the square, the carriage had suddenly lurched to a stop; the road was blocked by people streaming into the square to listen to the preacher. His voice boomed through the thin carriage walls.

"We have left the age of kings behind," Conrad had heard him saying. "And invite those who were lauded as such to join with us, arm in arm, as equals and friends!"

Conrad's coach was plain and black, as nondescript as they came; the man couldn't have known the Renaltan king was being transported inside. And yet . . . Conrad had a distinct, undeniable feeling that he did. That he wasn't speaking to the gathered crowd, but directly to him.

Since glimpsing the man from the carriage, Conrad had felt an ever-increasing pull to return to the square to find him, to listen to him. It was as if the thought had been dropped into the center of his mind, overriding his better judgment. He was a fish caught upon a line of inevitability, and no matter how hard he tried to swim in the other direction, he knew he'd be reeled in eventually. So why not now?

As Conrad approached, the preacher was pointing to the clock behind him. "This will be the first sign, as predicted by High Mage Fidelis the First, in the Midnight Papers, over one thousand years ago!" He raised an old book high over his head. "*Verily I say unto thee, when in the last moment of the shortest day, the Grandfather's two hands*

point to the sky and stay, thou shalt know that the Empyrea's return to earth is finally upon us! Tonight is Midwinter, friends. When this clock falls silent at twelve o'clock that night, may you all remember that I, Fidelis the Fourteenth, teacher of the Circle Midnight, foretold it to you."

Conrad elbowed his way closer, squinting at the man, scrutinizing him. There was something mesmerizing about him, about the cadence of his voice and the fluidity of his mannerisms. And his eyes, too—in the darkness, they were impossibly bright.

And when those eyes drifted across the gathered listeners, Conrad felt the same uncomfortable jolt he had in the carriage, like his skin had been pulled back and his skull cracked open. Like all of his thoughts and memories and wants and fears were exposed. On display.

Fidelis the Fourteenth smiled, as if he had eavesdropped on that thought, too, and found it amusing. Then he lifted his medallion so that all could see it. It was a disc of white gold with strange pictograms ringing the outer edge. "We of the Circle Midnight have been watching for these signs for centuries! Long have we suffered in silence as the Tribunal pursued and persecuted us, but we have lived to see the end of their tyranny and their false teachings!"

This pronouncement elicited a rumbling affirmation from the somber crowd.

The medallion settled back into its place against the man's chest as his voice dropped to a conspiratorial hush. "Be warned, my dear friends; the clocks will be the first of many signs, many sufferings, to come. The Empyrea has looked over this fallen world and found it wanting. She sees your tribulations and it grieves her. This world —this sad, squalid, *broken* world—has failed her. Has failed *you!*"

He nudged his horse forward, and it moved sedately through the crowd. "The Goddess's most cherished wish is for her devoted sons and daughters—the righteous, the *chosen!*—to cast off the filth of this world, to defy those who would seek to control us, to rule us, and to submit ourselves wholeheartedly to her will. And when we have proved ourselves, she will gather us up unto her bosom and give us a place within her heavenly palaces for all eternity. Look around you. Look at the misery you have been forced to endure. You have already passed the first test of devotion unto her: humility. And you have borne it so beautifully."

A woman near the front was staring up at the preacher with a look of hungry fervency in her eyes. "But what of the wicked? What will happen to *them?*"

The man smiled, bending to take her hand. "Fear not, dear friend. For when the Empyrea cleanses this earth, it will be with a slow and brutal vengeance. You and I will watch the annihilation from safety, secure in the knowledge that we will never have to be subjected to the petty sins and vile trivialities of humanity ever, *ever* again."

The woman gave a rapturous sigh, fully ecstatic at the idea of watching her neighbors experience an agonizing, torturous end at the Empyrea's hand. Conrad was disturbed, but he was also intrigued. What was it about this preacher that had all of these people eating from his palm?

His voice was rising, bursting across the square like a bullhorn. "The stilling of time is but one sign of many written in the Midnight Papers. There will be floods and fires and famine. Sickness and suffering. But it will all be in the Empyrea's name, and for her glorious purposes. Come, dear friends. Join with us, and be saved."

Just then, Conrad felt a hand on his shoulder and a powerful tug drawing him backwards into the murky shadows of an alleyway beside a tavern hung with a placard of a broken lyre.

He squirmed and kicked against his assailant, first afraid of what they'd do if they knew he was the king and then afraid of what they'd do if they *didn't*. "Let go of me!" he spat, punching and snarling, arms flailing.

The grip on him suddenly loosened, and he whirled around wearing his most kinglike expression, cheeks reddened by imperious outrage.

His anger morphed into shock when he saw his attacker. He didn't know what he expected—a threadbare pickpocket? A cutthroat mercenary? A brawling drunk?—but certainly not this . . . animal.

The creature was covered in patchy fur, standing a foot taller than Conrad, but with its head bent low, as if it were frightened. Under his stare, it scuttled further into the sheltering darkness, but it didn't run away. It didn't smell like an animal either; rather, the scent he caught was floral, like violets. "You're not supposed to be here," it said. "You're not prepared."

Conrad was startled. The voice, coming from the ducking, furry head, did not belong to an animal at all. Rather, it was that of a human *girl*. A young woman.

As his eyes adjusted to the dimness of the alleyway, he began to see the human shape underneath the strange skins. It was a cloak, he realized, of hundreds of different furs and leathers, haphazardly patched together. It was too big for her; beneath the drag of the heavy hood, Conrad could only just make out the smudgy smears that, in good light, might make up a face: nose, eyes, mouth . . .

"You need to stay away from the Circle," she said. "You can't let yourself get pulled in. They are dangerous. To you. To Renalt . . . to everyone."

"Who are you?" Conrad asked, finally finding his voice.

"A friend," she said. "Or I was. Used to be."

"You know me?" he asked, and then realized she had said "friend" with a strange emphasis, like a title. Like it began with a capital *F*.

A *Friend*.

"You should not engage with the Circle unprepared," she said, avoiding the question. "Fidelis," she said, lifting an oversize sleeve to point to the mouth of the alley, "the *current* Fidelis. He reads thoughts. Sometimes he can give them to you, too. Make you think things you wouldn't normally think. You need to know that. You need to protect yourself."

He thought of the man's too-canny stare. "Okay. How?" he asked.

She shrugged, a benign human gesture that belied her inhuman costume. "I don't know how," she said. "I just know that you must be careful. Because—"

She didn't get a chance to finish. The clock had begun to chime; it was midnight. The fur-girl froze as she listened to each toll, quivering like a cornered rabbit.

It stopped at eleven and did not start again.

"Dear stars," she whispered. "It's happening." She grabbed him by both arms and said, "Don't trust them. Don't let them get close. You and Sir Greythorne must get out while you still can."

Before Conrad had a chance to say a word, she darted clumsily off into the darkness, knocking a moldering crate from its perch on the edge of a barrel. She was gone before the crate hit the ground, the crash of it covering all other sounds of her escape.

As Conrad trudged back to the castle, his mind spun like a potter's wheel, trying to force his muddy thoughts into a sensical shape. She was familiar enough with him to call Kellan by his last name, but was not close enough to know that Kellan was no longer in his employ. The more he considered her words, the more they seemed weighted by a sense of inexorable certainty. She had spoken truth, he felt it. The man on the black horse *had* planted the compulsion to return to the square and listen to his preaching into Conrad's mind . . . which meant that Fidelis, like everyone else, was jockeying for control of a weak, childish king.

If there was danger on the horizon, Conrad would have to confront it on his own.

Though still grappling with these thoughts, Conrad made it through the gate and inside the side servants' entrance without trouble, but by the time he came to the castle's third floor, his distraction had morphed into carelessness. He didn't hear the footsteps until they were nearly upon him. He'd stumbled right into the middle of a guard's nightly rounds. And while he'd certainly be able to lie and posture his way through the discovery, seeing the king alone in an abandoned hallway after midnight and dressed in streetwear was sure to make a memorable impression and news of the encounter would spread to every corner of the castle before the sun came up tomorrow.

Conrad sprinted and ducked into the first bedroom he came to, then pressed his ear against the door as the guard walked past, whistling an off-key rendition of "Don't Go, My Child, to the Ebonwilde."

When the footsteps and the whistling faded away, Conrad sighed in relief, turning his back against the door, only to realize that the room in which he'd taken cover was not a bedroom after all.

It was Onal's old stillroom and study.

He wandered among the tables, which were still littered with the healer's potion-making paraphernalia. Onal was everywhere in this room, as if all her years spent walking up and down this floor had permanently imbued the floorboards with her essence.

She was his grandmother, he reminded himself. His father's real mother. The woman who had borne King Regus, and then raised him like a governess, without any acknowledgment of her true role. Not that Onal needed such appreciation; she was never one to over-indulge in sentiment or feelings. She had been very much like the remedies she brewed: she'd do you great good if you could get past the caustic and bitter taste.

When Aurelia was Conrad's age, Onal had taken her under her wing and taught her a bit of herb lore. He would have loved such an opportunity; he could have made it a game like the ones Aurelia had shown him. He moved through the shelves and squinted at the faded labels on the bottles, written in Onal's own hand. The most basic concoctions were at the front: an aloe and honey tincture for burns, marshmallow root and bromelain for cough. But the farther back on the shelf he went, the more obscure the remedies became. Boiled salamander eyes for fevers, ground tern bones for seasickness, brewed frostlace flower for forgetting, badger milk for nightmares . . .

Conrad paused, then went back half a step, picking up the dark purple bottle, second to last on the shelf.

Frostlace for forgetting, he thought.

And suddenly, he had an idea.

5

NOW

AURELIA

10 DAYS TO MIDWINTER
1621

"Liar," I said through gritted teeth. "Zan would never abandon me."

"I am telling you the truth," Castillion said. "And I can prove it to you, if you'll let me. Please, Aurelia."

Reluctantly, I followed him. I couldn't force myself to take a final glance at the dais, so instead, I looked up at the constellations in the domed ceiling. They seemed to spark as we left them behind.

Inside the Night Garden, the air had been sweet and warm, pervaded with the soft scents of a spring evening in the Ebonwilde. But outside, it was winter. My assessment of the frostlace blossoms had been correct: Midwinter was coming soon. I could feel the bite of the cold through my thin gown, my flimsy slippers. Where did I get slippers? Had I been wearing them when I went into the casket? I couldn't remember.

Castillion removed his heavy cape—crimson velvet, lined with white fur—and settled it over my shoulders, fastening it with a brooch in the shape of his signet spider. The spider's body was made of a smoky luneocite stone that gave off a dim glow.

"Won't you need this?" I asked.

"I'll be fine," he replied. "I'm well-adjusted to the northern climate."

I wanted to tell him that I didn't really need it either; what harm could the snow do me now? But his castoff warmth, already permeating the fabric, was more pleasant than the cold and so, selfishly, I kept it.

Specks of frost drifted weightlessly around us as we walked. Heavier snow must have fallen in the last few days; it had been cleared from the walkways but was still collected in mounds on each side.

Castillion led me down the paths between them. "The Night Garden was built first," he said. "Before even Fort Castillion itself. It was made to commemorate Adamus Castillion. He was a powerful mage, it was said. Favored by the Empyrea. Destined for great and glorious things."

"And did he? Do great and glorious things?"

Castillion shook his head. "He died young. Didn't get much of a chance."

I thought of the man and woman in marble at the Night Garden's center. "Was that his statue on the dais?"

"That's him," Castillion said. "Him and his beloved, Vieve." He was quiet for a moment, watching me, as if waiting for a flicker of recognition at the name. Then he said, "You're descended from her, actually. On your mother's side. It was even in her name. Genevieve: from the line of Vieve."

"Are you saying I'm . . . related to you?" I made a face. I'd wanted to call Castillion many things over the course of our acquaintance, but I never imagined one might be *cousin.*

"No, no," he said hurriedly. "They died before they could marry or have children. You're descended from the daughter of her sister. I'm descended from the son of his brother."

I stiffened. *One or the other. One or the other. Daughter of the sister, or son of the brother.* How many times had that face in the mirror said those words to me before the Day of Shades?

We had come to an overlook atop a sheer cliff. No, not a cliff; the telltale square zigzag of battlements rose like blunt teeth from the snowy edge. It was a wall. Fort Castillion, it seemed, had been built more into the mountain than upon it.

Below, the cold winter moon glinted off the obsidian waters of an inlet bay, where dozens of ships lined the harbor. Huddled close to the cliff's edge was the town, a cluster of buildings constructed of dark Ebonwilde timber, their steeply pitched roofs fringed with icicles. The fort was penned in by a wooden palisade, and where a moat might once have flowed, a ring of fire now burned, orange against the indigo night.

And across the expanse outside the wall, a sea of tents.

"Not long ago," he began, "this was a simple village, one-tenth the size of what you see now. As far back as our records go, there were never more than a hundred families living in the Castillion province. And now . . . just look. People are arriving faster than we can build houses to keep them."

"It never occurred to you, while you were laying waste to the rest of Achleva, that eventually you'd have to take care of the people you conquered?"

He smiled grimly. "These are not people I conquered, but those who have fled to my door out of desperation, looking for help. And hope."

"This"—I waved my hand across the landscape—"is where people come for hope?"

"Yes," he said. "Now imagine what the rest of the world must look like for that to be true." He turned toward me again, his white hair buffeted by the chill wind. "That line of fire burns all day and all night, continually fed by the day's dead. Some from the cold, but most from fever. But at least here there is food, and a small modicum of protection."

"Protection from what?"

He didn't answer, but something about the way he looked at me then—the uncharacteristic tightness of his mouth, the sudden rigidity of his back . . . it made him look strange. Vulnerable, perhaps? Or young.

No, scratch that. He looked *old*. Not in his face, but in his eyes. There was a weariness in them that belonged to a man of seven decades, not a mere two and a half.

But by the time he glanced at me again, the expression was gone.

"This way," he said.

At the battlement's edge, stairs spiraled up to the door of a pinnacle turret. The room at the top of the turret seemed to serve many uses: study, library, observatory. There were shelves and shelves of books; tables cluttered with half-burned candles, hardened wax drippings overflowing tarnished brass holders; and an oversize pine desk that was piled with paper: scribbled notes, maps, schematic drawings. The chamber smelled of polish and leather and old books. There was a bed on one side, made up with a plain, homespun quilt, then a tall mirror, and a large copper basin for bathing.

If I'd had any blood, my cheeks would have flamed crimson. "You brought me to your bedroom?" I coughed.

"My study," he said without missing a beat. "But I do sleep here sometimes, when I am up very late and too tired to make it across the courtyard to the main part of the keep. It's something of a sanctuary for me, separate as it is from the rest of the fort. I thought you'd appreciate the solitude."

I wandered around the perimeter. There were four tall windows anchoring each direction of the circular room. From the first window, I had a view of snowy terrain and the northern night sky, where the aurora rippled across the darkness in streaks of luminescent color. An enormous brass spyglass had been wheeled to that window and pointed toward the heavens. It was as thick as a ship's mast and longer than I was tall.

The western window had a view of the courtyard, where the Night Garden shone like a jewel in the middle of a radiating spiral of crisscrossing paths. The eastern window at its opposite showed the town, the tents, and the burning moat.

From the last window, the one facing south, I could see nothing. Well, not *nothing*—just the eerie Ebonwilde, stretching endlessly into the distance, black wood and bleak horizon blending so seamlessly, I could not make out where one ended and the other began. It was vast, unchanging, unknowable.

Castillion cleared his throat and I turned. "I was hoping you wouldn't ever have to see this, but . . ." He had a folded parchment in his hand. A letter, bearing a broken seal of gold-colored wax, imprinted with a raven—the Silvis raven, from Zan's family ring. "I won't deny you the truth."

I took the letter, hoping Castillion could not see the quaver in my grip. As I opened it, he continued, "You told me to join with Valentin to wake you, and I tried to follow those directions exactly. Before I retrieved your body from the Assembly, I attempted to reach him—even offering a substantial reward for information about his whereabouts. And after I brought you here, I sent him several correspondences, telling him of my success. Twice, he did not respond. On my third attempt to contact him, he sent me this. And your vial of blood with it."

I unfolded the letter and began to read.

My dear sir—

I regret to inform you that the girl of which you speak, Aurelia Altenar, died on the last day of Decimus, 1620. She is buried in the *crypt beneath the sanctorium chapel at Greythorne Manor. As she died in my arms, I can assure you that whatever ghoul you're intending to raise from the dead **is not her**.*

I am enclosing this vial of the real Aurelia's blood so that you might have no further reason to contact me about this matter.

Let the dead remain in the ground where they belong.

Valentin de Achlev

I read the letter three times, examining every turn of phrase, every stroke and curve of his pen, but I already knew: this was Zan's bold and unmistakable script, written by his own hand and sealed with his ring. And the last, most final proof of his abandonment now hung on a cord around my own neck.

Let the dead remain in the ground where they belong.

Zan knew. He *knew* that Castillion had found me. He *knew* that Castillion wanted to wake me. He *knew* and he chose not to come.

Whatever ghoul you're intending to raise from the dead **is not her**.

He'd underlined that part hard enough that his pen had nearly gouged through the paper.

I scoured the letter again, certain I was missing some vital piece of information that would allow me to decode its true message. Or that it was a cipher of some kind, and would only become clear with the right context, the right key.

But the letter was frank. No hidden meanings, no subtext to unravel.

To my great shame, I found myself missing the grief I'd felt when I thought Zan had died in Stiria Bay. It was a simpler, more innocent agony, untainted by the corrupting sting of rejection and betrayal.

Castillion said, "I'm sorry, Aurelia. I truly am. I know you had a deep, sincere belief in him. I take no joy in proving him unworthy of your high regard."

"I have yet to see you take joy in anything," I said under my breath.

"You don't know me very well," he said quietly.

I shoved the letter into his chest. "You should have listened to him," I said, wishing that my voice didn't sound quite so feeble, so broken. "You should have left me where you found me."

"I couldn't have, even if I'd wanted to."

"That's right. You made a commitment, and you had to keep it," I said. "Ever the slave to your precious virtues."

"No," he said. "It's not that. Not wholly." He was watching me again, gauging my reaction with his usual imperturbable calm. He had removed a scroll from one of the shelves and brought it to one of the larger tables in the center of the room. With a quick *whoosh*, he unrolled the paper, which unfurled across the entire length of the table.

As he weighted the edges of the document, I approached it cautiously. "What is this?" I asked.

"This," he said, "is the new world."

It was a map. I leaned over the table to scrutinize it. Castillion's protectorate, carved from the northernmost part of what was once Achleva, was marked in blue. On the opposite end, my own nation was divided by a thick line. The smaller part, on the southeastern side, was outlined in red and labeled RENALT. The larger section stretched from the southwestern side of the island, through the Ebonwilde, and up past Stiria Bay. There was no indication of field or river or city left on that side; it was a crosshatched patch of black ink. To the side was written THE MIDNIGHT ZONE.

"What's this?" I asked, running my finger along the jagged line.

"The land staked by the Circle Midnight," Castillion replied from over his shoulder. He had moved across the room and was rummaging on another table, shifting around papers and mathematical instruments. "It's a doomsday cult that swept into power when things started to go bad. They worship the Empyrea obsessively, following the writings of a pre-Assembly high mage named Fidelis the First. By the time anyone else understood what was happening, they'd spread like a stain across the entire western coast, gathering followers and violently laying claim to everything in their path. Aha!" He'd uncovered a crystal decanter and two glasses.

I raised an eyebrow. "No longer espousing sobriety, I take it?"

He gave a grim laugh and flopped into a large leather chair. "I do my best," he said, crossing one lanky leg over the other. "But some allowances must be made when one is facing such circumstances as these. Would you like one?" He lifted the bottle, and amber liquid sloshed inside.

I shook my head.

He shrugged. "Are you certain? Because you might need it in a minute." Then he set both glasses down and took a large draft straight from the decanter itself.

"Why?" I asked. "What could you possibly have left to tell me that is worse than what I already know?"

"You saw the map," he said slowly, avoiding my eyes. "You saw Syric?"

"If the map is correct, Syric is in the Midnight Zone. Does that mean that the Tribunal is gone?"

"The Tribunal was ended after the Day of Shades. Syric had an uprising, and then the citizenry attacked and hung them all, which made way for the king to return to his court."

I froze. "Conrad went back to the capital?"

Castillion nodded. "He did. And . . . he was still there the night an earthquake struck, causing the failure of the dam north of the city and a tsunami in the ocean south. Syric was overcome by a wave on both sides." He looked at the rug under his boots, an antique red Marconian piece, decorated with interlacing gold swirls. "King Conrad did not make it out." His eyes flicked up to mine, full of an infuriatingly gentle pity.

"He's dead?" I asked, barely audible, sinking into the chair opposite him. "Are you trying to tell me that my brother is dead?"

"I'm very sorry."

Conrad! My beautiful little brother, gone? My soul screamed its rebellion at the thought. How could that be? How was the world still spinning without him in it?

Every other heartbreak paled into nothing compared to this loss. Zan's betrayal, Renalt's destruction, my shock at waking to the face of my former enemy in a frightening, foreign world. All of it was nothing compared to this.

My hands were like claws, gripping the arms of my chair. My eyes burned, but were barren of tears. I wondered, obliquely, if in my new body I could still make them.

"You know this for certain?" I asked in a strangled voice.

"I know nothing for certain," Castillion said. "Certainty is another rare commodity in this new world." He took another long drink. "There is no diminishing the cruelty of your brother's likely passing, but you must know that you are one of *millions* to face such circumstances. In the past year there have been floods and fires and food shortages, and illnesses on such a grand scale, it can be hard to fathom." He paused. "You'd be hard-pressed to find someone out there whose life has not been altered by such a loss."

"And you woke me, in the middle of it? Why? Why not just let me remain in my oblivion?" The numbness, the endless blackness . . . I longed for it now.

"Because," he said with a careful calm, "in your brother's absence, *you* are the rightful queen of Renalt."

I went still as a statue. Still as ancient stone. I looked back at the map. "But there is no Renalt," I said. "Not like it was before."

"It could be restored to its former glory. Renaltans just need someone to rally around. Someone who could remind them of who they are, to make them believe that they can fight. Aurelia," he said, shifting to the edge of his seat in his earnestness, "we can send the Circle Midnight back to the shadows from whence they came, but we have to stop fighting each other first." Leaning forward in his chair, his dark eyes were fervid. "Imagine what you and I could do if we were *united*."

"United?" I whispered. There were implications in that word I was not yet prepared to consider. My reflection's rhyme suddenly re-formed itself in my memory.

One or the other, one or the other. Daughter of the sister, or son of the brother.

When I glanced at Castillion again, it was as if I were seeing him for the first time. He had always been a striking man, with his dark eyes and shock of white hair, his impeccable dress. But had he always been so . . . earnest? So intense? Had his mouth always been shaped like that, with one side curved up into a sardonic half smile, like he was holding a sly secret on the tip of his tongue? I had to admit that it was not . . . unpleasant . . . to look at him. But now that I was, I wished to the stars I could stop.

I said, "The people of Renalt have always loathed me. They would never accept me as their queen."

"They will," Castillion said. "I know they will. I have invited Renalt's lord protector—the closest thing displaced Renaltans currently have to call a leader—to meet with us tomorrow. If *he* can be convinced that you're capable of reclaiming Renalt's throne, everyone else will, too."

"Lord protector? Which of the courtiers stepped in to seize that outrageous title? Gaskin? Graves? Hallet?" I scoffed at the thought.

Castillion's tone was measured. "Greythorne."

Kellan. Merciful Empyrea! I closed my eyes, trying not to think about how the last time I saw him, he was cradling his bleeding arm in shock, his face marred with an expression that was equal parts hatred, hurt, and disbelief. He was my loyal bodyguard and most devoted friend, and I had chosen to ruin his life over letting him lose it.

I was *terrified* to see him again. He probably hated me. But at least, with Kellan, I wouldn't have to wonder why.

In a strangled voice, I said, "You saw what I did to your men. I am barely holding myself together. Even now, there's a part of me that wants to hurt you." I dropped my voice. "You need to know that."

"I'm not afraid of you," he said.

But even as he said it, I saw his body tense up. He could say he wasn't afraid of me, even convince himself of it, but the rhythm of his heart and the pace of his breath told another story.

I was just like his seven-legged spider: damaged and dangerous, and better off left alone.

6

THEN

ZAN

The Canary girls must have seen him coming; Jessamine was waiting for him on the tavern's stoop. Her arms were crossed over her chest, her eyes heavy-lidded, an I-told-you-so ready on her lips. When she saw his face, however, her initial smugness was quickly supplanted by concern. "Merciful Empyrea, Zan. Are you all right?"

"Not really," he said, wearily rolling from Madrona's back. He had to fight to keep his knees from buckling when his feet hit the ground. "I think I might be losing my mind."

She raised an eyebrow and tilted her head. "Oh?"

"You're supposed to look surprised and say, *No, of course not, Zan. You're completely fine!*"

"Well." She shrugged. "Spending weeks on end alone in a crypt isn't exactly *normal* behavior. Honestly, I expected you to crack a lot earlier."

He wanted to laugh. Here in the cool light of morning, grounded by Jessamine's gentle deprecation, he could almost forget the encounter with the phantom of Father Cesare—who'd then turned into Isobel Arceneaux—the night before.

Almost.

"All right," she said, hands on hips. "Come in, then, Your Highness. I'm sure we can find some use for you."

★

The rest of Zan's day was spent on the roof of the Canary, nailing tin shingles back into place while the chill wind of the Renaltan moor buffeted against his skin. In the fields below, the children were playing games with each other, laughing and tumbling through the brittle grass. These were the orphans from the Achlevan refugee camp near Greythorne—his people. His *subjects*, were he to actually lay claim to the title of Achlevan king. He did not see how such an event would help anyone, though; as hard as their circumstances were now, they would not improve with him on a throne.

As night fell, Delphinia donned a fringed blue shawl and tromped out through the fields to collect the children. Rafaella stuck her head out of the door, calling to them, "Hurry! Hurry! Dinner is ready!" The evening sun gave her brown skin a burnished glow.

She glanced up at Zan on the roof and smiled. "You too. Time to come down and eat. You've done plenty of work today, and despite what Jessamine says, there's nothing wrong with saving a few tasks for tomorrow."

"I heard that!" Jessamine's voice came from inside.

Lorelai joined Rafaella on the porch, counting the heads of the children as they came back inside. "Torrance, where is your hat? I just knitted you a new one! Heloise, mind those muddy shoes."

He could see why Aurelia had loved these women. He couldn't help admiring them—they had not asked for this responsibility, but they had risen to meet it, uncomplaining, while he had ignored it, too busy nursing his own wounds to consider anyone else's.

He climbed down from the ladder and followed the children inside as they assembled in the dining hall.

Bone-tired, Zan flopped into a chair in the farthest corner as Jessamine went from table to table, ladling broth into a dozen waiting bowls. The hall, full of giggling children, was no less raucous than it had been mere months ago when it was populated with travelers and rowdy tradesmen. He pulled a thin sketchbook and a stick of charcoal from a pocket, distracting himself from the memory of kissing Aurelia in the room above where he now sat by drawing the view of the Renaltan grasslands from the Canary's roof.

He felt a small tug on his sleeve and turned to find a girl at his elbow, gazing up at him from beneath a fringe of sandy hair. Heloise of the muddy shoes, he remembered.

"I heard Miss Jessamine call you 'Your Highness,'" Heloise said, lisping through the gap left by a missing front tooth. "Are you a king?"

Zan grimaced and shook his head. "I'm not," he said.

Her face fell, and he added, "Sorry."

She screwed her mouth to one side, then shrugged. "I didn't think so. You don't look like a king."

"What does a king look like?" Zan asked, curious.

"Probably taller," she said slowly, considering. "With a crown and a big beard like my papa used to have."

"Your papa?"

"Yes. Miss Lorelai said he's with my mama and the Empyrea now."

"I see," Zan said. "I'm very sorry."

She shrugged again. "He used to say that when our rightful king was on the throne in Achleva, maybe we could go back home. We used to live in Achlev, you know. Where it never got cold. Not like here."

"I know," Zan said. "I used to live there, too."

"Do you miss it?"

Zan was flooded with a torrent of memories. Of a bloodleaf-clad tower and a cottage lined with yellow flowers, of traversing tunnels in the dark and watching a witchy princess work midnight magic on the wall high above a sleeping city. The memories were as clear and sharp as cut glass. *Stars!* He wished he had something to drink. "Sometimes," he said finally.

She nodded sympathetically and said, "Me too," before scampering to rejoin the boisterous pack of children.

"She's right about that, you know." Jessamine set a bowl down in front of him and began filling it with soup.

"That I'd look more kingly if I were taller and had a beard?"

"Yes," she said. "But also that if Achleva had a king, she could go home."

Zan said, "There's no going home. Not for any of us."

★

During the day, Zan helped with odd jobs around the Quiet Canary. After supper, he usually sat with a few of the children and taught them art. Nothing too advanced; it was mostly showing them how to observe and render. He'd set an object on one of the Canary's old gambling tables—a mug, a coin, one of Jessamine's stickpin brooches —and tell them to describe it. "What do you see?" he'd ask. The answers were always logical at first: *A cup. It's pewter. The coin is flat and copper. A pin, brass. Shape of a butterfly.*

Then he'd ask, "What else?" It would always take a minute or two for them to let their understanding of what the thing was used for slip away, allowing them to see it again as what it was in space. "Where is the light?" he asked. "Where are the shadows?" And "Yes, it's gray, but what other colors can you see? A hint of orange along the side there, reflected from the fire. Yes, there's purple in the darkness. See here, where the light shines from the rim? It's almost white."

They'd scrunch their faces and squint, their stubby sticks of colored wax making squeaks and scratches as they rubbed across the fine parchment of Lorelai's donated stationery.

It was amazing how well he was able to teach the Canary's young charges how to see contrast and color while drowning in a sea of gray himself.

The Canary girls gave him Aurelia's old room, the little closet too crabbed for anyone else to have staked a claim. It had been left untouched. The quilt was rumpled; there were still strands of her hair in a comb on the dresser. There were whispers of her presence everywhere he looked, which he found comforting and disquieting in equal parts.

By night, he drew. Sketch after sketch after sketch . . . he always started with something safe, like the Canary's crooked weather vane, or a smattering of crows scared into flight from the frostbitten fields by whooping children. But his drawings always eventually drifted to more painful things: Kate and Nathaniel's cottage in Achlev, a re-creation of his mother's portrait that used to hang outside his bedchamber, and, of course, Aurelia. Her hands, delicately stretched out across a book, or fingering a glass knife, or dripping blood into a bowl for a spell. Sometimes it was her neck, long and graceful, and the soft slope of her shoulders. Her lips, too, frowning in concentration, quirked to the side in frustration, or softly parted as she whispered his name between kisses. It was a slow, self-inflicted torture that usually ended with him asleep at the desk. He'd wake with a pounding head and aching back and bleary vision, but *anything* was better than spending every night alone in Aurelia's bed, staring into the darkness. He was tormented by his own thoughts, and the persistent voice in his brain that reminded him, over and over, that had he only been smarter, stronger, braver, better, Aurelia would not now be buried under a half-finished painting beneath the Stella Regina.

He wanted to go back to finish it; every morning he woke up resolved to do it, and every morning he found some excuse to stay. He told no one of his hallucination of Father Cesare and Arceneaux, and even managed to rationalize that it was a product of bad wine or tainted grain . . . but still could not convince himself to return and find out for certain.

He was a coward, through and through.

One night, after he'd been there nearly a month, he had knocked a piece of charcoal on the ground and, when he bent to retrieve it, saw a piece of paper that had slipped between the desk and the wall. He tugged it free and found himself looking at another of his own drawings—the one he did the night he and Aurelia had sought refuge here, after the events of Conrad's coronation. It was of the horseman who saved his life.

He touched his fingers to the rider's shadowed face—Aurelia's face. He knew her now. Knew it was *her* breath that had coaxed life into him that night on the shore of Stiria Bay, *her* voice that brought him back from the brink. *Her* words that had filled him, however fleetingly, with a sense of noble purpose. *Si vivis, tu pugnas.* While you live, you fight.

Fighting, it turned out, was easy. It was living that was hard.

7

THEN

ROSETTA

Syric's clock tower was an imposing structure, looming over the city square with all of the dispassionate severity of a mirthless governess. If it were still working, it would likely have noted the hour as sometime between one and two in the morning. The streets were mostly empty now, save for the scuttling of rodents in the gutters and the muffled, drunken laughter leaking into the air from beneath tavern doors. But the hour and minute hands had both gone still on the twelve, pointing endlessly toward the sky.

Rosetta stared at the weak glow of the clockface from beneath her hood for a long while, again willing the hands to move. *Just a tick*, she thought. *The smallest inch.*

When it became clear that no amount of wishing would reanimate the clock, Rosetta crossed the square toward it, her dark cloak billowing in the cold air. She didn't really notice anymore; she was always cold. It had been that way for so many years now, she hardly remembered what it was like to be warm. To be human.

What warmth she did feel was always faded and fleeting. Sitting in front of a roaring fire or resting in the arms of an ardent lover could make her remember, for a little while at least, what it was like to be alive. Those moments were like tiny drops of honeyed mead on her parched tongue, a small relief that was gone too soon, and only served to leave her thirstier than before.

Kellan was different from any of her other lovers, though. She felt something deeper for him—she could not deny it. Deeper even, perhaps, than the feelings she'd once held for his ancestor Mathuin Greythorne. She could still feel the heat of their encounter under her skin, like a sunbaked stone that holds its warmth long after nightfall.

"Rosetta!"

She turned at the sound of her name. Kellan was hurrying toward her, his face full of concern. It sent another painful flare of fire in her chest. She wished, not for the first time, that he was less noble. Less brave. Less beautiful.

Things would be much easier for her if he were.

"I *told* you—" she began as he got near.

"You *told* me nothing," he said, touching her arm with his good hand. "You left without so much as a goodbye. But why?"

She turned again to look at the clock. She whispered, *"Verily I say unto thee, when in the last moment of the shortest day, the Grandfather's two*

hands point to the sky and stay, thou shalt know that the Empyrea's return to
earth is finally upon us."

"What does that mean?"

"It's a prophecy from the Midnight Papers," Rosetta said. "A very
obscure piece of writing, made over a thousand years ago." Her voice
caught in her throat. "It predicts the end of the world."

Kellan's legs were long, but he had to dash to keep up with her
pace. "What are you going to do? Climb into the clock? Try to repair
it yourself?"

"If I have to," she said. "Because if this is what I think it is . . ."
Her yellow eyes flicked in his direction. "You can't imagine the devastation to come. The Empyrea has been waiting a long, long time to
enact her plans. Long enough I had come to believe, foolishly, that she
might never get the chance."

"The Empyrea doesn't go out of her way to bless anyone," Kellan
said, "but she also doesn't seem too inclined to punish 'the wicked'
either."

"If you think that," Rosetta said, turning on him, her breath coming out in an angry, icy cloud, "you're as naïve as a newborn child."

They were at the foot of the clock tower now. Rosetta moved
around to the back, where a rusty, fist-size iron lock hung from the
door's latch. She cursed under her breath. "Iron. Stars, I hate iron."
Metal was always the most unforgiving of mediums upon which to
exert feral magic, and of the metals, iron was the worst.

Wearily, she began to summon her strength to work a spell. Then
Kellan came up behind her and slammed his new metal hand down

upon the lock. The old iron gave way easily, and Kellan used his other hand to unhook the broken lock and toss it aside.

She turned a yellow glare on him. "If you knew how much work that hand took to make . . ."

He shrugged. "At least I can be good for something."

As dark as it was outside, it was darker still inside the clock tower, which smelled of dust and damp and old grease. Cobwebs were abundant; it had been a long time since anyone set foot inside here.

"What now?" Kellan said.

"We go up," Rosetta replied, her gaze following the switchback stairs that led to the top.

Their footfalls on the metal stairs sounded like the slow, sonorous clanking of old chains, but otherwise the tower was silent. There was no whirring of gears, no clattering of cogs, no hum of mechanical workings. When they reached the top platform, the moon was suspended on the other side of the luminous clockface glass, one pearly disc framed perfectly by the other.

Rosetta strode across the platform to look out through the glass. To the north, she could see the rise of the rocky hills. To the south, the ink-black line of the quiet ocean. And below, the sparse glitter of lights from candlelit windows.

This was a vantage point normally reserved for falcons and crows, seabirds and sparrows. She was a creature of the forest and its footpaths, more at home beneath the sheltering trees than above them. The sky was unnerving in its infiniteness. Too big, too cold, too unfeeling. Just like the goddess who was said to rule it.

With a sigh, Rosetta began tracing out the spell lines against the backward clockface. Up, down, turn, across. Loop here, twist there. Back around. In. Out. The glass warmed beneath her fingertips as the little rivulets of power began to stream out from the knot pattern. *Move*, she told the clock as the spell crept from the glass into the pin fulcrum at its center and then began the agonizingly slow coil around the metal hands. *Move*.

They did not obey.

She pushed and strained and gritted her teeth, forcing her power down the center shaft into the giant gears suspended in the cavernous vault behind her. "Move!" she commanded again, this time aloud.

"Rosetta," Kellan said, concern clear in his voice. "Rosetta, stop."

The gears groaned, scraping hideously against each other, but still refusing to give even an inch. Desperately, she reached for more power, drawing this time from the reservoir given to her by the warden's mantle.

It wasn't there.

She pulled her hands away, severing the spell.

"We should go back," Kellan said, coming up behind her and putting his arms around her. Then, "Rosetta, you're shaking."

"It's gone," she muttered. "The mantle is gone. The prophecy is here, coming true right before my eyes, and I have none of the power I need to stop it."

"Calm down, Rosetta," Kellan said. "It's *just* a clock. Just one broken clock." But despite the conviction of his words, when he glanced back up at the clock, now laced with a web of meandering hairline cracks across its face, doubt began to tighten his throat.

"It was Aurelia," Rosetta said. "She must have taken the mantle, that night in Greythorne. She is the only one who could have done it —a daughter of the woods. But how did I not realize it was gone?" Rosetta asked herself. "How did I not know?"

She knew the answer, though: she had been too preoccupied with Kellan for all these weeks. Trying to fix what Aurelia had broken in him, and what had sprouted between them.

The Ninth Age had begun, and brought Fidelis the First's prophecies into fruition along with it. Even in the darkest of her imaginings for the future, she saw the world ending slowly, over centuries, millennia, eons . . . this meant they had a year.

The Reckoning of the Midnight Papers was here, and the earth was left with no warden to lead the war against it.

"Come back to the Minstrel with me," Kellan coaxed. "We can get something to eat, try to sleep, and talk more in the morning, when we're rested . . ."

An inane laugh bubbled up from her. "*Rested?* I haven't been 'rested' in a hundred years. Know why? Because I have responsibilities. Real ones that can't be abandoned just because I'm angry or feeling sorry for myself."

Kellan's expression darkened. "Isn't that *exactly* what you tried to do? You lied to Aurelia about the Ilithiya's Bell because *you* wanted to use it to cross into the Gray and finally die. Who did you intend to take the warden's mantle then? And let's not forget this." He lifted his right hand. "I lost everything because of your lies."

"Go ahead and blame me, Kellan. Blame me, or Aurelia, or Arceneaux and the Tribunal . . . whatever you need to do to get through the day. But do you know who doesn't deserve any of your blame? Conrad. He—"

"I'm done with this," Kellan said darkly, starting down the stairs. "I'm done with you."

"That's right, run away!" She leaned over the rail, calling down the dark void at his retreating figure. "Wouldn't want you to have to actually face your failings!"

The sound of the tower door clanging shut spiraled up the column, and Rosetta moved to look out the cracked clockface glass. Far below, Kellan's cloak was little more than a gray blotch as he strode across the square to the tavern.

★

She waited for him to look back, to pause, to turn around—*something*—but he never did. It didn't hurt as much as she thought it would; perhaps, after all of this time, she really was better off alone. "Farewell, Kellan," she whispered.

8

THEN

CONRAD

The first thing Conrad did when he awoke was track down Pelton, the castle's reedy, high-strung seneschal, for a comprehensive list of the city's most powerful players now that the Tribunal was gone. "In particular," Conrad said, "I'm looking for information about an organization called the Circle Midnight, and of a document called the Midnight Papers."

Pelton's upper lip dwarfed his bottom lip, and when his expression became pinched, it turned his mouth into a petulant, upside-down pout. "Where would you have heard a name like that, Majesty? I hardly think you need to trouble yourself with such—"

"I hardly think *you* need to trouble yourself with questioning me," Conrad retorted, molding his face into its most imperious expression. He didn't enjoy putting on the "haughty king" persona, but it seemed to be the only way to nip this kind of head-patting patronization in the bud. "I require only your compliance, Pelton. Should I ever want your opinion, I'll ask for it. Until then, I suggest you keep it to yourself."

"My apologies, Majesty," Pelton said, bowing low, "I will see what information can be gathered about this 'Circle Midnight.' Anything else I can do for you, my king?"

"I'll take my evening meal in my room tonight," he said. "See that it gets sent there."

He spent the morning in the library, collecting books that caught his interest. History, mostly: *A Pre-Assembly Account of the Western Realms* and *The Feats and Failures of Thirteenth-Century Renaltan Kings*, but there were a few religious tomes mixed in as well, such as *Our Beloved Empyrea* and *Meditations on the Goddess of the Sky*. The selection was appallingly limited; the Tribunal's oppressive hand was felt everywhere, but especially in libraries. There is little a tyrant fears more than unfettered access to a collection of ideas; ideas, left unattended, can bloom into beliefs, and beliefs into rebellions.

So, they replaced the people's desire for truth with fear of it.

By swiftly and brutally punishing those caught with forbidden books or expressing dissonant opinions, and rewarding those who informed on their friends and neighbors, the Tribunal had essentially made their oppression of ideas self-sustaining. Only the bravest and most reckless still traded in contraband books after they were purged from the open marketplace.

Aurelia, of course, was one those people. He knew about her secret trove of reading material under the royal sanctorium altar. No child who enjoyed games and hiding as much as he did would have missed it. He used to use his time in worship to look at the ones with pictures. Even after he was convinced that Aurelia was going to have him assassinated, he never told anyone about her hidden books.

Now that he was king, he vowed to make sure no one would have to resort to such extremes again.

Apparently, his kingly posturing to Pelton had proved fruitful; when he arrived back at his room that evening, his dinner was already waiting for him.

After piling his books on his desk, Conrad palmed a rosy apple from the tray and munched on it while he removed his uncomfortable waistcoat, only to see a folded piece of paper flutter from his breast pocket. He dropped the apple back onto the platter and the jacket onto the bed so that his hands were free to fish the note from the floor.

It read: *There is a loose floorboard two paces to the left of the fireplace. Go see what is under it.*

Confoundingly, it was in his *own* handwriting.

Heart thumping excitedly, he walked the requisite paces from the fireplace and was delighted to discover that there was, in fact, a floorboard loose. He dropped to his knees and pried it free.

There he found a small, hollowed-out compartment, wherein was hidden a sizable bottle of purplish liquid and a sheaf of small papers just like the one he'd discovered in his pocket, tied with twine.

Most were blank. The top one was another note.

Ultimus 23rd, 1620, Midwinter Night: You snuck out of the castle to listen to a Circle Midnight preacher named Fidelis the Fourteenth. You were warned by a "Friend" that he reads minds and implants thoughts, which is why you feel so compelled to go and listen to him and his message. As this Friend identified the Circle as a threat to your country, you have decided to get closer to them and become familiar with their inner workings, but you are wary about the thought reading. But then you realized—he can't read thoughts you didn't have.

You found this bottle of frostlace potion in Onal's old study. The bottle says one drop will erase approximately thirty minutes of memory. After writing these notes, you will take six drops.

Could this be true? He *did* remember sneaking out to the city, though it was a little bleary—like a muddled dream. But after that, nothing. It seemed that his consciousness had filled in that time with mundanities—he could recall possibly eating, but would not be able to describe the cuisine. And going to sleep, but not what he'd thought about before drifting off.

This was a game, he realized, euphoric. Just like the ones he used to play with Aurelia, only this time he was playing it on—and with —himself. Hurriedly, he took the charcoal pencil from the compartment and moved to the next paper in the pile, which was blank.

He began to write, following the same pattern as the first note, again addressing his future self as "you" rather than taking the more journalistic route of "I." After all, Past Conrad was writing to Future

Conrad, and if he viewed those two versions of himself as different entities, this would be the best way to structure the messages.

Ultimus 24th, 1620: You found the note. This seems to be working. Tonight you will hide it in your breast pocket again, but you'll have to figure out something better soon; the maids have been launder- ing our clothing with astonishing regularity, and you don't want to lose it, or them to find it.

Then he set the pencil and papers back into the hole beneath the loose plank and removed the bottle of frostlace potion. In the fire- light, he could see the swirling liquid through the dark glass; it was nearly full to the top. He untwisted the lid and lifted the glass dropper over his mouth.

The potion fizzed a little as it dissolved on his tongue. It tasted of snow and cold metal and something vaguely floral . . . like lavender, but sweeter.

Because he wasn't sure how much time he had before the memory erasing could take effect, he closed the bottle and crammed it back into the cubby, settling the floor plank overtop of it. Then he tucked the note into his pocket and hung the jacket up in his wardrobe, where it would be ready for tomorrow.

His tray of food was waiting for him next to the bed, but as he approached it, he wrinkled his nose. With a sigh of indignation, he wheeled the tray to the door.

Hector and Pomeroy were at attention in the hall. "You, there," he said to Pomeroy. "Would you be so kind as to take this back down to the kitchen and bring me up a new one?"

"Is the food unsatisfactory, Majesty?" the guard asked.

"Look at that apple!" Conrad said, pointing. "It appears that someone has taken a *bite* out of it."

9

NOW

AURELIA

10 DAYS TO MIDWINTER
1621

Castillion left before dawn, though it was hard to know the time for sure since the only clock I could find in his study was apparently broken. Before he left, he told me to get some sleep so that I could be rested before Lord Greythorne's arrival; I nodded placatingly, uncertain I *could* sleep, even if I wanted to try.

And anyway, I'd done enough sleeping for a lifetime already.

Finally alone, I began to explore the study. I wasn't sure what I was looking for exactly, only that I'd gone to sleep in a world I knew and awoken in another I didn't recognize, and that I needed something —*anything*—to help me reconcile with a reality in which Zan was a stranger and Conrad was . . . Merciful Empyrea, *Conrad* . . .

I had to stop rifling through papers to lean against the table, my head suddenly swimming.

I could *not* let myself think about Conrad.

Across the way, the mirror mocked me with its emptiness, as if saying, *What does it matter that things are different now? You're not real anymore. Not human.* I stormed over to it, ripping the blanket from the bed and tossing it over the top in a huff.

Most of my search was fruitless; the only useful thing it turned up was the set of clothes I found in the back of a drawer next to the bed. They'd be a little big on me, but not terribly, and at least I could get out of the blood-spattered garments I'd worn out of the coffin.

And then my eyes slid over to the copper basin.

When I turned the spigot and heated water began to flow from the pipes, I was delighted, letting it fill up halfway before I could stand it no longer and stepped into the water with a sigh. I might have been like a dragon now, or any other cold-blooded creature unable to create its own heat, but the warmth of the bathwater proved that I wasn't sensationless. That I was, at the very least, still capable of *feeling*.

In the water, I was finally able to inspect this strange new body, shaped exactly like my old one and yet somehow unutterably foreign. The scars on my knees, gained from a thousand rough-and-tumble childhood exploits, were erased. Gone, too, were the nicks and punctures of hundreds of past blood spells, and the puckered slash on my abdomen from the alleyway assailants in Achleva. The arc of Arceneaux's knife, the last and worst physical wound of my mortal existence, was no longer there, either. I was pristine and unblemished, not a mark upon me.

I closed my eyes and lay back into the water, letting it overtake me inch by inch until I was fully submerged, the beating of my heart —a slow, sonorous thrum—surrounding me on all sides, the sound amplified by the water. It was an echo of my former humanity, my new body mimicking the workings of the old one, though it had no more blood to pump through it. I almost wished I knew how to make my phantom heart go still, so that I could be content with warm water and unblemished skin and would not have to be reminded of how much emotion and magic it used to hold.

That was when I heard the voice.

Aurelia.

I sat up with a gasp, swiping the wet strands of hair from my eyes, and pulled myself from the tub, dripping water all across the polished floors of Castillion's study.

With one hard yank, I ripped the blanket from the mirror. Then, I stepped in front of the sheet of silvered glass without waiting to wonder what I might see within it.

The room was reordered in a perfect opposite: the bed, the compass-point windows, the ceiling-high shelves of books, the curving banister that led from the upper level to the lower. But though I was only inches away from the glass, there was no sign of me within it.

I must have imagined hearing my name, I thought, squeezing my eyes shut and putting two fingers to the bridge of my nose.

When I opened them again, a face was looking back at me.

She had large, lake-blue eyes and a proud mouth, the streaming strands of waist-length black hair clinging to her pale, naked skin.

She was supposed to look like me, but she didn't. She was too symmetrical, too perfect and doll-like, as if conjured by a rose-tinted memory and not reality.

I stepped back, and the reflection followed, just slightly out of sync. "What do you want?" I asked.

The doll-girl tilted her head and replied in a voice not unlike my own,

You'll go, my child, to the Ebonwilde
For there your fortune waits.
When the midnight strike on the longest night
stop the clocks, you'll count the days —

Though it was framed in the same eerie rhythm and rhyme scheme of the familiar Renaltan folk song, this felt less like a warning and more like a prediction — or a promise.

A knock sounded, startling me and drawing my attention to the door. When I glanced back at the mirror, she was gone. The frame was empty once again.

Who would be knocking at this time of night? But it wasn't night, not anymore; the first early rays of morning were beginning to show in the eastern window. Was Castillion already returning? "Just a minute!" I called, struggling to wrangle my damp limbs into the dry clothes.

To my surprise, it was not Castillion waiting on the other side of the study door, but a soldier, dressed in a full suit of leather, including an ostentatious lavender-plumed helm and a breastplate stamped with the seven-legged spider.

"Lord Castillion commanded me to come here," the soldier said. "He thought you might need—"

"Protection?" I scoffed. "I don't think—"

"No," the soldier said, reaching up to lift his helm from his head. "A friend."

"Nathaniel?" My hand went to my mouth.

He smiled. "Hello, Aurelia."

He had changed so much. It was hard to pinpoint *how* at first, as he was just as tall and broad, face still strong and handsome as ever. His hair was shorter, shorn close to his deep brown skin, and he had grown a dark beard, but his eyes were still soft. He was still the man my dear friend Kate had fallen in love with—the soft-spoken warrior. But the way he held himself was different. He looked . . . weary.

The biggest change, however, was in his eyes: once a deep, warm brown, they were now fully black, as if there was no iris at all.

I hugged him fiercely. His was the first familiar face I'd encountered since waking—other than Castillion, who didn't count—and it filled me with so much joy to see it. I finally understood how desperately *alone* I'd felt.

"How are you?" I asked, pulling away. "How is Ella? Why are you working for Castillion? I have so many questions . . ."

He nodded. "I know. There is such a great amount that has happened since the last we saw each other."

I ushered him into the study and sat him down in one of the chairs, as if I were the hostess here, and not a hairsbreadth away from hostage.

"If Castillion wants you to convince me of his goodwill and upstanding intentions, you can say so. You don't need to lie to me. I doubt you could change my mind anyway; I know well enough what kind of man he is."

"He is a good man, Aurelia," Nathaniel said. "And that isn't a lie."

I frowned at him. "All right. So he has drugged you, then?"

"Sorry, but no."

"Blackmailing you, perhaps?"

"Afraid not. Dominic Castillion is, without doubt, the reason I'm alive right now. After what happened in Morais, he took me in. Gave me food, water, shelter. A job in one of his most trusted regiments. And all of that despite the fact that I had been quite dedicated to his opposition up until then."

"No, Nathaniel. Don't tell me that. I want so very much to despise him." I gave a deep sigh, thinking of Zan. "I guess it's not the first time I've misjudged someone's character." I stopped. "What happened in Morais?"

"Eight months ago," he said, "it was part of the first territory grab done by the Circle Midnight. They struck in the middle of the night," he said. "It was over before it began." There was something about his expression . . . the way his eyes pinched in the corners, the grim line of his mouth . . .

"Nathaniel," I said, my voice barely audible. "Ella?"

"I'd left her in the care of Kate's parents while I tried to help Zan's resistance efforts." His head hung low. "She was happy with her grandparents in Morais. Safe. Healthy. Growing like a weed. I should have stayed with her. Should have said no when Zan asked for my assistance. But I hated it there. Kate's parents loved Ella, but they could barely stand me. I should have lived with it. I should never have left. Then, at least, we could have died together."

Hand to mouth, I felt this revelation settle over me like a suffocating shroud. "Ella is . . . ? No."

"I was sick with the Bitter Fever when it happened—near death myself," he said. "That's why my eyes look like this. They tell me I was lucky to have survived, but it doesn't feel like luck." He glanced away, the muscles in his jaw tightening. "By the time I had recovered enough to go after her, it was too late."

"You went back for her?"

"I tried. I only made it as far as Percival, but I saw enough of what the Circle did to the people there—it was brutal. Horrific. Anyone who didn't immediately surrender and join them was lined up and executed. But with a prayer first, like a ritual. Or a blood offering." He shifted in his chair, sagging as if he carried the weight of those events on his back, like bricks. "Castillion had a boat in the water near Silvis, the *Endurance*. Just a small transport vessel, it wasn't equipped to fight, but he still took it down the coast, collecting as many refugees as he could. I was one of the last, rescued right before the Circle's ships began to give chase. We were able to outrun them and their cannons, but only barely. The *Endurance* lived up to its name, too; by the time we arrived back here, it was hanging together by a few nails, far too much damage to fix. Had to be scuttled in the bay."

After a long, subdued silence, I finally ventured, "I am so sorry."

He nodded. "As am I. For both of us. I know about Conrad."

I took a deep breath and voiced the hope that had been sustaining me. "Castillion said that no one knows for sure if Conrad was still in Syric when the flood hit. His body wasn't found. There could still be a possibility that he got out somehow. Went into hiding, maybe . . ."

Nathaniel looked at me, black eyes soft and sad. "Perhaps," he said, but he didn't mean it. He thought I was deluding myself.

"Castillion has arranged for Kellan Greythorne and me to meet today," I said. "My former bodyguard, who is now leading what is left of my country. I'm hoping he'll be able to tell me more about what happened to Conrad; it's the only reason, really, I'm going along with Castillion right now."

Nathaniel nodded solemnly. "I know of Lord Greythorne," he said. "His boat, the *Contessa*, docked this morning."

"He's here?"

Nathaniel said, "He's with Castillion now. Wait, Aurelia, you can't just—"

But I had already bolted to the door.

10

THEN

ZAN

The carriage arrived in the middle of the night.

Zan was still awake, laying the last few strokes down on a drawing of a frostlace bloom, requested by little Heloise, whose mother used to grow and sell them to apothecaries when they lived in Achlev. He nearly dropped his charcoal at the sound of approaching hoofbeats; in all the time he'd been there, the Canary hadn't seen a single patron or passing merchant. Between the usual winter lull and the loss of Greythorne as a destination for trade, the Canary's old business as an inn and tavern had withered into nothing. During the day, the building was full of life and noise from the children, but at night . . . Zan had gotten used to the stillness. Which was why the after-dark arrival of a four-horse coach was so surprising.

He raced down the stairs, Jessamine ahead of him and Delphinia behind while Lorelai and Rafaella went from room to room to make sure the children were still sleeping.

"If it's someone looking for a room," Jessamine said, "I think we'll have to send them away."

"But why?" Delphinia asked. "We can move the children around to free up some beds. We haven't had any news from the rest of the country in ages. I feel so cut off."

Zan and Jessamine exchanged looks. Something didn't feel quite right. "Do you have any weapons?" he asked.

"Weapons?" Delphinia asked, moving for the door. "Why would we need weapons? We're an *inn*. It's probably just someone looking for a room for the night."

"There are a few knives in the kitchen," Jessamine said. "I'll get them."

"I don't think we need anything like that," Delphinia protested. "We have no reason to think anyone would come here to hurt us. What if they need help?"

"Maybe we don't," Zan said. "But we can't take chances."

Someone pounded on the door, and a man's voice broke through the thin cracks of the wooden planks. "Is anyone there? Please! Please open the door. My wife and daughter are sick. They need help!"

"Delphinia," Zan said, his feeling of dread growing, "don't—"

But she had already unbolted the door and let it swing open.

The man on the stoop was of middling years, his dress mostly workman's wear. His hair was gathered into a ponytail at the nape of his neck, wiry wisps swept across a bald patch on his crown. He saw

Delphinia in the doorway, the lamplight haloing her blond waves, and fell at her feet, clutching at the hem of her skirt.

"Oh, are you an angel?" he wept. "Most glorious woman! Will you let us in? Will you save us?"

"Of course," she said gently, bending to help him back up to his feet. "You are welcome here, sir. We don't have much, but we do have a solid roof over our heads and some food to eat."

"Thank you," he said. "Kind lady."

Jessamine had returned, and Zan could see the hilt of the kitchen knife tucked into the waistband of her dress. Reluctantly, he allowed Delphinia to escort the distraught man inside.

"You said your wife and child are sick, sir?" he asked. "What ails them?"

Delphinia seated him near the fire and removed her shawl from her own shoulders to wrap around his.

"A fever," he said. "It came on quite suddenly. They're waiting in the carriage."

"I'll get them," Zan said after a beat. "And help them inside."

"I'll go with you," Jessamine said, though her eyes were trained on Delphinia, who was filling a mug of ale for the man.

Outside, the horses were agitated. Jessamine put her hand on one of their muzzles, attempting to calm them as they stamped. "Look," she said to Zan. "They're hungry. I wonder how long it's been since they ate."

Zan had come up to the side of the carriage. "Do you know of a tavern that uses a broken lyre emblem?"

"The Scheming Minstrel," she said. "It's located in Syric."

There was something strange in the air—an odor at once sweet, sulfuric, and putrescent. It was coming from inside the coach.

Stomach knotting, Zan put his hand on the handle and yanked.

The stench barreled into them like a battering ram, causing Zan to stumble away, coughing. Jessamine doubled over and retched into the dirt.

There was, indeed, a woman and child in the carriage, but they were long past needing help. Their faces were pallid and waxy white, with black streaks dried upon their cheeks, like tears.

Zan and Jessamine looked at each other.

"Dear stars. *Delphinia*," Jessamine gasped. They took off back toward the tavern.

Delphinia was sitting down across from the man, pushing a bowl of leftover stew toward him. When he saw Zan and Jessamine reenter, he said, "Where's my wife? Where is Martha? And Sibby? Aren't you going to bring them in? Aren't you going to help us?"

"Sir," Zan said, moving closer, his hands raised in a calming gesture. "I think you know that there's nothing we can do for your family."

"What do you mean?" Delphinia asked, blue eyes darting from Jessamine to Zan. "What's going on?"

Whip-fast, the man pushed the table over and yanked Delphinia up by her hair, pulling her in to his chest. She whimpered as he drew a dirty knife from his shirtsleeve and held it against her cheek. Sweat poured down his livid face. His pupils seemed unnaturally large, and dark.

"You lie. You are liars! We don't have the sickness. Fidelis *promised* me. We're the blessed! We're the saved."

Delphinia's eyes were glassy with terror. "We mean you no harm," Zan said, inching closer. "We *do* want to help you. But first you have to let her go."

The blackness in his pupils had spread beyond the irises and was now pooling in the corners of his eyes. "Martha," he said, addressing Delphinia, "Martha, I'm the head of the family. I know what is best for you and Sibby. For *us!* Martha!"

Delphinia was crying now. "I'm not her," she said in a small voice. "I'm not Martha."

He backhanded her, the knife narrowly missing her eye. "I told you not to speak to me like that, Martha!"

Delphinia sobbed as he shook her, and Zan moved closer still. The knife was almost in his reach. Just a few more inches . . .

But the man saw Zan from the corner of his eye and let go of Delphinia to lash out at him with the knife. Zan blocked the blow with his forearm, but felt the skin part against the blade. Delphinia used the distraction to dart into Jessamine's waiting arms.

Blood spilled hot from the cut, and Zan's anger welled over with it. When the man swiped at him again, Zan, fuming, swung his fist and funneled all of his rage into the movement. *"Get back!"* he cried as the blow connected, and the man's body flew backwards into the wall before flopping bonelessly to the floor.

He gave a final, gurgling breath, two tears making slow, black tracks across his sallow cheeks.

Zan cursed, clutching his bleeding arm, and saw Rafaella and Lorelai at the top of the stairs. Doors began to open down the hall and a little voice said, "What's happening? We heard noises—"

"Nothing to worry about, dears," Lorelai said, hurrying to shield them from the scene downstairs. "Back to bed, all of you."

While Lorelai tended to the children, Rafaella began to come down the stairs, but Delphinia barked, "No! Stay up there!"

"But," Rafaella protested, "we have to clean up before the children —"

Delphinia was looking at the corpse. "This is a sickness, make no mistake. I should have known, after the clocks stopped working, that this could be next. We've already been exposed, but you haven't. We have to keep it that way, and treat it like we would the plague."

"What should we do?" Lorelai asked in a strangled voice.

Delphinia looked at Jessamine and Zan. "We'll collect the bodies and burn them. You will don gloves and cover your faces and clean this whole place—scrub anywhere this man touched with as much soap as we have to spare. Afterward, you will burn the clothes you wore and the cloths and brushes you used. The children must stay upstairs until it's done."

"What about you?" Rafaella asked, looking anxious.

"My favorite sister is a healer," Delphinia said, "in Fimbria. We'll go to her. She'll know what to do."

"We'll go to her, then," Jessamine said reassuringly. "We'll go straight for Fimbria."

"All right," Lorelai said. "I'll pack things for you and drop it to you from the window. A change of clothes and some money, a few supplies . . ."

While Lorelai and Rafaella collected what they'd need for the journey, Zan and Jessamine dragged the man's body across the tavern floor and out the door. Ignoring the sharp pain in his injured arm, Zan hoisted the corpse into the cab as Jessamine released the horses from the carriage and led them to a pile of fresh hay.

Jessamine helped Zan to push the benighted carriage away from the building. In the frosty field, Zan struck a match and held it to the carriage curtains. They caught quickly, and soon the entire thing was engulfed in flame. Delphinia joined them to watch it burn.

"We'll go to Fimbria and return when we know it's safe," Zan said to her as the red-tinged smoke rose up to the night sky.

"If this is what I think it is, I don't know if we'll be coming back," Delphinia replied.

"But you told Rafaella and Lorelai—"

"That was a lie," she said bluntly. "I don't want them to see us suffer."

THEN

KELLAN

"No one's gonna want t' fight you with that," Malcolm said, inhaling from the pipe dangling from one side of his mouth while letting a slow stream of smoke dribble out the other. "It's an unfair advantage."

Kellan looked up, trying to control his exasperation. "You didn't think it was unfair to make me fight one-handed."

"Made for a better show. But this . . ." He motioned to Kellan's silver gauntlet. "This just isn't sporting."

"If I knew how to remove it, Malcolm, I would."

"Shoulda thought o' that before you put it on," Malcolm grumbled. "You've been our top moneymaker the last couple o' weeks, too. Damn shame to lose you." He closed his ledger and picked up his chair. "Fight's gonna start soon," he said. "Might be a seat available near the front if you hurry. Place a couple o' bets if you like. Maybe make some coin that way." He laughed.

Kellan grabbed the man by his grubby collar and pinned him against the wall, metal hand pressed into his throat just under his stubbly jowls.

Malcolm's pipe fell from his gaping mouth.

"I need to fight," Kellan said in a low voice. "I *have* to fight."

Malcolm made a strangled, gagging sound and Kellan realized he'd gone too far. He released him and stepped back. "Sorry, sir. Sorry—"

But instead of exhibiting anger, Malcolm rubbed his bruised neck thoughtfully. "Maybe we can think of some . . . new . . . kind of arrangement." He retrieved his pipe from the cobble and polished it on his shirt. "I might have another idea for you. Come back in a week, boy, and let's see if we can't work something out." He patted Kellan on the shoulder and then opened the arena's back door, momentarily flooding the alleyway with the sounds of the first fight's bells and the crowd's responding cheers before slamming shut and sealing the lively noise behind it.

In its absence, the alleyway was doubly quiet. Kellan punched the brick with his silver hand. This left a crumbling divot in the wall, but not a scratch on the luminous silver.

Malcolm was right—if he wanted to make money, he could just go around the front and find a seat at a table in the audience. He knew the fighters better than anyone; a few well-placed bets, and he'd make double or triple what he could have gotten by taking to the ring himself. But it wasn't the money that he craved. It was the adrenaline. The triumph. And the validation that came with each conquest.

What he wanted was proof that he didn't need two good hands, not really. He didn't need a fancy title. He didn't need a medal of bravery or a royal pat on the back.

He didn't need anyone or anything.

He didn't need Aurelia.

When he got back to the Scheming Minstrel, Ivan was just closing up behind the bar. He was wearing his nicest set of clothing, too: a tunic of blue linen, sewn with silver trim on the hems, though it was starting to look a little threadbare at the elbows.

"You're closing up early," Kellan said. "If you're going to the fights, they've already started."

"By the stars, no." Ivan draped his damp rag over the edge of the sink basin. "Going to take Martha and Sibby to hear that preacher in the square again tonight. You should come too. Man's got a lot of interesting things to say. Really eye-opening."

"I'll pass," Kellan said.

Ivan shrugged. "Oh," he said. "This came while you were out." He slid a folded parchment across to him. "A palace messenger brought it. In a real big rush. Couldn't wait to get going."

The note was very short.

Your services are required.
  Must meet to discuss.
  Mausoleum. Tonight.

The throng in the square was bigger this time, with people like Ivan clamoring to get close to the man mounted on the black horse.

Kellan skirted the edges, keeping his head down, as the preacher's words rippled across the audience. He spoke quietly, almost gently, and though he was on the far side of the square, Kellan could hear his words as clearly as if he had pulled his horse right along next to him.

"Friends, the first sign has come to pass! Just as Fidelis the First wrote so long ago, the Grandfather's hands pointed to the sky and have not moved one inch since midnight on Midwinter. Not even *time* can stop the Empyrea's great work! I pray, my friends, that you join with me, for only those who have entered the Circle will be safe from what is to come next!"

The man's voice hummed in Kellan's ear like a persistent gnat long after the sight of him was lost behind huddled buildings.

There were two sentries stationed at the castle gate, but Kellan didn't bother with them; he'd followed Aurelia to and from the royal grounds enough times to know where to slip in and out unnoticed. Though the iron fencing around the grounds was nearly thirty feet high and topped with sharp, fleur-de-lis-shaped spikes, there was one section of bars on the southern side that looked sturdy at a glance, but was loose enough to lift straight up from the ground, creating a gap large enough for a human to slip through. He'd thought about reporting it dozens of times but he knew if he did and it was repaired, Aurelia would just find another way out. In the end, he decided that he liked the escape he knew about far more than the one he didn't.

The royal mausoleum was a building of austere marble, simple in its ornamentation but massive in its size; the Renaltan commitment to austerity had never extended to the afterlife, and it became something of a competition among the wealthy families to outbuild each other, each memorial more ostentatious than the next. There were some Renaltan lords whose family tombs doubled the size and scope of their actual homes. Compared to those, the Altenar family's resting place was rather modest and meek.

The lamps in the entry were already lit, and Kellan could see Conrad inside already, standing quietly between his mother's and father's tombs, one hand on each stone slab. He looked so small, so young . . . it was easy to forget that, underneath the trappings of kingship, Conrad was still just a lonely little boy, not even a full decade old.

As if sensing Kellan's thoughts, Conrad whirled around. "Took you long enough," he said in a huff. "I've been waiting here for at least an hour. There are plenty of other things I could be doing with my night."

Kellan grimaced at the tone. Not ten years old, but still a king. "Where are your guards, Majesty? It is dangerous to be out here without protection."

"I gave Hector and Pomeroy the night off," Conrad said with a shrug.

"Roland Hector and Thurmond Pomeroy?" Kellan asked, eyebrow shooting up. "*That's* who you've made your bodyguards?"

"After the Tribunal's purges of the guard units," Conrad said haughtily, "my options were . . . limited."

"Surely you could have done better than two drunkards who waste all of their money and time making bad bets on fighting matches." He'd seen them at the arena more than once, swilling down tankards of ale and pawing at the serving maids. That was probably where they were now.

"They weren't exactly at the top of my list." Conrad lifted his chin. "But my top choice told me in no uncertain terms that he could no longer be bothered with royal service."

Kellan protested. "After what happened at Greythorne, I was in no shape to—"

Conrad nodded to the end of Kellan's right shirtsleeve. "Looks like you've got that straightened out well enough."

Kellan lifted the hand, letting the lamplight glide over the slick silver surface. "Rosetta's doing," he admitted. "Sure, it's pretty. But it is still useless." Worse than useless, because it had kept him from the fighting ring.

"Well." Conrad straightened his doublet. "I see this meeting was a waste of both our time, then." He strode past Kellan out of the mausoleum, starting across the lawn toward the castle.

"Wait—" Kellan hurried after him. "Is there something in particular you're worried about? If you really need my help—"

"Something . . . in *particular?* Have you taken a walk through the city recently? It's a mess. People are tired, hungry, scared. They need a leader to help them through it. A *real* one. But they got me. A kid." He kicked at the ground with his gold-buckled shoes. "I hate court, Kellan. I hate being called 'Your Majesty.' I hate people bowing and pretending like they care about me. No one tells me anything important, and when they do speak to me, it's mostly lies and compliments they don't mean. I wish I didn't have to be a king at all. I wish I could be something . . . greater."

"What is greater than a king?" Kellan asked.

"I don't know," Conrad said, shrugging. "A rescuer, maybe. A hero. Like Aurelia."

Kellan tried to smother his resentment with forced indifference, and said tightly, "Aurelia was brave, yes. But she was selfish."

Conrad, however, wasn't listening. He had suddenly stopped still and was standing motionless at the edge of a large, round patch of ground that was devoid of any grass. The dirt within that section was scorched black.

"What's the matter?" Kellan asked.

"I remember this spot," Conrad said quietly. "I remember what happened here, on the night we left."

Kellan remembered it too: orange tongues of fire, reaching up, up, up into a black sky as a girl in the center of them screamed.

Everything, Kellan thought, *everything since that day has been so terribly wrong.*

Aurelia had wanted to go back for the girl—her maid, her friend —and he hadn't let her. He'd pulled her onto his horse and ridden away as she sobbed into his shirt.

He didn't feel sorry for the girl who'd died here that night, though he knew he should. Her end had been terrible, but it had been quick.

He looked at the thick, useless metal fingers on his right hand.

Perhaps she was the fortunate one.

"Empyrea keep you," Conrad murmured solemnly, but whether he was speaking to his sister or the girl who had burned here in her stead, Kellan did not know.

"Listen," Kellan said, "if you want authority, you can't ask for it, or wait for someone to give you permission. You must *take* it."

"Oh?" Conrad said. "And if I order you to come back to work for me, right now? What then?"

"That's not—"

"Even *you* won't listen to me. Even *you* don't see me as a king." He squared his shoulders. "You know what? It's fine. I don't need you or anyone else telling me what to do. I need to rely only on myself. So thank you, Kellan, for bringing me all the way out here to teach me that lesson."

"*I* brought *you* out here?" Kellan asked incredulously, but Conrad was already storming away across the lawn, too far to hear.

✱

That night, Kellan dreamed he was trapped in a maze, but not of hawthorn hedge like at home in Greythorne. This was a labyrinth of Syric's alleys, damp and narrow and smelling of mold. And he was being followed; he could see the shadow lurking, always only a few steps behind him. If he looked hard enough, he could see the rippling fur of some kind of beast, herding him further and further toward the center of the maze. At the end of it, however, the only thing waiting for him was an eerily empty square and its broken clock.

When he turned around, he saw the shape of the creature outlined in the darkness, accompanied by the smell of violets.

"Don't let them get him," it said.

12

NOW

AURELIA

9 DAYS TO MIDWINTER
1621

"Wait!" Nathaniel cried, hurrying after me. "They're in the immigrant camp. You don't know the way."

"Maybe not," I said. "But you do."

"It's rife with the Bitter Fever," Nathaniel said. "It isn't safe. I can't catch it again, but you . . ."

"I have no fear of illness," I said. "Not anymore."

I had come to the upper gate, looming over the thick-timbered buildings of the town. One of the gatesmen eyed me warily, dressed as I was in Castillion's clothes, and his red cloak and spider brooch.

"Lower the drawbridge," I commanded.

The guard looked to Nathaniel for guidance, unsure what to make of me.

Nathaniel gave a long, relenting sigh. "At ease," he told the soldier. "Do as she says." Under his breath, he said, "Castillion's not going to be happy about this."

"He's your commander," I said. "Not mine."

"Can't wait to hear you explain that to him."

The chains clinked as the portcullis was raised and the drawbridge came slowly down on the other side of it, bridging the gap between the upper gate and the lower one. It was a steep gradation, and the planks were marked with bolts at regular intervals for better traction through the ice and snow. The drop on either side was a long one; a bad slip could mean a broken neck or getting skewered on the rooftop weather vane of one of the buildings below.

I peered over the edge of the drawbridge at the village houses, where lamps were coming on in the lavender light as the earliest risers began their day.

"Is this the only way in and out of the fort?" I asked.

"There are other ways," Nathaniel said, "through the tunnels in the rock, and they are like a labyrinth. Easy to get lost. And Castillion keeps them locked down, since that's where he keeps the food and supplies that the settlement depends on to survive. If something happened to the Trove"—Nathaniel shook his head—"none of us would likely make it through the winter."

We'd come to the second gate, where another gatekeeper had already begun to lower the remaining bridge. From this vantage point, Fort Castillion loomed larger than the mountain it was built upon, turrets jutting like tusks from solid stone. If both gates were up, it'd be almost impossible to penetrate from below. This second bridge crossed above what was once a moat, but was now a deep channel of smoldering refuse. Through the smoke, I could see men offloading long, shroud-wrapped bundles from a cart and tossing them into the burning trench.

"Are they burning . . . ?" I couldn't form the word *bodies*.

Nathaniel nodded and said, "Victims of the Bitter Fever. It's a terrible disease. Kills most of the people it infects, and those who *do* survive are permanently marked by it." He pointed to his eyes. "No one wanted to be around us survivors at first, but Castillion won't let us be turned away. He treats us just the same as anyone. Makes sure we have useful jobs. Like them. And me."

The men at the cart stopped their work for a moment to watch us trundle down the bridge. Even from a distance, I could see that each had no iris at all; they stared with large, obsidian pupils.

The tents that made up the encampment were made of rough canvas that sagged beneath the heavy snow. There was one cobbled road down the center, but everywhere else the snow had been trodden into a thick soup of cold mud. Women were emerging from inside the flimsy shelters to stoke up cookfires as soldiers moved wagons through the sludge, handing off small, paper-wrapped parcels to each as they passed.

"What's in them?" I asked Nathaniel under my breath.

"The day's rations," he replied. "From the Trove. It isn't much, but it's far better than starving." The door of the tent nearest us swung open for a moment, revealing an interior packed tight with people huddled together on floors strewn with straw. "A little better, at least."

One tent stood out from the others; it was taller, octagonal, and dyed a deep cobalt blue—Renalt's color. A thin plume of smoke rose from a hole in the top, and two flags bearing the Renaltan fleur-de-lis waved on each side of its entrance. My father used to use a tent like it when he toured Renaltan cities, setting up a chair in its center to act as a makeshift throne. With no king left to rule, it would be Renalt's lord protector occupying it now.

I slowed to a stop, suddenly nervous. "Kellan's in there," I said to Nathaniel. "The last time I saw him . . . I . . . I . . ." I couldn't finish.

"Come on, now," Nathaniel said, gently teasing. "I don't believe it. Aurelia Altenar, losing her nerve?"

"Don't tell anyone," I said. "I have a reputation to maintain."

The tent was divided into two parts, the first being a smaller antechamber hung with two canvas flaps that acted like doors to the central section. Between them, I could see Castillion leaning over a table with a look of concentration on his face. "How reliable are your sources?" he was saying. "Because if what you say is true, the whole game changes . . ."

"Very reliable." I could not see the second speaker's face, but I knew his voice as intimately as my own. Kellan. "The person who gave me the information is someone I trust. Someone who risks their life every day for our cause. If they get caught . . ."

"I've seen the Circle Midnight's work," Castillion said darkly. "You don't have to explain the danger to me."

"Aurelia," Nathaniel whispered by my ear. "Are you going to go in?"

I put a hand up to quiet him.

"My source in the Midnight Zone said that they keep the boy

isolated, and they've never been able to get close enough to make a positive identification, but the signs are all there." Kellan had moved next to the table, giving me a partial view of his shoulders and back. "It is my belief that the child in question is, in fact, Conrad Altenar."

"What?" I gasped.

Both Kellan and Castillion's attention immediately snapped to me. I parted the canvas flaps and stepped into the inner chamber.

"Aurelia," Castillion said, "what in all the stars —?"

"Sorry, Commander," Nathaniel said apologetically. "We should have announced ourselves before —"

"Is it true?" I demanded. "Is my brother alive?"

I looked at Kellan, heart in my throat. Despite his ostentatious new moniker — lord protector — he was dressed in dun-colored traveler's clothes, worn and stained from a long and arduous journey. His woolen cloak was draped over his right shoulder, shielding my Day of Shades handiwork from view.

There was no exchanged apology or salutation between us, no hugging or cursing, no shaking of hands or raising of fists. We simply studied each other quietly, best friends and total strangers both at once. Those contradictory truths turned the thin air that separated us into a wall more impenetrable than the one Achlev built to protect Aren's tower.

It was Castillion who finally broke the silence, saying reluctantly, "There are . . . indications . . . that King Conrad did not die the night of the flood in Syric, but is, instead, being held captive by the Circle Midnight. How they got ahold of him and for what purpose they keep him—if it is him at all—are still mysteries. As I told you before, there's very little we can know for certain."

"But," I sputtered. "There's a *chance?*"

"Yes," Kellan said. "I think there's a chance."

"All right," I said, moving closer to the table where a map similar to the one in Castillion's study was laid out. "Tell me where he is, and how we're going to get him."

"Aurelia," Castillion said. "We can't. You only just woke up—remember what happened in the Night Garden? You need time to get your feet under you. Not to mention that it's the middle of winter, and we have more and more refugees to care for arriving on our doorstep every day. Some sick with the fever, some starving, all in need . . ."

"But—" I began.

"*But* also . . . we know so little about the Circle's intentions. Right now, things are tense, but at least they are quiet. We can't risk breaking that tension. We can't risk starting a real war. Not even for your beloved little brother."

"Kellan?" I asked. "Please. It's *Conrad.*"

Quietly, Kellan replied, "No one feels more regret about what happened to Conrad than I do. But Lord Castillion is right. It is too dangerous. Our personal feelings are irrelevant. This is about the greater good." He reached his right arm from behind his cloak to place his hand on my shoulder. Not a real hand, of course; it was a solid silver replica of the one I'd taken from him.

This was a brutally calculated gesture on Kellan's part: Chastisement disguised as comfort. A weighty metal reminder that decisions driven by personal attachment sometimes come with devastating cost.

And it worked, to an extent. Inside, I felt myself crumpling. But on the outside, I simply nodded. "I understand," I said.

Kellan removed his silver hand from my shoulder and Castillion rapped his knuckles on the table. "Good," he said. "It's for the best. We'll give it some time, gather more intelligence, and when the chance comes to make a move, we'll be well prepared." He moved around to my side of the table and added, "We can talk more tonight. In a more formal setting, after Lord Protector Greythorne has fully debriefed me."

"Of course," I said, mollified. Then: "I'm very sorry to have interrupted. If you'll excuse me."

Nathaniel hurried after me, weaving through the tents to keep up. "You took that rather well," he said. "I expected more of a fight."

"Fighting would be a waste of effort," I said briskly. "I'd rather put my energy to better use."

"*What* better use?" he asked.

"I'm going after Conrad."

"I will agree that this news is good—that it should give you hope," Nathaniel said. "But that is all it is! A hope."

"It's enough," I said.

"Please," he begged. "Consider what you're doing. Castillion wouldn't—"

"Damn Castillion," I said. "I saved him, he saved me. We're even. I'm going after Conrad, I don't care if I have to scour every inch of the Midnight Zone to find him." We were at the lower bridge again, and

I lifted my chin as if in defiance of the fortress itself. Then I looked over my shoulder. "Are you coming or not?"

"Aurelia," he said softly. "I . . ."

"I know it's easier to believe that Morais is gone. That Ella is gone. But you said yourself that you never got close enough to *see* the proof with your own eyes. Don't you want to know?"

"It's impossible," Nathaniel said, wavering. "I tried already, and nearly died . . ."

"The last time you tried," I said, "you did it alone."

"Merciful Empyrea," he cursed under his breath.

"You don't need the Empyrea," I replied. "This time, you have me."

PART II
THE ENEMY DRESSED AS FRIEND

13

THEN

ZAN

*Z*an and Jessamine buried Delphinia by the roadside.

She had first started feeling sick two days after they left the Quiet Canary. A headache, she said, and a dry cough. At three days, she began to sweat. At four, the hallucinations began. She would cry, and then sing, and scream, and chatter on and on about things they could not make sense of, to people they could not see.

On the morning of the fifth day, she died, with her blue eyes wide open, obsidian tears streaking her alabaster cheeks.

Watching Delphinia's lovely face disappear beneath the cold dirt was difficult; it hardly seemed fair that someone so full of life and energy would meet such a fate, while he—a mere shade of himself —was still stuck aboveground. But the Horseman's motto was caught like a burr in his thoughts. *While you live, you fight.* Which meant carrying on no matter what.

"Do you want to say something?" Zan asked Jessamine, as she stood at the foot of her friend's fresh grave, auburn hair whipping wildly in the cold wind. "Some Empyrean prayer?"

She shook her head. "I was raised by a witch," she said. "A feral mage. We worshipped the Ilithiya. And while Delphinia had a definite liking for priests, she had little regard for religion itself." She paused, and then removed a deck of cards from her skirt pocket. Betwixt and Between, he saw. She rifled through the myriad of characters, before finally settling on one and pulling it free from the deck: the Saintly Sinner.

In place of a headstone, Jessamine stuck the card upright in the soil. "It was her favorite of the deck," she said, her eyes shining. "She was very much like that—the sweetest of sinners. Kind, and loyal, and beautiful. And *very* good in bed. She'd want that noted." Jessamine sniffed and looked away to pull another card from the deck. "Here," she said, thrusting it at him. "If I go next, use this one for me."

The Metamorph. It depicted the evolution of a caterpillar into a butterfly. He wanted to reassure her that she had nothing to worry about, that they'd both be just fine. But she was too pragmatic for comforting platitudes, and he was too tired to construct any. "Fine," he said, tucking it into his pocket. "If the time comes."

"I have one for you, too," she said, holding out another.

He cocked his head to the side. "Sad Tom? Really?"

"What? It suits you," she said.

"Don't worry about burying me," he said. "Just roll me over the edge of a cliff and call it good."

"Exactly something Sad Tom would say." Jessamine hooked her foot into the stirrup of her mare, Nell, and hoisted herself into the saddle. From the higher vantage point, she looked toward the horizon. "This road will take us to Fimbria," she said.

"That's a long way to go," Zan said, looking again at the fresh-turned earth, "especially now."

"We owe it to Delphinia," Jessamine stated. "Her family should know what happened to her. And I have a few of her effects . . . she'd want her sister to have them, I'm sure."

"And if we have the fever, too?" Zan asked.

"Her sister is a healer," Jessamine said.

Zan shook his head, thinking of those trickling black tears marring Delphinia's pale cheeks. "I'll go with you as far as Fimbria," he said after a long moment. "That's all I can say for now."

Jessamine regarded him thoughtfully. "You know, if Delphinia had done what Aurelia did for you, and told me there might be a way to rescue her from this, I'd be searching the world over to find it. I'd never stop, never rest. Just on the mere chance . . ." Her words trailed into the wind.

Zan's fingers closed over Aurelia's blood vial. "Death is death. It can't be undone."

"Can't it?" Jessamine said. "Your eyes are gold now, but weren't they once green? Tell me, how did that change come about?"

Zan said nothing.

"It would take nothing short of a miracle," Jessamine said. "But Aurelia was something of a peddler of miracles." Then she shrugged. "Come on now, Sad Tom. We'd best be on our way."

★

The town of Fimbria was quiet as they rode in, but that wasn't so unusual on its own. A seaside community like this one was always susceptible to the whims of the weather, but this was more than an off-season lull in travel; there was a strange smell—something sickly lurking beneath the salt and brine of the coastal air. Their horses ambled down the mostly deserted streets, headed north, until Jessamine pulled to a stop. "This is the address Delphinia gave me."

"Looks empty," Zan said. "Do we know anything else about this woman? Her name, even?"

"Cecily," Jessamine replied. "Cecily . . . Cartwright, I believe. But she won't know Delphinia as Delphinia—she was born with the name Prudence."

Zan snorted; if there was anyone less unsuited to the name Prudence, it was Delphinia.

"And what are you going to tell her?"

"I'll give Cecily a few of her belongings, and tell her how honored I am to have known her sister. Delphinia was a sister to me, too, in all of the most important ways. Wait, where are you going?"

"Anywhere else," he said, trying to make his voice sound flippant. "Preferably somewhere that can offer a drink."

She swore at his back, but he didn't know what epithet she chose; he was, thankfully, too far away to hear it by then.

★

Fimbria's town center was small, but unlike the rest of the town, it was bustling. Not with the typical market fare of merchants hawking their wares; most of the permanent shops were empty and shuttered. No, the square was awash with ordinary folk selling the trappings of their everyday lives. One woman was clutching the corners of her apron, which was full of old tin cutlery and chipped teacups, as if she had overturned a kitchen drawer into it while she held it like a hammock. "A copper apiece," she said, when she saw him looking. "Five coppers for the whole lot." He shook his head and continued walking as she shouted at his back: "Fine, then! Four. Maybe three?"

He passed a man selling mismatched kitchen chairs, and a woman trying to offload a washboard and laundry bucket. A little girl in a checkered pinafore was sitting next to a bench lined with an assortment of well-loved rag dolls. Her eyes were red, as if she'd been crying. "Buy a poppet for your little ones, sir?" she asked with a sniff.

"Oh, I don't have—" Zan began, but seeing her watery eyes, he screwed his mouth to the side and crouched down beside her. "These are all so lovely. Why are you selling them?"

"Mama says we need coin to buy passage to Castillion," she said in a small voice. "Right now there's only enough for me and her, and if we don't get more soon my papa will have to stay here, where everyone's getting sick." She sniffed, and then forced a smile. "A penny for Margaret." She touched the top of a doll with hair of braided black yarn. "A penny for Tippy." She touched one wearing a dress of faded blue flowers. "And a copper for Francine." The last one was so threadbare, little bits of straw were poking through the lopsided stitches of its smile.

"If you were me, which would you choose?"

"Francine is my favorite," she said. "She's a very good friend."

"Tell you what," Zan said. "I think I've taken a shine to Margaret, but all I've got is a silver. Will that be enough?" It was at least double what could purchase passage on a merchant ship.

She nodded vigorously, and he placed the coin in the center of her small palm. She gave the doll a final squeeze and then placed it tenderly into his arms, as if it were a real baby. "I hope your daughter likes it," she said.

"Oh, I don't—" But she had already gathered up Tippy and Francine and was scampering away, zigzagging through the packed square.

He tucked the doll into the pocket of his coat and stood to go, but stopped suddenly when his gaze snagged on a woman on the other side of the market, just past where the little girl had disappeared into the crowd.

Blond hair piled atop her head, with little wisps teased out by the wind, a fringed shawl wrapped around her shoulders, and the lovely curve of a round cheek, turned just enough to hide her full face.

The resemblance to Delphinia, even from behind, was striking. Was this the sister they'd come to Fimbria to find?

He began to make his way toward her, tugging Madrona along by her lead rope while she whinnied in protest. By the time he got to where he'd first seen the woman, she wasn't there—but he caught another glimpse of her hair another twenty feet away. He continued after her, pushing through the throng, always several steps behind.

He followed the woman all the way to the pier, where people were waiting in lines up and down the docks, hoping to secure a spot on one of the departing ships. Seamen were shouting their boats' destinations to the clamoring people, taking bribes for a better position in their lines. Zan slowed at the edge of the cobble, and Madrona bumped her nose against his shoulder in irritation; the only thing she disliked more than being made to move was being forced to stop after she got going.

Delphinia's sister was nowhere to be seen. Zan shook his head, cross at himself for losing her.

"Are you lookin' to get aboard the *Contessa*?" a young man nearby asked him. "The cost for passage is highway robbery, of course, but at least it's slightly cheaper than the rest o' them boats."

"Oh?" Zan asked politely, still scanning the crowd.

"Yeah. They're stopping in the isles first to pick up a load of spider silk from the Sisters of the Sacred Torch before they go on to Castillion, so they're knocking a few coppers off o' the total price, on account o' the extra sailing time."

Zan nodded distractedly, not really listening, but the young man kept on. "See? That's the *Contessa* right there. Nothin' fancy, but serviceable. Worth it to save a few coins, I think." He pointed to a carrack up the row, a stout, sturdy vessel with striped sails.

Zan felt a flare of shock go through him as he followed the line of the young man's finger and saw the woman he'd been following standing on the *Contessa*'s deck. As he stared, she began to slowly turn, inch by inch, until her face came into full view.

Golden hair, eyes the color of a summer sky, pink lips pulled into a coy smile, and a black streak on each cheek—the mark of the fever that had taken her life. Not Delphinia's sister—it was the shade of Delphinia herself. But as he watched, the black tears stretched into black veins, and soon it wasn't Delphinia he was looking at. It was, again, Isobel Arceneaux.

14

THEN

CONRAD

One week after Midwinter, Conrad called for a banquet.

"Why?" Pelton asked from behind his desk in his nervous, wheedling voice. "What do we have to celebrate?"

Conrad said, "The new year, of course. I've been reading about the kings of the past and it occurred to me that the best of them all have one thing in common: they forged relationships with the other leaders in their city. I'm not talking about courtiers," he added. He couldn't think of anything worse than sitting at a table with Gaskin or Hallett or any of their ilk. "I'm talking about city leaders you mentioned in the reports I requested. Influential merchants and ministers and shopkeepers."

Pelton gaped. "You want to call a banquet for . . . regular people?"

"Outstanding citizens," Conrad said. "People with clout."

"Majesty," Pelton said, "I hope you're not talking about that preacher again. If you read my reports, you would have seen how very questionable he is . . ."

"What do you mean by questionable?" Conrad asked.

"I mean that Fidelis is not the sort of person you invite to a banquet in your hall. He has a strange effect on people. They follow him. Like rats to a piper's song."

"Sounds like a man I want to fight alongside, not against," Conrad replied. He had a vague feeling of necessity stirring inside him. This was an important connection to make. He just knew it. "Invite him. And any others you deem worthy. The celebration will take place tomorrow."

"But there are so many things to consider," Pelton protested. "Will there be music as well? Dancing? What shall we serve? Surely these common folk and their untrained palates won't appreciate the same sorts of things we would prepare for the gentry . . ."

"Whatever you would provide for a nobleman's event, you will provide for this one," Conrad said firmly.

"Captain Greythorne would not approve—"

"Captain Greythorne doesn't work for me anymore, remember?" Conrad's mood soured immediately; he was still quite cross that Kellan had sent a note asking to meet him at his parents' tomb just to reiterate his unwillingness to return to royal service. He crossed his arms and gave Pelton his most imperious expression. "If you're not careful, neither will you."

"Fine," Pelton said in resignation. "If you want a banquet for"—he cringed—"*ordinary* folk, I'll see that it's done."

As Conrad was about to leave, he saw something strange out of the corner of his eye: the bearskin rug under Pelton's desk was oddly shaped, puckered around a seam, as if someone had cut a large strip from the center of it and then tried to sew it back up again. "Pelton," he asked, "what's wrong with your rug?"

Pelton glowered. "Pranksters," he said. "Rabble-rousers. Some of the kitchen boys or stable hands trying to get my goat. My great-grandfather killed this bear. It was a family heirloom. I had one of the seamstresses sew it up for me afterward. She did her best, I'm sure, but the damage was done." Reluctantly, he added, "I'll have it removed if it offends you, Majesty."

"Just curious," Conrad said. "Were the responsible parties ever caught?"

"I never got a confession," Pelton said. "But most of the accused left their positions soon after the Tribunal took over."

"Ah," Conrad said. *Drat*, he thought. He'd have liked to make friends with them.

The rest of that day, however, Conrad began to notice similar oddities wherever he looked. The head of the great twelve-pronged buck that hung over the grand hall's fireplace was missing a patch of fur from the back of its neck. The suede-covered bench under the window in the library had been similarly defaced. All over the castle, little bits of leather and fur had been carefully cut away from furniture and hunting trophies and wall hangings . . . not even books were safe. He counted at least four with blank patches in their leather covers, and six from which the covers had been completely removed.

It was a riddle, but Conrad couldn't escape the niggling feeling that he, somehow, already knew its answer.

That night, during his weekly worship in the royal family's private sanctorium, he knelt beside the altar and tried to quiet his mind enough to recite a half-hearted prayer when, from the corner of his eye, he saw one of the curtains flutter, and smelled a sudden whiff of violets. The sanctorium had no windows that could produce a draft or a breeze, and Conrad had watched Hector and Pomeroy inspect the room from one end to the other before letting him set a foot over the threshold, so there was no way someone could have hidden inside until he was alone. Still, his heart began to hammer furiously—from excitement or fear, he couldn't know which—as he unclasped his hands and stood up from the altar. "Hello?" he asked the air.

Was there something wrong with the painting across from the altar? It was of devils and cherubs, representing the battle between sin and righteousness, and he'd never liked it. But now it looked almost distorted, somehow. Like he was seeing it through water . . .

He sprang suddenly across the altar and grabbed at the shape. The distortion warped further, and there was a distinct female cry before the illusion faded altogether. Conrad nearly fell over when he realized that it was a creature with a bizarre, patchy hide.

Her arms were up defensively, and the sleeves of her cloak slipped down to reveal a pair of human hands, covered in angry, puckered scars. A human girl, he realized, in a highly unusual cloak.

"Well," he said, "I guess that answers the question of where all the pieces of fur and leather are going."

When she realized that he wasn't going to strike her again, she hurriedly dropped her hands to her sides, pulling them inside the cloak.

"I feel like I should remember you," Conrad continued. "But I can't recall how."

"It's the frostlace," she said, slowly inching back toward the nearest shadow, still keeping her face obscured by the heavy hood. "It was gone from Onal's stillroom. I know you've been taking it."

Frostlace for forgetting. He could almost see the bottle in his mind's eye, but it was blurry and indistinct, like a half-remembered dream.

"I know what you're doing, too," she said. "You're playing a game with yourself and the Circle. I'm here to tell you again: *don't.*"

He ignored her warning, his attention fully caught by her patchwork garment. He was a full head shorter than her, but she still shrank from him as he got closer and closer. "Extraordinary," he said, lifting the hem of a sleeve. "The lines you've sewn into it. The patterns. It's a spell, isn't it?"

As if to answer his question, the air around her seemed to shimmer, and within seconds she was no longer a girl in a monster cloak, huddled in the shadows, but a fair maiden in a gown of woven moonlight, her hair tumbling down her back in silvery waves.

"Will you listen to me now?" she asked, her voice like tinkling bells.

Then her face began to elongate, her teeth began to sharpen, and her dress stretched and took on emerald hues. Soon, she wasn't a girl at all, but a serpent with knifelike claws and diaphanous wings that shifted between cerulean and viridian.

"How about now?" Her voice was rumbling and low, and her forked tongue flicked out as she spoke.

A dragon.

In awe, Conrad reached up a hand to her long, twisting neck, but it passed right through.

"Incredible," he said. "It's an illusion."

"Listen to me," the dragon hissed. "The Circle is going to be responsible for some terrible, terrible things." The illusion slowly dissipated, and soon she was just a girl again, hiding in her bulky fur robe. "Please. I know you think the frostlace will keep you safe from having your thoughts read, but it's too risky. You must stay away from them altogether. *Promise* me."

"Who are you?" Conrad asked.

He couldn't see her expression, but her voice was small and quavering. "I—I can't say. I don't dare. You're in too far already. And if they find me in your thoughts . . ."

"Why should I trust you if you won't even tell me who you are?"

"If you can't trust me, you must put your well-being in the hands of someone you do trust. Bring Sir Greythorne back into your service. Please," she begged. "Let someone with more worldly experience help you . . ."

Conrad clenched his fists into tiny balls, trying to keep from losing his temper—that was exactly what a child would do, and he wasn't a child anymore, he was a *king*.

"I am quite capable of handling things on my own," he said. "I don't need Kellan Greythorne, or you, or Pelton, or *anyone else* telling me what to do." He smoothed out his jacket, and added imperiously, "I could call my guards in here right now, and have you dragged away and put in the dungeon . . ."

"No," she said, shrinking further toward the wall. "No, please! I—"

". . . *But*," he continued, "I recognize that you are trying to look out for my safety, however misguided your methods might be. So I will let this little infraction slide. I am going to leave now, and when my guards and I are gone, you may slip out of here quietly and go your way in peace. That said, if you infringe upon my privacy again, I will have no choice but to see you arrested."

He did not wait for her answer, instead swiveling on his heel and marching to the door. On the other side, Hector was waiting with a bored expression on his face. "How was your worship, Majesty?"

"Illuminating," he replied with a quick glance over his shoulder. But the girl had worked another illusion, and was nowhere to be seen.

Ultimus 30th, 1620: You saw that strange girl again today—the one you wrote about in the first entry. And even though she—like everyone else—wants to treat you like a baby, you do think you need to be extra careful when dealing with Fidelis and the Circle Midnight, especially now that you're holding a banquet with the specific goal of getting to know more about them.

If they are as dangerous as she seems to think they are, it will be all the more glorious when you conquer them — and all on your own.

Still, she was very afraid of being discovered. You're going to take an extra few drops of frostlace tonight to erase the encounter with her from your memory, just in case.

15

THEN

ROSETTA

112 YEARS AGO

"Do not worry, my little Rosebud," Grandmother said as she shouldered her pack. "We won't be gone long. Only a couple of days."

"To camp in the snow?" eleven-year-old Rosetta asked, piqued. "You'll miss Midwinter!"

"We can light the candles and ring the bells upon our return. No harm in waiting a little bit."

"But," Rosetta protested, "if it's such an important thing to teach Galantha, why can't I come, too? I won't be the warden like she will, but that doesn't mean I can't learn . . ."

"No buts. I need you to stay here and care for Begonia. Can you do that for me?"

Rosetta nodded sullenly, knowing that eight-year-old Begonia had discovered a tangle of frostlace buds several leagues to the east, and would not be convinced to leave until they had bloomed and were properly harvested. She had no need of a babysitter.

Grandmother had turned to Galantha, who was waiting patiently by the kitchen door. She was thirteen, and "beginning to bloom," as Grandmother put it. Rosetta was all knees and elbows, every awkward inch covered in freckles. She envied Galantha's grace and blushing prettiness, even while she detested it. And Galantha would someday soon follow Grandmother into the wardenship, which meant she was given extra lessons in the feral magic that Rosetta adored and Galantha endured.

It was hardly fair that Rosetta, who relished her magic and hungered to use it, was passed over for the wardenship simply because she was not born first.

"Make sure to do your chores," Grandmother said as she and Galantha headed out the door. "Don't let Saffron sleep in my bed . . . she left a dead mouse between my sheets last time and I'm still mad about it." Curled up next to the kitchen hearth, the fox pricked her ears up at the sound of her name, and she gave a bored swish of her tail in response. "And"—Grandmother pointed her finger at Rosetta's nose—"leave that spider in the kitchen window alone; she's a lovely little thing, and I won't have her bothered."

"As you wish it," Rosetta said.

Behind her back, her fingers were crossed.

As soon as they were gone, Rosetta turned to Saffron and said, "Get up, you lazy thing! We've got to hurry if we don't want to lose their footprints in the snow." She left a note for Begonia, just in case.

It wasn't hard to follow them; Rosetta was very good at moving through the forest unnoticed. Saffron was reluctant to leave her warm place at the hearth at first, but couldn't retain her gloominess for long. As Rosetta walked, Saffron joyously jumped and rolled in the powdery snow alongside her, snowflakes clinging to her coat and gilding the fringe of eyelashes around her amber eyes.

Rosetta was careful to keep plenty of distance between herself and her grandmother and sister during the day, but during the nights she ventured closer, drawn by the glow of their campfire and the possibility of overhearing a lesson in feral magic. She was disappointed; for two days, Galantha and Grandmother only spoke of the travel, and what was on the cookfire, and what the weather might look like tomorrow. Rosetta gnawed glumly on the strips of dried meat she had brought for herself as she listened from behind a tree, periodically tossing bits to Saffron, who slurped them up with gusto, even though she'd been tracking and catching mice and voles beneath the snow all day long.

Saffron was an excellent travel companion, just as content in the snow as she was by the kitchen hearth, good-naturedly plodding across the miles even as Rosetta started to tire. Which was why it was so surprising when, on the third day of travel, she stopped, stock-still, and began to growl at a strange-looking tree.

That was when Rosetta saw the sigil for the first time: a spider with only seven legs, carved deeply into the bark. No matter how many cajoling flatteries—or angry admonishments—Rosetta offered, she could not convince the vixen to take even one step past that mark.

"Fine," she had said. "Run back home if you like. I'm going without you."

It didn't take her long to understand why Saffron had balked; there was something . . . off . . . about the place. An intolerable emptiness that only got worse the further past the boundary she trekked. Winter was always hard on workers of feral magic; just like bears and bees and bats, the energy they used became sluggish and slow to answer after snow started to fall. But *this* was not a winter magic's drowsy reluctance to wake to a mage's call; it was its absence from the landscape altogether.

Ahead, Grandmother and Galantha had come to an opening in the trees and were standing under a purpling evening sky.

"This place is terrible," Galantha said, and Rosetta could hear strain in her words. "It feels like death."

"Worse than death." Grandmother usually spoke so gently, but here her voice went hard and grim. "For death is a part of the natural cycle of things. It is a transition from one plane to another. What you are feeling is not death. It is the absence of life."

"But there are trees," Galantha protested as Rosetta ducked behind a juniper.

"They *were* trees once," Grandmother said, "but not anymore. They do not live, or breathe, or grow. They died when the Spinner died at this same hour, at this same place, over a thousand years ago. In any other part of the forest, the trees would have been subjected to the natural processes of decomposition and replaced by new growth.

But there is nothing left here to maintain the balance—no worms to churn the soil, no insects to consume the wood, no fungi or moss to hurry the decay—and so here they sit, untouched by the ages."

Rosetta looked closer at the juniper behind which she was hiding; its needly leaves were not the lovely silver-green of a juniper bush in winter, but a sickly grayish black.

"Who, or what, is the Spinner?" Galantha asked. "In all of my lessons, I've never heard you mention that name before."

"Since the beginning of recorded time, high mages who were able to glimpse the future wrote about a child who would be born under a certain configuration of stars. A child who could practice all three types of magic—the Malefica's blood magic, the Ilithiya's feral magic, and the Empyrea's high magic—and plait them together, to wield them at once. Such power, it was said, would rival that of the goddesses themselves. It could be used to create worlds . . . or destroy them. Long ago—even before the creation of the Assembly—there was a group of mages who dedicated their lives to this prophecy. They tracked the omens, mapped every change in the stars, and when the time was right, they triangulated a location from them. It took them years of searching, but they found her: Vieve."

As if awakened by the name, the air within the glade began to stir, and an icy wind whistled through the trees. Rosetta's whole body went rigid, the hair on the back of her neck pricking up as if someone was standing behind her. She stole a glance over her shoulder, wondering if Saffron had decided to join her after all, and was surprised to find the woods empty. Nothing there but secrets and shadows.

Grandmother continued, "The mages raised her, trained her to use each kind of magic in turn. And then they brought her here, just as I have brought you. Under the same configuration of stars that had accompanied her birth, and on the longest night of the year, she began to weave a spell for them."

"What kind of spell?"

"It is believed that they were trying to steal divinity from the Empyrea. That with her light and Vieve's power, they could become like gods themselves. Immortal."

A chill started across Rosetta's scalp and then skittered down her neck and arms, raising her hackles, and the sound of the wind morphed from a whistle to a murmuring hum.

Grandmother had wandered to the gnarled, misshapen apple tree at the glade's centermost point and was looking up at the sky through the boughs. "The Empyrea herself was moved from her heavenly throne and began to descend to the earth to take retribution against them. And in great fear and awe, the mages ended the spell the only way they knew how: by killing its maker."

"You mean . . . she was murdered by the men who raised her?" Galantha had a tender heart, and this story had brought an impassioned empathy into her voice. "For doing the thing they asked of her? How dare they! That poor, poor girl."

"It was a sin, yes," Grandmother replied. "But it did not go unpunished. The Verecundai got what they asked for. They were, indeed, granted immortality. Just not the way they expected. One of their number, you see, a blood mage named Adamus, loved Vieve, and he used his own lifeblood to curse them, turning them into bodiless wraiths, trapped with their shame in this glade for all time."

"They're . . . here?" Galantha's eyes began to scour the darkness between the trees, and Rosetta shrank further behind her cover.

"Yes," Grandmother said. "But do not worry, they cannot hurt us. Not in the daylight."

"Could they ever get free?"

Grandmother waited a long while before answering. "Such a thing would be near impossible." But her voice was edged with an uncharacteristic doubt that made Rosetta quail. Grandmother was over three hundred years old, and had withstood as many trials: bloody wars, brutal regimes, and calamities of a scope Rosetta, at the time, could hardly have fathomed. She was an ornery old battle-ax who approached challenges with the unimpressed impatience of a woman who had seen everything and had no time for it.

Which was why it was so troubling to see her uneasy . . . if *Grandmother* found something frightening, that thing must be fearsome indeed.

"Near impossible is not impossible," Galantha said, warily watching the shadows. Rosetta hunkered down even lower to keep from being seen.

"There is a prophecy—though I'm not sure you can even call it that. More like . . . a story. Written by a mage called Fidelis, a madman obsessed with the story of Vieve and Adamus. He believed that the Spinner and her consort would someday be reborn. He said it would start here, where it began, with the Verecundai being freed by a man descended from Adamus's family line. Then, all the clocks will stop at twelve o'clock on Midwinter Night. Following that, a year of unrest: plagues, floods, famine, and fear. And then, exactly one year later, the Empyrea will come down from the heavens and cleanse the earth of the filth of man, and begin a new world free of sin and death."

"What does any of this have to do with us? The wardens?" Galantha asked.

"Think about that word, Snowdrop. *Warden*. We are tasked not only with keeping people out of the Ebonwilde . . . we must also keep some things *in*."

"I don't understand," Galantha said.

"Night is falling," Grandmother replied. "You will soon enough. Come now, we want to be outside of the border before the light is gone."

The deepening darkness allowed Rosetta to move a little more freely, and she tiptoed at a steady pace behind them as they trudged north through the snow. Grandmother continued Galantha's lesson as they walked. "Every one hundred years, Adamus's family sends one of their sons to the glade. The practice was started on the belief that when Adamus is reborn, the Verecundai will be the first to identify him, and that he will take his place as their lost eighth member . . . only this time, they will not be his equals, but his servants. Over time, however, much of the true meaning of the practice was lost, and the family began to believe that the sacrifice was being made to the Verecundai to ensure the safety and prosperity of their lands for another hundred years."

"What made them believe that?" Galantha asked. They had just reached the northernmost edge of the blighted, lifeless valley, also marked by a tree with a spider sigil.

Grandmother looked at Galantha, her eyes glinting in the moon-light glancing off the snow.

"We did," she said.

It was then that Rosetta saw another figure moving slowly toward them, head bent low.

"Grandmother," Galantha whispered. "What is going on?"

"I'm sorry for this, my Snowdrop," Grandmother said, taking Galantha's chin in her aged hands. "This time you will only watch, but one hundred years from now, when I have gone to the next plane, it will be your responsibility to carry on this tradition, detestable and difficult as it is. The Empyrea cannot be allowed to undo every beautiful thing that the Ilithiya brought to life with her love."

Galantha pressed her lips together and nodded, as bravely as she could.

On the horizon, the aurora was beginning its nightly display, as feathery fingers of turquoise and violet began to twist across the lapis sky. And as the women watched, the approaching person became more defined against the snow, moving slowly but steadily in their direction, toward the Verecundai's cursed glen.

It was a man. An old man, actually, with a back bent like a shepherd's crook, shambling on legs like brittle twigs. He kept his head down, his fur cloak flapping in the wind.

When Rosetta looked back at her grandmother and sister, Grand-mother was tracing a spell of concealment into the air. Rosetta could see them, but she had been taught to discern the reality behind such misleading enchantments; to the man, they would be all but invisible, no more than a slight shimmer in the shifting air.

Her grandmother's visage was as thin and flimsy as parchment, but there was no mistaking the knife she removed from her belt.

Dread left a bitter flavor on the back of Rosetta's tongue. She hoped that she was wrong. She hoped Grandmother—the woman who had raised her, who spared window spiders and thanked raspberry bushes and planted extra carrots for the forest rabbits to steal—could *not* be about to kill someone. Could she?

The man never made it past the spider sigil.

Grandmother pounced on him as he hobbled by, drawing her knife across his throat with a grim precision. He died without making a cry, blood dripping from the sides of his mouth and into the white whiskers of his beard.

Rosetta's horrified shout was smothered by Galantha's keening; blood had erupted from the man's neck and splattered across her hands, which were shaking violently. "It's all right," Grandmother said, trying to comfort her. "Cry if you must. We have done a terrible thing tonight, but we did it for the greater good."

Rosetta did not cry; she ran. She picked up her skirts and plunged straight past the spider sigil into the waiting darkness beyond.

16

NOW

AURELIA

9 DAYS TO MIDWINTER
1621

We had to move quickly. I roved Castillion's study, filling a satchel with anything I could find among his bric-a-brac that might prove helpful on a journey through the wintry Ebonwilde. Besides the map, there wasn't much: some matches, a compass, and a flask of strong whiskey I found tucked away in the back of a drawer. Before going out the door, I stopped to grab the fur-lined red cloak, swirling it around my shoulders before fastening it with the spider brooch.

Kellan was to meet me outside the Night Garden, but I got there a few minutes earlier than we'd agreed to give me a chance to look over the cloister for my ring a second time. I was certain I'd had it when I went into the casket; if it wasn't removed prior to my waking, it had to have fallen free during the frenzy of my waking. Now that the disorientation and mania had abated, I hoped to search with clearer eyes.

True to its name, the Night Garden retained its twilit ambience even in the full light of day. I strode through the trees until the maudlin statue of the center cloister came into view. The frostlace buds were swelling just a little bit more now, their light, feathery scent tickling my nose as I approached. It was a good thing that the forgetfulness they caused was transmitted through consumption, not scent.

Sometime in the last hours, someone had come in and cleaned up the scene. The glass casket had been rehoisted upon its pedestal, set like a jewel into a scene of otherworldly beauty. I could imagine what I must have looked like, lying in repose under those luneocite panes. I felt a pang of pity for the poor people who'd gathered with Castillion, expecting to wake a maiden, only to be accosted by a monster.

Well, I didn't exactly get what I expected, either. I closed my eyes and let my mind drift for a moment to what I had pictured, going into the box, would be waiting for me when I came out of it again. I imagined feeling a gentle kiss on my lips, then letting my eyes flutter open to find Zan leaning over me, his face awash in brilliant light, as beams of sun were caught by the glass and fractured into a thousand dancing colors.

It felt like truth. Like something that *was*, not something that might have been.

Don't do this to yourself, Aurelia, I chastised. *He let you go; you must figure out how to do the same.*

I clutched the vial of my blood, willing it to give me strength. And then I went back the way I came, letting the ring stay lost in the Night Garden, my fruitless wishes with it.

By the time I made it out of the greenhouse, Nathaniel had also arrived. He had changed from his Castillion livery into plain clothes in a mostly unsuccessful attempt to appear unobtrusive, but he was too tall, too dignified, too handsome to ever truly blend. "I guess that will have to do," I said. "Though I'd hardly call you 'unnoticeable.'"

"Speak for yourself," he replied. "Have you looked in a mirror lately?"

"Unfortunately," I said with a shrug, "mirrors don't really work for me anymore."

"Probably for the best," he replied, shouldering a pack.

"What is that supposed to mean?" I huffed. "Do I look so terrible? Is it the clothes? They're Castillion's."

"We can discuss your fashion choices later," he said, furtively scanning the empty courtyard. "We have a slim window of opportunity right now to get into the Trove before the porter realizes his keys have gone missing." He lifted a hefty key ring and jangled it. "Don't know which one it is, so we'll need time to try as many as we can."

I followed him into the keep, carefully dodging any of the other Castillion soldiers or attending staff. The first level was like Castillion's study, stately and well-furnished, made up of a massive entrance hall and several smaller parlors. The level below seemed to be more utilitarian: the kitchens, the scullery, the larder and broom closets. The next one down was the servants' quarters, mostly. "If you go that way"—Nathaniel pointed down a well-lit hall—"it'll take you into the Fort Castillion village." He tilted his head to another hall, not lined with brick but seemingly cut directly into stone. "This way leads to the Trove."

The way was narrow and dim, first gradating slowly down and then becoming a set of steep, slick stairs. "Nathaniel," I said, "are you taking me to the dungeon?"

"The dungeon is down here, just the other direction." He chuckled. "Castillion was originally founded by miners," he said. "Most of Achleva's ore came from their mines. Which is why, when looking for a place for their fortress, Castillion's predecessors just decided to plop a building over the top of one." We came to an iron door, and he took out the nicked key ring and began trying each one in turn. "As it happens," he said, "it makes an excellent location in which to stockpile all the necessary resources for surviving an apocalypse. Aha!" One of the keys made a click, and he turned it in the lock.

I gasped.

"Welcome," Nathaniel said, "to the Trove."

Inside was a cavern of black stone, three stories tall and honeycombed with branching alcoves and corridors. At the apex, a circular window let in air and a narrow shaft of daylight. It, like many of Castillion's other engineering marvels, seemed to be operated by a series of wheels and pipes and pulleys, allowing it to open and close at will. Wooden stairs and balconies connected each level to the next, and as Nathaniel led me forward, I saw that each offshoot of the main cavern housed something different from the last. One was a collection of cloth and thread of innumerable varieties. Another held barrels of ale, the next grain.

"How is this possible?" I asked.

"Remember all of those territories Castillion overtook, one by one? Everyone thought he was just a new despot, eager to fill a vacuum of power left by the fall of Achlev. But every time he moved on a region, the first thing he did was collect and catalogue whatever resources they had in abundance, bringing them here for safekeeping. Had he not done that, hundreds of thousands of refugees, Achlevan and Renaltan alike, would have died this last year. After the floods, and the fever, and the Circle's rise."

"I hated him," I said. "Fought against him. And all the time he was doing this."

"You weren't the only one, Aurelia," Nathaniel said. "The good thing is, he knew people would hate him . . . but he did it anyway. So many are alive today because of his foresight."

"Foresight?" I mused. This was more than simple shrewdness. It was . . . uncanny. Supernatural, even. I thought of Aren, the high mage queen whose spirit had guided me to Achleva, who showed me little glimpses into my future. Because of her, I had been able to kill Cael and save Zan's life. But Castillion was a blood mage, and the magic disciplines never overlapped.

"Come on," Nathaniel said, hanging the key ring on the door's handle for someone else to find later. "Let's go before my guilt overcomes me, and I lose my nerve to leave."

We worked from the top to the bottom, first collecting tools for travel: ropes, a knife for me and a sword for Nathaniel, flint and steel, fishing line and fishhooks. On the second level down, where the dry goods were kept, we had managed to collect some tea leaves and a handful of dried beans when we heard a voice from the entrance above. "I swear, m'lord, I don't know how this could have happened!"

A second voice had joined the first. "Look," Castillion's said, "they can't have just disappeared!"

Nathaniel pulled me into one of the off-shooting corridors, pressing a finger to his lips. Then he murmured, "This is the beginning of the back exit. We should go. Now."

"But we don't have enough food," I protested in a whisper. "We need what's on the bottom level. I saw dried meat, and rounds of cheese . . ."

"We have tools," he said. "That will have to be enough."

"Aha!" Castillion said triumphantly. "Looks like they didn't make it very far after all."

My chest went tight. Had we been caught? But then I heard the jingling of keys.

"They're right here," Castillion said. "You left them in the lock. Tell the truth, Porter. Have you been sampling the Trove's ale again?"

Relieved at the reprieve, I nodded to Nathaniel. If we didn't go now, we might not get another chance.

"Where are we going?" I whispered. It was getting darker and darker the farther we moved away from the central part of the Trove. "I feel like I'm being swallowed by the mountain. Like someone could get lost down here and never be found."

"Not to worry," Nathaniel said. "Part of my training in Castillion's forces included memorizing the Trove's tunnels. The exit isn't that far."

"Oh, good," I said, relieved. "So you've been this way before."

"Not exactly." I could hear the sheepishness in his voice. "I memorized a map of the tunnels. No one is actually allowed outside of the center Trove cavern. Too much risk of shaft collapses."

"Are you *serious?*" I hissed. "At least *you* can die! I could get stuck under a rock *forever.*" I shuddered.

"If it comes to it, I give you permission to use my blood for a spell to get yourself free."

I felt my bloodless body stir at the suggestion, hungry for a taste of the magic it lacked. I was glad, right then, that it was too dark for him to see my face.

"Look," he said a minute later. "Light."

The exit was only three feet high, a half-circle outlet that might once have funneled water away from the mining tunnels. We had to crawl out on our bellies, finding ourselves on a very narrow ledge on the other side. It was colder on this side of the mountain, the wind off the arctic water assailing us straight-on. The clouds overhead were thick and iron gray; there would be more snow here soon.

"What's that?" I asked. The light was weak and dreary, but compared to the darkness of the caves, still blinding. I squinted at a line stretching long across the expanse of white, and as my eyes adjusted, was able to make out the shape of wagons and carts and horses struggling on the snowy, roughshod road.

"More refugees," Nathaniel said. "These ones are probably coming up from Renalt by way of the Ebonwilde; twice as long a journey, but safer than trying to sail past the Circle Midnight. Come on, we need to make it down from here before nightfall. I paid off one of the stable hands—there should be a pair of horses waiting for us at the bottom."

I nodded absently, still focused on the Renaltan refugees. Unbidden, the lyrics of that old folk song surfaced in my mind: *Don't go, my child, to the Ebonwilde, for there a witch resides . . .*

Renaltans were an absurdly superstitious people. How bad must things have been for them to willingly venture through the woods that they had, for centuries, feared so greatly?

It would not be long before I found out.

17

THEN

KELLAN

"There's someone waiting for you," Ivan said from behind the bar as Kellan trudged into the tavern dining hall, rubbing sleep from his eyes. It was past midday, but what reason did he have to get up at the crack of dawn? One of the benefits of not being a soldier anymore was that he could sleep in as long as he wanted. And every day, that meant waking up later and later.

"Who is it?" Kellan asked, palming a pear from a bowl on the countertop.

"See for yourself," Ivan said, jerking his head toward the corner, where a fussy-looking man wearing an overstarched tunic was listlessly drumming his fingers on the tabletop. "Do you know him?"

Kellan sighed. "Unfortunately, I do."

He trudged over and slid into the booth across from him. "Seneschal Pelton," he said, sniffing the man's floral, violet-scented perfume. "What can I do for you?"

Pelton's eyes darted around the mostly empty dining room before settling on a spot just over Kellan's shoulder, as if afraid to look him directly in the eye. "I've come to talk to you about King Conrad," he said in an uncharacteristically quiet voice.

Kellan folded his arms and flopped back against the bench. "Not sure there's anything left to say."

Pelton didn't seem to notice Kellan's silver hand. Surprising . . . when Kellan delivered Conrad to the castle, the vain little man—always meticulous and obsessed with perfection—had gawped openly at his missing right hand.

Dropping his voice further, Pelton leaned forward and said, "He's letting himself be . . . influenced . . . by some unsavory characters."

Kellan grunted. "Not surprising, really—the entire court is populated with unsavory characters."

"I am not talking about Graves or Gaskin." Pelton cast a worried glance over his shoulder, where Ivan was drying cups behind the counter. "I'm talking about the Circle Midnight." The last words were so quiet, Kellan had to strain to hear them.

"You mean the weird preacher from the square? The one with the horse?"

"Yes."

"I don't see how Conrad's religious interests are any of my concern."

"Is his continued existence any of your concern?" Pelton hissed. Then, "The Circle Midnight is not some trifling, self-indulgent juristocracy like the Tribunal. The threat they pose, not just to the king, but to Renalt . . . and perhaps to humanity itself . . . is *substantial* and *significant*."

Kellan's eyebrows lowered into a V, and he studied Pelton from under them with an astonished, quizzical alarm. Never, in all of his years working at the palace, had the seneschal demonstrated a mere *shred* of that kind of passion or intensity. Even Ivan, all the way on the other side of the room, had stopped his polishing to eye them inquisitively.

Pelton checked himself, taking a steadying breath and folding his hands on the table in an attempt to regain some of his composure. "Obviously, I feel very strongly about this. But no matter what I say, Conrad will not listen to me. He's made up his mind, and refuses to hear reason."

"Mule-like stubbornness does run rather strong in that family," Kellan said, casting his eyes at the ceiling. "What do you expect me to do about it?"

"Talk to him. Stay close to him. Don't let them get him."

Don't let them get him. Hadn't he heard those words before? Troubled, Kellan gave a slow, reluctant nod. "All right. I suppose I can try to talk to him, at least. But you should know, the king and I aren't on particularly good terms at the moment. I'm not sure he'd let me across the palace threshold, let alone bend his ear."

"There's an event coming up. Day after tomorrow." Pelton slid a folded parchment across the table. "Banquet and ball, being held at the king's request, in honor of the city's most influential citizens. I've procured for you an invitation. You can talk to him there."

Kellan unfolded and scanned it. "This says it is a costume ball," he said, looking up. "And that no one uncostumed will be allowed through the gate. You must be joking."

"I don't care how you manage it." Pelton sighed. "Just see that you do."

★

Kellan chose to dress as an Ostrothian gladiator, with his hair tied up in a bundle of tiny black braids and wearing a long tunic and leather armor that looked quite powerful yet showed off a rather uncomfortable amount of his thigh. He was able to carry a sword and shield with this costume, and even if they were just cheap wooden replicas, he felt better having them, especially since he could use the shield to cover his silver hand.

As he climbed the stairs to the banquet hall, Kellan realized that this was the first time he'd ever attended an event like this as a guest, and not a servant of the crown. How many times had he stood steadfastly behind Aurelia as the food was served and the dancing began, wishing he could reach out a hand and lift her from her chair? To take her in his arms and sway to the rising lilt of the court musicians' strings? But the Aurelia with whom he'd envisioned dancing was a daydream—a figment of his imagination. The real one was far more flawed, more willful, more irritatingly independent. In getting to know *that* Aurelia, he'd learned to love her differently . . . and admired her, perhaps, more.

Until she had raised his own sword against him.

It was a lesson in mistrust he would not soon unlearn.

No one from the Renaltan landed gentry had been invited, but it hadn't stopped those who were already in Syric from coming. Lord Gaskin's mother and aunt were serving sizzling glares from the corner by the roast goose; the Marquess of Hallet's daughter was dancing with her new stepbrother in a decidedly unsisterlike manner near the wine fountain; and Lady Fonseca's four dour female cousins were eating candied fruits in perfect synchronicity along the wall behind the dessert table. The aristocrats were not accustomed to having their parties infiltrated by the middle class, but Kellan could see that Conrad's idea to appeal to that sector was a good one. The rest of the attendees were less polished in their manner, but were far more powerful in their influence.

Pelton, dressed as a jester, looked only slightly more ridiculous in curved-toe slippers and a bell-trimmed red cap than he did in his everyday uniform. He jingled over to Kellan, motioning proudly at the crowd. "Ah, Lord Greythorne. Surprised to see you here."

"Yes, I'm sure you're completely shocked. Where is this Fidelis?"

"Not yet arrived," Pelton said. "But I'm sure he'll be along soon enough, since this entire rigamarole was put together for him—and he doesn't seem the type to pass up an opportunity for more clout and power."

"Before that happens, I should probably go make my presence known to the king," Kellan said. "Get it over with."

He pushed through the array of costumed revelers—a winged Empyrea, a pink petunia, a lion with a mane of yellow-and-orange yarn—toward the king, who sat in the oversize Renaltan throne with his feet dangling six inches from the floor. The young king's eyes, however, were keen; he was observing the gathering with an eagerness that surprised Kellan. Despite his assertions to the contrary, Conrad seemed to very much enjoy his position as the master of the gathering.

Before he could get within a few yards, however, Kellan was flanked by two men in uniform, each lifting an arm to cut off his path to the king.

"Well, if it isn't the errant knight himself."

Kellan summoned his patience. "Hector," he said. "Pomeroy."

"We've been missing you at the fights," Hector said, grinning. "Heard you got canned."

"Just not the same without the Gryphon in the arena," Pomeroy added. "No one to root against."

"I'm sure you are both losing plenty of money without my help."

"The Mastiff has been helping us clean up nicely," Hector said. "Couple more big wins, we won't need to work for the kid anymore."

"King," Kellan corrected in a tight voice.

Pomeroy shook his head. "Oh, you can drop the act. Everyone knows you can't stand the brat either. No reason to stay now his filthy witch sister is counting worms—"

Kellan's left hand closed on his prop sword as a red haze clouded his sight. *Not your fight,* he reminded himself. *Save it for the arena.* He took a slow, cleansing breath.

"Look at this!" Hector grabbed the Ostrothian shield away. Kellan's silver hand was immobile and useless to stop him. The guard rapped his knuckles against the metal, laughing. "Malcom was tellin' the truth! How much did it set you back, Greythorne? Is that why you're here tonight? Gonna beg for work now that you spent all your coin on this fancy new appendage?"

"Don't worry," Pomeroy said, exchanging a cunning smile with Hector. "Malcolm's got something new in the works for you. An opponent perfectly matched for the Gryphon."

Kellan looked between their two heads and saw Conrad happily chatting up a man dressed as a rooster, with large, multicolored feathers protruding from the back of his pantaloons, and realized, belatedly, that this was all a monstrously ridiculous joke.

There was no danger here—not unless you could drown in frills and foppery. Kellan sheathed his sword and used his free hand to yank his shield from Hector's grasp before making an about-face and heading for the door.

"See you in the arena, Gryphon!" Pomeroy called after him, before he and Hector burst into laughter.

He didn't take the main exit, choosing instead to use one of the back ways Aurelia used to frequent, through the kitchen and down another hall, whispering curses as he stripped off the costume. First the cheap cape, then the useless sword, and then the shield. He tossed them all in a heap at the edge of the corridor.

Fool, he told himself.

That's when he saw her: a girl hovering outside the back entrance to the grand hall, looking as if she were unsure if she wanted to enter or make a run for it. She was dressed in a gown of gold, with lines of shining white radiating out from a ring woven into her bodice. A sun, Kellan realized. Her mask was gold, too, covering her eyes and half of her face, with a circle of golden spikes jutting from her hair, which was also bright blond. It was half-piled in golden curls at her crown, the rest falling in a wave over her shoulder.

She was beautiful in a way he had never quite seen before. She was . . . incandescent, and not just because she was dressed like the sun. He found himself moving toward her. "Are you lost?" he asked. "This is not the main entrance."

She whirled to face him, mouth dropping open in surprise. "Lord Kellan," she said. "I mean—Captain Greythorne. I didn't think you . . . I mean . . . what are you doing out here? Shouldn't you be in there? With the king?"

She knew his name. It sent an odd shock through him. "Do I know you?" he asked, tilting his head, and thinking how familiar her perfume smelled, too . . . like violets. "Yes," she said. "I mean—no. I mean . . . I know *of* you. Everyone knows of you."

The musicians had begun the next song, an old ballad played slowly on the lute. Suddenly, Kellan was in less of a hurry to go. "I can escort you inside, if you like," he said.

"No," she said quickly, nervously wringing her gloved hands. "No. You should get back to your duties. Conrad . . . King Conrad, I mean . . . he needs you."

"He really doesn't," Kellan said, but she wasn't listening; her attention had been dragged back to the hall. The women were curtsying on one side, the men bowing on the other, and directly down the line, Kellan could see Conrad on his throne, speaking with a man in a purple robe. The man bent down to Conrad, as if to show his respect, and a silver medallion swung from his neck.

"No," the girl breathed, taking a step back, then another. "It's too late." She turned on him, pointing a finger accusingly. "Why aren't you there? You were supposed to keep Fidelis from getting close!"

"What?" Kellan was in earnest now. "How do you know—?"

Just then, the purple-robed man—Fidelis, apparently—looked up, his head snapping toward their direction.

"Bleeding stars!" she whispered, spinning on her heel so suddenly that he had to stagger backwards a few steps to keep from getting ramrodded.

"What's the matter?" Kellan asked as she bolted past him into the shadows. "Wait," he called. "Don't go!" The girl was running now, trailing rivulets of shimmering light. He followed after her, reaching out with his silver hand. "I just want to talk."

She was quick—very quick. And though the palace was a winding maze of corridors, she seemed to know exactly where she was going, darting down one dark hall after another. As she went, light bled away parts of her image. Soon the golden crown, the mask, the dress . . . all · were gone. And underneath was . . .

Stars save me, he thought. *Is that a . . . a . . . bear? Or something else? Is she a shapeshifter, like Rosetta?* But Rosetta's change was visceral, a shift in her entire bodily form. This was an illusion, and soon it was gone completely.

And just like that, so was the creature. Or . . . whatever she was. One moment she was sun, and the next she was merely shadow. A puff of smoke. A dream.

There was a startled noise behind him, and he turned to see one of the kitchen maids. She had dropped a plate of food she was obviously smuggling from the party.

"Did you see?" he asked, breathlessly. "Did you see her?"

The maid stammered, "She won't hurt you, I promise, sir. I know she looks frightening, but I swear, she means no harm to no one. She's a sweet girl. We give her food sometimes . . . but it isn't breaking any laws. Please don't be angry, Master Greythorne. Sir."

She prostrated herself over the scattered contents of the fallen tray.

"You know who she is?" Kellan asked, kneeling beside the nervous maid.

"Yes. Yes, sir. Sort of. I . . ."

"What's her name?" he asked. Because even now, he could not shake the feeling that she—creature, girl, magician, whatever she was —knew him. And he her.

"We call her Millie," the maid said. "Because of what she wears. Like *mille peaux*. Thousand furs."

18

THEN

CONRAD

The preacher of the Circle Midnight had finally arrived.

Conrad wasn't sure *why* he wanted him to be there at the ball, exactly. Just that he did, very badly. And that this man—Fidelis the Fourteenth, as he was now introduced—was the reason for throwing this party.

Up close, Fidelis had a gaunt face and a large forehead, and pale eyes of a murky blue. His hair—what was left of it—was shaved close to his head. He bowed to Conrad, and his medallion swung to and fro in front of him.

Overall, there was nothing about the man's appearance that made him interesting enough to arrange an entire ball for, but he had a mesmerizing way about him that intrigued Conrad.

"Your Majesty is curious," Fidelis said. "About me and my . . . organization."

It was as if the man had pulled the thought right from his head. "I am," Conrad said. If Fidelis was so good at reading people, what use was it to lie? "I heard your preaching the other day. It intrigued me."

"I saw you there, Your Majesty. In truth, I was mostly speaking to you. My fellows and I . . . we would very much like to teach you more about our message, if you are amenable to it."

"And what is your message, exactly? Are you Tribunal?"

Fidelis shook his head firmly. "The Tribunal went astray long, long ago. They served a false goddess. The goddess of death. Of darkness. But not us. We worship the *true* Goddess. She Who Lives Among the Stars. The *real* Empyrea."

"And how do you know?" Conrad asked. "If one faction could be mistaken, could not you be mistaken also?"

"His Majesty speaks his mind," Fidelis said congenially. "We appreciate the forthrightness. But no . . . unlike the Tribunal's violence-hungry blood mage Cael, *our* founder was a man of great wisdom and peace. Fidelis the First was his name, born with the gift to hear the Goddess's voice, whispering all the secrets of the universe, telling him of what was, and is, and will be. *Our* teachings are true, because they came directly from the Goddess herself. She spoke to Fidelis. And through his writings, she continues to speak to us."

"Would she speak to me, do you think?" Conrad asked.

"She would," said Fidelis. "She does already, actually. But you must be taught how to hear her whispers. Let us teach you to listen, Majesty. Let us call you Friend."

Friend. The word hummed in his ears.

"I think . . ." Conrad began slowly. "I think I might like that."

"If that's true," Fidelis said, "you are ready to cross the second level of initiation into the Circle."

"What must I do?"

"The second level is all about letting go of worldly things," Fidelis said. "This costume party is a start . . . you've recognized that true power comes from the common folk and have invited them here, honoring them over the out-of-touch, wealthy elites that comprise the nobility."

"But . . . ?" Conrad asked.

"But look around, Majesty. Look at all this . . . pomp. The fine foods, the outrageous opulence. The flamboyant dress." Fidelis leveled a side-eyed glance at Conrad's costume, which was meant to be a ship captain's apparel, but had been constructed from velvets and silks, sewn with gold thread. A real sea captain would never dream of wearing such ridiculous finery aboard his boat. "The Empyrea requires simplicity from her followers, to keep them from becoming susceptible to pride, gluttony, vanity, and greed."

Conrad shifted in his throne, suddenly embarrassed. "I can do better," he said. "From now on, I will swear off excesses."

"Wonderful!" Fidelis said, clapping his hands in delight. "I will be watching to see how you do. When I believe your effort is sufficient, I will send a message with an invitation to the third level of initiation. I do so look forward to it."

Conrad asked, "Should I expect to wait long?"

Fidelis rose from his genuflection with the sliver of a smile on his lips. "That depends on you," he said.

That night, when Conrad was pulling every suit coat and vest and pair of pantaloons from his closet, he found a note in one of his pockets, and followed it to a hole under the floorboard that held a cache of several more notes just like it. He read each one with glee, and then added one more to the pile.

Primus 1st, 1621

Tonight you met Fidelis at the costume gala, and he has directed you to free yourself from your worldly belongings in order to advance into the next stage of initiation.

It's beginning.

The next morning, he had a string of servants in and out of the castle, removing the pretentious trappings that came with kingship. Pelton watched with dismay, wringing his hands. "But, sir," he argued as a butler walked past with a gold-painted vase in hand, "some of these are priceless antiques! They've been in your family for generations!" His frown drooped nearly off his face as he saw a maid go past with a bundle of damask curtains in her arms. "This is outrageous!"

"What is outrageous, Pelton," Conrad said, "is that we have gone so long like this, lording our wealth over our people while they go without. I've instructed the servants to take all of these things and give them away in the town. And then I'll dismiss the servants," he said. "I do not need anyone waiting on me hand and foot."

That made Pelton turn a shade of beet red. "Sir, many of the servants rely on this employment to feed their families. Would the Empyrea want these poor people to starve because you became so preoccupied with your own salvation you neglected to care for the people within your sphere that do not have your resources?"

That made Conrad pause. "Fine," he said. "We'll keep most of the staff, and let them go a few at a time, after they've had time to seek other employment." He didn't want anyone to suffer unduly on account of his attempt to perform the abnegation rite to a sufficient level. He hoped Fidelis would not judge him too harshly for it.

Pelton looked relieved, but only for a minute, until a maid passed by carrying a patched-up bearskin rug. "Wait!" he cried, hand up in admonition. "That's mine!"

✹

Three nights later, Conrad was studying alone in the library when everything went suddenly dark as a rough sack was thrown over his head and his arms were pinned behind him. "Do not fight, nor cry out, Friend," a soft voice whispered. "The third trial of initiation into the Circle has begun."

He tamped down his initial terror and tried to relax as he felt himself being moved. *You wanted this,* he reminded himself. *You must be brave, like Aurelia.*

When the sack was removed from his head, he found himself in a room without windows or flat walls—it was built in a circle, with a moon shape carved into the center, surrounded by an eight-pointed star. The floor seemed to rock beneath him, and at first he blamed it on the disorientation caused by the blinding hood. After a moment, however, he realized that the movement was caused by waves—he'd been brought onto a ship.

He was sitting in one of ten black, high-backed chairs arranged around the moon, upon which Fidelis stood, his hands lost in the sleeves of his robe. There were nine other initiates besides him, each blinking blearily from their chair. Around the edge of the room, dozens of faceless, torchlit figures waited for the meeting to begin.

Even in his simplest attire, Conrad was grossly overdressed; everyone else wore threadbare work shirts and patched-up breeches; they'd probably had a much easier time proving their dedication to abnegation. He found his eyes drawn to the boots of the man sitting in the chair to his left—they might once have been made of good leather, but were so well-worn, Conrad could see the color of his stockings through the holes left when the creases began to split. When the man glared at him, he blushed in embarrassment and quickly averted his gaze.

Fidelis began with a flourish. "Welcome, dearest Friends. You have all been invited here today because, of all the people in this city who are desirous to hear our message, you have been singled out by the Empyrea herself as the *most* elite of her chosen. Those with the courage and fortitude to take the news of her coming to the masses, and to bring the like-minded you find among them into the fold with us."

The hooded listeners stomped the floor and Fidelis smiled again. "When the clocks stopped at midnight and did not move again, you were among the first to bear witness. Because of your great faith, the Empyrea has directed me to conduct you through the third-level rite of initiation. Your third-level initiation will be different than that of those who came before you, or those who will come after, because *your* rite of fortitude will coincide with the coming second sign of the Empyrea's reckoning."

Fidelis moved around the circle, taking hands and touching heads as he passed. "The Midnight Papers tell us that a plague will spread throughout the land. A fever far worse than any we have ever known before. It will strike the young and the old with equal vengeance, claiming men . . . women . . . *children*." Fidelis paused briefly in front of Conrad, as if to emphasize his point. "None shall be safe," he said, "except *you*."

From his robe, Fidelis produced a palm-size amphora, lifting it for all to see. In the torchlight, the glass sparked red, but the contents behind it seemed to reflect no color at all. The closest thing Conrad knew to call it was black, though it was unlike any black he'd ever seen. Not onyx or ebony or obsidian . . . it was deeper than that. Like a shadow's shadow. Or the empty nothingness between one star and another.

Fidelis swirled the liquid inside the amphora, saying, "It is written that when Fidelis the First heard the Empyrea's voice, he was so filled with her divine light, there was no room left inside him for sin. He wept at the beauty, and his tears turned black as they carried away his every impurity, every iniquity, every want, every jealousy. He collected those tears in this jar, knowing that one day, you and I would be standing here, staring down the coming calamity, and that we, too, would need to be cleansed of our sins so that we can be prepared to face it." He looked up and said, "I ask you, Friends, who among you is ready to partake of that selfsame light? To let it work within you like a purifying fire?"

The listeners began clamoring for his attention. "I am ready!" one woman said as she fell rapturously at his feet. "Praise the Empyrea!" said another man, who stood on his chair and clasped his hand to his heart. "Let me be cleansed!"

But Fidelis's attention landed on the man sitting beside Conrad, the one with the worn-out boots.

"You," Fidelis said. "Come here."

The man stood and bashfully shuffled over and knelt before the preacher, removing his cap and twisting it in his hands. "The Empyrea has seen your devotion, Friend Ivan. She wishes to bestow upon you a great blessing."

The man's eyes widened in surprise that Fidelis knew his name. "But, sir," he said, "I'm just a humble tavernkeeper, of no consequence."

"Of no consequence? No, Friend Ivan. I daresay your influence will soon be felt the world over, as you have been invited to be the *first* to partake of Fidelis's bitter tears." Fidelis broke the wax seal on the amphora and pulled the stopper, pressing the glass to the man's lips. "Drink, Friend, and let the Empyrea's spirit work within you so that you might carry it across the land and spread it to every corner of the world."

Ivan's eyes were reverent as Fidelis tipped the amphora and the liquid filled his mouth. He swallowed, and then smiled. "I can feel it," he said in both pain and awe. "I can feel it working!"

"A man of lesser fortitude would not be able to speak after partaking of the bitter tears, Friend Ivan. You are already proving the Empyrea's faith in you is well placed."

Fidelis went clockwise from one supplicant to the next, offering each a sip of the black fluid in turn. Conrad mustered up his courage; he had no desire whatsoever to drink something that looked like liquefied tar, but he did not want to make a spectacle of himself by refusing, either. In the end, however, he didn't have to. When Fidelis came to him, the amphora was already empty.

"Worry not, Friend Conrad," Fidelis said, putting a hand on his shoulder. "You may not be able to pass the fortitude initiation rite tonight, but that is because the Empyrea has other plans for you." He smiled. "*Magnificent* plans."

19

THEN

ZAN

"Couldn't find that drink you were looking for, I take it?" Jessamine's arms were crossed in front of her as Zan reined Madrona up next to her. "Well, I didn't find the sister I was looking for, either. Because the woman we're trying to find isn't actually Delphinia's sister. She's 'Sister Cecily.' A *nun*. She used to run a small healer's practice here, but a few years ago she was ordered back home to—"

"The Abbey of the Sisters of the Sacred Torch?" Zan asked.

Jessamine pursed her lips in consternation. "I spent all day trying to figure that out! No one wanted to talk to me. I had to bribe people for information, which is humiliating—I'm an *accepter* of bribes, not an offerer. I'm completely out of money now!"

"I'm sorry that you had to abandon your ethical standards," Zan said. "If it makes you feel better, I used the last of my money, too," he said, pulling two tickets from his jacket, "buying us passage on a ship set to make a stop on Widows' Isle . . . home to the Abbey of . . ."

". . . the Sisters of the Sacred Torch." She snatched the tickets from him. "Well, aren't you full of surprises today, Sad Tom? And here, all this time I've been thinking you were just mopey and useless."

"Thank you?" Zan said, raising a perplexed eyebrow. "I think?" He did not tell her about how the apparition of Delphinia had led him to the right boat, or how she'd turned into Arceneaux before disappearing.

"All right," she said, letting out a long breath. "I can't believe I'm saying this, but: let's get ourselves to that nunnery."

★

They set their horses free before boarding the *Contessa* that evening. As Jessamine had used her money for information and Zan had used the last of his for passage, it would have been better if they could have sold them first, but the market was awash with desperate people peddling their goods for pennies. No one who could have bought them wanted them, and no one who would have wanted them could have bought them. Especially not Madrona, surly old nag that she was. She even tried to kick him as he said goodbye.

"I'll miss you," he told her. "Even if the feeling isn't mutual."

The captain of the *Contessa* was a sea-weathered Renaltan by the name of Gaspar. He watched his passengers shuffle up the gangplank with narrowed eyes, burly arms crossed over his chest as two of his subordinate sailors inspected each person before they were allowed aboard.

"Any signs of fever?" the first sailor asked Zan, prying his mouth open to get a good look at his teeth and then down his throat.

"No," Zan said.

"Any coughs? Trouble breathing?"

"No, none."

Next to him, Jessamine slapped the other sailor away as he reached toward the hem of her skirt. "Touch me with that hand and you'll lose it," she warned.

"No weapons," he replied, pointing to the knife hilt sticking from the top of her ankle boot. She glared at him, refusing to break eye contact as she retrieved the knife and dropped it on the plank in front of her. "Happy?"

Zan's sailor asked, "Have you been exposed to anyone afflicted with the Bitter Fever within the last three days?"

"Not in the last three days, no," Zan said. "But—"

"Passengers stay below deck. You'll be assigned a bunk. Meals are served three times a day, at nine, noon, and six. Move along," the sailor said, already turning his attention to the man in line behind him. "Next!"

Zan and Jessamine were ushered down a short flight of rickety stairs and into a dim hold where beds were little more than thin boards stacked three high. "This looks promising," Jessamine said dryly as she laid the small bag containing Delphinia's effects beside one of the bunks. She sat down on the plank and grimaced as it groaned in response. "How long is this voyage supposed to be again?"

"Only a few days," Zan said, wishing he'd had the sense to stay at the Stella Regina—sharing space with Father Cesare's eviscerated ghost seemed less and less unpleasant with each passing hour. The other passengers were filing in in twos and threes; it would be very close quarters soon. A man who'd claimed the bottom bunk three spots over had caught sight of Zan's beautiful companion and had flashed a grin in her direction that revealed a few brown teeth and a vast expanse of gum.

"We're doing this for Delphinia," Jessamine said, averting her eyes. "We're doing this for Delphinia. We're doing this for Delphinia."

A woman in a worn dress took the bunk across from Zan's, giving him a mistrustful glance from behind wispy russet hair, holding a bundle to her chest so protectively he thought it was an infant at first. It wasn't; it was a bottle of spirits, swathed in a blanket to, apparently, shield it from prying eyes when she wanted to take a furtive nip. She saw him looking at her and scowled, shouldering away from him, exposing the little girl who had been watching him from behind her mother's skirts. She was still very young, probably only three or four years old, and obviously terrified.

While the woman's back was turned, Zan removed Margaret the rag doll from his pocket and set it next to the foot of the woman's bunk. The little girl watched him do it warily, and when he turned his head, he saw in his periphery a skinny arm reach out and snatch her up.

The ship set sail shortly before sunset, and the evening meal for the passengers—of which Zan estimated to be over thirty—was a thin, fishy-smelling soup and a cup of weak ale. Thankfully, before they'd left the Quiet Canary, Lorelai had wrapped up a loaf of sweet bread in wax paper and left it on the stoop for them to take with them, and Zan removed the last hunk of it from his pack. He gave half of it to Jessamine and had settled down against his bunk to eat his portion when he saw a pair of owlish eyes watching him from one cot over.

The eyes belonged to the same man he'd talked to on the docks before he saw Delphinia. A boy, really, no more than fourteen or fifteen, whose gangly appendages had long spurted past the tattered hems of his clothing. He'd already finished his paltry meal; the bowl of unpleasant soup had been licked clean.

Zan reached across, depositing the bread into the youth's waiting hands.

"Many thanks, sir," he said between hasty bites. "I ent had nothin' to eat since I sold me chickens two days ago."

"Where are you headed?" Zan asked.

"Fort Castillion," the boy said, licking crumbs from his lips. "Ma said it's the only place to find good work these days. She was goin' to be a cook and I was goin' to see if I could get on buildin' those big ships o' his everyone talks about."

Zan's blood went chill. *Castillion*. The man who'd tried to kill him in Stiria Bay and very nearly achieved the goal. He wanted to warn the lad to run, *run* in the other direction, but instead he asked, "Where's your ma now?"

"Had to stay in Fimbria," he said through one last, big muffled bite. "Even with the money for the chickens, there weren't enough left for two tickets. So she made me get on ahead, and said she'll catch up to me later, when she gets up enough coin for the journey. She weren't feelin' so great this morning, neither. Hot, then cold. Probably better for her t' wait."

Zan nodded slowly, glad that the boy didn't know the slim odds of ever seeing his mother again. At least his final memory of his mother wouldn't be of her crying bitter black tears.

Come and find me.

The sound of Aurelia's last words blew into his thoughts like a caustic wind, and he was instantly retransported to that moment on the Stella Regina's stage, where he watched the first and last person he'd ever love slip from the warm Here into the cold After.

It took a moment for him to realize that the boy was still talking. He shook his head. "I'm sorry, what?"

"I asked you your name," the boy said, wiping his hand on his trousers before extending it. "I'm Lewis."

"His name is Tom," Jessamine cut in, leaning casually against the bed. She was tall enough that she couldn't stand to her full height in the cramped quarters.

"Nice to meet you, Tom," Lewis said, shaking Zan's hand with a timid grip. "And you are . . . ?"

"Jenny," Jessamine said. "Pleasure."

"Are you married?" Lewis asked.

Zan and Jessamine cringed in unison. "Stars, no," Jessamine said. "Brother and sister, actually."

"You don't look like—"

"Different mothers," Jessamine said quickly. "Our father married sixteen times, can you believe the old bastard? Can I see you for a minute, Tom?"

Zan shrugged and got to his feet, and she lugged him to a corner where there were fewer ears to overhear them. "Our father married sixteen times? Really?"

"I didn't see you offering any helpful alternatives," she said. "You were just about to tell that kid your actual name."

"That's what a person usually does when asked for it," he said.

"I'm not sure you want anyone in here knowing who you really are. One of the women over there was staring at you. And while you do have a certain . . . brooding, tortured, shaggy-orphaned-spaniel look about you that some women *might* find appealing . . . she kept looking at something in her bag. So, when she was distracted getting her cod-water slop, I took the liberty of nicking *this* from her things." She handed him a crumpled piece of paper. "Looks to me like a bounty," she said. "On *you*."

"I'm seeing that, *Jenny*," Zan said through gritted teeth.

Dominic Castillion was offering 100 gold pieces to anyone who could give him information that would lead him to one Valentin de Achlev, and 150 gold pieces to anyone willing to turn him in to the commander directly at Fort Castillion. A fairly accurate rendering of his face was included, along with the preference that the erstwhile king of Achleva be brought in alive if possible.

How reassuring, Zan thought, crumpling the paper before looking around for someplace to dispose of it. Finding nothing, he stuffed it deep into the pocket of his jacket.

"What are you doing?" Jessamine hissed. "I've got to put that back!"

"Why would you put it back?" Zan hissed in response. "We don't want her to have it."

"She'll be suspicious if she realizes it's gone."

"I'd say she's probably plenty suspicious already. *Bleeding stars!*" he cursed. "We can't let that get into the hands of the crew, or they'll sail right on past Widows' Isle and up around the northern coast to drop me at Castillion's feet."

"We just have to make it to the Sisters. That's not very long. Can you stay low and unobtrusive until then?"

"I can try," Zan said, in a voice as dismal as his chances.

★

The first night aboard the *Contessa* passed without incident, and so did most of the second day. But by the second evening, Zan noticed more and more people hovering on his periphery with an odd, too-intent look in their eyes, like a farmer with an approaching trip to market, protectively watching over a fattening lamb.

His nerves that night were taut, his mind restless. He knew he needed sleep, but was unable to achieve it. He needed food, too, but couldn't seem to keep from giving his portion of the rations to Lewis, who'd grown more sallow and withdrawn with every passing hour. Zan thought at first that it was the rocking of the boat across rough waves, but the boy managed to keep his food and water down well enough. It was something else.

The first two days, Lewis was happy to chat about his hopes for the new life he'd have in Castillion, or about his late father, who died when Lewis was eight, from whom he had inherited a talent for carpentry and woodworking. About his mother, too. A woman who was sometimes gruff and strict but whose work ethic and dedication ensured her son never went hungry. But on day three, his stories slowed. By that evening, they'd stopped.

In the dark of the third night, Zan woke to see Lewis tossing and turning on his bunk, drenched in sweat so heavy, it caught the dim lamplight and made him look as if he were made not of flesh, but fragile porcelain.

"Lewis?" Zan said.

Lewis mumbled a nonsensical response. Filled with dread, Zan yelled to the rest of the folk in the cabin, "Someone, quickly! Fetch the captain, find out if there's a healer aboard! This boy is sick. He needs help!"

"Zan," Jessamine whispered, hand on his shoulder. "I think the captain's already here."

Captain Gaspar's wide form was silhouetted on the cabin stairs. The woman from whom Jessamine had stolen the bounty flyer stood just behind him, pointing at Zan.

"That's him," she said to the captain. "That's the man Castillion wants."

Gaspar moved closer, rubbing the stubble on his boxlike chin.

"Listen," Zan said, putting his hands up beseechingly. "I don't want any trouble."

Gaspar grasped the front of Zan's shirt, his clenched fist as square and solid as a sledgehammer, and pushed him next to the nearest lantern, hung from a hook on a splintery beam. Then he jerked his head toward the tattling woman, who reached into Zan's jacket and removed the ball of crumpled paper. She smoothed it out and held it up next to Zan's face.

"I think you're right," he told her. To Zan, he said, "You're going to earn us quite a pretty penny, Your Highness."

"You want me?" Zan said dangerously. "Fine, you've got me. I'll go willingly, you won't have to ask me twice. But only if you find someone to help that boy over there *right now*."

Jessamine had knelt next to the boy, peering into the wan face beneath the sodden fringe of hair plastered to his forehead. She looked up at Zan, still pinned by Gaspar to the post, and shook her head. "I don't know if there *is* any helping him now," she said softly.

Gaspar let go of Zan to lean over Jessamine, inspecting Lewis in his bunk. Then he lurched backwards, clamping his arm over his mouth.

"It's the fever," he said, calling to his crew. "Cover your mouths! You! And you! Pick him up. We'll have to throw him overboard!"

Zan swiped the sword from Gaspar's scabbard with a metallic *shink*. "You'll do no such thing."

Jessamine produced a second knife from deep within her bodice and wrapped her right arm over the captain's right shoulder, aiming its thin and wicked point at the bulging vein in his throat with the other.

Zan tucked Gaspar's sword into his own belt and moved to lift the boy—who was flushed and gaunt, and far lighter than expected —into his arms.

"Wait—" Jessamine protested. "You'll be exposed."

"Likely I already am," Zan said. "And I can't let them toss him overboard."

Jessamine nodded and fell in step behind him, yanking her hostage along with her. "One move from any of you," she warned, "and the captain dies."

Her threat was unnecessary; every passenger and crew member was rooted to their spot, too scared of catching the fever to get close.

Zan, Lewis in his arms, made it up the stairs and onto the deck first, with Jessamine and the captive captain behind. The night wind was brisk and cold, and laden with moisture from a gathering storm. Through the darkness a tall building loomed, a dusky silhouette against the midnight sky.

A lighthouse.

Zan laid Lewis down in one of the *Contessa*'s longboats, then jumped in himself before waving for Jessamine to follow. She tightened her grip on the captain's neck until he lost consciousness and slumped over, then dropped his weighty body to the floor and stepped across it to the boat. As soon as she was in place, Zan used the captain's sword to cut the ropes, and they plummeted into the water below.

20

THEN

KELLAN

"She comes and goes as she pleases," the maid, named Cora, said, snapping the proffered coin from Kellan's outstretched fingers, even while she kept her eyes trained on the fallen tray. "We don't say nothin' to her, and she don't say nothin' to us. But we leave her food, and scraps of fur and fabric when we can find it, and then sometimes we find our chores done before we'n even get to 'em."

"But where did she *come* from?" Kellan asked, picking up one of the fallen biscuits and placing it on the tray as a display of good faith, proof that he wouldn't turn her in for the stolen food. "What purpose does she have here in the palace?"

"I don't know," Cora said, "none of us do. But she's been here, hiding in the walls and hauntin' the back passageways, ever since I been workin' here, goin' on two years now. Only saw little glimpses o' her here 'n' there when the Tribunal was around. If they'd caught her . . ." She shivered.

"What does she use the fur for?"

She shrugged. "Gretel—the old, mean laundress with the big boil on 'er nose—she thinks Millie sleeps in a hole in the ground outside somewhere. Y'know, a burrow or a nest or somethin'. So she needs the fur to keep warm at night." Her nervous eyes darted toward the door as if longing to bolt toward it. "I didn't see what she did or said to you, m'lord. I just came 'round the corner an' only saw her for a second before she got away." Then she said timidly, "I don't think she means no harm, m'lord. If it's known what she does, they'll put her out for sure. Them streets is unkind to us orphan girls. 'Specially now, with so many so angry all the time."

"She is not in any kind of trouble," Kellan said, replacing another biscuit, then a sad-looking chicken leg. "Nor do I have any authority with which to punish her. I only want to talk to her. If there's any way you can relay this message to her, I would be much obliged."

Cora nodded. "And if I do, where can she find you?"

"The Scheming Minstrel," he replied. "Room seven."

★

Kellan left the tavern before nightfall the next day and headed toward the arena. The line to get in was already long—longer than he'd ever seen it, and it wasn't even dark yet. By the time he got up to the front, it stretched down the block. *All these people coming to see the Mastiff?* he thought sullenly, letting himself be herded toward the north entrance with the rest of the crowd, his gladness at not being recognized eclipsed only by his irritation at it. Already, the Gryphon seemed to be old news.

At the door, a large man stopped him. "No weapons," he said. "Items can be retrieved as you leave."

Kellan muttered under his breath as he unbelted his sword and plunked it on the table.

"Excuse me, sir," the man said, giving his right arm, which had become visible when he moved his cloak aside to retrieve his sword, a meaningful look. "*All* weapons must be surrendered."

Kellan glared at him and raised the metal hand. "I'm afraid this one isn't removable."

"My apologies, sir," the man said quickly. "Two coppers entrance then. All money goes to pay the winning pot."

Kellan fished the money from his pocket and tossed it at the man, hurrying toward the aisle that funneled people to their seats.

The fights had already begun when Kellan pushed through the crowd on the mid-level viewing platform and sat down near the rail. A barrel-chested man with a red beard was pummeling a thin competitor, who then bent and charged headfirst into his midsection, only to be knocked flat on his back. The arena dirt flew up around him in a cloud.

"Ale, mister?" a girl asked, coming up beside him with a mug and a pitcher. "Only a half copper."

"No, thank you," he replied.

"Place a bet?" she asked without missing a beat.

"Hardly seems like a fair fight," he said.

"Oh, they're not betting who will win," she said, "but how long it'll take to knock him out."

Malcolm was diversifying his repertoire, it seemed. Kellan shook his head, and the maid shrugged. "Come find me if you change your mind. The next bout is s'posed to be even more exciting. Could pay handsomely."

"Who are the fighters going to be?" Kellan asked.

She winked. "Stick around and find out," she said, and she moved to the man next to him.

Kellan leaned against the rail as the bigger man landed a last punch across the jaw of the smaller one, sending him rolling. He came to a stop spread like a starfish across the floor, staring glassy-eyed at the ceiling, blood trickling from his nose.

The crowd roared, some clinking their mugs together while others huffed and muttered oaths at their loss. The ale-serving women went around giving coins to some and taking them from others as the victor made a lap and the unconscious man was dragged away.

"And now." Malcolm had entered the arena, his booming voice rattling in the rafters. "The moment you've all been waiting for! Tonight, my friends, you will witness a spectacular display of brute against beast! Of might against metal. Of man . . . against *monster!*"

The excitement inside the arena reached a fever pitch, and with a flourish, Malcolm bowed. From one side, the Mastiff stomped, curling his thick-muscled arms in front of him with a howling bellow. He was not wearing the boxing gloves that used to be part of the uniform, but metal gauntlets. His chest and shoulders were bare save for two crisscrossing strips of leather, studded with tiny spikes.

Kellan found himself at the edge of his seat. What could the purpose of such armoring be? The battles were brutal enough when they were gloved fist against gloved fist.

And then, the opponent appeared.

Tonight, the Mastiff would be fighting his own namesake.

The dog was of an abnormal size, likely the result of targeted breeding and growth-promoting feral magic, with paws the size of plates. And if that wasn't bad enough, he, too, was outfitted in metal armor, spikes marking the line of his spine and over the top of his head. His real teeth were fearsome, but he was wearing a mask, too, edged with razors. Beneath it, the dog was snarling and foaming, straining against his chain.

Kellan looked at Malcolm, who had removed himself to the safety of the tally box. The fightmaster caught his eye and grinned. *Maybe we can think of some . . . new . . . kind of arrangement,* he'd said.

Kellan jumped to his feet with an audible gasp, but no one heard it over the sound of the bell and the clapping and shrieking of the crowd as the dog's chain was released. He could not watch this. He could not, in any way, be a part of anything so exploitive and sick.

Malcolm must have seen him go, because he caught up to him outside. "Didn't want to stay for the whole show, Gryphon?" he needled. "Brilliant, isn't it? I have to thank you—without you, I'd have never thought of it."

"Piss off, Malcom," Kellan said.

"I've got a special opponent for you, too, you know. All outfitted and ready to go. Don't you want to meet her?"

Kellan kept walking, and Malcolm called out after him, "If not you, it will be someone else. Someone real special. Maybe . . ." He blew a puff of smoke into the cold air. "Maybe we'll have to bring *witches* back to the arena. What a spectacle that would be!"

Malcolm's taunting laughter followed him all the way down the street.

21

NOW

AURELIA

9 DAYS TO MIDWINTER
1621

Nathaniel and I rode for a full day and into the night, always keeping one eye on the road behind us to make sure we weren't being followed.

As much as I disliked Castillion, I felt oddly regretful leaving him behind without so much as a goodbye. But this wasn't about him. It was about Conrad.

The night of our first encampment, Nathaniel shivered beside a small and sickly fire.

"This was a mistake," he said. "You were right, we needed the food on the third level."

"We'll make do," I said. "This isn't the first time I've been lost in the Ebonwilde."

"Was the last time in the middle of winter?" Nathaniel asked, still shivering.

I unpinned the spider brooch at my throat and handed him the red cloak. "Here," I said gently. "I don't need it; I don't feel the cold like I used to."

"Are you certain?" he asked, and I nodded. It was only partly a lie; the chill I felt now was *worse* than when I had flesh and blood, because I couldn't generate my own heat anymore. But, unlike Nathaniel, the cold couldn't kill me.

"Maybe it won't be so bad, freezing to death," Nathaniel said glumly, donning the cloak, though he declined the ostentatious brooch. "It would be better than what awaits when Castillion realizes I stole from him."

"He's got bigger things to worry about than some pilfered beans and tea leaves," I said.

"I wasn't talking about the beans or tea leaves." Nathaniel gave me a meaningful look.

"Ah," I said, bristling. Nathaniel was right; to Castillion, I was a commodity. A useful means to a convenient end.

And yet . . .

He's nothing to you, Aurelia, I reminded myself.

I let Nathaniel rest until the first rays of morning. As the dark hours passed, I tended to a small fire and tried to soak up its feeble heat, even as frost began to crystallize in my hair and the fringe of my eyelashes.

In the dawn's light, the woods were much altered from what I remembered. Before, the forest grew so thick and lush that, from the ground beneath its canopy, the only sky was green and made of leaves. Now the barren trees sat in forlorn clusters, stripped down to their crooked bones.

I, who had traversed the Gray, found this realm far more desolate in its stark black-and-whites. The emptiness felt almost hungry, like it had eaten up the life within it and was still ravenous for more.

"Not what you remember, is it?" Nathaniel asked when he woke. I had pulled a tin cup and some of the tea leaves from the saddlebags and had melted some snow over the fire. The cup was steaming now; I handed it to him as he settled in next to me.

"No," I said, looking around. "It isn't. But nothing is how I remember. Or what I expected."

"What *did* you expect to wake to, when you laid yourself into that coffin?"

"I thought that . . ." But I didn't finish, instead choosing to bite my lips together, as if doing so would seal Zan's name behind my teeth. "It doesn't matter what I thought. It didn't turn out that way."

During the next night, when Nathaniel slept, I tried to find enough food to keep him alive. I'd watched Kellan setting snares plenty of times, and attempted to mimic what I remembered. On the third night, I actually caught something—a bony, half-starved winter hare. A pittance, but enough to keep Nathaniel going another day.

I was on my way back when I came across the pond. It was frozen over, thick enough to hold my weight. I nearly cried from relief, trudging to the center of it so that I could punch out a fishing hole. I was scraping snow aside when I caught a glimpse of something moving beneath the ice. I peered closer, thinking it might be a fish, and found myself looking into the eyes of my own reflection.

Not my reflection, though; I had no reflection anymore. This was the same doppelganger I'd seen in Castillion's mirror . . . a girl who looked like me, but was not me. She regarded me for a long minute before speaking. It was another rhyme, another riddle.

> *Beware, my child, in the Ebonwilde,*
> *For the enemy dressed as Friend.*
> *For good or ill, 'tis the final hill*
> *Before your journey's end—*

"Who are you?" I asked the girl. And she opened her mouth as if to speak, but the sound I heard, low and eerie, came drifting instead across the cold horizon. *"Aurelia!"*

I gave a start. That was a real voice, saying my real name.

When I looked back at the ice, the girl was gone. But my name came again, closer this time. "Aurelia?"

I hurried away from the icy pond, wishing that I could still invoke the invisibility spell I used to rely so heavily upon. Instead, I was forced to settle with watching him from a distance. The caller was leading a horse through the trees, his cheeks ruddy from the cold, his white hair waving over the top of his woolen head wrap.

Castillion.

He was less than twenty feet from me, but the sound of the wind was loud and without the red cloak to give me away, I blended into the surroundings rather well.

Go away, I thought. But he only moved closer, his breath bursting from his mouth in pale clouds. He looked weary.

While I watched, he tripped on a root hidden beneath the snow and fell to his knees. He cursed, and waited a long beat before forcing himself back to his feet. I didn't want to have to deal with him, but I didn't wish him to wander in the snow forever. It seemed cruel to just stand by as he struggled. So, sighing, I stepped from my hiding spot into his view.

He was staring at me open-mouthed; to him, I'd materialized out of thin air. "Aurelia?" he asked. Then he *hugged* me. "Thank the stars."

I stood motionless, stiff and awkward, until he stepped back.

"You shouldn't have come after me," I said. "And you definitely shouldn't have come after me *alone*. Where are your guards, your soldiers? I'm almost insulted you didn't bring an army."

"They are still at the fort," he said. "The fewer people who know you're out here, the better. Please, Aurelia. Come back with me, right now. You'll be safe behind the walls of the fort."

"Safe?" I scoffed. "What on this earth can hurt me? Thank you for the concern, but I'm on my own errand now."

"Stars above," Castillion cursed, his eyes rolling to the sky in exasperation. "Even if that report is true, and Conrad is alive . . . have you, for one moment, stopped to consider that the Circle might *want* you to come after him? That they might be using him as bait?"

"Conrad is *everything* to me. The only good thing I . . . I . . ." I swallowed, recentering myself. "He is my only family."

"He's not the only thing good left in your world, Aurelia," Castillion replied softly. "Nor does he have to be your only family . . ."

"And what would you know about it?" I snapped. "You have no family. Nor friends. Only servants, hostages, and subjects."

"That's true," he said. "I have no blood relatives left, but that doesn't mean I don't understand what family is. I respect and honor your devotion to your brother, I do. But if you knew what was at stake . . ." He turned the other way, his profile becoming a dark carving against the moon's white light, which was drifting in long, shifting beams across the snowy meadow.

"If I don't know what is at stake, it is because you have chosen not to tell me. Is there something that I need to know?"

He went quiet and still, as if he were balancing on a thin rope and a misstep here might mean a terrible fall.

I lost patience. "Go back home, Castillion."

Unfortunately, Castillion was about as good at following orders as I was. When I appeared back at the camp with him in tow, Nathaniel was awake and shivering next to a pitiful fire. He said, "Looks like you caught something after all." But despite the lightness of his voice, I could see the concern wrinkling his forehead.

"Don't worry, Lieutenant Gardner," Castillion said. "You're not in trouble for going with her. If I'd known she was going to leave, I'd have insisted upon it."

I ignored him and knelt to skin the coney, but Castillion said, "Stop, please. You might as well try eating your own shoes. Here." He went to his horse's pack and began to unload it, pulling out salt meat, cheese, bread. "Some real food."

Nathaniel accepted the offering gratefully; it was the first decent meal he'd had in days. Castillion fed our horses, too. "We won't make it home from Morais if you're all starved to death."

"We?" I asked, lifting an eyebrow.

"If you insist on going, then I insist on going with you," Castillion stated. "If we follow that ridge over there, it's less than half a day to Morais." He pointed. "And that's only because the snow and the weary horses will make us slow."

"I think he's right," Nathaniel said. "I've never come at it from this direction before, but that does look like the Morais range."

"See?" Castillion said. "I'm already proving useful."

I took a deep breath and let it out slowly. "Fine," I said. "You can come. But only because you have better food."

★

By midafternoon, we'd reached the ridge. But where there once was a narrow canyon valley between two peaks, there now was a blockade of man-size rocks and rubble. The two flanking mountains both bore deep scars from the blast sites. Our horses began to pace fitfully. "Listen," I said. "Do you hear that?"

"I . . . hear nothing," Nathaniel said.

"That's exactly it: There's nothing here. No life. No birds in the trees, no insects in the soil beneath the snow, just . . . *nothing.*"

Castillion looked uneasy, and distractedly rubbed his left shoulder, just above his heart. "Well," he said after a minute. "Let's get this over with."

"How?" Nathaniel asked. "It's completely blocked."

"See that?" Castillion said, pointing to the snow. "Footprints. And not ours. Someone comes and goes from here. We just have to follow their lead."

He was right—again. There was a tunnel through the debris, and we followed through it, fully aware of the precarious state of the rubble above our heads. The feeling of oppression, however, of being confined to a narrow space with the mass of a mountain above, did not diminish after we crossed the passage and emerged into the territory on the other side. If anything, it became heavier, as if the air were weighted by despondency.

We'd left our horses tied to trees outside the blockade and so were forced to go the rest of the way toward the Morais holding on foot. It was for the best; the horses would have been driven to distraction by the wrongness of the place. Even the amorphous Gray, where time had no meaning and everything happened all at once, felt more real than the territory inside the Midnight Zone.

A choking, congealed soot cast the entire valley in a dismal monochrome; all the rich color of tree and field and river and sky had been leached away. The acrid scent of ash and sulfur was so strong it could be tasted.

Castillion's mouth was drawn down into a tight frown. "I knew it was supposed to be bad in the Midnight Zone," he said at last. "I just didn't expect this."

"Come on," I said, finally. "We can't stay here and stare. We have things to do."

"This way," Nathaniel said, and we quietly followed.

★

The Morais manor was probably beautiful once. It had been built of pink sandstone, with breezy, terraced walkways surrounding a long and elegant pool of turquoise water. I could easily imagine Kate as a child here, leaping from stone to stone, her eyes alight with glee, and her wavy hair flying like a banner behind her.

But, like Kate, that version of the manor lived only in the past. The pool was a sunken mess of brown sludge; the bright tiles of the outdoor corridors were broken and lined with grime. The windows were nearly opaque with soot, and mold had begun to creep across the plaster walls like leprosy. And from every side, I was bombarded by the last sickly gasps of magic from old, unwilling blood. People had died here. Many people.

I snuck a glance at Nathaniel, who took it all in with a stoic expressionlessness that made me regret bringing him with me. When I'd asked him to come, I'd been riding the high of learning my brother might be alive. Seeing Morais like this quelled any notion that the same could be said for Ella. It was a cruel thing I'd done, removing an amorphous uncertainty and replacing it with such a hideous reality.

We went inside. At the end of the second floor, Nathaniel worked the iron handles of a set of double doors. "This was Kate's parents' suite," he said as the doors swung open. "They set up the nursery on the other side, so Ella's grandmother could keep her close by."

The smell that hit us was horrific; a stench of rot magnified within a closed-off space. Nathaniel stepped in first, but I grabbed his shirt-sleeve. "I can go in and look," I said. "You don't have to—"

"I *do* have to," Nathaniel said quietly. I didn't dare contradict him.

The first room was an antechamber parlor, and all around the floor there were signs of a struggle: broken vases, overturned furniture, drag marks across the ornate rug. I passed a golden mirror that was broken into a dozen radiating shards. There was blood on the glass at the center impact point; I could almost hear the sound of a head cracking against it.

"Someone was killed here," Castillion said, pointing to a brown, splash-like stain across filigree wallpaper. "And then they were dragged . . ." He moved into the bedroom, where a four-poster bed stood in the center of the room, swathed in a closed canopy of moth-eaten silks. ". . . here."

Nathaniel swallowed hard and grabbed the cord, pulling it down hand over hand. The curtains parted slowly, creaking down the track.

"Bleeding stars," I said, knuckles to mouth. Two skeletons lay side by side on the bed. Their flesh had liquefied and slid away from the bone, leaving oily stains on the silken sheets upon which they lay. Nathaniel carefully lifted the hand of the skeleton on the right, pulling a heavy silver signet free of the pinky bones.

"Kate's father," he said quietly. "Baron Antunes Morais. And her mother, Baroness Juliana Morais."

"Empyrea keep you, Antunes and Juliana," Castillion murmured solemnly. Nathaniel pocketed the signet, and turned his eyes toward the slightly ajar side door we'd all been trying so hard not to see: the entrance to the nursery.

I grabbed Nathaniel's hand and squeezed it. "Whatever we find in there," I said softly, "I'm here for you."

He gave me a brief nod, and then his hand slipped from mine as he took two steps forward. Then three. Then four. He put both hands against the door and gave it a soft push.

Unlike the main bedroom, the nursery was in perfect order. A small, doll-size replica of the Morais manor stood on a table by the door, the front façade resting open on its hinges, revealing the interior of the manor in perfect detail. Inch-tall dolls were scattered throughout, going about their daily business — cooks in the kitchen, laundresses bent over washboards, and butlers perusing the pantries. A little girl in pigtails stood with a mother and father doll, representative of Kate with her parents.

An oil painting of Kate as a young woman — perhaps seventeen or eighteen — was hung on the wall behind it. She was smiling brightly, a yellow flower tucked into her wavy hair, hands folded in her lap. Beside that was a portrait of another child: a baby with plump cheeks and black curls wisping out from beneath a white bonnet. Ella had Nathaniel's hair and beautiful brown skin, but she took after Kate in every other way, including the dimples in her cheeks. Her eyes were silver-gray, the color they'd turned when I gave her drops of bloodleaf flower potion as a newborn infant.

Nathaniel stared at the portraits for a long time before he was able to turn toward the silent crib, trimmed in lace, and guarded by woolly animals in the shapes of rabbits and bears and elephants and lions.

I held my breath as he leaned over and peered inside.

"It's empty," he said finally, his voice barely audible. "She's not here."

I came up behind him to look for myself and, sure enough, there was a soft indentation in the bedclothes from where a child had once slept, but there was no child.

I didn't know whether to rejoice or despair. She wasn't here! But if not here, where?

I heard a noise behind me and turned to see Castillion climbing up on the table to reach the two paintings, taking them both from the wall and then stepping down to lay them on the floor. He removed a knife from his boot and sliced along the edges of the frames until the canvases came free. Then he rolled them up and, wordlessly, handed them to Nathaniel.

22

THEN

CONRAD

The morning after his unfinished rite of fortitude with the Circle Midnight, Conrad's breakfast tray was delivered with something extra: a package containing a purple robe, and a letter sealed with the moonlike hallmark of the Circle Midnight. It read:

Dear Friend Conrad,

Last night, I told you the Empyrea has marvelous plans for you. Tonight, I would like to give you the first glimpse into what those plans might be. Meet me on the North Road outside of the city at nightfall for the second part of your initiation into our ranks.

Tell no one of your plans; as with all righteous work, there will be those who would oppose your choice to join us.

After you have read this note, burn it.

Your fellow Friend,

Fidelis XIV

There was a candle on the table beside him. As he lowered the corner of the paper into the flame, he heard a voice.

"Conrad, don't."

The letter flamed, and by the time he'd dropped it into the fireplace grate, *she* was peeking out at him from the other side of his bed, by the door. The girl in the furs . . . she must have snuck through the door when the messenger brought him the letter. He knew, instinctively, that this was not the first time they'd crossed paths, even if those memories were so indistinct, they were more like half-forgotten dreams than actual memories.

"Don't go with them," she said, louder. "This isn't a game anymore. You are proving nothing by going along with their plans."

Conrad moved slowly to the windows. Hadn't Fidelis just said that if anyone knew about his involvement with the Circle Midnight, they'd try to stop him? "You shouldn't be in my rooms," he said. "My guards are just outside the door."

"I mean you no harm," the girl said. "It's the Circle you must be wary of."

"If you mean me no harm," he said, "why are you hiding, over there in the shadow? Come here. Show me your face."

"If you see my face," she said, "*he* will see my face. And I don't . . . I *can't* . . ." She paused. "You know all of this, Conrad. We've talked like this before. It's all recorded right here," she said, moving to a certain spot on his floor, where one of the boards was a little loose. As she did, Conrad threw the curtains open, flooding the entire room with blinding sun.

She let out a cry, hands going up over her face as she flinched away from the revelatory light, only to stumble backwards into his breakfast tray, sending it crashing to the floor.

The door burst open at the sound, Hector and Pomeroy charging in behind it to see what was the matter. Pomeroy dragged her up by the back of her strange cloak, twisting her arms behind her. He tried to pull her hood back, but she writhed and snarled and twisted in his grip; it was all he could do to simply hold on to her.

"What should we do with . . . this?" asked Pomeroy.

"Take her to the dungeon," Conrad said, scrambling to appear authoritative. He would have just sent her away, but now that his guards were involved . . . "Let her sit there for a day or two. After that, we'll see about giving her a proper trial . . ."

"But sir," Hector argued, "you've just been attacked in your own room! That is an unforgivable offense. Under the old Tribunal law, punishment should be served immediately."

"She will see a trial, and in time, appropriate punishment." Conrad figured that if he put off the "trial" long enough, he could quietly release her later—at present, he just needed a reason to get them all out of his hair. He had a feeling that whatever happened with the Circle Midnight tonight, it would convince him of their legitimacy, or provide him with enough proof of treachery to call for dismantling their full operation. "But for now, take her to the dungeon. And then, you must go to Pelton for an extra gold coin each, and take the rest of the day off, both of you. You have earned it, and my great thanks for your bravery."

"Come on, then, you mongrel," Pomeroy said, now grinning from ear to ear. Conrad suppressed a cringe as his guards hauled her into the hallway, where one of the castle maids was carrying a bundle of firewood to another room. She stared at the men and their struggling quarry, mouth agape, and then back at Conrad, only catching a glimpse of the boy-king as he disappeared behind his chamber door.

★

From the tenor of Fidelis's note and the directive to meet outside of the city, Conrad assumed this would be more than just a casual evening meeting and began to the gather a few articles he might need for an overnight venture. While he was packing, he found the message in his jacket. *There is a loose floorboard two paces to the left of the fireplace. Go see what is under it.*

After reading through all of his notes, he pondered the fur-girl's warnings, and felt another pang of guilt, sharper this time, for having Hector and Pomeroy keep her in the dungeon, dank and awful as it was.

Perhaps she was right: it was dangerous to play this game, both with himself and with the Circle. But what would happen if he ended it all now, and ignored Brother Fidelis's invitations? At least this way he could observe what was going on from within the organization while satisfying his own curiosity. And . . . he admired Fidelis. He had no title, no riches, nor any other claim to authority, but when he spoke, people *listened*. Conrad had never even met his own father.

Never got the chance to observe or emulate the king who had come before him. Perhaps this was the next best thing.

Before letting the frostlace remove the day's events from his memory, he added another note to the pile:

Primus 5th, 1621: You encountered the girl in the fur cloak in your room today. Hector and Pomeroy will keep her out of the way until you can make it out of the castle and to the rendezvous with Fidelis on the North Road.

You're getting very deep now, but you are the one in control.

Aurelia would be proud.

As a precaution, he removed the contents of the space beneath the floorboard, rolling the notes up around the bottle of frostlace before hiding them all inside the puzzle box Aurelia had gifted him last year. Better to have them with him, in case something went awry. They were his memories, after all. He tucked the box alongside his other things and waited until nightfall, when he would make his escape.

★

Fidelis was waiting for him in a carriage on the north side of the city. "Sorry I'm late," Conrad puffed. "Since you wanted me to come alone, I had to walk."

"No matter," Brother Fidelis said mildly. "I'm just happy to see you. I see you received my gift?"

"I did," Conrad said, pulling at the purple cloak. "And I am looking forward to whatever you've got planned for tonight's gathering."

"This," Brother Fidelis said, smiling, "is more than just a simple gathering. It is a demonstration of our devotion to the Empyrea, and a working of her power through us." He tapped his cane against the roof of the carriage, and in response it creaked into motion. "It is the start of something wonderful."

They followed the river northeast for an hour—enough distance that Conrad began to squirm thinking of how long it would take to get back before anyone noticed he was gone—but Fidelis filled the time with diverting stories of Fidelis the First, founder of the Circle Midnight.

"He lived a few hundred years after the start of the Assembly," he explained. "He was a mage gifted with the most powerful and incredible of magic: the ability to hear the voice of the Empyrea herself."

"I looked all over the castle library for writings about him," said Conrad, "but I found nothing."

"Already trying to immerse yourself in our prophet's teachings?" Fidelis said approvingly. "Good lad. But no, you won't find him in any archive or library. Only a very few copies of the Midnight Papers remain. We, as a group, only have one. And the original has long been lost to time."

"I would love to read it sometime. I am interested in his prophecies to quite a great depth," Conrad said. "Especially those concerning the end of the world."

"The end of *one* world," Fidelis corrected, "in favor of another, better one. A world free of all humanity's foibles and flaws. It was for this cause that the Circle was created, and the one for which we still strive. Put all other distractions from your mind, Friend Conrad. For tonight, you will truly see and understand the great work the Empyrea has waiting for you."

The moon was high in the sky when they, at last, reached their destination at the foot of the dam. They left their carriage at the base and climbed the steep, upward trails on foot. When they reached the top, they were greeted by twenty or thirty other Circle Midnight members who were sitting around an enormous knot-like symbol that appeared at first to be painted onto the stone. But as Conrad got closer, he saw that it was not paint—it was lines of black powder.

"Welcome, Friend!" Conrad was greeted by a Midnighter who clasped his hand and said, "My name is Eustacia, first doyen of the fourth faction. We are very glad that you have decided to join us on this wondrous occasion. We know what it is you have left behind. The Empyrea recognizes your sacrifice and will remember it and reward you well in the world reborn."

"So you know who I am?" Conrad asked with curiosity.

"We know who you *were*," she said, stressing the last word. "Now you are as we all are: a Friend. Equal with the rest of the Empyrea's devoted, and transcended far above the rest of lowly mankind."

Eustacia led him to a ring of other Midnighters just outside of the black powder knot. She greeted others as they went, and explained to Conrad who they were. "Over there," she said, "you'll see Friend Junius beginning to gather the members of the second faction around the sacred knot to work the spell."

"Are they feral mages?" Conrad asked.

"Oh, we don't use those Assembly terms here," she said. "But yes, the second faction are those of us who possess the gifts of pattern magic. The third faction is made up of those who possess mortal magic, what you might have heard called blood magic." She sniffed, as if she found the term reprehensible. "We don't have many—the third faction is our smallest."

"Then is the first faction . . . high mages?"

"Mind magic," she corrected, "those who have extrasensory perceptions."

"And what is the fourth faction?" Conrad asked. "You said you were part of the fourth faction."

"The fourth faction," she said, "is the largest one. And it consists of those of us who do not possess any power outside of our keen love and devotion for the Empyrea." She smiled, hand to her bronze medallion. That must be how they differentiated between each other, Conrad mused, when they all wore the same robes and short-cut hair. Bronze for the fourth faction, copper for the third, silver for the second, and gold for the first. And Fidelis, leader of them all, wore a medallion of platinum.

"You'll make a wonderful addition to our fourth-faction ranks, Friend Conrad," Eustacia said, patting his shoulder in a warm, motherly way. "Look! Tonight's blessed events are about to begin!"

Twelve members of the second faction—feral mages, Conrad mentally noted, only discernible by the fact that their medallions were silver—took their places around the black powder pattern on the rock. Far below where they stood at the top of the dam, the river rushed along at its normal pace. The dam loomed over the valley, the reservoir at capacity behind it. In the very far distance, Conrad thought he could see Syric's glow.

"How will the city see the demonstration this far away?" Conrad asked, puzzled.

"Worry not, my young Friend," Eustacia said. "They will see it. And they will know the full extent of our might."

Each of the second faction now placed a stone at their feet at equal intervals around the knot's outer circle. The rocks were mostly clear, but glowing faintly blue. Conrad knew well what they were: luneocite. Then the second-faction Midnighters all put their hands together and began a low hum. At the same moment, they started to wave their arms in the space in front of them, drawing perfectly synchronized loops and swirls in the air.

The light of the stones seemed to be dragged toward their motions, leaving trails of soft blue. The hums grew louder, deepening from a faint buzz to a vibration Conrad could feel in his chest. The light weaving grew more elaborate, involving every part of the Midnighters' bodies, like a dance.

And slowly, slowly, the luneocite light began to seep across the lines of black powder, causing it to give off blue sparks.

"This is it!" Eustacia bent to his ear, so he could hear her over the sound of the humming, which was quickly causing the very stones beneath his feet to vibrate.

He'd thought this was just a demonstration, a showy display for the sake of enticing new recruits, like himself, to the cause. But when the earth started bucking beneath his feet, he began to understand the enormity of what was happening.

The Circle Midnight wasn't watching for the signs of the Empyrea's return . . . it was *instigating* them.

He had no fear for himself—even as the rocks shook, it was clear that the Circle Midnight's spell would not allow the ground upon which they were standing to buckle—it was all for the city he'd left behind.

Eustacia was watching the spell take shape with an ardent joy. Across the knot, Fidelis was staring at the sky as if caught in some blissful rapture. The humming became a roar, and the ground groaned as it heaved. An earthquake. The blue light had made it to the center of the black powder pattern, and now veins of blue were streaking across the stone, toward the dam.

Merciful stars, Conrad thought. He was frozen in place.

As the light reached the dam, it set off a series of explosions that added to the earthquake's cacophony of sound. Chunks of rock splintered outward, raining spear-like shards down below, followed by cylindrical torrents of water. One after another, after another.

And then, the whole of the dam gave way.

The Midnighters finished their spell and ran to the ledge, whooping and cheering their ecstatic, impious glee.

Conrad stood still. Beside him, Eustacia began to intone a passage of what had to be a prophecy from the Midnight Papers.

And then, I say unto you, the earth will tremble,
And the sleeping sinners choke and drown
As the salt and snow meet together
And bring the mighty city down.

Understanding dawned upon Conrad slowly and painfully: the salt was the ocean, rising into a destructive wave following the earth-quake, and the snow was the meltwater held back by the dam.

Pinned between the two was Renalt's capital city, Syric.

He had allowed this to happen. And for what? If there were reasons for his involvement in this outside of curiosity and hubris, they were buried too far in his subconscious to reach.

Fidelis had come up behind him, placing his hand on Conrad's shoulder. "This is your rite of fortitude, Friend Conrad. You are, undoubtedly, quite hurt and afraid to see this city ended in such a way. But you must bolster yourself up, and take comfort in the knowledge that it is all done in accordance to the Empyrea's will, and the lives lost tonight are in her hands."

Conrad nodded, but he could not speak. He couldn't even pray. What point was there in asking the Empyrea for her blessing when Fidelis had made it very clear that this was the enactment of her own relentless will?

Abandoned by both Goddess and king, the people of Syric would die doubly betrayed.

23

THEN

KELLAN

"You're leaving?" Kellan asked as Ivan dragged a trunk across the tavern's floor toward the open front door. Outside, a carriage marked with the Scheming Minstrel's insignia was waiting, Ivan's wife and daughter already sitting inside.

"Yes," Ivan said, wiping sweat from his brow as he hoisted the trunk onto the back of the carriage. "We've been directed by the Empyrea to spread the Circle Midnight's message." His hair was plastered to his forehead, his shirt nearly soaked through. His hands, as he closed the cart's door and latched it, were pale and trembly. "We have heard her call, and we are answering."

"Ivan," Kellan said cautiously. "You don't look well."

"It's my sins," he said, with a glassy-eyed smile. "I'm displaying fortitude as they are purged from me. Soon I will be as pure as the Empyrea herself. I can tell you more if you'd like to know—"

Kellan sidestepped. "How long will you be gone?"

"I'm not certain," Ivan said. "But you may stay on here as long as you need, no payment needed. I've moved past the desire for worldly goods." He stuck out his clammy-looking hand for a parting hand- shake. Kellan eyed it, arms folded. "Empyrea keep you."

Just then, a girl came barreling toward the tavern, eyes wide and panicked as she ran. "My lord!" she said breathlessly. "My lord! They've got her! They've got her and I don't know what they're going to do to her."

Ivan climbed up into the driver's seat and snapped the reins. The carriage rolled away as Kellan took Cora by the shoulders. "Calm down. What has happened?"

"Millie's been caught," she said, words tumbling out in a torrent. "She was found in King Conrad's bedroom this morning. They said she was going to attack him, and he told them to take her down into the dungeon. I waited until my chores were done and went down there to take her some food and talk to her, but when I got there, *they* were taking her out of the dungeon. And the things they were saying, my lord . . . they were awful."

"Take a breath," Kellan said. "Who was taking her from the dun- geon?"

"The king's bodyguards," Cora said. "Hector and Pomeroy. They were smiling and laughing, saying that according to law, an attempt on the king's life was an immediate sentence of death. They said, 'Say what you want about the Tribunal, they knew how to take care of witches.' And then they laughed, and talked about how much they would get paid for bringing her to someone . . . I can't remember the name exactly. Milton? Morton . . . ?"

Kellan asked darkly, "Malcolm?"

"Yes! That's it! Malcolm. Malcolm is going to pay them, they said. I went to the king's quarters first to warn him about what they were doing—he had told them just to jail her, not hurt her—but he wouldn't answer. M'lord, I'm so frightened! What will they do to her?"

"I think I might know," Kellan said. He went for his cloak. "You should go back to the—"

"No," Cora said. "I told you, Millie is my friend! I'm going with you."

"Then we've got no time to waste."

★

It was another big night for the fighting arena, but Kellan did not wait in line this time. Instead, he went around to the back of the alley, Cora trotting along on his heels. The fighters' door was already closed and locked for the night, but Kellan wouldn't let that stop him. "Stand back," he warned Cora, before kicking through it in a shower of splinters.

While the upper part of the arena had been built for entertainment, the lower part had been built for utility—this was where the witches were penned while awaiting their trial, in cramped cells lining either side of a dingy, dark hall. When Kellan was fighting, the cells had been empty. Now, they were occupied. There was an eagle in one, a bull in another. Then a bear, and a wolf. The dog that had fought the Mastiff was in the second-to-last cage. The obscene armor had been removed, making the angry red cuts crisscrossing his hide plainly visible.

Kellan's upper lip curled back in disgust.

At the end of the hall, one of Malcolm's men spotted them. "Hey!" he shouted. "You're not supposed to be back here!" He was about to draw a sword when Kellan ducked, sweeping his foot low and knocking the man's feet out from under him. Then he rolled, wrapping his arm around his neck and squeezing until his opponent went limp in his arms.

The move had never failed him.

On the arena floor, Malcolm was beginning his spin-up speech.

"The king himself handed us this unusual next contender, a monster unlike any other, with the order that no man raise a hand to her." He smiled and lifted his arms to the crowd. "And so, no *man* will. Tonight, we will all bear witness to a spectacular display of monster against monster. Of beast against beast!"

The crowd gasped as one of the dungeon doors opened and another soldier—Hector—led a strange creature covered in a thousand different bits of fur and leather onto the court's floor by a rope looped around its hands and neck.

Her hands and neck, Kellan corrected himself. He knew that underneath that cloak was the girl Cora had called Millie. The girl who hid in the castle's shadows and did chores for other maids in exchange for bits of food. The girl who'd appeared at Conrad's costume ball dressed like the living sun.

"Wait!" Kellan called, but the sound was drowned by the roaring of the audience.

Malcolm was shouting, "And now, here comes the competitor!"

A monstrous creature emerged with a bloodcurdling roar. A hulking lion that had been outfitted in wings of jagged metal feathers and gauntlets that turned its great paws into scythe-like talons. Beneath the lion's livid amber eyes, a pointed metal mask had been affixed, turning its enormous maw into a deadly, sharpened beak.

It was a lion no more. It had been turned into an unholy imitation of another, more mythic beast.

A gryphon.

"Bleeding stars!" Kellan cried.

In the arena, the girl was frozen to her spot as the armored lion circled. Maids all around the court were hurriedly scribbling wagers from clamoring bettors while the circling lion was making quick, testing swipes at the girl, teeth snapping behind the metal beak, taloned paws batting at her. A few times, it came away with chunks of fur.

It was playing with her, Kellan realized. How many times had this same place borne witness to the methodical teardown of an innocent victim, only to repeat that history in a new and literal way? The girl seemed to understand that her fate was inevitable, and instead of attempting to fight back, she went totally still, holding her bound hands in front of her as if in a silent prayer.

At that moment, Kellan leaped from the bottom row barricade.

He hit the dirt and rolled, and the lion swiveled around to stare at him with lambent orange eyes, tail flicking.

Kellan reached for his sword and broke into a run toward the girl

—Millie—and then had to spin out of the way of the razor-edged beak as it drove into the dirt.

This, he thought to himself, *was a truly terrible idea.*

"Here!" someone called—it was the serving maid who had tried to get him to place a bet the last time he'd watched a fight, throwing her serving tray in his direction. The hammered disc fell short and rolled, and Kellan dove toward it as the lion charged him, knocking his sword out of reach. The armored beak scraped across Kellan's metal hand, showering sparks. It roared angrily and reared up on its back legs to swipe at the air with its taloned front paws.

While the animal roared its anger, Kellan grabbed the tray with his left hand and managed to get it up over his face before the lion's claws made contact, sliding through the thin metal as if it were paper.

Is this it? Kellan asked himself. *Is this how I go?*

How very fitting, he thought, *that I should meet my end this way, undone by a gryphon, the specter of who I once was.*

"Here!" Millie was screaming. "Over here!"

The lion turned toward her voice, giving Kellan time to toss the shredded tray aside and get back to his feet. The lion was headed toward the girl, who was backing away.

He had to get between them. It was the only option.

He ran full force ahead, aiming for the gap between Millie and the charging predator, ducking as the lion leaped, pulling the girl down and rolling together as the animal went over them, skittering on its metal claws before making an abrupt about-face, snarling and foaming.

When they came to a stop, Kellan was lying with his back to the dirt with Millie's body stretched out overtop of him. He could see the shadowy shape of her face within her backlit hood, but it was hard to focus on discerning her features, as a jeweled pendant had come untucked from her cloak and was swinging over his head like a glittering green pendulum.

He didn't have time to consider that oddity; the lion was coming their way again, its mail screeching.

They scrambled to their feet, both weaponless. "Untie my hands!" Millie cried. "Hurry!"

But it was too late; the lion was already upon them, leaping with both taloned paws extended.

They were cornered.

With an angry, guttural roar, Kellan stretched his right hand forward, as tingling sparks shot down from his shoulder, through the silver gauntlet's boundary at his elbow, and into his wrist, where the current broke into five points of crackling power that pooled at each of his fingertips.

He could feel it. The silver was a part of him, alive. Awake. And as the razor-beak slammed into his metal palm, his silver fingers began to stretch around the creaking mask, bending it beneath his grip. Then, almost without meaning to, he felt the silver begin to curve and sharpen, becoming claws of his own, piercing the metal. When he had it fully in his grip, he yanked the beak mask away from the lion's face.

The lion bellowed and scrambled backwards as Kellan's claws retracted, leaving him on his hands and knees, panting for breath and staring in shock at his right hand, now back to its clunky solid form. But something had changed; now that he had used it once, he knew he could do it again.

"My ropes!" Millie shouted again as the lion adjusted to the light without its mask and crouched low to spring again. Kellan concentrated, and the hand morphed into a fist, then a knife grew from behind it, wide and sharp. He placed the edge of it against the ropes at her wrists and it slid through them like soft butter.

While she shook the binds off, the animal sailed forward again. Kellan reached out with his right hand, willing it into the shape of a sword. With one slice, he felled its left wing, which creaked as it came off and crashed on the ground.

The crowd was surging, feeding off the energy of the spectacle. Some of the railings were loosening against the press of the people clamoring for a better view. The lion, beginning to tire of Kellan and Millie, was taking notice.

"Get back!" Kellan tried to yell at them. "Get back!"

Malcolm, who had reemerged from behind the gate, was running toward them, shouting. "What are you doing? Do you know how much I paid for that armor? It was a fortune! Maybe even more expensive than the lion itself, and you just went and ruined—"

The lion had recognized that voice, and was hurtling toward Malcolm, whose eyes had gone wide as he lost his footing and then scrabbled backwards through the dirt like a crab. The lion pounced and took his head in its mouth, and there was a muffled scream followed by a sickening crunch and a spray of blood.

The lion was dragging its kill toward the side of the arena when the mid-level railing gave way, sending hundreds of watchers sprawling into the dirt below. The lion abandoned Hector's mangled, headless body and began to stalk toward its plentiful new targets. Kellan felt helpless; he'd never be able to rescue them all.

Just then, he saw Millie standing calmly in the middle of the court, her hands weaving a complex pattern into the air. And as she did, the image of her shimmered like sun on a tin roof, growing taller and slimmer, her face elongating into a sharp, pointed snout and hundreds of gleaming teeth. Slitted eyes the color of rubies stood out against the expanding emerald scales. Soon, she had stretched above even the highest viewing levels, almost bumping into the eaves of the roof. Then she opened her mouth as if to scream, but instead she let out a torrent of livid orange fire.

The illusion had an intense, immediate effect on both the lion and the onlookers.

The people were scrambling to escape, stampeding over any-one who had the misfortune of standing between them and the exit doors. Within minutes, the Tribunal's court had emptied and the lion had retreated into the pen from which it had emerged. It had taken Malcolm's corpse with it, leaving a line of gore and blood behind it in the dirt. Kellan pulled the gate down after it, locking it in, and then turned back to the girl just as her illusion began to waver and diminish, and she collapsed into a heap of shredded fur and leather.

Kellan went to her side and began to pull the pieces of cloak aside; they were sticky with the girl's blood. She tried to push him off. "No," she begged.

"You're injured," he replied, using his soldier's voice. "It has to come off so I can see the damage."

"It's nothing," she said, but her voice was tight with pain. "I've been through wor—" But the sentence devolved into a shriek of agony as Kellan helped her sit up and undid the clasp at her throat, tugging the entire cloak away by the hood.

For a second, all Kellan could do was stare.

Beside the lion's livid scratches, her skin was covered in a strange pattern of old scars, twisting up her limbs, under her linen shift, across her chest, and up onto her left cheek. Not just any scars, either . . . *burns*. But it wasn't the scars that shocked him so completely. It was her eyes, bright and familiar, and the necklace with a dragon charm settled against her chest.

He had a matching one under his own shirt, a gryphon.

Her name wasn't Millie after all.

It was *Emilie*.

The girl who had switched places with Aurelia the night of their escape from the Tribunal.

The girl who had burned at the stake for her effort.

As he gaped, they felt a strange rumble beneath them.

"Oh no," Emilie whispered. "It's happening."

He hoisted her into his arms, as careful with her wounds as he could be. Cora was standing at the mouth of the cell block, waving them to follow her. Meanwhile, a group of Malcolm's men stalked toward them. He recognized some of them as his own former opponents: the Grizzly, the Raptor, the Serpent . . . all had drawn swords or were swinging chains menacingly.

So much for the "no weapons" rule.

A second tremor, stronger than the first, rolled through the dirt under his feet. What was happening? Kellan wobbled, but did not fall. He caught up to Cora and they ran together down the dingy hall. The shaking of the earth had disquieted the captive animals, and they were squawking and growling and banging against their cages.

"Can you walk?" Kellan asked Emilie, and she nodded. He set her down and she and Cora ran the rest of the way down the corridor as Kellan held out his right hand and concentrated again. *Change,* he willed it. *Change.*

Their pursuers were already to the mouth of the corridor when the hand began to re-form into a knife. Without waiting for it to solidify, Kellan struck at the lock on the first gate, slicing it free. The wolf behind it padded out, growling. But not at Kellan—it was looking at the men pouring into the passage behind him. Kellan moved to the next cage and the next, letting each creature out in turn, trying to ignore the shrieks coming from behind him.

When he caught up to Emilie and Cora at the alley exit, a third wave of earth shaking had begun, this one so powerful, they had to cling to the wall as they staggered from the arena. Clay shingles slid from the roof and shattered in shrapnel-laden bursts on the ground at their feet. It was the longest of the quakes, and the earth roared and groaned in anger.

"No, no, no," Emilie was muttering. "It's too late. It's too late. It's over. I've failed."

"What do you mean?" Kellan demanded.

She recited, but the words felt very real. *"And then, I say unto you, the earth will tremble, and the sleeping sinners choke and drown, as the salt and snow meet together, and bring the mighty city down."*

Kellan's eyes went wide. "The dam."

She nodded.

"We're all goin' to die, ain't we?" Cora asked, quavering. And when no one answered, she turned and ran.

"Wait! Cora!" Kellan cried after her, but she wouldn't stop. She sprinted down the street until she had disappeared. Kellan swung Emilie's arm over his shoulder and started to pull her along in a run.

"Stop," she said tiredly. "It's no use. In minutes, this entire city will be underwater. There's nowhere to go. Nothing we can do."

"We're not dead yet," he said. His eyes caught on the clock tower, peeking out from above the buildings. "And while we live, we fight."

24

THEN

ZAN

*Z*an and Jessamine each took an oar and rowed toward the looming, unlit lighthouse, against the heave-ho pull of the waves on their rickety vessel. Above, lightning wove in and out of the dark storm clouds like a needle through coarse wool.

Halfway to land, the rain started. It fell in heavy sheets, soaking them both to the bone and making it almost impossible to see more than a few feet in front of them. They were nearly pitched free when they hit the first rock along the outer edge of the isle, barely managing to stay inside the boat. The water outside of the lighthouse was a gauntlet of ruthless, razor-edged reefs, and the timbers of the longboat groaned with every splintering scrape and blow.

Zan and Jessamine battled for each inch of progress. The wind whipped the waves into a foaming white frenzy, sending stinging salt spray into their eyes. He tried to shield Lewis's inert form from the bulk of the onslaught, but it did little good; the waves were attacking from every side, allied by rain from above and the hungry sea from below.

Zan's existence condensed into the moments between each pull. One, heave, two, ho. One, heave, two, ho, as he tried not to remember the deep, dark water of Stiria Bay. Drowning the first time was not a pleasant experience; he had no wish to repeat it.

With water creeping up past his ankles and no hope of a horseman to charge out of the mist to save him this time, Zan consigned himself to the prospect of a watery grave. At least, he rationalized, Jessamine wouldn't be able to use Sad Tom to mark his resting place there.

I'm sorry, Aurelia. He cast the thought into the sky. *I failed you. I failed you. Forgive me.*

And then—land.

They were lucky; they had rowed up on a rocky incline that acted like a ramp. They didn't bother finding a place to tie the irreparably damaged boat; it was half-capsized anyway.

Zan struggled to lift Lewis, but the youth's sodden weight and the weakness in Zan's weary arms were too much for him, and just as he thought he pulled him free, he realized that he'd come away with a strip of torn fabric alone; the boy and the boat had both been sucked back into the swirling water of the surf, lost to the depths.

Zan stared in shock, but Jessamine was yanking on his arm. "He was already dead, Zan! We have to let him go! Get up! Get up! Hurry, before the sea pulls you in, too!"

The incline was slick and treacherous, and the cold water sucked at their hems, unwilling to give them up without a fight. Somehow, they managed to reach the bottom of a switchback path that zigzagged up to the base of the lighthouse. The rocks on either side of the narrow way were sharp; by the time he reached the top, Zan was covered in cuts.

The lighthouse, when they reached it—thank the stars—was dark but not locked. They got the iron door shut and bolted behind them, and sank down against the thick wall, drawing heaving breaths. Jessamine recovered first. She gave Zan a sideways look. She motioned to the drops of blood peppering his arms, and the gashes in his arms and cheeks, and said, "I'm glad that's you and not me. I've made it this far without any disfiguring scars on this beautiful skin. Don't want to go to my death looking like . . ."

"Looking like death?" Zan suggested with a bark of a laugh. Then he stopped. "Did you hear that?"

He got to his feet, hand clamped to his bleeding arm.

"Hear *what?*" Jessamine asked, scrambling after him. "It's just the storm."

But Zan was already making his way up the lighthouse's spiraling staircase, his way lit in staccato bursts by lightning seen through the lantern glass at the apex of the cylindrical tunnel.

He had a strange recollection, as he ascended, of another climb in another tower, in what felt like another life. And though it had been a long time since he had felt the tightening of his chest, the weakness of his lungs, the shooting pain in his heart, he remembered it well. He remembered the fear—not for his own life, but that he might be too slow, too late to stop her from jumping.

Aurelia.

That had been when he knew he loved her, though it wasn't so well-formed a thought as that. Rather, his vision had gone fuzzy and faded, compacting onto a single point: a girl at the top of a tower, her ashen hair loose and waving as she approached the precipice. And he ran, because he could not bear to lose her. Not then. Not yet. Not *ever*.

And despite all of the odds, and the screaming pain in his lungs, and his diminishing sight, he had made it in time. He'd pulled her from the ledge of Aren's tower, and then she, in turn, pulled him back from the edge of mortality.

"Aurelia!" he cried as he reached the top and saw her. "Aurelia, don't—"

But it wasn't Aurelia at all—it was the hideous, black-veined version of Isobel Arceneaux. She pointed at him, opening her mouth as if to speak, but no sound could be heard over the shriek of the wind.

"Zan!" Jessamine had caught up to him, was shaking his shoulders. "Zan! What is going on?"

"Do you see that?" he asked, his eyes riveted to the apparition. "Do you see her?"

"See who? Bleeding, cursed, *stupid* stars. You can't lose your mind, Sad Tom. I'm not ready to toss you off a cliff."

"I'm not sick, Jessamine," he insisted. "I swear it."

But Jessamine wasn't looking at him anymore; her eyes had caught upon something beyond the ghostly nun and the lighthouse glass: the

Contessa, caught in the mighty push and pull of the tempestuous sea, getting closer and closer to the island's deadly barrier of rocks.

"They're going to be dashed to pieces," Jessamine said. "They won't make it through. They can't see the way."

Arceneaux reached out again, and this time, Zan followed the line of her finger to the base of the lighthouse lamp, where a series of brass-plated knobs waited in a line, all pointing down.

He crouched down and turned the first, and was answered by the hiss of gas moving through the fittings. Then the second, which gave a click, and then the last, which made a spark.

And suddenly, the whole world went up in a blaze of blinding light.

25

NOW

We were deep into Circle Midnight territory now. We'd left the manor and snuck into the valley below, darting between the stark barracks buildings that were arranged in a nondescript grid as far as the eye could see. There was no snow on the ground, and the further we descended, the hotter it became, as if the blanket of choking smoke trapped all the heat beneath it even as it shut out all the light.

The Midnight Zone truly lived up to its name.

The Circle Midnight's troops were going through formations, marching and stopping, marching and stopping, pantomiming slaughter in between.

"I had no idea," Castillion said under his breath, "just how many of them there are."

"How do we stand a chance against this?" asked Nathaniel.

"Shh," I hissed. "Something is happening."

The formations were coming together around a central platform, where several figures stood in a row. These people were wearing robes in the same purple-black color as the soldiers' armor. One of them, a man, began to speak, and though he must have been at least half a mile away from our hiding spot, his voice was crystal clear in our ears.

"My dear Friends," he said, lifting his arms. "One thousand years have passed since the time of Fidelis the First. Like our beloved master, our cause was relegated to darkness while the corruption of mankind continued to spread across the earth, poisoning everything they touched with their wants and their hedonistic desires. With their selfishness, and their fickle, feeble, easily breakable hearts. Until now.

"In these last few months, we have done what our predecessors could not: We've brought this world to its knees before the Empyrea. We've reminded the population who is really in control. We stand at the precipice of our final hour. The hour in which we provide our Goddess with the final sacrifices she needs to remake this sorry world into something far better. On Midwinter Night, the sun will go down upon this earth and it will not rise again!"

"Aurelia," Castillion said in a low, urgent whisper, "what are you *doing*?"

"I have to get closer," I said. "Stay here." And I darted from our hiding spot and tripped down the hilly incline toward the gathered troops.

I stuck to the outskirts of the buildings, working my way toward the front in little jolts. Even while they all seemed to be listening to the speaker with the same blank, inane stare, I couldn't count on their senselessness for my safety. In such a sea of conformity, I stood out too much. If I was seen, I was already caught.

One of the barracks doors was open a crack, and I slipped through it. The inside was low ceilinged and dark, with double-bunk cots stretching the entire length of the building. There was nothing to distinguish one from the next, and barely a foot of space between each one. There were no tokens or mementos, no alteration in the type of fabric or color, nothing that could be mistaken as personal property. But there were robes folded underneath, and I snagged one as I moved from one end of the barracks to the other, hastily pulling it over my clothes. By the time I reached the other side, with the purple hood obscuring my unshaven head, I was indistinguishable from any other Midnighter.

And all the while, the man's speech droned on. There was no difference in the sound in the barrack building or outside it, no lift in volume as I drew nearer to the front. It remained an even level no matter what distance away I stood.

He was speaking into our very minds, I realized.

This man was a high mage. And a powerful one, to be able to project his thoughts across so vast an audience.

I wondered if that was the cause of the vacuity in the eyes of his listeners. How much power did he have over them? Could he make them move, too? Could he lift one arm and know they'd follow? Could he tell them to dance and watch them pirouette in sync? How far did his control go?

And, perhaps most importantly, did it go in reverse?

Still hidden behind the corner of a barracks, I searched the depths of my memories for something I could use. I tried first with the worst sound I'd ever heard: the shrill scream of a witch burning to death on a stake. I let it ricochet inside my head until it was louder than the preacher's words, and then sent it back along the connection toward him.

Was that a pause?

I tried a few more things: the sound of half-dead wolves howling in the night, the crunching thunk of a body hitting the ground after falling from Achlev's wall, the wails of frightened children watching Toris execute their parents in Achlev's square. And though a slight murmur started up among the Midnighters, the preacher did not miss a beat.

I felt certain it was working; the reaction of the crowd was proof enough. The sounds I was sending to him were being passed along into his listeners' minds. But he himself seemed unperturbed. Was it the content or the effort that was lacking? I wondered how many horrid things this man had witnessed to hardly notice when they were being injected into his brain.

So I tried another tactic, and reached for the old Renaltan folk song my mother used to hum to me and Conrad.

Don't go, my child, to the Ebonwilde, for there a witch resides.
Little boys she bakes into pretty cakes,
Little girls into handsome pies.

It was a sonorous, sad melody. And before I knew it, I could hear it being hummed by a few of the soldiers nearby, and left my hiding place to hurry past them and get closer to the obverse side of the gathering.

The preacher was now struggling to keep his composure, and though he kept muddling through his speech, the sound of the song grew louder and louder.

Don't go, my child, to the Ebonwilde, for there a horseman rides.

I was almost to the front by then, and was finally close enough to see the faces of the Midnighters lining the stage behind the leader. They were all dressed so similarly in their thick, loose purple robes and closely shorn hair, there was very little to distinguish one from the other.

Except for height.

One Midnighter on the far left was shorter than the others. He was younger than them. And though his eyes bore the same glazed emptiness as the rest, his face was achingly familiar.

Conrad.

Seeing him was confounding, washing me in joy and devastation both at once.

Conrad! I shouted across the preacher's connections.

"Conrad!" the crowd yelled aloud. "Conrad!"

But my brother did not move; he did not even twitch at the sound of his name being bellowed across the field of thousands. Only his gaze shifted, his eyes moving slowly from one side of the crowd to another.

I willed him to look at me. To distinguish my face from all of the others . . . and he did.

For a single second, we locked eyes with each other. I scrambled to find another scrap of familiarity to send him, something that might reach him, and thought of the game we used to play.

Black, I thought, *means something is within ten paces, and hidden from sight.*

I saw something flicker in his eyes, so I kept going.

White means something is within twenty paces, and in plain view.

Yellow for up, blue for down, red for north, green for south, purple for east, orange for west.

But before I could send more, the preacher finally snapped. "Silence!" he cried, both aloud and in our minds, with the force of a sudden thunderclap. The rest of the crowd obeyed, their mouths and minds falling still at once, but not mine. My thoughts were tangled and angry and hostile, and they drew his attention inexorably toward me, like a thrashing trout at the end of a fisher's line.

And then, an enormous explosion sounded from one of the barracks on the other side, belching a fireball into the air and sending the Midnighters into their attack positions. I felt myself being yanked backwards. A hand clamped over my mouth to stifle a yelp as I was pulled down behind another Midnighter building.

Castillion put his finger to his lips before removing his hand from my mouth. He waited until a second explosion came from the other side of the valley and then waved me to follow him. At the top of the slope, I saw Nathaniel running toward the edge of the trees. He was trying to lead their attention away from us, and it was working too well.

"There!" The preacher on the stage pointed toward Nathaniel's fleeing form. "Archers, ready!"

I screamed in horror as ten thousand arrows flooded the sky toward my friend.

Without conscious thought, I tore the top from my vial of blood and poured a stream of it into my hands. I grabbed Castillion and cried out Nathaniel's name, too desperate to formulate a command. My magic had always been able to read my intentions.

We flashed across the space just after the first volley hit the ground at Nathaniel's feet. We arrived in front of him and he threw himself over us, using his body to shield us from the arrows that found their target in his back. I could feel the force of each one as it hit: one, two, three.

The magic in my blood spent, I reached around Nathaniel's back and used his, screaming *"Ut salutem!"* just as another volley streamed down toward us from the sky.

26

THEN

CONRAD

First, they shaved his head.

It was an extension of the abnegation rite, they said, the part where he left his old life behind him and embraced the new one ahead.

It should have been easy to let them take his hair; his city had been destroyed while he'd watched — and participated in its destruction — and he hadn't shed a single tear. Why, then, did his eyes sting so much now, watching hanks of curling, golden locks fall at his feet?

Eustacia gave him a gruff pat on his back, motioning for him to stand up and move on down the line, where another member of the fourth faction was waiting to present him with a bronze Circle Midnight medallion and a new name: Chydaeus.

It meant "common." *Ordinary.* Nothing.

They were determined, it seemed, to remind him that here, he was not a king. There was no room for kings inside the Circle; there was only the Empyrea. And of course Grandmaster Fidelis, who, as doyen of the first faction, was the Circle's highest-ranking member. He, the Circle members said, was the fourteenth reincarnation of the first Fidelis, the one who'd written the Midnight Papers and established the initiation rites that the Circle had practiced in secret for a thousand years.

Conrad was lucky that they did not search his purple robe; the nine-sided puzzle box remained well hidden within the heavy velvet folds. After the waves were called up and the subsequent celebration of death was over and the rest of the Circle had gone to sleep next to the broken dam, Conrad snuck the puzzle box out and, in the dim light, opened it.

He remembered writing something down after that, but he couldn't *quite* recall what it was. Still, it comforted him to know it was there.

The next day, a boat arrived, black as coal and flying the Circle's banner. It sailed right over Syric, navigating deftly around the clock tower and the few city spires tall enough to break the waterline. The Circle's secret members, those who'd been part of the long history of hidden rites, were a diverse group: merchants and millworkers, shipbuilders and sailors. And now that they'd been called out of concealment, the Circle's true might was beginning to become clear. With the Tribunal's gaze trained elsewhere—likely by the Circle members embedded within its ranks—the organization had collected everything it needed to stage its coup.

"Where are we going?" Conrad asked Eustacia as she herded him toward the vessel.

"Hush, Friend Chydaeus," she said coldly; all of the effusive kindness she'd displayed the night before had utterly vanished. "You'll know what you need to know when you need to know it."

✦

Aboard the boat, the Circle followed a strict schedule. And though every part of him wanted to rebel against it, he allowed himself to be moved along with the Midnighters' comings and goings, eating when they ate, sleeping when they slept. He walked the deck during the day, feeding bread crumbs to seagulls or helping to pull up fishing nets for the night's dinner. The other Midnighters began to get used to him. And in getting used to him, they also began to ignore him.

Two days after leaving Syric underwater, they came upon De Lena. When they left the next morning, the city was on fire and their numbers had doubled. Then they hit Gaskin, to a similar success. They had a very simple mode of operations: those who could not be convinced to join their cause, through fear or by Fidelis's silver tongue, were destroyed.

Under the Tribunal's regime, the Circle had survived like termites in the darkness. And, also like termites, now that the Tribunal was gone they'd emerged from the woodwork to propagate, chewing up and spitting out everything in their path.

Other than Fidelis and, to some extent, Eustacia, it was hard to know who was in charge on the Circle Midnight's ship. The crew members went about their duties without ever speaking to one another. They moved from chore to chore with a glazed, unfocused look in their eyes. The ship's workings were timed with the precision of cogs in a clock, each person's tasks a tick in a string of ordered, rhythmic movements.

Tick, tick, tick.

They seldom used names, either, calling each other only "Friend" on those rare occasions they were forced to speak. "I've come to relieve you of your post, Friend," said one man to another. "Thank you, Friend," was always the reply.

Conrad had never been so miserable, itching at every second to disrupt the tedium with a scream. Anything—*anything*—would be better than this monotony.

Order in all things, he thought, watching them. Hadn't that been the Tribunal's motto? And despite the many atrocities the Tribunal committed in the name of that ideal, this distillation of that phrase into its purer form was unsettling in a way he couldn't have fathomed before. Anger, he could understand. Brutality, he could understand. Animosity, he could understand . . . all of those things were rooted in emotion. But *this* unfeeling adherence to perfection? It was unnerving to the point of being inhuman.

In realizing this, he came to the satisfying conclusion that despite his predicament, he still had one power to use against them: chaos.

He started one morning by tapping his foot in a regular, repetitive rhythm. Every now and then, however, he'd miss a beat or two, and then add a few extra to catch up.

Every time it happened, the Midnighters nearest him would flinch —just a little. It was all the incentive Conrad needed to throw himself

227

into the effort with full force. When they brought him bread, he'd eat it from the middle. When he used the privy, he made sure to veer a little off the mark. While everyone else wore their robes starched to a crisp neatness, Conrad made sure his was always a little rumpled.

After several days of this—exactly how many, Conrad had lost count—he woke to find Fidelis sitting idly by his cot.

"I've been told that you are creating several disturbances, Friend Chydaeus," Fidelis said calmly. "That your assimilation into our culture has been . . . rocky."

"I don't know what you're talking about," Conrad said. "I've been doing my best." The puzzle box, tucked inside his robe, was poking his ribs; he tried not to think about it, lest Fidelis pluck the thought from his head.

"I have the ability to ensure your full compliance," Fidelis said. "But I've found that things always go a little smoother if I gain your submission to our order naturally, willingly. The Empyrea believes you could become one of her finest followers. Which is why I have decided to give you a few more responsibilities in preparation for your next rite."

"What do you mean?" Conrad asked.

"We'll make port again in two days, up the fjord toward an Achlevan territory called Morais. The land between Aylward and Morais is where we'll set up our base and begin to enact our plans in earnest."

"Aren't those who live there going to be opposed to our overtaking it?"

"Almost certainly," Fidelis said. "Though we have plenty of our members there already, waiting for the signal." He stood. "You will be accompanying Eustacia to the Morais manor. Once there, she will assign you a task she believes you will find particularly difficult—all of the initiation levels are meant to stretch your capabilities and commitment—and will report back to me about how you handle this responsibility."

Conrad wanted to spit in his face, but he tamped down the impulse and said instead, "I would be honored, Grandmaster."

Fidelis's smile did not reach his eyes; Conrad was certain he was reading his mind again. He lifted his chin and focused his thoughts on the many ways in which he might prove himself a loyal Midnighter in Morais.

"It is a great work we're doing," Fidelis said. "Cleansing the world of imperfection." He sighed. "You should know ahead of time, Friend Chydaeus, that it is likely to get a little bit messy. Our methods are not always ideal. But from chaos comes order." He put a hand on Conrad's shoulder. "As you will soon see and understand. Eustacia will collect you when the time is at hand. And I'll send down a new, better-fitting robe for you. It seems as if there's something about this one that is bothering you quite a bit."

★

The new robe Fidelis produced for Conrad was a much smaller size, which made it impossible for him to conceal his puzzle box. Though it pained him to have to do so, Conrad shifted it to a hiding spot beneath his cot mattress. Even though he couldn't remember what was important about it, exactly, he did not like being physically separated from it.

Just as Fidelis had promised, they made port on the fjord two days later, and Eustacia came to fetch him for the mission.

"Come, Friend Chydaeus," she said. "We have work to do."

✶

They approached the Morais manor house in a group of twelve, led by Eustacia. They didn't slink or try to hide themselves, choosing instead to walk right up to the baron's front door, passing a rectangular pool full of crystal water. It was still early in the year, so there were no water lilies blooming yet, but at the bottom of the pool was a mosaic of tiny circular tiles arranged into the form of the white-winged Empyrea. Eustacia bent her head and said "Blessed be the Empyrea. May she look down in favor upon our devotion today."

Conrad was beginning to feel sick.

A butler opened the door after Eustacia's polite rap. She bowed to him respectfully. "We are humble travelers," she said. "Religious pilgrims, you might say, and we would like to pay our respects to the lord and lady of the house, as we are passing through their lands."

"One moment," the butler said, disappearing for a minute. When he returned, he said, "Baron and Baroness Morais will greet two of you in their parlor. The rest may wait in the foyer. Follow me."

He led Eustacia and Conrad up the stairs and around the plaza terraces to a pretty room furnished with several velvet-upholstered couches. A tray of sweet wafers and tea was set out on the table. Conrad's mouth watered; the Circle's rations were spare, mostly unseasoned strips of dried meat and crisp bread. He longed to swipe up the whole tray of wafers and stuff his face full.

Eustacia did not speak. They waited for several minutes before the baroness swept in. She was of late middling age, wearing a crepe satin dress of a bright pink color and onyx-and-gold earrings in her ears. "Hello, pilgrims," she said cheerfully. "We welcome you to Morais."

"Where is the baron?" Eustacia asked. "We had hoped to be met by him as well."

"He'll be along shortly," Baroness Morais said, slightly taken aback. She lifted the teapot. "May I interest you in a cup of tea while we wait?"

Conrad began to reach out for one, but Eustacia answered for both of them. "No, thank you, mistress. We follow principles of austerity, and do not indulge in such things."

Baroness Morais gave a curt nod and poured herself a cup instead. Stiltedly, she asked, "To what site do you come as pilgrims? Morais is not well known as a crossroads; the only feature of note is the nearby Ebonwilde." Her tone seemed to indicate that no one would want to visit that.

"It's the Ebonwilde we seek," Eustacia replied.

The baroness gave a sound of astonishment behind her teacup. "What is there in that dark wood that you would wish to find?"

"Death," Eustacia said. She lunged for the baroness.

The baroness tried to flee, but Eustacia grabbed the hem of the woman's pink dress before she could make it over the couch and she fell instead, cracking her head against a mirror behind her. She collapsed with a cry. Eustacia pulled a thin athame from her belt and stalked toward the woman. Running footsteps sounded. The door burst open, and a man in a mauve dress coat barreled in.

"What is going on here?" the baron bellowed. His eyes fell to his wife, groaning on the ground.

"Juliana!" he cried, rushing to her, but Eustacia nabbed the heavy silver teapot from the table and smashed it into his face. Then she kicked him in the chest and he, too, collapsed.

Eustacia tossed her athame to Conrad, procuring a dagger from the baron's own belt instead. "Bring her," she commanded. She hoisted the baron by his arms and dragged him into the adjoining room.

The baroness was bleeding from the wound in her head. As Conrad shakily pointed the athame at her, she lifted her hands into the air. "I'll go," she said in a quavering voice.

More shouts and screams could be heard from deeper in the house, as the rest of their company roved through it. Conrad tried not to pay attention, but the sounds rang in his ears. He followed the baroness into the bedroom, holding the athame to her back, feeling utterly terrified.

"Here," Eustacia said, dumping the baron against the wall. "We've got to kill them right if their deaths are to strengthen the Empyrea."

Baroness Morais fell to her knees. "Please," she begged. "Please don't hurt him."

Eustacia was mumbling a prayer. "Dear Goddess on high, accept this humble offering and let it strengthen you."

And then she stabbed the baron in the heart.

She wiped her dagger off on her robe and looked at Conrad.

"Your turn," she said. "This is the task I've chosen for you. Slit her throat, Chydaeus, and pass the fourth level of initiation. The Empyrea commands it."

Conrad clutched the athame, swallowing his fear and disgust, and had taken the first steps toward the weeping baroness when a strange sound came from behind another set of doors. A cry, but not like the ones coming from the first floor.

A child's cry, Conrad thought, about to vomit. *There's a baby in here.*

Eustacia's eyes swiveled toward the sound. The child's cry came again.

The baroness tugged the sleeve of his robe. "Please," she whispered. "Please. You can kill me. Just don't hurt her."

The athame was slick in Conrad's sweaty grip. He looked into Juliana's eyes and knew he'd never be able to kill her—no matter how much his position within the Circle relied on his passing the fourth initiation.

She saw his hesitance, saw him glance back at Eustacia, and through her tears, she gave him the tiniest nod that she understood.

He handed the baroness the knife.

Eustacia lived just long enough to understand what had happened. She pulled the athame from her neck and stared at it for a second as blood gushed from the wound. She looked at the baroness first, and then to Conrad, her eyes registering shock and rage at his betrayal before they rolled back into her head.

Conrad felt suddenly calm. He knew what needed to happen.

"Hurry," Conrad ordered Baroness Morais. "Put on her purple robe."

He went into the nursery and found a tiny girl standing in the crib, holding on to the bar and gazing at him with a quizzical expression. Her hair was a lovely cloud of dark curls.

"Hello," he said, carefully lifting her free. "I promise I won't hurt you, but you've got to be very quiet, understand?"

She couldn't be more than a year old, but her eyes were clear and bright. They reminded him of Aurelia, and it strengthened his resolve.

Back in the bedroom, the baroness was already dressed in Eustacia's robes. She held out her arms to the baby, and Conrad handed the child over. The woman clutched her tightly to her chest. "Oh, my darling Ella," she said. "Oh, my sweet girl."

"Do you have any frostlace flower?" Conrad asked with urgency, dragging Eustacia, now clad only in her underclothes, to the four-poster bed. Stars! Though a thin woman, she was heavy. He had to use his back to push her onto it. He dreaded having to do the same with the baron, but when he looked up, he saw the baroness had set Ella down and was lifting her dead husband onto the bed beside Eustacia.

"I have a small dropper of frostlace," the baroness said, giving her husband's forehead a caress of farewell. "I've had bad dreams since my daughter died and Ella came to live with us."

"I'll need to take whatever you have, right now," Conrad said. It was the only way Fidelis would not be able to pluck these memories from his mind, he knew it. He didn't know *how* he knew it, but he knew it. "If they find out what I did, they'll kill me. You and your granddaughter will have to escape through the Ebonwilde."

The baroness was already rummaging around on her vanity. Blood still dripped from her scalp, but she didn't seem to notice. Conrad thought she was probably fueled by shock. "Come with us," she said to Conrad as she searched. "You're just a child yourself."

"He'll find me," Conrad replied. "You're better off going on your own, especially if I can't remember how you got away or which way you went."

The baroness unearthed a little glass dropper. "Here," she said, thrusting it into Conrad's hands. The sounds of mayhem elsewhere in the mansion seemed to be coming closer. The baroness picked up the baby again, pulling a blanket from the bed and wrapping the child in it.

"Good luck to you," he said.

"Empyrea keep you," she replied tremulously, and then slipped out onto the terrace, leaving him behind with the bodies in the bed.

He tipped the bottle into his mouth and swallowed its full contents. Then he hid the bottle back in the vanity and, as the antechamber's door burst open and the Midnighters strode in, he lay down on the floor in a contorted position and closed his eyes, waiting for his "Friends" to find him.

✶

That evening, back at the ship, Fidelis summoned Conrad.

"I have been informed that things did not unfold as planned at the manor," he said in a flat voice. "A pity about Friend Eustacia."

"I don't know what happened, exactly," Conrad said truthfully. "I remember going in, and talking to the baroness, and then Eustacia killing the baron . . . but after that it's just . . ." He shrugged. "Gone."

Fidelis eyed him from beneath heavy lids. "Yes," he said after a minute. "You truly don't remember. I wonder why that is?"

"I must have gotten hit," he said, "when the baroness got away."

"And yet you bear no marks or bruising upon you," Fidelis said. "Strange."

Conrad shrugged again, uneasily this time. "It's been a long day, Grandmaster Fidelis," he said. "I'd like to go to my cot now."

"You know," Fidelis said thoughtfully. "Come to think of it, there *is* one way such lapses of memory can happen. Have you ever heard of a plant called . . . frostlace?"

Conrad didn't know why, but he froze.

"Strangest thing, frostlace," Fidelis said. "Very expensive. Only blooms on Midwinter Night, in the cold."

Slowly, languidly, Fidelis produced a familiar, nine-sided puzzle box.

"Leave that alone," Conrad said. "That is my private property."

"Ah, that's the thing, Friend Chydaeus. We in the Circle Midnight have neither privacy nor property."

"You don't know how to open it," Conrad said confidently.

"If you know it," Fidelis said, "I know it. But I recognize in this moment an opportunity for your advancement within the Circle. What do you think, Chydaeus? Is now the time for your fourth rite? To prove your honesty to me and to the Empyrea?"

Conrad swallowed. "What would you have me do? I am telling you now, I don't know what is in that box."

"I believe you," Fidelis said. "Because I can read your thoughts. But I can also tell that you do not want me to open it. Is that true?"

There was no use lying—and doing so would mean failing the fourth rite. "Yes, Grandmaster. I do not want you to open it, though I do not know exactly why."

Fidelis handed the box to him and said, eyes glittering, "You open it for me, Chydaeus. Surrender this last secret so that you might stand honestly and forthrightly before the Empyrea."

Hands fumbling, Conrad turned the cogs on the puzzle box until it sprang open.

Fidelis pulled out a roll of papers and a purplish bottle from the puzzle box, then plucked the top paper from the stack and read a line from it. *"Ultimus 23rd, 1620, Midwinter Night: You snuck out of the castle to listen to a Circle Midnight preacher named Fidelis the Fourteenth."* Then the next. *"Ultimus 24th, 1620: You found the note. This seems to be working."* Then the third. *"Ultimus 30th, 1620 . . . you need to be extra careful when dealing with Fidelis and the Circle Midnight."*

Smirking, Fidelis said, "You've been a busy boy, Friend Chydaeus. Smart, though, using these notes as your memory." He stood and walked to the pipe stove. He opened the door and tossed in the papers, sending the puzzle box in to follow.

And even though he could not quite remember what any of those notes said, Conrad still wanted to cry as he watched them crinkle and blacken on the coals.

Fidelis did not destroy the bottle of frostlace. Instead, he snapped his fingers, and a dozen other berobed Midnighters appeared from the shadows. They all laid hands on him at once.

"What are you doing?" Conrad yelled. "Stop! Don't! Let go!"

The Midnighters stretched him out into a reclined position, forcing his jaw open and his head back. Overhead, Fidelis uncorked the bottle of frostlace and smiled.

"Since you like frostlace so much," he said, "I want you to have it *all*."

And he poured the bottle's entire contents down Conrad's throat.

27

THEN

ROSETTA

Rosetta had tried to forget what happened that Midwinter Night a century ago. To box it up and push it so far back into the recesses of her mind that it felt more like a cobwebby relic of someone else's past than a traumatizing piece of her own.

She had only gone back one other time since, thirteen years ago.

But now that she was here again, staring at the spider sigil carved into the bark of that old tree, the memory of that night reemerged from its corner, just as terrifying as when she had first lived it. And every step she retraced brought it into sharper focus.

Here was the spot that Saffron stopped, refusing to go even an inch further.

Here was the juniper I hid behind, listening to Grandmother weave the sad story of the murdered Spinner to Galantha.

This was the direction from which the old man came walking.

This is where Grandmother was standing when she caught him.

This is where the snow turned red with his castoff blood.

This is the direction I ran.

And here . . . Rosetta stopped at the foot of the apple tree. *Here is where I first saw the faces in the mist.*

But now . . . they were gone. There was no stirring in the air. No cavernous eyes nor long-toothed smiles. No trailing fingers plucking at her dress or hair, no taunting whispers coiling around her ears.

She had thought there could be nothing as frightening as the Verecundai, but as dusk settled over the glade, she realized that their absence from their interminable prison was far, *far* worse.

The wardens had performed their terrible duty for one thousand years, keeping disaster at bay despite paying such a high cost themselves . . . until Rosetta took up the mantle.

She did not change back into a fox for the journey home; it was too easy to forget herself in that form, and she deserved to feel the full weight of her folly. Through snow and mud she trudged, pulling her guilt behind her like an iron ball and chain. A journey that should have taken days instead encompassed weeks. The first tender shoots of crocus and tulip should have been poking up from the ground, but even as the snow melted, there was no sign of a returning spring. It was as if the lifelessness of the Verecundai's glade had also slipped its confines, and was slowly consuming the forest it had been kept apart from for so long.

Once inside her homestead's protective boundary, Rosetta paused for a moment alongside the southern edge, where a large stone jutted from the snow. A marker for a mortal body long gone, separated from a spirit that still lingered.

Rosetta tarried at the spot, her red hair lashing her cheeks, wondering why Galantha thought that giving up her life to salvage Rosetta's sorry soul was a worthy trade. She'd made such a mess of everything. At least with the warden's mantle on her shoulders, she had a role to pretend to fill. But now . . . Begonia was dead, her connection with Kellan had flared and burned out, and even the Ebonwilde was being taken from her, inch by inch.

Nothing left to do but sit back and wait, hoping that when the Empyrea finally got her way and razed the earth of life, Rosetta would meet her end with it.

Still fully submersed in those dark thoughts, she heard something strange.

A cry.

She thought at first that it was perhaps the mewling of an animal, transmuted into a humanlike sound by the wind. But when she heard it again, louder, she turned toward the source and was shocked to see a flicker of soft light coming from within her own cottage.

She ran toward the house, kicking up mud and unpleasant recollections of the last time this sanctuary had been infiltrated. There was little left in the world that could actually hurt Rosetta, but as she mounted the steps and pushed open the door, she could not help the fear that calcified her quicksilver heart into rigid stone.

The kitchen, as she stepped inside it, was mostly dark and still very cold. The light was coming from the parlor beyond.

"Hello?" she called. "I know you're here. Come out! This is my house; you are not welcome." She raised her hands like weapons, readying herself to weave a spell at the first sign of trouble.

The crying, which had stopped at the creak of the door, began again.

Slowly, slowly, Rosetta crept across the kitchen floor until the parlor came into full view.

The first thing she saw was the crumpled shape of a woman, who appeared to have crawled to the fire and was able to get a small flame going before collapsing beside it. She was dressed in a strange robe of deep purple and bloodstained silk slippers, holes showing the frostbitten skin of her feet underneath. Her hair was peppered silver and gray, and there were earrings of gold and onyx dangling from the lobes of her ears. Rosetta moved closer and realized with a chill that the woman no longer breathed. Her body was curled around a blanketed bundle; she'd died clutching it to her breast.

Gingerly, Rosetta reached down and pulled a corner of the blanket aside. She found herself staring into a pair of wide, translucent eyes.

A baby.

★

Rosetta buried the woman alongside her own grave in the back end of the homestead yard. The child, despite her soiled clothing and cold-chapped cheeks, seemed to be in relatively good health. She was not quite a year old, Rosetta guessed, and not yet able to walk. When Rosetta got her washed and fed and tended to her scrapes and bruises, she fell asleep quite easily in the cradle Begonia had once used for her dolls.

While the baby slept, Rosetta followed the dead woman's footsteps to the edge of the homestead, where she found that one of her wards had been partially unknotted, likely by a bird scavenging fiber for its nest. She tied it back up and replaced it on the tree, returning to the cottage just as the child was waking once again. Softly, though; after their first encounter, the little girl did not cry again.

"What shall I do with you?" Rosetta asked the child, warming some milk in a pan. "You can't stay here."

She wondered what her sisters would do in this situation. Galantha, likely, would have scoured the earth to identify the deceased woman and deliver the child to her rightful next of kin. Begonia would have been enamored with the baby and probably would have decided to keep her.

Rosetta had neither Galantha's nobility nor Begonia's caretaking instinct. She was as ill-suited to motherhood as a field mouse to pulling a carriage.

It took her days to decide. Just long enough for her to feel a pang of regret when the matter was finally settled in her mind. In another world, perhaps, this cottage would get to watch another girl grow into a woman; these woods would get to see another daughter take up the mantle. But not this time.

The Quiet Canary was still as Rosetta approached it, basket in hand and baby strapped to her back. She folded several blankets into the basket and laid it softly onto the stoop before settling the sleeping child into it.

"You be good," Rosetta told the little girl, brushing the back of her finger across her round cheek. "The women here are very kind, but I'm trusting you to not give them any trouble, all right?"

The baby's dark lashes fluttered just a little as Rosetta placed a kiss on the top of her dark hair, but her eyes did not open. She slept on.

Then Rosetta gave a quick and heavy knock at the door and dashed away, transforming at last back into a fox as she went.

28

THEN

ZAN

His dreams that night were fraught, filled with flashes of things he'd tried to forget: the feel of his father's backhand against his lips, the red sap of broken bloodleaf stems marking the place his mother's body had fallen from Aren's tower, the smell of Lisette's gardenia perfume as she died in his arms, blood bubbling from her lips.

And always, there was Aurelia. She was in every thought, every memory, watching his struggles from a safe distance, accusations glittering in her eyes. *Come and find me*, she'd say, over and over, first as an invitation, then a question, and then a plea, and finally a demand.

And eventually, her words morphed into the shape of an eight-legged creature, glossy black save for a white, moon-shaped sliver on its abdomen. The spider crawled up his leg and across his torso as Zan trembled, too weak to move and swat it away.

Finally, when it reached his neck, the spider sank its fangs into the soft flesh.

Zan woke with a scream.

"Shhh." A soft, soothing voice came from beside him. "Don't try to get up. You're safe. You're in the Sisters' hands now."

A woman leaned over him, wearing a mild smile that belied the firm strength of her hands as she pushed him back against a pillow. He was in a light and airy room, with a high stucco ceiling and no furnishings save for the bed he was occupying, her chair, and a plain side table.

She wrung out a washcloth in a basin of cool water, and then used it to mop his brow. "What did you see?" she asked. "The venom of a crescent silk spider is said to awaken memories. And from the look on your face, son, I'd say not all of yours were pleasant."

She called him "son," though she could not be more than a handful of years older than him. Beneath the bone-colored silk of her wimple, her skin glowed a warm, sable brown. "We should probably thank you," she continued. "For lighting the lighthouse lamp. Our keeper died three days ago, and by the time the storm hit, it was too late to send anyone out there as a replacement." She poured him a cup of water from a glass carafe.

"The ship we came in on," Zan rasped, accepting the water gratefully. "The *Contessa*. Did it make it?"

"I'm sorry to say that I don't know. It's not uncommon, after a big storm like that one, for there to be shipwrecks on our reef, even if we've got the lighthouse fully lit. We can find salvage up and down our shores afterward. Not this time. That could mean they kept on going, made it out just fine. Or . . . it could mean that there's simply not enough of it left. Were it not for you and your friend, we'd never have known a ship even passed by."

"My friend," Zan said suddenly, attempting to sit up again. "Jessa —Jenny. Is she—?"

"Alive," the nun said. "Though quite a bit worse off than you, I'm afraid. She's in the infirmary, with the other fever patients. You're fortunate; all you got was a spider bite. We're pretty good at keeping the spiders contained, but there are one or two wild ones out there."

"The Bitter Fever? It's here, too?"

"We think it came with a merchant ship from Syric that stopped here to buy silk two weeks ago." She looked away, wan and wistful. "Indeed, that's what took our lighthouse attendant, Sister Devereaux, Empyrea keep her soul. It's been very hard."

Zan was puzzled. "My friend and I were both exposed to it. How is she ill and I am not?"

The nun shrugged. "Some seem to be naturally immune."

"You?" he asked.

She nodded reluctantly. "We're the lucky ones, I guess."

"Luck? You don't think the Empyrea has blessed us?" he asked sardonically. "That is generally the go-to answer of religious establishments such as yours."

"Perhaps she has," the nun said. "But it sure doesn't feel that way to me."

"You're very honest," he said.

"It's a failing of mine," she replied. "I'm still working on it. Don't hold it against me. Um . . . ?" She trailed off, waiting for a name.

"Tom."

"Nice to meet you, Tom. I'm Sister Cecily."

★

By the middle of the day, Zan couldn't stand being alone in that tiny, nondescript room anymore. He knew he should wait for Sister Cecily to return before he went wandering around the abbey alone and without permission, but after her grief-stricken reaction to his news about Delphinia, he wasn't sure when—or if—she'd be ready to talk to him again. So he forced himself up and got to his wobbly legs, feeling a lot like the wrung-out washrag still sitting on the stand next to the bed: limp and drained.

The abbey was a sprawling complex of housing and gardens—some for growing vegetables, some for raising the spiders from which the nuns derived most of their income. The largest part of the compound was where the silk was collected and processed into thread and then dyed and woven into the fabric that merchants from all over the Western Realms and the continent would sail half the world around to purchase. Zan's own father, Domhnall, had favored the Sisters' silks, and spent lavishly on collecting every opulent variety. He supposed it was because of those bolts of rose-and-gold damask and vermilion quatrefoil that he assumed the place that produced them would be just as lavish, but that couldn't be further from the truth. Everything about the abbey was austere, simple to the point of plainness, and designed firstly for function.

Zan shuffled alone through the complex's halls, peering into spinning rooms filled with silent spinning wheels and weaving rooms with quiet looms. It was enough to make him wonder if Sister Cecily wasn't just another ghost, or figment of his imagination.

Then he found the infirmary.

The Sisters had set up their sick bay in what would normally have been the abbey's sanctorium, with cots where the pews might once have been and tables piled with nursing supplies lining the transept. There were a handful of nuns weaving through the cots like determined bees through a hive. They had to be efficient; they were outnumbered five to one by their patients.

One of them hurried over. "You shouldn't be here!" she chastised, chasing him off with a flip of a towel. "Out with you!"

Behind her glasses, her eyes were an unnerving black, with no distinction between her pupil and her iris.

"Leave him alone, Sister Aveline," Cecily said from across the room. "He wants to see his friend."

"He could be exposed!" Sister Aveline protested. "And . . . he's a *he*."

"Oh, hush now," said another nun, bending to help one of her patients sip some water. Her eyes, too, were black. "If you don't look under his clothes, there's no difference."

"Sister Beatrice!" Aveline said, scandalized.

Beatrice looked at Zan. "Apologies," she said. "Sister Aveline is quite unused to menfolk."

"I don't want to disturb anyone," Zan said, retreating. "I will go."

"No," Cecily said, rising to usher him to her chair at Jessamine's bedside. "It's good you're here. She's been fighting quite hard, but I'm not certain how much time she has left. It's better we don't have to go looking for you. Gives you more time to say goodbye."

Zan's heart sank. He sat down beside Jessamine. "Hello, there, Jenny," he said, taking her hand.

"She's been hallucinating for hours," Beatrice said. "I'm not sure she'll be able to respond."

But Jessamine turned her face toward him. "Pretty," she murmured, and Zan realized that she was actually looking at Cecily, standing at his back.

"She's definitely hallucinating," Cecily said, but her cheeks ripened to the rosy color of harvest apples.

Sister Beatrice straightened the pillow beneath Jessamine's head and said softly, "Look. Her eyes. Probably won't be long now."

Beatrice was right; Jessamine's pupils were widening at a steady rate, the warm amber color of her irises narrowing to a thin ring.

"Come on, now," Zan said, his throat constricting. "Don't do this, Jessamine." He dropped the pretenses and used her real name. "You know I'm completely helpless on my own."

Her glassy gaze fell upon him. She said in a slow mumble, "Don't be sad, Tom."

Cecily patted him on his shoulder and said, "Take heart. She doesn't want you to mourn."

But Zan knew better. What Jessamine had said was not *Don't be sad, Tom.* It was *Don't be Sad Tom.*

Even at the very precipice of death, she couldn't let that joke go.

Jessamine's eyes became unfocused, blackness swallowing the last sliver of color as her breath slowed. Zan ground his teeth together, and he clung to her hand. It was light and fragile in his grip; holding it felt like cradling a wounded bird.

He drew in a breath and locked it in his lungs, bracing for the black tears to start pooling in the corners of her eyes. Waiting to add another name to the long list of people he'd loved and lost.

But it didn't happen. One moment passed, then another, and another, and slowly, he allowed himself to exhale.

Cecily touched the back of her hand to Jessamine's forehead. "By all the stars!" she said gladly. "It's broken. The fever has broken! We must say an extra prayer of thanks tonight."

29

NOW

AURELIA

6 DAYS TO MIDWINTER

My spell for transport to safety had landed us squarely in the center of the warden's homestead, where Rosetta's ire at our sudden, disconcerting appearance at her doorstep was quickly supplanted by urgency when she saw Nathaniel's dire condition. She immediately took charge, leading us into the cottage and shoving things from her table to make room for his body. "Quickly, now. Lay him here." Castillion and I set him down upon it as carefully as we could, with his back facing up so she could access his wounds.

I paced as she worked, crossing floorboards between the hearth and the hallway enough times to wear ruts into the wood grain. Castillion sat to the side, watching me make my rounds, uncharacteristically quiet. But Nathaniel's skin continued to gray, and after an uneasy hour, Rosetta said, "I'm losing him, Aurelia. The damage is just too severe."

"No," I said shrilly. "Just keep going—"

"Aurelia," she said, lifting her hands away. They were streaked with red all the way up to her elbows. "There's time enough to say your goodbyes."

"No," I said again through gritted teeth, as if by denying reality I could change it. "You can't let him die! You're a warden! Isn't this part of your job?"

"I *was* a warden, but I am no longer," she said coldly. "Perhaps you recall why that is?"

It was because of me. Because I had taken her mantle and given it to Arceneaux, just before trapping her in the Gray. But this was not the time to explore the ramifications of that action, nor to indulge in self-recrimination.

"You can yell at me all you want later." I grabbed one of her hands and pushed it back down to his skin. With her hand under mine, I tried to force it to resume the pattern. Up and down, then across again. "Do the spell, Rosetta," I yelled. *"Do the starsforsaken spell!"*

"Aurelia!" she chastised, trying to pull away, but I kept mimicking the shape of her knot, until I felt a jolt move from my hand to hers, and then down into Nathaniel.

I blinked, and the room that had been empty was now covered, every inch, in glimmering threads, like a dewy spider's web caught from behind by morning sun.

"Bleeding stars," I breathed.

Rosetta's eyes went wide. "You can see them? The connections?"

Mutely, I nodded.

Instead of fighting me, Rosetta moved her hands to the tops of mine. "Follow my lead, all right? Let the power move through you. Channel it, don't try to control it."

It was like a graceful dance, moving those gossamer threads of power around in three dimensions. Up, down, through, around, down and back. Where we touched Nathaniel, the energy followed. When it was clear that I was getting the hang of it, Rosetta let go and let me continue on my own, while she began a new spell, working overtop of mine.

Using feral magic was unlike anything I'd ever felt. Using blood magic had been like . . . breaking down a dam and trying to harness a flood. It was an explosion . . . passion and power released in a dazzling burst, bright and blinding, but lasting only a moment before fizzling to nothing fast.

This was its precise opposite. It was magic of method and precision, made inch by careful inch. I didn't know what I was doing, or how . . . but I dared not question it too closely, because by some mighty miracle, it was *working*.

Castillion had moved closer, and was watching our movements with quiet interest. After a moment, he said, "Look, Aurelia."

I dared to steal a glance at Nathaniel's face, and felt my chest tighten when I saw the warmth returning to it.

"Careful," Rosetta warned. "Keep those emotions in line. You can't let yourself get distracted. Not yet."

The two spells were working in tandem with each other; I was keeping Nathaniel's life force flowing while Rosetta pinned the

broken pieces inside of him back together. I could see now how difficult—if not impossible—this would have been to do alone.

I don't know how much time passed while we worked, but when
Rosetta made the last twist in her spell and said, "All right, Aurelia.
You can stop now," it took several moments for my hands to acknowl-
edge my head's signals and finally go still.

Castillion, who had been sitting with his head on his arms by the
hearth, snapped to attention. "How is he?"

"We've gotten him out of any immediate danger," she said, wiping
her hands on a clean rag before handing another one to me. "Now we
have to wait for his body to respond. *He* must take it from here. He
can make it through this, if he has the will."

I took a deep breath, studying Nathaniel as he slept. He wasn't the
same man I had met on the streets of Achlev two years ago. His face
was leaner now, his features more defined, chiseled into sharpness by
the strike of each successive tragedy. He'd lost his wife, his home, his
daughter . . . I wanted so much to bend down and beg him to *hang in
there*, to *keep going,* to *fight.* But was that a selfish impulse? Was it cruel
to ask *him* to endure more misery and pain simply because *I* might
similarly suffer at his loss?

Castillion had come up behind me, placing a calming hand on my
shoulder. "He's a soldier," he said. "He won't give up yet. Not when
there's still a battle to be won."

"Let him be," Rosetta said. "He needs to rest. We all do now."

We moved into the parlor, where Rosetta put a kettle on the hook
over the fire for tea. She took the rocking chair, and Castillion sat
on one side of the settee, leaving the other side open for me. I chose

instead to sit alone on the braided rug in front of the fire, pulling my knees up under my chin.

We were all quiet for a while, listening to the snap and pop of the wood in the grate and lost in our own thoughts. Then Rosetta said, "I can't figure it out."

Only half listening, I asked, "What?"

"How is it possible that you, a blood mage, could work a feral spell?" she asked. "If I hadn't seen it for myself . . ."

"Maybe it's because of this," I said, motioning to my quicksilver body. "I'm like you now."

"That's not it. Magic ability isn't attached to the physical body. It's part of our souls. Our very essences," she said. "Blood mages must use blood for their magic, but it does not have to be their own blood. Likewise, there *is* magic in all blood, but only a blood mage can wield it." She hesitated, shaking her head as if about to give voice to an absurdity. "I think maybe . . ." But the kettle had begun to wail.

Castillion hurried to lift the kettle from the hook, removing three teacups from the hutch by the kitchen door. "We're all very tired," he said briskly. "It has been a taxing day. But Aurelia, we cannot linger here. Not after what we saw in the Midnight Zone. We have to get back to the fort immediately, and begin preparations for an imminent attack."

I nodded, but looked toward the door behind which Nathaniel was resting. How could I leave him in such a state?

Rosetta's eyes narrowed at him. "You seem very familiar. What did you say your name was?"

He handed her a steaming cup and said, "We never got as far as any formal introductions. But my name is Dominic. Dominic Castillion."

"The great commander himself, in my humble cottage?" She looked at me. "You do keep strange company, Aurelia. Isn't he the one who tried to kill your beloved prince?"

Castillion ducked his head in embarrassment, but not because of the attempt on Zan's life. It was because of his confession, on board the *Humility*, that it was meant to be an attempt on *mine*.

They told me you'd be the end of me, he'd said.

"Yes," I said, choosing the simpler explanation. "But he is also the one who woke me, when Zan chose . . . otherwise."

"I see," she said. "Well, Dominic Castillion. My name is Rosetta." She extended her hand, as if she were a queen and not a crotchety hedge witch.

Ever the chivalrous diplomat, he took her hand and bowed to kiss it.

It happened in a flash: Rosetta yanking his hand down and twisting it behind his back, giving her the opening to kick in the back of his knees. He let out a cry of pain as she forced him to the floor and then straddled him, pinning him to the ground with her knife of bone, drawn so quickly from some hidden compartment in her clothing that it looked as if she'd pulled it from thin air.

Castillion was breathing in startled gasps, his eyes bugging. His white hair fanned out on the rug, both hands raised up in acquiescence.

"Rosetta!" I hissed. "What in all of the bleeding—?"

"Your hair is different," she said to Castillion. "That's why I didn't recognize you at first."

"W-wait," I stuttered. "You know each other?"

"We've never met!" Castillion said in a rush, before Rosetta quieted him by pushing her knife further into the soft flesh at the conjunction of his neck and his jaw.

"You were my greatest mistake," she said in a soft, dangerous voice. "Of all my many regrets, *you* are the one that will haunt me."

"Castillion," I said, "what on *earth* did you do?"

"Nothing," he said in a choked whisper as blood began to trickle down his throat. "I swear it, Aurelia. I swear."

"You're hurting him, Rosetta," I protested. "Put the knife down, and maybe we can figure this out . . ."

And then, to my shock, she ripped open his shirt, each button giving way in a series of *pop pop pop*s.

Castillion looked at me, his dark brown eyes full of some unnameable emotion. Indignity? Humiliation? Shame?

No . . . it was defiance.

On his chest, over his heart, was the scarred purple mark of the seven-legged spider.

30

THEN

KELLAN

Kellan and Emilie were only on the second flight of stairs when the wave hit. It burst through the iron door and crashed inside the clock tower while the building groaned. Water hungrily lapped at their heels as they climbed the stairs in the dark, up and up and up. Emilie's injuries slowed her, but Kellan would not let go; he kept his arm wrapped around her torso and lifted her when her strength failed or her feet slipped on the slick metal.

"I've got you," he said. "We're almost there."

Making it to the top was the only goal he allowed himself to focus on, but the real question—the one he did not dare give voice—was how far the water would keep rising after they ran out of stairs to climb.

They practically leaped up the last few stairs and tumbled onto the platform, breathless and wheezing. They peered through the holes in the platform grate at the water churning on the other side, writhing like an angry animal behind the door of a cage. Three feet away, then two, then one . . .

"Bleeding stars," Kellan said as it began bubbling up through the holes. He pulled Emilie back to her feet, her sodden cloak of animal furs weighing nearly as much as the girl beneath it. "Hold on to me."

They waded through the now ankle-deep water toward the clockface, where the hands were still stuck in their skyward perpendicular orientation. By the time they were underneath the center pin, the water was up to their waists and had pushed Emilie out from Kellan's arms.

The water slammed her body against the glass of the clockface and pinned her to it. She struggled uselessly against the torrent, caught like a moth in the cobwebbing cracks glinting in the glass circle.

"Kellan!" she cried, her eyes round with helpless terror as the *snap-crack-snap* sound of buckling glass rose over the roar of the thrashing waves.

Not again, he thought, remembering the night he last saw her, with her face turned up in agony, lit red by flame as he rode away. She'd somehow survived the fire of the Tribunal's pyre; he'd die before he let her be claimed by water.

He let the water lift him from his feet and carry him to her, but just before he hit the glass, he threw his right arm toward the center clock pin, willing the metal of his quicksilver hand into a new shape. He cast out with his left hand to grab the collar of Emilie's cloak just as the glass gave a final groan and shattered into a thousand glittering pieces that burst outward with the frothy surge of water.

He felt his right hand catch and hold, and when he looked up, he saw that it had formed into a gryphon's talon, each one of the claws hooked three inches deep into the foot-thick diameter of the clock pin. With his left arm, he hoisted Emilie from the pull of the flow, straining every muscle, until she was able to wrap her arms around his neck. She clung to him, coughing and spluttering as the current splashed over their heads, trying to suck them both into the whirling maw of black water and broken timber on the other side of the submerged clock tower.

"I can't hold on!" he yelled. He felt his claws slipping, sliding slowly through the iron, leaving gouging tracks with every lost inch.

"I'm too heavy," Emilie called back, and he thought for a minute that she was going to let go. Instead, she unfastened the fur cloak and let the water drag it from her narrow shoulders until it disappeared into the abyss.

The load lightened, Kellan gripped Emilie tighter and willed the claws to grow longer, deeper, to wrap around the iron bar and farther around his own arm. Bands of liquid silver began to crisscross past his elbow, up his straining biceps, and across his chest and neck. It gave him the strength he needed to hold on until slowly, slowly, the water began to recede. When it went down enough for them to be able to put their feet back down on the solidity of the platform floor, Kellan finally released his grip, first on Emilie, and then from the clock's center pin. The quicksilver re-formed into the shape of a hand and fell to his side, as lifeless and heavy as a hunk of rock.

Emilie was shivering in a plain linen dress that clung wetly to her thin frame. "Th-thank you," she said.

Kellan found that he, too, was shaking . . . but whether it was from the wet and cold or the sudden abatement of adrenaline, he could not be sure. He looked at his silver hand and said, "Th-thank the m-mage who made th-this for me."

"If I ev-ver m-meet h-her, I will," Emilie said. Then, "My sk-skill is m-much more limited—I'm only any g-good at illusion—but I c-can do this."

She took his left hand in hers and began tracing a pattern into it. A feral spell. He'd seen Rosetta work dozens of times, making complicated loops and whirls with delicate, dancing fingers. Emilie's spell was far more rudimentary, consisting of a simple, repeated array of lines: a circling spiral, followed by a stroke from top to bottom and side to side. Like a sun, or a star. The effect, too, was slow . . . a creeping warmth that passed from her fingertips into his skin.

She smiled shyly at him as the magic began to work. It was a lopsided smile, tugged down a little on the left side by scars, and the loveliest thing he'd ever seen.

★

They stayed the night in their frigid perch, huddled together while the floods slowly abated, trying not to think about what kind of devastation awaited them on the other side of the night. "I'm sorry about your cloak," he said, putting his arms around her to help alleviate some of her shivering. "I'm really wishing you still had it right about now. Was it . . . important?"

"A project my mother started before she died. A cloak of protection, made of the pelts of a thousand different animals and sewn together with feral spells. I had to figure out how to finish it on my own, using whatever bits of fur and leather I could find."

"Protection?"

"From the same people I tried to warn you and Conrad about. The Circle Midnight."

"The message left in my room. The rendezvous with Conrad at the tomb. Pelton's invitation to the ball . . . that was all you?"

She nodded grimly.

"And I was too ignorant to see it. And now . . ." Through the clockface's empty circle he could see the spires of the castle, the only parts left unsubmerged. "It's too late."

"The Circle does not easily let go of the things that it wants, nor do they squander a resource that might prove useful in the future," Emilie said. "If they have him, we can trust that they will keep him alive. Fidelis wouldn't want to drown a king if he could recruit him first. That should be some comfort, at least."

"How do you know all of this?"

"Because," she said sadly, "I was one of them."

Kellan tensed, and Emilie looked the other way. "I was raised in the Circle. In secret, of course; they had to go underground after the Tribunal's organization and rise to power, but the Circle's practices never died out. They have thrived in the dark, with small sects in every city, members in every court. They even had agents within the Tribunal, who worked covertly to protect the order. When I came of age, my mother and I were sent to Syric on the express mission to get me close to Princess Aurelia somehow. Fidelis wanted me to watch her and report her movements back to them. To gain her trust, if possible, and insinuate myself into her inner circle. It took years—by the time the goal was reached, my mother had been tried and hung as a witch."

"I don't understand," Kellan said. He stood up, head spinning. He began to pace. "You helped Aurelia. Stars, you were burned at the stake for her—"

"She was kind to me." Emilie's eyes misted, and she tugged the dragon pendant around her neck. "She did not see me as just a servant, or a . . . a pawn, like the Circle did. So I helped her. And I paid the price, yes, but I wouldn't change anything. Nor would you, I expect."

Kellan's eyes dropped to his silver hand.

"That night, I used an illusion to escape the pyre, and then to hide in the castle afterward. I stole salve and gauze for my wounds from Mistress Onal's stillroom. She never said anything, but I think she knew I was there somehow, and went out of her way to replenish what I needed and keep it stocked on her shelves. I'm alive because of her."

Kellan nodded. "That sounds like something she'd do."

"When the Tribunal clerics who tried to kill me realized the pyre was empty, they decided it was better to cover up my disappearance than admit they'd let me get away. So they filled an urn with ash from the pyre and buried it in a Tribunal potter's field. A piece of luck, I thought, to be able to heal without fear of pursuit. I thought that when I was recovered, I'd return to Fidelis and the Circle and tell them what I'd done, and how I'd kept the princess alive, but he arrived at Syric first. When I went to see him, I was told by one of the Circle's first-levels that he'd gone to visit my grave.

"I was touched. And I thought—I'll surprise him there. Make myself invisible, and then drop the illusion just at the right time. I convinced myself that he'd be impressed. Maybe even advance me within the ranks of the Circle. Had I not shown good judgment? Had I not been obedient? Had I not exemplified endurance?"

"What happened?" Kellan asked, gentler now.

"I was wearing that illusion when Fidelis stood with other Circle members over my empty grave and *lamented* at what a disappointment I'd been. He said I'd squandered the opportunity they'd made for me when they turned my mother in to the Tribunal." She took a quavering breath. "Until then, I didn't know . . . They'd had my mother executed, you see, for the express purpose of ingratiating me with the princess. So that we might have some common ground."

Kellan said, "I'm so sorry."

"Don't be," she said, setting her jaw. "Fidelis's high magic gift revolves around the manipulation of thoughts, but he's become so good at the art of subjugation that after the first few encounters with someone, he doesn't even have to use his magic to control them. He strips people of everything that makes them who they are . . . home, family, history, identity . . . and breaks them down in a never-ending cycle of punishment and praise. And they become hollow little puppets, trained to follow his every order, to submit to his every whim, so full of fear and love that they can no longer tell which is which. I'd been away from his influence long enough by then that I was no longer constrained by his magic, and learning that he had purposely had my mother executed . . . it was enough to jolt me out of the last of my conditioning."

She paused here, collecting herself. Then she swallowed hard. "I finally understood why my mother had agreed to bring me to Syric, so far away from his influence, and why she had begun making the cloak that could protect a person from the effects of high magic. She wanted to get me away from the Circle. Even so, were it not for what I'd already been through, I'm not certain I would have had the audacity to leave that day in the potter's field. But by then, I'd gone through fire and come out alive on the other side. I was changed."

Kellan was staring at her, hardly able to comprehend what that must have been like.

"After that, it was like a veil had been lifted from my eyes, and my thoughts were entirely my own for the first time in my life. I began to think that I was safe. But then the Tribunal fell, and Fidelis got bold. He started recruiting in earnest. He set his sights on Conrad, and I knew I couldn't stand by anymore."

"You are very brave," Kellan observed quietly.

"I thought I was," she said, "but at the ball, Fidelis took one look in my direction and I went fleeing in terror." She lifted her face. Two tears were running in thin streaks down her cheeks, one soft and smooth, the other marked with the uneven patches of healed burns. "What spell can protect you from your own past?"

"I wish I knew," Kellan said, sitting beside her once again. "Perhaps time?"

"There's not much of that left, I'm afraid," she said, resting her chin on her arm. "For any of us. The clock was the first sign of the Reckoning written in the Midnight Papers. This flood is the next. Soon, the Bitter Fever will spread across the land, followed by unrest and ending with a great battle. Then the Empyrea will descend, cleansing the earth in fire. The Circle believes that all of it—the flood, the fever, the war—is a sacrifice for her. An offering of blood. And if she accepts it, they will be rewarded in the world to come."

"Is it true?"

"What does it matter?" Emilie said. "*They* believe that it is. And they will stop at nothing to ensure it all happens exactly as Fidelis the First foretold it."

"And what role does Conrad have to play in all of it?"

"It's not Conrad they want," Emilie said. "It's Aurelia. They believe that she is the reincarnation of the Spinner—a mage who could work all three magics at once. The Spinner is the ultimate offering; a human with power nearly equal to that of the Empyrea herself. I suspect they want Conrad because they know they can use him to gain control over Aurelia."

Kellan was shaking his head. "Aurelia is dead. I was there when they put her body into its grave."

"Her *mortal* body," Emilie said. "That's part of the Spinner's lore, too. That she will shed her mortal skin and reemerge, triumphant, in humanity's final hours."

"To save them?"

"To rule them. To become queen of the Empyrea's new world,

with the reincarnation of her beloved consort, Adamus, by her side."

Kellan was silent, aghast.

"The Circle doesn't want to kill her," Emilie said, rising to look out upon the submerged city. "They want to *crown* her."

31

THEN

CHYDAEUS

Chydaeus knew Grandmaster Fidelis did not trust him, though he wasn't quite sure why.

As a member of the Circle, Chydaeus was without equal in his devotion to the Empyrea. He was always the first to kneel at worship every morning, and the last to leave. He was diligent in his tasks and careful in his words—a model Midnighter in every way.

Why, then, did Fidelis continue to keep him at arm's length? For months now, Chydaeus had been made to watch as other initiates passed him in the ranks. Many who'd come into the Circle after him were already past the sixth rite of their initiation, while Chydaeus had been stuck at four since they overtook Morais.

The answer, he finally determined during one of his day shifts hauling timber to the shipbuilding sites, must be his age. He knew he was young, but he was also remarkably sharp. And he was a hard worker, putting twice as much effort into his daily tasks as others double his age. That was not a boast, either, as vanity was one of the frailties of men most vexing to the Empyrea. It was truth. Truth was an intrinsic factor of order.

At the next worship, he vowed to say as much to the Grandmaster.

"Friend Fidelis," he said, approaching the Grandmaster after the requisite prayers and prostrations were complete, "I wish to speak to you. It has come to my attention that I have not been permitted the same level of involvement in the ministrations of the Empyrea's will as others who are of an equal footing as me here among the Circle. I wish to know why that is."

"Come now, Friend Chydaeus," Fidelis said. "It is unseemly to wish to rise above your peers, for are we not all equal in the sight of—"

"I have no wish to rise above my peers," Chydaeus interrupted earnestly. "Only to raise them up alongside me, so that we may all be glorified by the Empyrea together. Challenge me, Grandmaster. Let me demonstrate the sincerity of my commitment to the Empyrea's cause."

Fidelis watched him, guarded, and then said, "All right. Tonight, the doyens and I will administer the fifth and sixth rites of passage unto you, those of judgment and obedience. If you fail, however, you will be demoted back to a two. Understand?"

Smoothly, Chydaeus said, "I do, Grandmaster." But inside, he was crowing. The fifth *and* sixth rites? There were only eight rites in total.

He would be only a few steps away from full membership in the Circle —perhaps he could even be considered for a position as a doyen in the fourth faction. He checked the notion as soon as it came to him, though; one never knew which stray thoughts Fidelis might pick up.

He finished his afternoon labor in record time that night, dropping his last load of lumber to the shipyard just as the sun was beginning to set, while the other fourth-levels were only on their second and third runs. This gave him enough time to wipe the sweat and grime from his face and change into his second set of robes before heading up to the Grandmaster's tent. He had to pass the fifth- and sixth-levels on their practice fields as he went, and tried to tamp down the envy he felt watching them move through their battle-training maneuvers. It was all in preparation for their seventh rite, because after judgment and obedience came endurance. At least, he reasoned, he was no longer a third-level, who had to do all of the heavy assembling required to learn fortitude. Or a second-level, who labored all day in the choking heat of the kilns, usually with only a small amount of food and water, to teach them abnegation. First-levels didn't even warrant that much responsibility; if they were lucky, they worked all day moving timber on their backs. If they weren't, they mucked out privies. It seemed cruel, but Conrad knew it was to teach them the humility they needed to pass the first rite. Some men had to be broken of their will in order to fully accept the Empyrea's.

And those who couldn't learn to submit . . . they were removed from the Circle's ranks.

It was how it had to be.

Grandmaster Fidelis and the rest of the fully-ascended mages resided in the building that had once been the manor house of Baron Aylward of Achleva. While Fidelis disparaged its grandiosity, he felt it was helpful to the lower initiates to visualize the heights to which they would be able to rise in the Empyrea's new world. When Chydaeus reached the door, a first-level initiate opened it, then stood aside with his eyes averted while Chydaeus stepped across the threshold into an ostentatious hall. It was absurdly large, with a twenty-foot ceiling and two red-carpeted staircases curving to a second floor, where Aylward's vain statue of himself had been replaced by one of the Empyrea in her equine form, great wings arced so high above her head they almost touched.

Another initiate, a second-level this time, wordlessly motioned him to follow. Ah, Chydaeus thought. He'd probably been given a trial of silence, abnegating speech for a predetermined amount of time. One of the more difficult tasks, usually given to the more obstinate Midnighters, those prone to curses and complaints. But failure meant being demoted back to a first-level, or worse: being expelled from the Circle altogether.

The second-level initiate stopped in front of an entrance to what was once Aylward's grand hall—the place he'd have held parties and banquets or conducted provincial business. Now it was empty, save for a quartet of black high-backed chairs situated on the dais. These were occupied by the first doyen of each of the four factions, with Grandmaster Fidelis's chair placed more prominently forward of the other three.

"Ah, Friend Chydaeus." Fidelis beckoned him in, and Chydaeus bowed deeply. Were he lower than a fourth-level initiate, he'd be expected to kneel or fully prostrate himself on the floor. Soon, he'd only have to give a nod when the Grandmaster spoke to him.

The next part was scripted; Chydaeus knew every word by heart.

"Welcome, initiate," Fidelis said and rose from his chair. "What is it that brings you before us this day?"

Chydaeus said, "I wish to demonstrate my loyalty unto the Empyrea and, by extension, fealty to the Circle Midnight, a society of her disciples devoted to facilitating her return to the earth, and the subsequent purification thereof."

"I acknowledge your request," Fidelis said. "Do my colleagues acknowledge it?"

The other three faction leaders gave solemn nods.

"The request has been heard and acknowledged. I, Fidelis the Fourteenth, do hereby grant permission for you, Friend Chydaeus, to proceed into the fifth task of initiation, which I have chosen for you and will now outline."

Chydaeus stood perfectly still as Fidelis approached him. "The fifth rite, as you know, is to ascertain your ability to soundly employ the Circle's values in passing judgment. To do so, we will present you with three individuals who have been recently caught breaking our rules. I will tell you the nature of their crimes and you will decide their sentences. Two of them will be exonerated. One must be convicted. It is up to you to decide which is which."

He waved at the second-level initiate waiting at the door, and he nodded and pulled it open. Two fifth-levels, dressed in their

Circle-assigned armor, herded three prisoners in before them, prodding them with the end of their spears like cattle. Two men, one woman, and all chained at their ankles and wrists.

Fidelis had said the people Chydaeus would be judging were members of the Circle Midnight, too, but these people were dressed like outsiders, in breeches and old tunics instead of their robes. Chydaeus tried to keep from sneering; it would not do to show any kind of premade judgment before he'd heard the prisoners' crimes, no matter their appearance.

"Latro, step forward," said Fidelis, and the first man obeyed. "Tell us, Friend Latro, what you did to land yourself in this . . . unpleasant . . . situation?"

Latro looked at his feet as he spoke, his voice mild. "I stole from you, Grandmaster."

"What is it that you stole?"

"Your medallion, Grandmaster. I was stationed here, as your personal attendant. And one night, when you were sleeping, I snuck to your bedside, where your medallion was set."

"And then . . . ?"

"I took your medallion, Grandmaster. And then I fled."

"What were you going to do with the medallion?"

"I thought of maybe sellin' it, Grandmaster. I don't know." Tears were running down his dirty face. "It was a mistake. I was caught almost as soon as I left the building. Please, Grandmaster. Demote me back to a level-one. I will work in the kilns. Or in the privies. No task will be too low for me. Let me show my humility."

"You may step back, Latro," Fidelis said with a wave of his hand.

"Caedis." He called the woman forward. "Friend Caedis, your question is the same. What crime did you commit to end up here?"

Caedis did not look down at her feet. Instead, she looked right into Fidelis's eyes. "Murder, Lord Grandmaster."

"Please elaborate."

"There was a woman I worked with in the armory. Another level-three like me. I don't know what her name is—was. While our fifth-level watcher was around, she was perfectly well-behaved. Obedient and quiet, but as soon as we were alone, she would begin to say things. All manner of things."

"What, pray tell, did the woman say?"

Caedis swallowed, and her mouth puckered. "I prefer not to repeat it, Grandmaster."

"In this one instance," he said, "you may."

Friend Caedis nodded. "She said that the Circle Midnight was a benighted organization, led by a charlatan."

"And then what did you do, Friend Caedis?"

"I took one of the swords from the armory fire," she said, "and I stuck her with it."

"Where did you stick her with it?"

Caedis did not flinch. "Right in her lying face."

Fidelis nodded. "Step back, Friend Caedis." He turned to the last man in the row. "Meraclus. Your turn. Tell us of your crime."

Meraclus did not look at Fidelis, training his eyes instead upon Chydaeus. "I can tell you what I was detained for," he replied. "Though I still cannot see how it constitutes a crime."

"Fine," Fidelis said. "Tell us what you were detained for."

"I—I am a member of the second faction, Lord Grandmaster. A feral mage."

"And?"

"I have been a member of the Circle for six years, Lord Grandmaster. I was approached by other Circle members after my brother —also a feral mage—was executed for witchcraft by the Tribunal. They recruited me into it. I was a fifth-level initiate within a year, and a fully vested member after two."

"And yet, here you are before us. Why?" Fidelis was tapping his finger on the arm of his chair, already impatient with the man's reticence.

"I am here," Meraclus said, "because I told several other members of my faction about a project I worked on with you last year. It—it was a poison, of sorts, with *blood* as its base—whose, I do not know. But we altered it with spells, turning it from a deadly poison to a full contagion. I don't even know all that was done to it, as there were people from every faction working on the project, and we were not allowed to fraternize with each other. As a feral mage, I've always been dedicated to balance, and to appreciation of the natural order of things. And this . . . thing . . . we created was the exact opposite. It was . . . unholy."

Chydaeus felt a shiver go down his spine as Meraclus turned again to him and said urgently, "When I heard about the fever that has been spreading across the Western Realms, I knew at once that it was that selfsame poison. How could I not know? How many sicknesses can there be that end with the infected crying tears of black? It wasn't the Empyrea's doing. It was *ours*."

"That's quite enough," Fidelis said.

The two fifth-level sentries stepped forward, stuffing a gag into Meraclus's mouth and pulling him back into line with the other two prisoners. They could not, however, muzzle the intensity of his gaze, which did not waver from Chydaeus.

"Well," Fidelis said, quickly regaining his composure. "You've now heard the crimes, Friend Chydaeus. Pass your judgment."

Chydaeus walked to the first prisoner, the man who'd attempted to steal from the Grandmaster himself. "Friend Latro," he intoned, "you are hereby pardoned." He took another step forward, coming to stand in front of the murderess. "Friend Caedis," he said. "You, too, are hereby pardoned."

In front of the last man, he paused.

Fidelis asked, "There is only one option left, Chydaeus, but you must still pronounce it. To Friend Meraclus, what do you say?"

"Condemnation," Chydaeus said, keeping his face a mask of calm.

"So be it." Fidelis stood. "Take those two away," he commanded the fifth-levels. "Leave the condemned here to receive his punishment."

Meraclus was whimpering behind his gag, wriggling forward in his chains in a pitiful attempt to snag Chydaeus's hem, like a worm.

"Tell me, Friend Chydaeus," Fidelis said. "What made you choose to condemn this man, and let the other two go free?"

"Latro and Caedis both did wrong, I will freely admit," Chydaeus said. "But Latro did not seek to thwart the Circle's teachings—he understood his place in it, and welcomed the opportunity to remain in it, even if it came with a demotion in initiate rank. Caedis's crime was even more grave, but it was done in defense of the Circle Midnight. But this man." Chydaeus cast a blistering glance at Meraclus. "He has been actively spouting lies . . . about our organization and about the nature of the Bitter Fever, which we all know was sent by the Empyrea herself, as a means of cleansing the earth in preparation for her imminent arrival. Even as he stood before me, he sought to sow doubt in me. No. Such a man will never be one of us. He is a blight upon the Circle Midnight, and must, therefore, be cut out."

Fidelis smiled. "Welcome, Friend Chydaeus, to the fifth level of initiation. You have passed with flying colors."

"You mentioned before that I would be facing the fifth and sixth rites," Chydaeus said.

"And indeed you shall." Fidelis produced a knife from within his robe and handed it to Chydaeus. "The sixth rite is the rite of obedience. You have soundly judged and condemned this man. Now, it will be you who metes out his punishment."

Chydaeus clutched the handle of the knife, and saw Meraclus's eyes go wide at the length of the blade.

"Obey, Chydaeus," Fidelis said. "Obey and become one step closer to full membership within our great order."

Chydaeus took a deep breath, and raised the knife.

32

THEN

ZAN

It was well past dark at the abbey when Zan paused at a window overlooking the outcrop from which the lighthouse jutted, and was surprised to see Sister Cecily alone on a flat strip of wind-scorched grasses. Her wimple was off, her sleeves rolled up, and her apron tied to keep from dragging in the dirt.

She was filling in a grave.

He hobbled down the steep, stone-cut stairs toward her, but she didn't look up as he approached. "You shouldn't be out of bed," she said, shoveling dirt over the shroud-wrapped body at the bottom of the shallow rectangle.

"Let me help you," he said. He grabbed a second shovel that was leaning up against the abbey wall. He was still a little weak, but he couldn't just stand there while she performed such a labor by herself. "It's a terrible chore to have to do alone."

"I volunteered," Cecily said, eyes misty. "Just to get away for a minute. And to render a service to these Sisters that I could not do for Prudence. You'd think after so many years, I shouldn't be so hurt about her loss." She sniffed. "But she was always my favorite, you know? Even after she had to leave."

"Let me guess," Zan said gently. "Priests?"

Cecily laughed, but it turned into a sob. "Now I *know* you knew her." She wiped her nose on her sleeve and said, "First Syric, and now this . . ."

"What happened in Syric?" Zan asked, shaking another shovelful of dirt onto the coffin below.

"A flood, it sounded like."

Zan froze with his foot on the back of his shovel, half buried in the mound of displaced dirt. "Did they say anything about the king?"

"No," Cecily said. "Nothing." She gave him a curious look. "Are you Renaltan? From your accent, I would have said you were Achlevan."

"I have . . . family . . . in Syric," Zan said. "I hope they're all right."

"If you want to send a message," Cecily said, "you can use one of our pigeons. Aveline is our bird keeper, but she probably won't notice if we borrow one."

"Is that a good idea?" Zan asked. "She already doesn't seem to like me much."

"She doesn't like anyone. Don't take it personally. Not on a good day like today."

"You think that today was . . . *good?*"

"Only three graves," she said, leaning on her shovel. "And with your friend's fever breaking, too? I'd call it a good day."

"How many others have you—?" he began, but stopped when he followed her gaze down the strip of grass, which was marked in regular intervals by patches of recently disturbed soil.

There were *dozens.*

"Things keep going how they've been going," Cecily said, "we won't have enough anchorites to keep the abbey running."

"I'm surprised you have enough already," Zan said. "I can't imagine spiders and celibacy are a big draw for new recruits."

That elicited a laugh. Cecily said, "How easily you have summed up our sisterhood into two words! Tell me, Tom, what do you think it is, this sacred torch that we have sworn our lives to?"

His eyes flicked to the lighthouse, strobing as the lantern turned upon its track.

"A good guess," Cecily said. "But a wrong guess nonetheless."

"All right," Zan said. "What is the sacred torch if not the lighthouse over which you keep watch?"

"You're thinking too concretely. What else might a torch be? What else brings light to darkness?"

Unbidden, Zan's first thought was of Aurelia. "Love?" he asked, almost inaudibly.

"Closer," Cecily said. "And commendably sweet. But no, the answer you are looking for is: knowledge. The founders of our sisterhood built the order to protect a sacred knowledge they feared would be lost to time or destroyed by oppositional forces. Seems a shame to have made it unscathed for a thousand years only to be undone by a fever."

Did "oppositional forces" mean the Tribunal? "Were the first Sisters mages?" Zan asked.

"Mages?" she scoffed. "Mages are too easily led astray by their power . . . too easily corrupted by its temptations, too easily controlled by their need *for* control. No, my dear. This settlement was begun by the *widows* of mages. Those who saw their loved ones lose their fight with and for magic, and were forced to carry on with the burden of pain afterward." She tilted her head, studying him. "What's the matter? Did I say something troubling?"

"No, no," Zan said hurriedly. "It's just that . . . I know what that feels like. To love someone . . . gifted . . . with magic. And then lose them. To it. Because of it."

"Well, then," Cecily said. "Perhaps you're in the right place here on Widows' Isle. Welcome to the sisterhood." She had laid the last of the dirt and was now smoothing it with the back of her shovel. "The abbess, I'm certain, would not approve. But we are rather short on staff these days."

"I've yet to meet the abbess," Zan said.

"Oh, but you have met," Cecily said, kneeling to pat the top of the new grave. "There you go, Abbess. May your soul find peace in the After."

Awkwardly, Zan asked, "I'd have thought that someone of such a station would have been laid to rest with more . . . pomp and circumstance."

"Usually, that would be the case. There would be a week of

mourning, with her body lying in repose upon the sanctorium altar, and every night a Sister would write and present a page of tribute to the deceased. At the end of the week, the late Sister's codex—her own writings, coupled with those tributes written after her passing —would be bound and laid in our Sacred Archive, where Incense of Aranea would be burned in her honor. But when you're burying several Sisters a day, all of those traditions go out the window."

"We could still do something for them," Zan said. "Even if it's small."

"I do know where the Incense of Aranea is kept," she said, thoughtfully tapping her chin. "Though it's not something we usually share with outsiders."

"But I'm not an outsider," Zan said. "You may recall that I was recently welcomed into the sisterhood."

"That you were," she agreed. "Well, Tom. Allow me to show you what the Sisters of the Sacred Torch have to offer outside of spiders and celibacy."

★

Incense of Aranea, it turned out, was a little more potent than the typical scented sachet or wooden taper. It was a coil of resin and wood powder imbued with aromatic herbs—seemingly innocuous at first sight—that the Sisters kept in a locked box in the back of a locked cupboard in the back of a locked room. And Cecily didn't have even one of the keys; she picked all three locks with two wimple pins.

That should have been Zan's first clue.

"Aha!" she said when the lockbox tumbler clicked and the lid popped open. "Now to the archive; that's where the braziers are kept."

She tucked the box under her arm and whispered, "Follow me, and keep *very* quiet."

"Should I be worried that what we're doing is going to get us in trouble?"

"Probably," she said, pulling a lantern from its hook in the wall and handing it to him. "But I'm pretty sure the abbess isn't going to object."

In the darkness, everything within the abbey's white walls was as though painted in shades of cool cobalt. Zan's lantern was a tiny pinprick of yellow against that tapestry of blue, weaving in and out of the abbey's meandering halls. He kept close to Cecily, knowing that if he got separated from her he'd never be able to retrace his steps again. When they stepped into an atrium, the light was caught and scattered by clouds of crisscrossing threads covering every surface.

"Sister Cecily," Zan hissed. "Is this . . . ?"

"Relax," she whispered. "Stay on the path and the spiders will leave you alone, I promise. We raise them to be docile so we can collect their silk without getting bitten. See?" She stopped and put her finger up to an overhanging branch, and a spider the size of a coin crawled onto it. Its abdomen was glossy and black, like a cabochon cut from polished onyx. Its legs were spindly and impossibly long, narrowing into delicate, daggerlike points. In the dark, the semicircular mark on its back shone the same ethereal silver as a winter star.

"Aren't they beautiful?" Cecily asked, lifting it for him to see.

Zan was mesmerized. How could something that had caused him so much pain have any right to be so lovely? And even though the bite on his neck still ached, he reached out and asked, "May I hold it?"

"Certainly," Cecily said, "if you're not afraid."

He stood very still as she coaxed the spider onto the back of his hand.

"They're very special," Cecily said as he let the spider slowly wander the length of his arm. "Can't find them anywhere else in the world. Abbey lore says that they were made when the Spinner was learning how to use her magic. The story goes that she was sewing strands of quicksilver and moonlight into a feral spell knot when she pricked her finger with her needle, drawing a single drop of blood. When the blood fell onto the spell, it transformed the knot into a spider—a creation new to the world, made without any goddess's permission or interference. Some would call it a miracle. Others, an abomination." Cecily tilted her head. "I think it is both and neither."

"The Spinner?" Zan asked, interested. He turned his hand over and the spider moved with it. "I've never heard that story or that name before, and my uncle, with whom I was very close, was an avid collector of such tales; he was an Assembly Mage before it fell."

Cecily said, "The Assembly fell because of its own hubris—believing itself to know all the answers when it didn't even have half the questions."

The spider came to rest in the hollow of Zan's palm, a black star of eight points. The longer he held it, the easier it was to believe that it *was* a spell brought to life with blood.

"Do you have all the questions?" he asked, lifting his hand to let the spider wander back to its home in the silk-swathed trees.

"No," she said. "But I'm finding more to ask every day." Then she beckoned him on. "This way."

In any other places of worship, the focus of the construction was always the sanctorium chapel. But in the Abbey of the Sisters of the Sacred Torch, the library archive was the centerpiece around which the rest of the complex had been built; in comparison, the sanctorium was barely an afterthought, more useful to the Sisters as an infirmary than a chapel.

Instead of timber and plaster, the library was built of quarried stone; even the shelves—of which there were hundreds—were made of marble instead of lowly wood. And underfoot, tiles of colored enamel were laid into every inch of the floor and lined with silver. The designs were as fantastical as they were graphical, with organic shapes of animals commingling with crisscrossing geometrical lines and alchemical figures—a celestial map, he realized as he walked, with all the constellations laid out in their corresponding quadrants, and old words lining the edge in a circle: *Humilitas, Abnegatio, Forti-tudo . . .*

"If you think that's impressive," Cecily said, noticing his eyes on the floor, "just wait."

They had come to the very center of the room, where a brass brazier waited on a circular stone table. She removed a coil of incense from the lockbox and placed it into the brazier, then took the candle from Zan's lantern to light it. It needed a second to catch, but then let out a smoke that smelled of bergamot oil and cedar, with a touch of juniper leaves and icy lavender . . . and something else . . . a rich and vivid scent he couldn't quite place. In fact, *all* of this had an odd air of familiarity to him.

While he was still trying to figure it out, Cecily had moved across the room and was touching the candle wick to another burner. This one sparked as it caught, and a line of flame climbed a column until it reached another burner, hanging twelve feet off the ground. The fire forked there, splitting in two lines that burned across a brass trough high over their heads. It met and split, met and split, and soon the entire room was aglow.

Zan's jaw dropped. Because, while incredible, the radiant lighting system served only to illuminate another marvel.

It was an orrery on a grand scale, stretching from one side of the library ceiling to the other. Brass planets, several feet in diameter, were mounted upon looping rings while stars of mirrored glass dangled between. It circled a center point on the floor, where a pedestal stood with an ancient book lying open under a sealed luneocite cloche.

"I've never seen anything like it," Zan said in hushed reverence, his gaze moving from the orrery to the pedestal and back again. It was impossible to take it all in at once. "Never in my life. Does it move?"

"It used to," Cecily answered. "In the Spinner's day."

"That is the second time you've mentioned the Spinner," Zan said.

"That's because this is where she was raised," Cecily said. "Before this became a nunnery, it was an outpost built by eight mages who believed that there would, one day, be born a mortal child with power that could rival the Empyrea's own. A mage who could use all three types of magic at once. This is her Codex," Cecily said, indicating the book on the pedestal. "All of the nuns make them now, but this was the first. It's a collection of her writings, done in her own hand."

"The Spinner," he said, stepping toward the book to peer at it through the glass. But it was hard to make out the words; the light from the radial brazier began to bleed into wisps that danced across his vision. He blinked several times, but the light only smeared more, this time taking new shapes. "Are you seeing this?" he asked.

"Yes," Cecily said, smiling. "It means the incense is working."

"What is in it," he asked as one of the light streaks morphed into a humanlike shape, "to make me start seeing things?"

"Little of this, little of that." Cecily was reaching out her hand to touch something in front of her that he couldn't see. "Essence of sombersweet, venom from the crescent spiders, virgin's blood, poppyseed milk."

"You said that you burn this stuff at funerals." Zan's head felt light, and his heart had begun to pound.

"We do," Cecily said dreamily. "What better way to say goodbye to our dead than to do it face to face?"

Zan coughed on the sweet-smelling smoke, suddenly angry. *"You're calling up the dead?"*

"Not the actual dead," Cecily said. "Not *ghosts*. Just the illusion of them. You said you lost someone, didn't you? Don't you want to see that person again? To tell them how much you miss them?"

And that's when Zan realized why the floor design had seemed so familiar. It was because he'd seen it before, on a smaller scale. It was the pattern that Rosetta had woven out of quicksilver string at the top of Aren's tower while she smudged the air with sombersweet smoke. The spell that had sent Aurelia into the Gray.

When he looked down at his feet, a pool of mirrorlike liquid had begun to spread across the floor.

33

NOW

AURELIA

6 DAYS TO MIDWINTER
1621

I tried not to look at the spider scar as I applied salve to the cut under Castillion's chin, but found my eyes kept straying to it anyway. It looked like a brand, puckered and purple.

"You wouldn't remember me," Rosetta was saying. "You never saw me. But I saw you."

Castillion's face had become drawn, listening to Rosetta so ably recount events that had existed, until now, only in his own memory. I tried to keep my own expression blank and calm, but each new detail of that night, thirteen years ago, made the task more and more difficult. The story came together in disparate pieces: Frost and snow. The tinkling of sleigh bells in the distance. A tree with the seven-legged spider carved into its bark. A glade in the Ebonwilde, something terrible sealed within it.

"That's why none of them ever returned," Castillion whispered. "It wasn't because *they* killed them. It was because *you* did. The wardens, I mean. Why?"

"If I knew all of the whys," Rosetta said, "I might have had an easier time keeping the tradition going. But I was made warden without training. I only knew what I saw my grandmother and sister do that night I snuck away to follow them. Imagine my surprise when I returned to the spot a century later and found that my quarry was not a man of eight decades, but a child of twelve years." She looked away, knuckles against her lips as she murmured, "I should have done it. I should have done it anyway. And now they're free."

"They are not what you think." He hissed as I dabbed a cold cloth on the cut, but kept his eyes trained on the ceiling. "The Verecundai is what we call them. Seven mages who were cursed by Adamus Castillion to remain trapped in that Ebonwilde glade as long as the Castillion line existed to maintain Adamus's spell. Every one hundred years, my family sent one of its sons to the Verecundai as sacrifice to keep it going. Usually, it was an older male of the line, but my father died in a mining accident a few months earlier." He shrugged. "I had two half siblings close to my age who might have qualified, but my stepmother chose me. I was the oldest anyway, and if I was out of the way, her sons would inherit everything."

"Stars above," I whispered.

"I wasn't angry," he said. "I went into it thinking I was doing something good. For the world. For my family. I expected to find death in those trees. What I found, instead, was truth."

"*Their* truth," Rosetta said. "You can't trust anything they've told you—"

Castillion said vehemently, "*They* helped direct me after my stepmother died and my half brothers drank and brawled themselves into early graves. Without the Verecundai's foresight, there would be no Trove. No stored grain, no livestock, no metalworks . . . Everything that we have at Fort Castillion now, we owe to their warnings."

"All that time you were conquering Achlevan provinces and subjugating their citizens to servitude . . . you were acting on the knowledge that eventually all of this would happen?" I tried to withhold my anger. "Why did you not say so? Why not warn everyone else?"

"And what would you or any other monarch have said if I brought such things to their attention?"

I bit my lip. "You could have at least tried."

"I did try once," he said. "I arranged a meeting with King Domhnall during Petitioner's Day right before the wall fell."

A memory came to me of Kate with me in the market square on Petitioner's Day, as she named the Achlevan lords on the stand and pointed out one with white hair, calling him Castillion. It was odd now, remembering it. Castillion was just a stranger then. Just a name. And now he was . . . what?

I glanced at him sideways, trying to figure out how this man and his dark eyes and white hair had moved from stranger, to antagonist, to ally, to . . . friend? *Was* he my friend now? Or just an annoyingly likable enemy? Or . . . something else altogether? It was a possibility I wasn't prepared to examine, let alone name.

Castillion was still talking, unaware of my eyes on him. "Domhnall laughed me out of the room. I left, and three days later, he was dead."

I finally asked, "All your ships and buildings and plans . . . those all came from the Verecundai?"

"They told me what was to come," Castillion said. "I had to decide what to do about it."

"So they helped you navigate these calamities," Rosetta barked, "but none of these preparations you made would have even been necessary if they'd stayed locked in the glade where they belonged."

"Nothing stays locked away forever," Castillion said. "Even if you had killed me that night, could you have kept going back every hundred years? To kill again and again and again? And who would have taken up the task after you? Your child? Your grandchild?"

"I'll never have a child," Rosetta said flatly.

"You see, then?" he said. "The system would have failed eventually, somewhere down the line."

Castillion was trying to comfort her, I realized in surprise. To assuage her guilt for choosing not to execute him.

"You were so small," she said, almost inaudibly. "So scared. Shivering in the cold and whispering to yourself. And I was so angry. At my grandmother and Galantha for leaving the task to me, and at you, for being so young. But if I had known you would set them free—"

"I did not set them free," he replied. "Not really. They are still trapped, just . . . trapped with me, instead of in the Ebonwilde. That's what this scar is." He tapped his chest, over his heart. "I can still call them, if I so choose. But I'm not sure how it will go if I do. You have some . . . history with them, Aurelia."

"I've never met them. How can we have 'history'?"

"Does that mean . . . Is she . . . ?" Rosetta said.

"Am I *what?*" I demanded. "What do I have to do with any of this?"

Rosetta was looking at me with a new expression on her face. "It makes sense now. Those dreams you used to have . . . the ones you told me about, back in Achleva? I thought it was just glimpses of the future you'd gotten from the Gray . . . a side effect of almost dying . . . but what I saw you do just now, with Nathaniel . . ."

"What are you *talking* about?" I asked, growing more exasperated with each passing second.

"And the healing," she continued. "Where you could take others' wounds as your own. It was an anomaly, to be sure, but I wrote it off. I didn't pay close enough attention . . . one impossibility after another . . ."

Castillion took my hand and helped me to my feet. "I should have told you before," he said. "That night on the *Humility*, probably. And when I woke you in the Night Garden, certainly. But there were always reasons to put it off . . . you were in such a state when you first woke, and then you ran . . ."

"Castillion," I said softly, pleadingly. "Please. What is this all about?"

"The statue," he said, "in the Night Garden. Do you remember it?"

"Yes. You said it was of a pair of lovers. Adamus and Vieve. And that you were descended from his brother's line, and that I am descended from her sister."

"You and I," he said, moving his hands to my face, "we are not simply descended from them. We *are* them."

I had no response, and Castillion continued.

"Part of the curse laid upon the Verecundai was that they would remain in their forest prison until those they had betrayed—Adamus and Vieve—were reborn into those family lines. The tradition my family followed, sending their sons to the Verecundai, originated as a test, to verify whether or not Adamus's soul had been reborn."

Rosetta was pacing now. "And my family must have begun their *own* tradition to prevent those sons from ever reaching the glade. So even if the eighth mage of the Verecundai was reborn, he'd never know his true nature, and the remaining seven would never be freed." Her yellow eyes gleamed in the firelight. "Until the task fell upon me, and I could not hurt a twelve-year-old boy, abandoned in the dark."

"So . . ." I started, trying to put the bizarre pieces together. "You think *I* am the reincarnation of . . . Vieve?"

"Vieve was known as the Spinner," Rosetta said. "Able to work all three types of magic at once, and weave them together. And from what I've seen you do . . ." She let the sentence trail off.

"I am certain that's who you are," Castillion said softly. "And not just because the Verecundai wanted me to kill you. Not just because your abilities are extraordinary and vast . . . I am certain because in the minute I saw you, I *knew* you." His voice dropped. "I know you, Aurelia."

✦

I spent that night in Galantha's room once again, though I only managed to tread the waters of the twilight stage of slumber, never sinking into deeper depths. Whenever my thoughts *did* manage to wander past the wispy edge into something close to dreaming, my thoughts invariably snapped back to the Spinner, Vieve—this formidable figure of the long-distant past, able to work all three types of magic at once, who was somehow tied to me.

No, not just tied to me. If what Castillion and Rosetta insisted was true, she *was* me.

I sat up in the bed and put my feet down on the floor, letting myself feel the solidness of it beneath my feet before going to the dresser where Galantha's mirror sat under a shroud.

Tentatively, I wound my fingers into the fabric and pulled it, inch by inch, from the frame. Then I sat on the stool in front of it and examined its empty reflection.

In a hushed voice, I said, "Show yourself."

And slowly, the uncanny version of me began to materialize in the weathered glass.

She lifted her hand and placed each finger against her side of the glass. I followed, until she and I looked like a true reflection of the other, hands pressed together, separated by two planes: one of glass, the other, a state of existence.

"Who are you?" I asked.

I am you, came the answer. And, across the mirror and upon the backs of my lids, images began to form.

I was seeing through a pair of eyes that were not my own, accessing memories of things I had never experienced.

Much of it was wildly wonderful—a golden machine of moving planets, the surge of joy upon casting a new spell, the taste of a kiss on my lips, the face of its giver blurred through half-closed eyes and a curtain of eyelashes—before it turned dark. Soon I was overwhelmed with memories of cold and flying snow, a sharp pain in my ribs and the sight of a sky roiling with the white fire of a Goddess's rage.

With a cry, I pulled my hand away from the mirror and everything diminished into the silvered glass. As it cleared, a series of distant thoughts came into my mind, unbidden, and in a voice not quite my own.

Be strong, my child, for in the Ebonwilde,
Bonds will break and blood will flow
Get up, my child, cast your fears aside
Steel your heart and strike the blow.

I grabbed my cloak and flew down the stairs, past Nathaniel still unconscious on the kitchen table and out the door into the snow. I headed in the direction of the sombersweet meadow. It was a magic place, the place where the Mother goddess, the Ilithiya, had died after making the world, leaving behind the sombersweet flower and a mortal daughter, Nola. When I was last here, the flowers were in full spring bloom even though it was nearing the end of autumn outside the homestead. It was a sacred, protected place, Rosetta had said at the time. One that never stopped blooming. And I needed a reminder that there was still beauty in the world, still life.

But when I reached it, the scene was not at all what I had hoped to see. Instead, a sea of shriveled blossoms and stalks bent low under the weight of snow.

Even this meadow, once full of the Mother goddess's divinity, was dead.

I heard the sound of his boots in the snow before I turned and saw him. "I know that it's a lot to take in," he said.

"My entire life," I said, "I've struggled against the ties that have bound me. With the magic I couldn't help, against a system I didn't build, propelled down one path after another that I didn't choose. And now you tell me that I'm not even *me*."

"You are still the person you've always been," Castillion said. "You *are* still you. You are just also . . ."

"The Spinner," I said.

"Yes."

"And you are . . . ?"

"The person who loved the Spinner." Seeing my expression, he asked, "Am I not allowed to care about you?"

"I wish you didn't."

"Do you care what happens to me?"

I said, "I wish I didn't."

He took a few cautious steps toward me, the slash of his dark brows making a V underneath the fall of his white hair. There had always been a regality to his features—high cheekbones, sharp jawline, generous mouth—but against the moon-gilt snow and the lavender-tinted shadows of the forest, he was something otherworldly. Slowly, carefully, he took my hand in both of his and then drew it to his lips. His soft kiss against my fingers sent warmth blooming across my cold skin, like the petals of an apricot rose.

"Command me, my queen," he murmured. "I will obey."

34

THEN

KELLAN

A farmer in a fishing boat found Kellan and Emilie two days after the disaster in Syric.

When he heard their shouts, and looked up to find two people waving at him from within the broken clockface, he'd nearly pitched backwards out of his boat in surprise.

They had to climb down the outside of the clock tower first, then swim several feet in the frigid floodwater to get to where he could reach them and pull them into his boat.

Emilie leaned over the edge of the boat to stare at the submerged city as they passed over it, its tin roofs and cobblestone streets visible only as ghostly shapes in the murky, bottle-green water. "Have you found many other survivors?" Kellan asked hopefully.

The farmer shook his head between pulls of the oars, sad and weary. "You're the first for me."

He brought them to a rendezvous point on a parcel of ground a mile or so outside the city, where folk from the surrounding towns outside of the flood path had gathered to see what they could do. There were rows and rows of sheet-covered bodies, lined up so that friends and family could peer at them in turn, searching for familiarity in the water-bloated faces. It was excruciating to watch, as the only thing worse than finding a loved one among the dead was *not* finding them, because that meant that they would likely never be recovered, leaving a maddening question mark where a definitive period should be.

Kellan and Emilie found the section for the bodies pulled from the palace, where the water had receded enough to allow rescuers to search the upper levels. Most of those who had been recovered were courtiers and serving staff, some of whom Kellan knew from his days at Aurelia's side. Emilie, too, knew more than a few.

Kellan joined her as she bent to pull the sheet from the last body in the palace's row. "Oh, Pelton," she murmured as the face came into view. "He was eccentric, but he was never unkind," she said sadly. "Empyrea keep him."

"No sign of Conrad," Kellan said, helping Emilie re-cover Pelton's face. "I've looked up and down these rows twice."

"I told you," Emilie replied. "He won't be here. He's with the Circle." As if saying their name could somehow summon them, she looked nervously around.

"Then that is where I need to go," Kellan said, knowing it to be true. "I have to find him, rescue him, bring him home . . ." He trailed off, and then said in a softer voice, "I would like you to come with me."

Her eyes glazed over with a base, instinctual terror. "No," she said, "I can't. I can't face them. You don't know . . ."

"I don't," Kellan said evenly. "I don't know. I need someone to teach me. I need someone to *help* me." Saying such a thing aloud felt strange; he was not used to asking for help from anyone. "Please, Emilie. Help me." Quieter, he added, "I will not let any harm come to you. I swear it."

She took two unsteady breaths and searched his face. Then she said, "All right, Lord Greythorne. I will help you."

"Thank you," he said, taking her hand in his good one. "And please . . . use my first name. Kellan."

With a wry smile, she said, "As you wish, Lord Kellan Greythorne."

In spite of himself—in spite of everything—he laughed.

★

They left the survivors' camp that same night, alone in the dark with no food, no clothing, no supplies between them. But this wasn't the first time Kellan had been forced to make the best of bad circumstances. On the way to Achleva with Aurelia, he'd hunted field grouse and made meals of rock cress. At least this time the foe was ahead of them instead of behind.

Emilie believed the Circle's next moves would be to sweep up the coast and take over as many cities and towns as they could as quickly as possible, leaving no time for word to spread and other settlements to prepare. With that in mind, they headed northwest, toward Graves and De Lena. After three days of walking and surviving on the nuts and seeds they raided from some poor squirrel's winter cache, they came to a lonely farmhouse. They stopped, hoping to beg a meal and a safe place to sleep for a night. When no one answered, they let themselves in.

Emilie had taken only a few steps inside the door when she stopped in her tracks. "Wait! Kellan! Do you smell that?"

The room was pervaded with the scent of decay, and it didn't take long to find out where it was coming from; the lady of the house was lying dead in the doorway to the kitchen, though there seemed to be no sign of trauma. Kellan bent to roll her over, but Emilie caught his arm before he could.

"Don't. Touch. Her," she said. "No skin-to-skin contact, understand?"

Kellan retrieved a thick stick from a tree outside and nudged the body over. He saw that the woman had black tears streaking down from her sightless eyes.

"What *is* this?" he asked Emilie. "What could do this to her?"

"The Bitter Fever," she said, as though the words were rusty on her tongue from disuse. "Fidelis the First wrote about it in his Midnight Papers. It's . . . a plague unlike any before it, a sickness that kills by showing a person their sins, and they die crying the impurities from their soul."

They slept in the hayloft of the barn, huddled close for warmth. In the morning, they harnessed the farmer's two horses and filled up the saddlebags with dried goods from the cellar before setting the house alight. The trail of smoke left in the sky was visible for miles down the road.

For weeks they traveled in the Circle's blackened, body-ridden wake, listening for any sign that the child-king of Renalt might be with them. But the more they saw, the more Kellan began to harbor the bleak thought that perhaps it would be better if Conrad had died in the floods of Syric.

They made it as far as Gaskin when the Circle started closing off their territory, sending troops of Midnighters to patrol the edges every night, looking for escapees who had eluded conscription and assimilation into the Circle's rigid hierarchy. Kellan and Emilie took to camping outside the patrol range, making plans about how to get to the other side, and what they'd do when they got there.

Kellan was returning from a successful hunt for that night's dinner, two quail slung over his shoulder, when he heard voices coming from their newest campsite. He ducked into the nearest trees just in time to watch a small squad of six armored Midnighters marching Emilie away from the campsite. Her small, pale face was rigid with dread, and Kellan felt his heart twist at the sight of it. He'd promised to keep her safe, and led her right up to danger's door.

There was no time to wait or plan; he could not let them take Emilie back to the cult she'd worked so hard to escape.

And so he set down the quail. He crept after them and within minutes attacked from behind, able to break one soldier's neck and embed his dagger in the back of another before the remaining four even heard a sound. But when the second soldier fell, he took Kellan's dagger with him, leaving him unarmed.

Well, mostly unarmed.

Kellan imagined himself back in the arena at Syric, letting the thrill of the fight drain the fear from his limbs. And, almost without his knowing it, his right hand became a blade, and his punches became punctures, blood flying with each stab and swing.

Soon, five Midnighters were dead on the road, but the sixth was backing away, with his knife pushed up against Emilie's ribs. "We don't have to fight, Friend," the Midnighter said. "Join us. Join us, and I will let her go. The Empyrea could use more fighters like you; she waits to welcome you both into her fold."

Kellan didn't have to look at Emilie's face to know that she would rather die than be returned to the Circle, but he relented anyway. "All right," he said, letting his quicksilver hand morph back into its regular shape and then lifting both hands in the air as a sign of acquiescence. "We'll do as you ask. Just let her go."

"Wise move —" the Midnighter began to say, but the words ended in a pitiful gurgle as a thin spear of metal pierced his throat and came out the other side, a splash of blood spattering Emilie's scarred cheek. The transformation of quicksilver had been lightning fast—so fast the Midnighter had not even seen it coming. It was almost reflexive; Kellan had thought what he wanted the quicksilver to do, and it had obeyed. The Midnighter crumpled into the mud of the road.

Emilie rushed into Kellan's arms and buried her face in his chest as he held her tight and stroked her hair. "I've got you," he murmured, laying his cheek against her head. He used his sleeve to wipe the blood off her cheek. "I've got you."

They returned to the camp and packed it up. "Where are we going now?" Emilie asked, climbing onto her horse.

"East," Kellan said, "to Greythorne."

"We're not going after the Circle anymore?" she asked, surprised.

"I promised you I'd keep you safe," Kellan said grimly. "And I failed you once. I will not let it happen again."

35

NOW

ROSETTA

6 DAYS TO MIDWINTER
1621

Rosetta heard the footsteps on the stair, one light patter that had to be Aurelia, followed shortly thereafter by Dominic Castillion's heavier step. The noise didn't wake her because she hadn't been sleeping. But that wasn't surprising; she never slept. Most nights she transformed into a fox and spent the dark hours patrolling the Ebonwilde. In that form, she could usually forget her humanity enough that it *felt* like sleep—a temporary rest from her worries, at least.

Since last Midwinter, however, her midnight travels had become less and less a respite and more a reminder of her continued failings. Animals and birds grew scarce, the flora never flourished past the first frail buds of spring, and the forest floor was quickly seamed with trains of ragged Renaltan refugees, escaping from the desolation of their fever-ravaged towns and their fallow fields and the looming threat of the Circle Midnight for the promise of prosperity in Dominic Castillion's realm. In any other year, she would have resented the encroachment into her quiet alpine refuge, but she could not blame anyone for it now. And so she lay awake in her bed, trapped in a never-ending cycle of anger, self-remonstration, worry, and fear.

When she heard the door close the second time, she gave up on even maintaining the appearance of sleep and slipped downstairs to stoke the fire before heading to the kitchen to check her ailing patient.

There, she was surprised to see Nathaniel's eyes open and trained on the kitchen ceiling.

"Hello," she said awkwardly; she had not expected him to be conscious yet. "I'm Rosetta. Aurelia's . . . cousin. This is my home; you're safe here."

His eyes flicked to hers. They were black from pupil to iris, a sure sign that he was one of the lucky few who had been afflicted with the Bitter Fever and lived. "Nathaniel," he croaked by way of introduction, and tried to sit up.

"If you must move, do so slowly," she said. "We patched you up well, and you should heal up pretty quickly, but the longer you can keep from putting stress on those stitches, the better. But, here." She hurried to pour him a cup of water, and put her hand under his head to help him bring it to his lips. "Quite the close call you had there, Nathaniel," she said, placing the empty cup into the sink basin. "You're lucky to be alive."

"Am I?" he asked. His voice was stronger now, a baritone rumble that gave her the feeling of bearskin cloaks and robust coffee—rich, and warm, and heavy.

She didn't answer, instead pushing her hair behind her shoulders as she leaned over his chest to check his bandages. She explored one with her fingers, and he inhaled sharply. "Sorry," she said, in a voice too curt to sound like a real apology. "I don't do this kind of thing often. I'm not used to . . . people."

"It's not you. It's not that."

"These accommodations do leave something to be desired," she said. "Your stitches seem to be doing all right. There's a couch in the other room. If you like, I can help you to it."

He nodded slowly, and she helped him maneuver into a sitting position. Then, she had him drape his arm over her shoulders as he put both feet on the floor. A slight groan escaped his lips as he shifted his weight, and she murmured, "Easy, easy," in response.

They hobbled slowly to the cushioned sofa next to the fireplace, and she was glad she'd thought to stoke it already, so there was a nice, steady flame crackling in the hearth when she got him onto it, stuffing blankets and cushions under his back to help prop him up. "Thank you . . ." he said, and after a moment of searching, found her name. "Rosetta."

She gave him a soft smile. "Good memory," she commented with approval.

"Where are we?" he asked, glancing around the room, taking in the heavy wooden eaves and the cracking, hand-painted plaster on the walls.

"My family cottage," she said in reply, suddenly conscious of the building's lived-in eccentricities. "In the Ebonwilde. Nothing fancy, I'm afraid."

"No, no," he said hurriedly. "I was just thinking how much it reminded me of another cottage I used to live in."

"So . . . small and humble?" She gave a tiny, embarrassed laugh.

"Very small," he said with a wan smile and a nod. "Very humble. I miss it. I was happy there."

There was a pause, and his eyes took on a faraway look, as he lost himself in those long-past happy memories. After a moment, he caught himself and cleared his throat. "Aurelia," he said. "Is she . . ."

"Still here," Rosetta replied. "She and Castillion have just gone out for the moment. I'm sure they'll be back soon. After what they told me they saw going on in the Circle Midnight, I'm sure they'll be wanting to get back to Fort Castillion soon. Preparations to be made, if an attack is imminent."

"Yes," Nathaniel said. "I'm sure you will be glad to have us out of your hair."

"Oh, no," Rosetta said. "I'm not sure you're in any shape to—that is, you're welcome to stay here as long as you need. To recover."

"That's very kind of you, but I'll go when they go. If there's a fight, I need to be there for it."

Rosetta knew that look, that tone: the pinched, unassailable compulsion to throw oneself into battle from the front line, despite—or perhaps, because of—injury or ill-preparedness or the impossibility of a happy outcome. She'd seen it before on Kellan, after he'd lost his hand. And it struck her, suddenly, that Nathaniel, too, had recently lost something irreplaceable. Something he thought he could not live without. And she frowned, wishing she was the type of person who knew what kind of words to say to give comfort. To give hope. Instead, she sat idly across from him, awkward and tight-lipped, as the firelight burnished his deep brown skin with warm, coppery glints.

He asked, "Do you know what happened to the pack I was carrying?"

"It's still in the kitchen, I think." And when he started to stand, she shot him a withering glare. "Sit. *Down*. We just got you settled—don't even *think* about trying to move until I give the go-ahead." She moved to the kitchen and found the pack peeking out from beneath the table; he had still been wearing it when they brought him in, and it had been the first thing discarded when they began their work to save his life. She picked it up, cringing. There were two arrows protruding from the leather; if they had made it through to the other side, it was likely that no amount of effort could have saved him.

She brought the bag in and handed it to him. "I do hope there wasn't anything important inside." She said it light-heartedly, but when his eyes fell on the arrow-pierced bundle, he let out a low, wounded, "Oh, no. No."

Without paying any mind to his stitches, he snatched up the pack and snapped the arrows at the head, pulling them free with a great deal more ginger care than she'd used when excising the arrows from his actual flesh. He tossed the freed shafts to the floor, and then carefully pulled a roll of canvas from inside. His eyes were wet as he fingered the tears where the arrows had pierced right through.

"What are they?" she asked cautiously.

"Portraits," he said, "of my wife and daughter. They're all that I have left of them." Slowly, he unrolled them, and Rosetta leaned over to get a better look. The first was split down the side, cutting across the neck and cheek of a woman with soft, doe-like eyes and a sweet smile. "Kate," he said, lightly touching her other cheek. "And Ella." He lifted Kate's portrait, revealing another one of a very small child, but the split went right down the middle of the little girl's face, rendering her featureless.

"May I?" Rosetta asked in a soft voice, and Nathaniel mustered a nod. She took the two canvases and laid them out on the braided rug, side by side. Then she began a spell of healing, not unlike the one she'd used on him. Her fingers danced slowly across the canvases, weaving, binding, rejoining the threads that had been broken. And slowly, the tears kneaded back together, the fragmented images made, once again, whole.

"Thank you," Nathaniel said when it was done. "Empyrea bless you."

"Actually," Rosetta said, lifting the canvases. "I don't worship—" Her words trailed off. "Nathaniel. I know this child."

"What?" Nathaniel asked, forehead wrinkling.

"This little girl," Rosetta said more urgently. "I *know* her."

Nathaniel was shaking his head. "Wait, no—Ella? You can't . . . that's just not possible."

"It was only a few months ago. There was a woman . . . an older woman, who didn't make it. But the baby . . ." Rosetta stared again at the newly mended portrait. "I'd know those eyes anywhere. Nathaniel," she said, her throat constricting. "Nathaniel, your daughter is alive."

36

THEN

ZAN

By lighting incense infused with sombersweet upon an ancient quicksilver spell inlaid into the floor of the abbey's library archive, Cecily had opened a portal into the Gray.

And Zan had gone tumbling backwards into it.

Zan had witnessed this ritual before, at the top of Aren's tower. He was only a spectator then, standing by in anxious agony as Aurelia lay down upon a spell knot of silver string that melted into a mirrored pool. He'd watched as her body went limp, her consciousness slipping from one dimension into another, on a mission to find and retrieve the wardens' lost relic, the Ilithiya's Bell.

Never, never, from her peaceful repose, could Zan have guessed what she'd been experiencing on the other side of that reflection.

The Gray was too simple a name for this world without rules. With no up nor down, no light nor dark. No time. No space. No *self*. Everything and nothing both at once. How had Aurelia faced this madness? How had she swum these impossible depths and come out alive on the other side?

Aurelia.

A ripple went through the clouds of chaos. *Aurelia*, he thought again, treating each soft syllable like a lifeline. He clung to the sound of her name, let it tether him to something he knew was real.

And then, he heard her voice.

"The frustrating thing about a firebird is that death never seems to stick."

Before he could stop himself, Zan turned to the sound as the colorless smoke swirled around him and solidified into white columns in a still sanctorium chapel, silvery moonlight streaming in from a window of colored glass.

No! Zan shouted, but it was too late.

A boy and a girl held each other on the steps of the Stella Regina's dais, caught up in a moment as fragile as a sunlit snowflake, its beauty more heartbreaking for its transience. Though they were ringed by the window's cool blue glow, the light bleeding from the girl's body was warm and golden. She gently touched her fingertips to the boy's face, bringing his forehead down to hers.

"You told me once to stop running and finally let you find me."

Don't show me this, Zan thought, heart in tatters. *Anything but this. I can't watch her die. Not again.*

But here, he was nothing. He was a ghost.

He buried his face in his incorporeal hands as she said her last words in a whisper, but it did no good; this event was etched indelibly upon his memory. He could still see her face turned up to his, her blue eyes brimming with pain he couldn't assuage, trust he didn't deserve, and a love too tender to endure.

"So come and find me."

When he opened his eyes again, the scene had changed. The boy and girl were gone and the stained-glass window was now a void, save for a few recalcitrant shards rimming the frame edge like ragged teeth. Still, Aurelia's coy challenge lingered in the empty air: *Come and find me. Come and find me. Come and find me.*

That's when Zan saw the priest. Father Cesare was framed by the shattered window, his expression mild and vacant, as if his entrails were not looping out of a gash only a few inches lower. It was just like the apparition Zan had encountered on Midwinter Night, the one that had turned into Isobel Arceneaux.

Father Cesare continued into the thorny maze, the light from his candle gleaming in tiny threads through the leafless hawthorn hedge.

"Wait!" Zan said, but his voice was strange and echoey. He turned to see another version of himself following after the bobbing light. He cringed at the sight of himself; he knew he'd been in a bad place, but seeing it made the extent of his wretchedness undeniable. The red-rimmed eyes surrounded by purplish circles, the dirty clothes, the lank hair and hollow cheeks . . . it was difficult to see.

He trailed close behind his Midwinter self, even though he knew what was coming next. And indeed, it happened exactly as he remembered it: He caught up to the apparition, thinking that it was someone who'd been thieving on the Stella Regina's property. The apparition had turned, showing itself first as Father Cesare before melting into the much-altered form of Isobel Arceneaux. He saw his other self retreat in terror, jumping to Madrona's back, and then riding off toward the relative safety of the Quiet Canary.

When his other self was gone, Arceneaux turned and locked her onyx eyes upon him. "Finally," she said, in a voice like the hiss of steam from the lid of a boiling kettle. "Finally, we can speak."

Her image changed once again, this time revealing her true self: a waifish woman, near skin and bones, with both of her hands pressed against the stone at the foot of the Stella Regina's clock tower. In the few months that had passed since the Day of Shades, she had aged decades. Her eyes were still black, and her veins still showed through her skin, but the truth of her was far less terrifying and somehow, far more terrible.

He approached slowly, and she stared up at him like a skittish animal through the thin strings of her once-dark hair. A necklace dangled around her bony neck—a metallic bell in the shape of a sombersweet blossom.

He knelt beside her, eyebrows furrowed. "Arceneaux?" he asked, trying to reconcile this pitiable creature with the powerful leader of the Tribunal who'd strung him up inside the Stella Regina and tortured him for hours.

"I was her," said the waif. "But I am someone else now. Someone . . . new."

"You're the Malefica," he said, understanding.

"That is the name of the other part of me. Or at least what *they* called her," she said. Her head twitched, and she scrambled into an improvised sitting position, folding her knobby knees between her immovable hands. "Those who have hated her. Her true name is much older, and unspeakable by the human tongue."

"What do you want of me?" he asked.

"Release," she said simply. "What you recognize as days has been, for me, years. Your weeks have been my centuries. Your months, my eons. I have been trapped here for a thousand human lifetimes, happening all at once. I wanted to live," she said, in the plaintive bleat of a starving lamb, "to know what it is like to wear mortal flesh. And now I do. I know pain. And cold. And hunger. And thirst. Such terrible, terrible thirst."

"I cannot release you," Zan said. "I have no magic with which to undo the spell."

"Then have mercy, boy, and end my life."

Zan shook his head. "I can't."

"It is what I deserve for what I have done. I did not know . . . before. I was not human, and could not comprehend. But human, I now am. And comprehend, I now do." Her tone sharpened, her lip twitching. *"Give me my end,"* she hissed. Then, "Please."

Zan stood, his eyes going to the fountain of the Stella Regina not far behind her. As he moved toward it, it changed through a multitude of iterations—now only half-built, now an empty field, now broken and covered in moss, now clean and flowing freely. He knew he was not real here, but he lowered his hands into the flickering water and willed himself corporeal enough to bring it out again. It took a few tries—he had to time it right, so that he lifted the water from the basin when the fountain looked most like the one of his own era—but he was able to bring a small amount of water over to the Malefica.

"Here," he said, extending his cupped hands toward her as she glared at him distrustfully. "Drink."

He went back three times to the fountain, and with each swallow of water, her expression lost some of its feral animosity. She did not thank him—he didn't think she knew how—but when the last drop had been drained from his hands, she said, "You have done me a service, even if it was not the end for which I asked. In return, I offer this." She bent her head, and the flower-shaped bell dangled forward. "It will allow you to move through the Gray without leaving your material body behind." When she sensed his reluctance, she added, "It will take you to where she sleeps, waiting for you."

"She?" he asked. "Aurelia? She is not dead?" Zan whispered the question and felt it transform on his tongue into a statement. "She is not dead."

The Malefica smiled, and the clouds of the Gray began to swirl and swell, overtaking them both in a tempestuous rush. When it cleared, the bony, bedraggled version of the Malefica was gone, replaced by an illusion of Isobel Arceneaux in all of her intimidating beauty, no longer pinned to the ground. She took a step forward, and Zan saw that they were not outside of the Stella Regina anymore, but inside a grand sanctorium chapel. The Assembly chapel, he realized as he glanced around in awe. It both matched his uncle Simon's description and still somehow far exceeded it in every way: its high ceilings were higher, its bright windows were brighter, its bold colors bolder. The pews were filled with the skeletal remains of long-lost mages, bowing as if in supplication to the gold-and-glass casket resting at the end of the nave.

"Look and see," Arceneaux said.

Zan's steps started out measured, but gained speed with every stride, until he was running—almost tripping over himself—up the aisle.

Through the glass coffin, he could trace the elegant lines of Aurelia's profile, and the cascading tumbles of her dark, dark hair. Her only covering was a cloth of ivory gossamer that pooled in delicate folds around her body. Her hands were resting softly overtop of it, between the dip of her navel and the swell of her breasts. As he approached, a beam of light caught the beveled edges of the top pane, fracturing into an array of a thousand colors. He held his hand up to shield his eyes from the brightness, and saw it:

Her chest was moving slowly, gently. Up and down. Up and down.

Aurelia was breathing.

Aurelia was *alive*.

Zan sank to his knees beside the casket, pressing both hands and his forehead to the glass as the Arceneaux illusion came to stand next to him. "Aurelia," he said breathlessly.

"That is the name by which you know her," the Malefica said. "But she, too, has many names. Aurelia. Vieve . . . the Spinner."

"What?" Zan tore his eyes from Aurelia in the casket.

"Aurelia is the Spinner. Watching time spool and unspool has made it all the more clear. She is the soul of Vieve, reborn into her sister's line and destined to be reunited with her beloved consort, Adamus. They will stand together, once again, at midnight on Midwinter.

And, one way or another, they will see the sun set on an old age and rise again on a new."

Zan fell back as the casket disintegrated into the Gray, and all his new and fragile hopes with it. "Adamus?"

"Him, you know as well." And Zan was treated to a vision of Dominic Castillion, coming out of a tent as an eager workman strode up to him.

"My lord!" the servant said. "My lord, we have found her! She is here!"

"No," Zan said, disbelieving.

The Malefica bent beside him, studying him with her obsidian eyes. "I tell you this not to hurt you, but as a kindness returned for the one you have offered. I am telling you the truth of her so that you will not be broken by the loss of her a second time." She placed her illusory hand on his shoulder in an awkward attempt to comfort. He stared at her hand; he could not feel it.

"Take the bell," she said after a long moment, and the illusion morphed from the beautiful Tribunal magistrate into the pale and sickly creature stuck by her hands to the ground of the Gray. "Take it and do as you will with it. Raise her, knowing you will lose her, or let her sleep in comfort until her reborn consort can do it for you."

Zan thought he could hear a voice in the distance—barking, worried. *Tom, Tom, wake up. Wake up! We have to go—*

"Hurry, boy. They are trying to bring you back to yourself. Take the bell, keep it hidden; you will need it soon."

Just as Zan's fingers closed around the silver chain, she added,

"Remember me here, boy. Remember the kindness I have bestowed upon you. Remember what I have—"

But he could not hear the rest; the instant he touched the bell, his spectral form was flung backwards through the whistling clouds of the Gray before crashing back into his material body, lying spread-eagle on the floor of the library archive.

Cecily was hunched over him, trying to slap him back into consciousness. "Tom!" she was saying. "Oh, thank the stars! Hurry, now. Stand up. Someone is coming . . ."

He groaned and rolled over, his hand trying to close upon the Ilithiya's Bell but coming up empty. Where had it gone? He rolled onto his knees, scrabbling to feel for it, but the overhead lights had burned out, and his vision was still blurry from the incense smoke.

Cecily wrapped her arms under his, trying fruitlessly to hoist him to his feet, but it was too late. A voice rang out inside the archive like the crack of a whip.

"*What* is the meaning of this?"

It was too late to hide, even if Zan had recovered enough of his senses to try. Instead, he blinked to dispel the clouds in his vision and found Sister Aveline's incensed face glaring back at him.

Cecily cleared her throat. "I can explain, Aveline—"

"No explanation is necessary," Aveline replied. "I can see everything quite clearly, with my own eyes." She turned to look at someone behind her, waving him forward. "Is this the individual you're looking for, Captain Gaspar?"

A man stepped out from behind the angry nun, a smile on his craggy face. "Yes, Sister. The very one."

37

THEN

CHYDAEUS

Chydaeus's endurance rite took place less than a month after his judgment and obedience rites; Grandmaster Fidelis, it seemed, had been quite impressed with his performance and was now actively looking to bring him into the upper echelons of the Circle's leadership, to make an example of him. "It will do the lower ranks well," he said, "to see what they can achieve by close adherence to the Circle's precepts, no matter their age or any other mitigating circumstance."

Once the endurance rite was completed, Chydaeus would only be one more step away from being a fully vested member of the Circle —eligible, even, to become a doyen within the fourth faction. He did not *want* that, of course, because wanting was the first step down the path to a litany of greater sins, but he couldn't say he would mind such a success. It was all to bring souls to the Empyrea, after all.

They will see what I am capable of, he thought. *Aurelia will be proud of me.*

Aurelia—where did that name keep coming from? No one within the ranks of the Circle had such a name. *The Empyrea* was the one he wanted to prove himself to. The Empyrea and no one else.

Fidelis was very quiet about what the endurance rite would entail. Chydaeus had heard other level-sevens talk of being deprived of food for several days, or forced to balance on a pylon for twenty-four hours, or scaling a cliffside without ropes. Most were physical trials that required perseverance and bravery, so he was surprised when he was led to a small room inside of the Grandmaster's house. It was on the highest floor, and was furnished far more grandly than the barracks, with a soft-looking bed and a large mirror, and a window overlooking the battle-training courses.

"I don't understand," Chydaeus said to the Grandmaster as he surveyed the room. "What am I meant to endure here?"

"Your endurance rite," Fidelis said, "is one that we save for the most important of our initiates. That is because it is the most difficult to pass. Your endurance rite, Friend Chydaeus, will be to go one hundred hours without sleep. It will start at moonrise tonight and end at daybreak in four days."

Go without sleep? It sounded easy enough, though far less impressive than cliff scaling.

Fidelis continued, "Pass this rite, and you are guaranteed a position as a doyen in the fourth faction."

Chydaeus's mouth dropped open, and Fidelis swept toward the balcony. "As I said, this is one of the most difficult. Because success is not simply judged by whether or not you survive, but by whether or not you survive with all of your faculties still intact."

"Are there any who have undertaken this test before me?" Chydaeus asked.

"One or two," Fidelis replied. "Vesanius, most recently."

Chydaeus's eyes grew wide. Vesanius had been a member of the first faction, a high mage who could move objects with his mind. He had passed his seventh rite, but before he could undertake the eighth, he broke into the armory and took it over, ranting and raving for hours before climbing to the roof and using his power to draw all the weapons of the surrounding Midnighters and impaling himself with them.

I am not Vesanius, Chydaeus told himself. *I am stronger than that.*

"In an effort to ensure a more . . . smooth . . . administration of this test," Fidelis said, "we have given you a more comfortable accommodation than the one Vesanius used. You might be pleased to know that this used to be the room occupied by one Meraclus! You remember him, don't you?"

Meraclus. The man he'd condemned during his judgment rite. He could still hear the man's final cry, still feel the knife in his hand, slick with blood. But he kept his face impassive and said evenly, "Of course, Grandmaster."

"If you pass this test, Chydaeus, this room will be yours to keep. How does that sound?"

"Excellent, Grandmaster. I hope to do you proud."

"I am certain you will." Fidelis called in an initiate wearing a silver medallion; a feral mage. "This is Friend Ensis. Hold out your arm, please, Friend Chydaeus. He is going to work a spell on you. Every time you fall asleep, the spell will step in and wake you up again."

Ensis traced a pattern around Chydaeus's wrist, and where he touched, a black mark appeared, leaving behind a hard-edged, interlocking design. When he was done, Fidelis dismissed him and said to Chydaeus, "Food will be sent three times a day, and there is a chamber pot in the corner for your usage. Now, it's not yet nightfall, but the rite begins at moonrise. It is my suggestion that you try to get as much sleep as you can until then."

"How will I know when the rite has started?" Chydaeus asked. "Will someone come to tell me?"

Fidelis smiled. "Oh, dear Friend, you'll know."

✶

Chydaeus's nervousness made his sleep fitful. He did manage to slip into a deeper sleep sometime after nightfall, but that made his awakening at moonrise all the more wrenching. He woke screaming, clutching his spell-marked arm, believing he was on fire. But there was no flame in that still, dark room, and as soon as he was fully awake, the agony instantly abated, leaving Chydaeus panting and relieved.

The first day went slowly as boredom crept in, but he kept himself occupied by exploring the room that had once been Meraclus's. There were a few papers left in a desk drawer, mostly scribbled feral spells and notes. The drawers still held his ceremonial robes; the man had been a fully fledged level-eight of the second faction. Just the fact that he had been given a room like this proved that he'd been a valuable Midnighter before his descent into apostasy and subsequent downfall and death. He could have been a doyen if he had put his mind to it. Instead, he'd turned against the Circle, blaspheming against the Grandmaster and sowing seeds of doubt. A fool if ever there was one.

Chydaeus was thumbing through Meraclus's books of feral spells when night began to fall. He set them aside to watch the sun set. One day down already, he thought to himself, rather smugly, before returning to the books.

He only nodded off once that first night, sitting at Meraclus's desk, after the words of the spell book began to blur and his head began to dip. It never hit the desk, though; as soon as his eyes closed, his arm felt as if it were being flayed apart by a sharp knife. He shook himself fully awake with a panicked wail, and the pain disappeared once again.

The second day was harder.

He'd gone through all of the books, read every scrap of paper, and turned the closets and drawers upside down and inside out at least twice by then. He fell asleep once, in the late afternoon, and woke to the sensation of a thousand simultaneous bee stings up and down his arm.

By the end of the second day, he'd lost his last scrap of self-assuredness.

He fell asleep three times that night, and each time the pain that woke him was worse than the last.

On the third day, he made up a game for himself. He removed his medallion and hid it by blindfolding himself and spinning around twenty times and letting the medallion fly somewhere in the room. Then he had to spin another twenty times before removing the blindfold to go searching for it, more dizzy and disoriented than he'd already been rendered by the sleep deprivation.

The fourth day was a nightmarish rotation between delirium and pain. He started seeing things—nameless faces with scratched-out eyes, ribbons of alternating color tied to trees that did not exist, wolves that spoke and a maze of thorny branches that led, over and over, to the window.

He found himself climbing out onto the ledge. He just wanted to sleep. If he jumped, he could sleep.

That was when he felt himself being pulled back into the room. Another apparition—this time, of a man dressed in a long black coat, with eyes that shone gold.

"Conrad," the man said, kneeling. "Conrad, can you hear me?"

Chydaeus did not know who Conrad was, but he couldn't find the words inside his addled mind to say as much. The man swore, and lifted Chydaeus like a baby.

"I can't take you away," he said, "not with that spell on you; they'd use it to torture you the instant they saw you gone. But perhaps I can give you some respite in the Gray."

Cradling Chydaeus, the man stepped right through the mirror into another room just like it, laid out in opposite on the other side, and set Chydaeus on the mirror-room's bed. He said, "From what I've seen, there's a split second of time between when you close your eyes and when the spell causes the pain to wake you up again. This is that moment. I will stretch it out as long as I can. Rest now, Conrad. I will watch over you."

The next thing Chydaeus knew, the pain in his arm had started again—like his skin was being eaten away by acid this time. He jolted himself fully awake and the pain stopped. He was alone in the room —the real room. His mind, though still fuzzy with confusion and weariness, was a little clearer than it had been.

When Grandmaster Fidelis returned the next morning, he found a weary Chydaeus curled up in a corner, tired and tense but with most of his senses still intact.

"You have passed the seventh rite," Fidelis said, and then paused, with a look on his face that meant he was trying to peek at Chydaeus's mind for a playback of the rite. A jumble of nonsensical delirium was what he got in return, and soon he nodded. "Congratulations, Friend Chydaeus. You may now sleep as long as you like. When you are refreshed, we will discuss the next steps on your journey."

That night, asleep in the soft bed, Chydaeus dreamed of a man watching him from the mirror, a man with black hair and golden eyes.

38

NOW

AURELIA

6 DAYS TO MIDWINTER

"Command me, my queen," Castillion murmured. "I will obey."

The words fell like stones into the still pond of my memory, sending ripples of recognition through me.

I stared at him, still bent over my hand, and whispered, "I've heard you say that before, haven't I?"

His eyes were hooded as he straightened. "It was one of the first things the Verecundai ever showed me. A vision of who I was . . . before. With you."

"Could they . . ." I began. "Could they show it to me?"

He blanched. "Aurelia, I can't advise such a thing. Not when . . ."

"Not when they want so much to kill me? I'm not afraid," I said.

"I believe it," he replied, lifting his free hand to my face. "I doubt you've ever been afraid of anything. But, Aurelia . . ."

"Please," I said, laying my hand over his. "Please, Dominic."

It was the first time I'd ever called him by his given name. It sent the final crack through his resistance. "All right," he said. "All right. If that is what you want. If you're *sure*."

"I am sure," I replied. "What must we do?"

"I'll have to call a fog," he said. "Part of the Verecundai's curse is that they cannot leave the dark. Over the years, I discovered that as long as they were not subjected to light directly—through sun, or lamplight—they could still form, even if they did not like it."

"The *fog*," I said, realization dawning. "While we were on the *Humility*, there was one day where we traveled through the most unearthly patch of fog. The other passengers called it a 'white day.'"

"I didn't know what else to do—I was so confused. I never expected to meet you in person, let alone have you show up out of the blue and beg me to take you aboard. I called upon the Verecundai for guidance."

"And what did they say?"

"The same thing they said before: that you'd be the end of me."

"And what did they say later when you told them that I was sleeping in a glass casket in your garden while you figured out how to wake me?"

"Nothing," Castillion answered sheepishly. "Because I never told them. That day on the *Humility* was the last time I called them."

"Why?"

He looked away, into the trees. "Because I had already decided what I was going to do, and I didn't want to be told otherwise. Sometimes," he added, "it's just better *not* to know."

"I won't be dissuaded," I said firmly. "If this is the only way to get answers, so be it."

"I just want you to be prepared," he said. "It's not easy. It certainly won't be pretty." He looked around. "This might be as good a place as any. At least the branches overhead here are thicker; less moonlight to worry about covering up."

He held the knife gingerly over his palm. "I might have been better at blood magic had it required less blood," he said. "But alas, drawing it seems to be an intrinsic part of the practice."

"Is it the pain you're afraid of?" I asked. "Or the power?"

"I've never been afraid of power," he replied. I supposed he was right. But to look at him now, head bent under the thatchwork of bare branches, in a plain wool coat and with no great castle, or fleet of ships, or army of soldiers nearby . . . it was hard to believe that this man, Dominic, was the same as the great conqueror, Lord Castillion.

"Here," I said, moving in closer. "You're holding it all wrong. You're going to cut too deep that way." I repositioned the knife, trying not to recall that time long ago when it was Zan teaching me this lesson.

"Thank you," Castillion said. "Now, you're probably going to want to stand back."

I watched him draw the blood, but had to look away when it fell in bright red splashes onto the white snow. The smell of it, an intoxicating mixture of sweet mead and metal, left my throat aching.

"Operimentum in nebula," Castillion said. *From clouds, a shroud.*

The mist collected first at our feet, as if rising from the ground. Soon, however, it began to descend from above and within minutes, I could not see the trees. Not long after that, I couldn't see my own hand in front of my face. Castillion, only a yard away from me, had been swallowed whole.

I felt both exposed and suffocated, as if I were being pressed down on all sides and still somehow weightless and adrift. I had the strange sense of being lost in utter isolation and watched by a thousand unseen eyes, both at once.

"Castillion?" I called into the mist, but he did not answer.

I stepped slowly backwards, all sense of direction erased as noises —cracks and rustles, wind and shuffling footsteps—bounced erratically around me.

And then, with a startled yelp, I knocked right into him.

He did not take notice of me; his eyes were blank and far away, as if he were in a trance.

"Dominic?" I ventured, waving my hand in front of his face, but he remained impassive, not acknowledging me at all. He'd opened his shirt halfway down and pressed his bloody hand against the spider scar on his chest, leaving a smear of crimson across the silvery-purple mark.

Then the whispers began.

"Who's there?" I called into the whiteness, but the voices took no notice of me. Instead, they continued in their soft, scraping murmurs to each other, like the fluttering beat of a skull-moth's wings. The sounds circled me, coming in closer with each turn, wrapping me up tight in the gossamer strands of their mutterings.

Welcome, daughter of the sister.

"Show yourselves," I said, taut with dread, not sure if I really meant it or if it was just something to say in order to hear the mundane, steadying sound of my own voice.

If she wants to see us, she has only to look.

I blinked, struggling to make sense of fleeting impressions seen only in the edges of my sight: a hand here, a face there. Long teeth, sharp fingers. And vague, scratched-out hollows where eyes might once have been.

"I see you," I said, my voice trembling in the back of my throat like a mouse too frightened to venture from its hole.

Good.

Now, we need a drop of your blood.

Reluctantly, I lifted the vial that hung from my neck and unstopped it, letting a single bead of blood roll from the narrow brim into the mist, which cleared as the drop fell, so I could see it splash against the snow. The ruby drop glowed against the white. It sank and spread into a streak of crimson light. I followed it as it moved under the snow until it came to the center of the sombersweet field, where a tree began to grow.

I circled in awe as black roots bulged from the frozen ground and a gnarled trunk stretched tall, unfurling bare, twisted branches. I watched as a single flower bloomed and then withered as the fruit beneath it swelled. Frost formed in glittering, daggerlike fronds around it, and when the apple was ripe, I had to break a case of glassy ice before I could pluck it from its stem.

I had never seen such a beautiful fruit, perfectly round and red as wine, glossy as a black widow's belly.

Eat, the voices said.

I tamped down my fear and raised the apple to my lips and took a bite. It was both sweet and bitter, and tinged with the coppery taste of blood. The apple's tender flesh dissolved on my tongue and slid down my throat, burning like frost and the strongest of spirits. It wasn't a real apple—it was conjured from the magic in my own blood.

Now, they said. *What do you see?*

The white mist churned. Scenes flashed by, impressions of a time long lost. I saw a library full of mechanical workings, and maps of the stars laid over feral spells, marked with gold ink and red blood. I saw a girl with dark hair, awoken in the night by her mother and ushered down the stairs, past her father, who was counting a bag of coin, and a younger child, who wept and tugged her mother's skirt. The girl was wrapped in a coat and led outside into the night air, where eight robed mages and three black sleighs waited to whisk her away into the night.

Watching it was strange and wrenching—more like a memory than a vision.

When she climbed into the second sleigh, the youngest of the mages slid into the seat beside her, letting down his hood to reveal a head of white-blond hair. When he smiled, the girl's apprehension dissolved like sugar into water, transforming into a dizzying concoction of nervousness and thrill.

I knew that's how she felt, because that's how *I* felt watching it.

Remembering it.

Time passed in a whirl of images. The pair grew together, learned together, trained together, lay together. They were threads of warp and weft, bound so tightly to one another they could never be unraveled again.

If I am to be a queen, she told him, tangling her fingers into his snowy hair, *you must be my consort.*

Command me, my queen, he whispered back, counting the stars reflected in her blue eyes. *I will obey.*

The next image was in another part of the forest, this time in winter. The woman stood in a snowy meadow. Eight-petaled frostlace blossoms were fully unfurled at the outside edges, marking the day as Midwinter. Eight mages surrounded her, like spokes on a spinning wheel. She was weaving a spell out of blood and starlight, working feverishly; white fire began to flash and gather in the sky overhead. A trickle of red started from her nose as light gathered beneath her fluttering eyelids and began to drip down her cheeks like molten tears. Through her glowing eyes, she watched the Empyrea coming down from the sky.

Her beloved broke from the circle and stole toward her, but it was too late. The other mages had ended the spell already; she had been impaled by their seven thin blades. Her spell ended with her life.

I saw him, broken and bewildered, gathering her into his arms, as her blood leaked apple red on the snow.

He took his own sword and held its point to his chest. Then he glared up at the other seven, and pronounced upon them a curse:

Even as you have taken from me, so will I take from you. You shall not die, but neither shall you live. You are cursed to walk this fallen earth until its end, when I and my love are born again and reunited, queen and consort, to reign in the Empyrea's perfect new world, free of pain and death.

The curse was sealed with his blood and hers, and the last trailing threads of her abandoned spell caught the mages like flies in a spider's web. Their bodies twisted into branch and root while their spirits, cleft from their flesh, were left wailing in torment, trapped in the spell until the day the boy and the girl—Adamus and Vieve—would be reborn.

When I opened my eyes, the vision ended and the apple fell to snow in my hand and dispersed like sand between my fingers into the fog.

Now you've seen it, the voices said. *You know the truth. Are you therefore satisfied?*

"No," I said, and found that not only was I not appeased—I was angry. "You showed me what happened, but not why. A cursory explanation of who Castillion and I are to each other, but not why you'd want me dead. Either then or now."

The fog hissed, and the forms concealed within it began to writhe and churn. *We think not only of ourselves,* they said. *But for all humankind.*

"I don't understand."

Better to kill the spider before it bites.

"I am no threat to anyone," I said. "I only want to be left alone."

What you want is inconsequential.

Power is poison.

Those who want it will find you, one way or another.

As we once did.

"I can defend myself," I said, stubbornly jutting out my chin. "I can fight back."

So says the Spider, came the reply.

Harmless until threatened.

Tell us, little Spider, what would you do for the ones you love?

For the brother, the lover, the friend?

The voices deepened, changing from whispers to wails. *It is your love that makes you weak.*

That makes you exploitable.

It is your love that stayed your hand one thousand years ago.

It is your love that condemned you.

The temperature, already cold, fell further, so that the very act of breathing was painful, like inhaling pins and shards of glass.

Your love condemned us all.

Vieve.

"No!" I cried. "I am not her! Her fate is not mine!"

As it was, so will it be again.

The clocks have stopped, but the wheels are turning.

Midwinter is nigh at hand.

The Empyrea will come, as she did afore.

And you will stand before her once again.

And choose:

Eternity or mortality.

Perfection or flaw.

Peace or pain.

Love . . . or death.

The wind became a shrill scream, whipping around me in a funnel, tighter and tighter, until I was trapped in a column of angry, twisting air, my hair flung up like black ribbons above me. I lifted my head and saw a circle of starry sky, enclosing the constellation of Aranea. The Spider.

. The last words were nearly lost in the fury of sound and snow, but they lodged quietly in my chest like the point of a stealthy dagger.

Ties will break.

Blood will flow.

Steel your heart.

Strike the blow.

39

THEN

ZAN

Sister Aveline answered Cecily's protestations with a haughty indifference. "As the most senior member of our order, I have the best claim upon the title of abbess. And as such, it is up to me to decide what must be done with interlopers and desecrators of our consecrated grounds."

"You cannot take that title simply because you *think* you deserve it!" Cecily argued as Gaspar and his men pinned Zan's arms behind him. "There must first be an election! It must be taken to a vote among all the nuns!"

"All, what, six of us?" Aveline returned, her weak chin wobbling with pent-up wrath. "An election would be a mockery now, when we have lost so many and been brought so low. Our last abbess was too permissive—turning a blind eye to the weak and wayward Sisters like you, allowing scum and riffraff into our hallowed halls. It was that misguidance that brought this sickness to our shores in the first place. I will not make those same mistakes."

"It's all right, Cecily," Zan said, thinking as quickly as his swimming head would allow. "Don't—" But he was silenced by Gaspar's fist, cuffing him on the side of his head.

"Stop that, you brute!" Cecily demanded, hurrying to Zan in concern. She made a show of checking him for broken skin and bruises, but used the opportunity to slip something small into his pocket— the Ilithiya's Bell.

"I'll tell Jenny what has happened," she said.

"Don't let her come after me," he replied. "When she's well, make sure she goes home to the Quiet Canary. Promise me!"

Cecily nodded, and Gaspar pulled Zan backwards by his ropes. He thrust a bag of coin into Sister Aveline's hands. She shook it, apparently unsatisfied with its weight.

"Hey," she protested. "You're trying to cheat me."

"Half now," Gaspar said. "The other half will be given to you after we collect the bounty. Is there a problem with that arrangement?" He shifted to make himself bigger, crossing his ham-haunch arms across his chest.

"No," she said, intimidated into agreeableness.

"Good," Gaspar said. "Pleasure doing business with you, *Abbess*."

★

The *Contessa* was waiting for its captain inside a tiny, mostly hidden inlet far enough down the isle that it could not be seen from the abbey windows. When Gaspar pushed Zan into the ship's lower holding, Zan saw that it was empty. He tried to tell himself that maybe Gaspar had dropped the other passengers off at Fort Castillion and returned to Widows' Isle to claim him, despite the fact that not nearly enough time had passed to allow for the *Contessa* to have crossed that much water and returned.

But Zan's hopes disappeared as soon as he saw the pile of discarded belongings at the far end of the hold. It appeared that someone had been recently sifting through them, for a smaller second pile was sitting next to the first, composed of pocket watches and jewelry and an odd assortment of Renaltan and Achlevan coin.

"Did you make them watch while you went through their belongings like buzzards?" Zan said in a tight voice. "Or did you at least give them the courtesy of tossing them overboard first?"

"Shut up, you," Gaspar said, cuffing him. "I can't let sickness spread among my crew."

Zan licked the blood from his lips. "I'd say there's a far worse sickness among you already." Then he bit his lips together, afraid that if he antagonized the man too much, he'd have his own pockets picked, and he did not want them knowing about the Ilithiya's Bell. Such a trinket looked plenty valuable, even without knowing its true purpose.

Gaspar raised his hand again, but thought better of it when his first mate said, "Best keep 'im alive, Captain, and let Castillion decide what to do wif 'im."

Castillion. The name alone was enough to deflate what little mettle Zan had left. He crumpled against the bunk post as the captain and first mate grunted back up the *Contessa*'s rickety stairs, locking the hatch behind them and leaving him in the lampless dark with nothing but a pile of dead people's effects and his own morose thoughts to keep him company. Soon, the ship was moving.

Aurelia is alive. Aurelia is the Spinner. Aurelia is alive. Aurelia is the Spinner. His mind was a whirlpool, circling around and around a new truth that was lodged like the blade of a harpoon in his heart: that the girl he'd loved so desperately and mourned so fiercely was both returned to him and lost to him forever.

★

He slept fitfully and woke with raw wrists and numb hands from the too-tight ropes when one of the sailors came to bring him a bowl of slop and a crust of bread for a meal.

"I won't be able to eat it like this," Zan said, raising his bound hands.

The sailor grunted. "Can't untie you. Cap'n wouldn't like it."

"The captain doesn't want to deliver me to Castillion all marked up—he'll lose money. Just loosen the binds a little, so they don't rub so much. What difference does it make down here? No place for me to go, no weapons of any sort nearby. Please," Zan said, as beseechingly as he could muster.

The sailor relented. "Fine," he said, wriggling the knot until the ropes slid free from Zan's wrists. "But if the cap'n doesn't like it, or you try any funny stuff, back into the ropes you go, only we'll tie yer hands behind yer back and get yer feet, too. Understand?"

"I understand," Zan said. "No funny business." He stretched his fingers and rolled his wrists before picking up the bowl that was his breakfast—or dinner. He had no idea what time it was. The sailor stalked back toward the stairs, and the light caught his face. Zan saw the sheen of sweat on his brow. "Sorry, friend, but . . . you don't look so good."

"I'm fine," the sailor said. "Mind yer own self, prisoner." And he spat on the floor as if to punctuate his point before slamming the hatch and leaving Zan alone once again.

Zan ate the gruel but pocketed the scrap of bread after fishing out the Ilithiya's Bell, careful to keep it from clinking. It was, in all, just slightly smaller than his own palm, and made of red-tinted metal that shone in the darkness, even without any light to reflect. The dewdrop jewel sparked as he turned it over, reminding him of the glass in Aurelia's casket.

The Malefica said the bell would help him move through the Gray without leaving his body behind in the material world, but she had neglected to tell him exactly how he was supposed to manage that without any quicksilver string from which to devise a portal nor feral magic with which to open it. Beautiful as it was, it was as useless to Zan as a lump of clay.

But, by its pale light, he could make out the shape and breadth of the holding, and managed to move to the end where the other passengers' effects were piled without bruising his shins on the bunks. Most of the real valuables had already been claimed by the captain and crew. All that was left here were the scraps: a rucksack containing a striped nightshirt and nightcap, a worn trunk containing patched-up socks and a poorly knitted scarf, a woman's toiletry case with a broken-handled horsehair brush and a cheap tin mirror that was too cloudy to return a reflection.

And then he saw the little rag doll. Margaret. He set the mirror aside and fished it from where it was hidden, under a bloodstained blanket wrapped around a broken bottle.

Seeing it was like getting a handful of still-hot cinders tossed into his eyes. They stung with heat, and he had to grit his teeth and count his breaths to keep from turning over bunks and bringing the sailors responsible for this back down to truss him up once again. Instead, he held the doll gingerly, hoping that it gave the child who'd last held it some small measure of happiness before the end.

He sat for a long while with his head in his hands, the Ilithiya's Bell slipping from his grip to dangle on its fine silver chain, still threaded through his fingers. He was surprised to see the movement captured in the tin mirror he'd set so carelessly aside; only minutes ago it had been too hazy to give him a proper reflection. Now, it shone with an impressive polish, and he saw his own face, bathed in the gentle light of the dangling bell.

Strange, he thought, gathering the bell up again to reach for the mirror, but as soon as he touched the bell, his reflection in the tin was swallowed up once again by a churning haze of gray. But when he held the bell by the chain alone, the tin cleared, and his own visage —drawn, bruised, and disheveled as it was—stared back at him.

With the bell in hand . . . the mirror became a window into the Gray.

He put the chain over his neck and tucked the bell under his shirt so that it was resting next to his skin. The mirror remained cloudy when he picked it up with both hands—a colorless screen. Curiously, cautiously, Zan touched the cold plane. He felt it give way, the smooth surface pooling around each of his fingers like liquid. His fingers could go in, up to his wrist, but then it stuck.

I'm going to need to find a bigger mirror, he thought.

★

Zan figured out rather quickly that though the tin mirror was too small to be useful for escape, if he concentrated hard enough, he could command the Gray to reveal itself within it. Little snatches at first —Jessamine and Cecily, their heads together in the abbey's sanctorium infirmary; the children at the Quiet Canary playing in the grass outside the tavern; Castillion and his men in the Ebonwilde, ostensibly searching for the Assembly. Most of what he saw was past, but he had no way of knowing if what he was seeing happened seconds, minutes, days, weeks ago. The future, when he tried to conjure it, was less easily discerned, muddled as it was by thousands and thousands of possibilities that morphed and twisted with every minute decision or pin-drop change of mind. But he found if he focused, he could catch a fleeting glimpse of the present, and could pin it down long enough to get a good look at it before it flitted away from him again.

It was through the mirror that he saw sailors on the decks above moving through their daily rituals in a well-worn rhythm, in time with the slow dip and swell of the placid sea. It was through the mirror that he watched the sailors sicken, first one and then another and another. The Bitter Fever moved through the ranks like wildfire, so quickly that, on the fourth day of his imprisonment aboard the

Contessa, Zan didn't have to wonder why no one came down to bring him his daily bowl of gruel. By then, no one was left. He was locked below deck on a drifting ghost ship.

If he didn't want to starve to death, he'd have to free himself. The closest thing to a tool at his disposal was the broken ale bottle, which he'd set aside on the off chance he'd need to use it to defend himself. Now, he wrapped his hands in some of the leftover cloth from the effects pile and used the sharpest shard of bottle to saw at the wooden door at the top of the stairs. The wood was old, and came away in long splinters. Soon, when he pushed his shoulder against it he felt the boards crack and bend away from the iron lock. A few well-placed shoves more, and he was able to bust all the way through the planks with one arm, cringing as he felt around for the latch and touched cold, clammy skin instead. It took some maneuvering, once the latch was turned, to push the sailor's body from the hatch and emerge, blinking, into pale light for the first time in days.

The scene that materialized as his eyes adjusted was a horror. The gun deck was littered with bodies. They were flopped over barrels, slumped against the cannons, hanging half out of tangled hammocks. The faces of the dead were twisted into grotesque masks of pain and horror, their purpling faces smudged with black tears. Zan gripped his bottle shard tighter and used his jacket to cover his nose as he picked his way through the corpses to the stairs leading to the open air above.

There were more bodies on deck, but these were in worse shape; for though the ocean spray had washed the bitter tears from their faces, seabirds had pecked out many of their eyes, leaving blank and staring hollows in the pallid skin.

The crew had enacted a horror upon their passengers, but the Bitter Fever had visited them anyway.

There was a creak on the deck behind him. Zan whirled around. He saw Captain Gaspar stumbling from the officers' quarters, his hands grasping at a stray rope to keep him from tripping on his dragging feet.

The captain raised an accusatory finger, his mouth opened in a silent cry of rage, and for a minute, Zan thought that this was another one of the Malefica's apparitions. But no—Gaspar was still alive, and frothing like a rabid, raging bulldog as he barreled toward Zan.

"You," he said in a rasping growl, finally finding his voice. "You did this. You . . . *cursed* us!"

His eyes were beady and black, but there were no tears on his cheeks. He'd lived through the fever, but it had not left him untouched; something had cracked inside him, and the malevolence that had been simmering beneath the thin veneer of his vocation's respectability was now freely flowing.

He'd survived the plague, but lost his mind in the process.

Zan, tired after days in the hold with negligible food and water, was slow to respond to Gaspar's swinging fists, only managing to duck out of the way at the last second.

"Listen." He tried to reason with the rabid captain. "It's just us now. I don't know if you can bring the ship into port alone, but I know I can't. We need each other if we're going to survive . . ."

Gaspar responded by throwing another punch, this time connecting with Zan's stomach. It knocked the wind from him. The move threw Gaspar off his balance, however, and he pitched over the inert body of one of the fallen boatswains. He grabbed Zan's boot and pulled him down with him. Zan struggled against the larger man's weight, but Gaspar seized his throat and started throttling him. Unable to draw breath, Zan swung widely with his broken bottle, and felt it connect.

Gaspar stared at Zan in shock as a fountain of red poured from the sidelong gash in his neck, and then his grip lessened and released. His black eyes rolled back into his head and he flopped overtop the boatswain's body.

Zan, gasping for air, released the bottle shard and scrambled, crab-like, away from the bodies until he hit the deck rail and could retreat no further. He waited there for a moment to let his racing heart slow, balancing his arms on his knees, before shakily pulling himself back to his feet. The bell and vial of Aurelia's blood had swung free of his shirt and he wrapped his fingers around them both, as if to draw comfort or strength when he had so little left inside himself.

Gaspar's blood was spreading steadily across the *Contessa*'s deck. Zan came to the edge of it, bell in hand, and saw that what glistened back at him from within the growing stain was not the steely ocean sky, but a strange, smoky swirl of crimson-tinted clouds.

With one last, steadying breath, Zan clutched the bell harder and stepped forward into the Gray.

40

NOW

AURELIA

6 DAYS TO MIDWINTER

The fog abated and Dominic sank to his knees with exhaustion. I tried to help him up, but he waved me off, saying, "I'm fine, truly. It always takes a minute to adjust afterward." He got to his feet slowly, cringing as he did, as if his bones were brittle. "Did you get the answers you were looking for?"

"I got a few answers," I said glibly, "and a thousand more questions. The first being: Why couldn't you have just *told* me who you thought I was when you woke me? Or at *any* point before now?"

"What was I to say? 'Hello, Aurelia. Good morrow. It's me, the reborn soul of your ancient lover.'"

"You're right," I said reluctantly. "I'd never have believed you. I still don't, even now."

"Yet it is true," he said. "All of it. And I know they are strange and frightening, but the Verecundai have spent hundreds of years paying penance for what they did to us . . ."

"And at least thirteen years muttering into your ear, trying to win you—*you!* The soul who cursed them in the first place!—to see them as your friends, guides, helpers . . . whatever it is you think they are now."

"I can see why you'd be skeptical of them . . ."

Quietly, I said, "They told you I'd be the end of you."

"You were once. You might be again. But do I look afraid?"

"Maybe you should be."

"If you hurt me, it will be because I let you." He tucked my hair behind my ear, then traced the line of my jaw with his forefinger. "I might even want you to."

"Don't."

"Don't what?" he asked quietly. "Let you hurt me? Or tell you I'd be glad of it? Do your worst, Aurelia." His breath hitched, his fingers drifting to my neck, his thumb soft against my lower lip. "Break my heart."

I put my hand to his, and then tugged it down from my face, but didn't let go—even though I knew I should have. He pulled our clasped hands into his chest and held them there for a moment with a solemnity that bordered on reverence, his eyes dark as an autumn wood.

When I finally withdrew my hand from his, it was to move the unbuttoned length of his shirt aside so that the blood-streaked spider scar was out in full view. There was something strange about the mark, and I let my fingers trail lightly over it. As my cold fingertips brushed against his skin, Dominic gave an involuntary shiver.

But at my touch, cutting through the spell of fog and forest and warm skin and white sky, I could hear the Verecundai's papery voices in my head.

Ties will break.

Blood will flow.

Steel your heart.

Strike the blow.

I pulled my hand back with a jarring jerk.

"I'm sorry," I said, nerving myself to look directly into his eyes instead of at the ground, where shame coiled around my feet and then wound its way up my body, slowly tightening around my chest.

"You can let your guard down now, Aurelia." He bent his head down, his lips a hairsbreadth from mine. "You can allow yourself to *feel* again."

Do it, Aurelia, I told myself, leaning in. *Let go of what* was *and embrace what* is.

Your souls have waited centuries to be reunited.

You can be those lovers you saw in the vision again.

Pretend. Pretend until you remember. Pretend until it's real.

His kiss was warm and sweet, and I returned it with as much heat as I could muster, trying not to recall Zan's face in the dark of his room in Achlev as he waited for his father's soldiers to come for him. Or the look in his eyes when he glanced up and saw me there, watching him. Or the unbearable radiance in my heart when he crossed the room and kissed me for the first time—so desperate and reckless and broken and brave.

When Dominic pulled away, his smile was exquisitely tender. I forced my face to mirror the expression, praying he could not see the unrelenting uncertainty behind it.

Pretend until it's not pretend anymore.

And so I kissed him again. I shuttered my heart's protest, buried my worries about what was past or might come next, and condensed the sum of my existence into that one moment. I lost myself in sensation without self-reproach, letting myself enjoy the simple warmth of his arms around me, the soft tickle of his breath on my throat, the reassuring thrum of his living heart beneath my cold fingertips.

"Aurelia!"

Rosetta's voice preceded her through the trees, giving us enough time to jump apart and try to smooth ourselves into some semblance of nonchalance, as if we had been only talking and not using our faces for any other mouth-related activities. "Aurelia," she said breathlessly, "Nathaniel is awake."

Avoiding Dominic's eyes, I thrust my hands deep into my pockets and allowed her to lead us back through the snow.

We found Nathaniel sitting upright in the parlor, the portraits of Kate and Ella on his lap. "Commander Castillion," he said, "I must formally request a leave of duty."

"Of course. You are granted to take as much time to heal as you need," Dominic said.

"Not for that," he replied, eyes shining. "It's because I need to go see my daughter."

". . . Nathaniel?" I asked uncertainly.

"She is alive, Aurelia." He beamed. "Look." He lifted a small blanket, hand-sewn with sunny little flowers. I recognized Kate's work immediately. I had sat with her when she embroidered it.

"Where did you get this?" I asked in shock.

"A few months back," Rosetta began, "I returned to the homestead to find a woman and child had managed to get past my wards. The woman was dead; she'd made it just long enough to see the little girl to safety." She tapped the edge of the painting in Nathaniel's hands. "*This* little girl."

"That's incredible!" I exclaimed. "Where is she now?"

"I left her in the hands of the Canary girls," she said.

"You could have chosen no better caretakers!" I replied. "We must go get her at once."

"Aurelia . . ." Dominic was shaking his head. "We can't afford another delay. We've got to get back to the fort."

"I've checked in on her periodically," Rosetta said, "and the last time I visited, they were about to join a caravan train to Fort Castillion."

"Will they be there already?" Nathaniel asked.

"No," Rosetta said. "They took a longer, but safer, route, up the eastern side of the realm. They'd still be several days out at least."

"Good," Nathaniel said, trying to get to his feet. "You two can return to the fort directly. I'll detour to the east, to see what I can find of the train."

"Nathaniel," I said, concerned, "you're in no shape to—"

Rosetta spoke up. "I'll go with him. I can look after him. His wounds, I mean."

Looking at Nathaniel's eager face stripped me of any desire to object. There was no rest nor medicine that would do more good for his health than seeing his daughter again.

"Do whatever you can for him," I told Rosetta, and she nodded solemnly. But then her eyes grew wide.

"What is it?" Dominic asked.

"The wards. At the border of the homestead. Someone is trying to dismantle them." She looked at me, apprehensive. "Someone is trying to get in."

We sped outside, where the sun was just starting to rise behind the towering trees, casting long, lavender shadows against pink-tinged snow. Rosetta made a beeline toward the northeastern quadrant of the homestead, where her ward-knots waved in the crisp breeze, each equally spaced along the line of the territory's edge. She moved with the same quickness of her fox-form, checking each one in turn. "I don't understand," she said after a few moments. "I *felt* a push against the spell. I felt someone testing its limits."

"Could it have been a bird?" Dominic asked. "Or some small animal?"

"No," Rosetta said in a tight voice. "Animals can come and go freely. It's humankind I ward against." A shadow crossed her face, and I remembered what I had witnessed in the Gray, when a stray group of Renaltan soldiers had infiltrated the homestead. They'd left her bleeding on the floor of her own home; the only reason she was here now was because her sister Galantha had worked a spell to save her life, sacrificing her own in the process. "Every so often, I'll have one fail—that was what happened when Ella and her grandmother got here—but I've been very vigilant since then, inspecting them every day."

"Aurelia brought us here pretty handily," Dominic said, "with a spell."

"I know," Rosetta said. "And when this is all taken care of, I shall have to strengthen my wards accordingly."

But Dominic wasn't listening. His eyes had caught upon something not far outside of the ward-line. "Do you see that?" he asked, stepping across the border.

"It's just holly," Rosetta said.

"No, not that." Castillion circled the holly bush. He reached through its thorny leaves to pull out a ribbon of a deep, rusted red. It had been tied into the branches, its two long tails waving softly down the side. *This.*

My breath caught as I came up next to him. "The ribbon game," I said, almost inaudibly. "I used to play it with Conrad. We'd tie colored ribbons around the palace as clues leading toward a prize." I reached to touch the ribbon and instantly recoiled, stumbling several paces before falling backwards into the snow.

"What is it, Aurelia?" Dominic said, hurrying to help me to my feet. "What just happened?"

"It's *blood*," I said, throat tight. "It was dyed that color with blood." From the angry, agonized magic I felt when I touched it, probably unwilling blood.

"What does it mean?" Dominic asked.

"It's from the Circle Midnight, most likely," I said. "We know they have Conrad. And when I was there, I tried to reach him by reminding him of this game. The ribbon colors had meanings, you see. Yellow for up, blue for down, red for north, green for south, purple for east, orange for west. Black means something is within ten paces, and hidden from sight. White means something is within twenty paces, and in plain view."

Looking from Rosetta to Dominic, I said, "It's a message, I think. And a threat." I gazed at the bloodstained ribbon. "They want us to go north, back to the fort."

41

NOW

CHYDAEUS

6 DAYS TO MIDWINTER

"Grandmaster," the fifth-level knight said with a deep bow. "The infiltrators were able to get away, but we were able to locate and apprehend the saboteur who caused the explosions in our kilns."

Chydaeus was still reeling from the events of the afternoon, when the sixth-sector rally went sideways after someone began sending messages back through Grandmaster Fidelis's thought connections, disrupting them with strange words and songs and pictures that were completely indecipherable and yet somehow bafflingly familiar.

This tour of the sectors was Chydaeus's first experience as one of the Circle's leaders. Fidelis was promenading him in front of the fifth- and sixth-level fighters so that they might visualize what they could achieve with dedication and perseverance. The tour was meant to be a high point for them all, a way to inject enthusiasm for the cause into the Midnighters' ranks before they set out for Fort Castillion—the last outpost of resistance to the Circle's power. Or, as Fidelis called it, the final jewel for the Empyrea's crown.

But now, everything was upended. They were back at headquarters, and Fidelis had taken to pacing up and down the grand hall, his purple robes swishing across the black-and-white tile. "Bring him in, then," Fidelis told the fifth-level. "Let's see who dares to thwart us."

The Midnighters dragged the man into the hall. He was dressed not in the robes of a Midnighter, but in a long black coat. His hair was dark and long, nearly to his shoulders, and when he looked up, Chydaeus saw that his eyes were gold.

He hurried to smother his surprise, keeping his face still so as not to invite Fidelis's attention and the exploration of his mind that was sure to follow. He knew him immediately: this was the man he'd seen in the midst of his endurance-rite delirium. A figment born of extreme sleep deprivation, he had thought, that was now standing before the Circle's leadership in full flesh and blood.

And of blood, there was plenty. It dripped from a cut in his cheek and was splashed across the linen shirt he wore beneath his long jacket. He wheezed as he stood there, and Chydaeus wondered if he had punctured a lung.

Fidelis stopped his pacing to circle the man, whose hands were tied behind his back. "Valentin Alexander de Achlev," the Grandmaster said with delight, "what a *pleasant* surprise. How honored are we in the Circle to be graced with the presence of royalty?"

"I should think you'd be used to it by now," the man, Valentin, said, shooting a look at Chydaeus.

Fidelis's smile puckered, as if he'd tasted something sour. He stared at Valentin for a long moment, with a look of rapt concentration on his face.

"If you're trying to read my mind," Valentin said, "it won't work. You see, a friend of mine showed me how to resist the influence of your high magic gifts."

"Well," Fidelis said, obviously irritated, "I guess we'll just have to do things the old-fashioned way, won't we?" He snapped his fingers, and the fifth-levels stepped forward. "Take him to the dungeon," Grandmaster directed. "I'll be down shortly. I would very much like to know more about what he and his friends were doing here this afternoon. Especially"—his eyes glittered—"the girl. Yes, dear Valentin, I am *very* interested indeed in your Aurelia."

★

Chydaeus had been ordered to stay away from the dungeon and the man they had captive within it. But he could not forget those gold eyes, nor ignore that name Fidelis had used: Aurelia. He remembered the face he'd seen in the crowd, among the sea of Midnighters: bright, earnest, unafraid. And *familiar*.

Aurelia.

His curiosity supplanted all of his instincts for caution. He crept down the stairs that led to the manor's small collection of holding cells, darting into an open one before Fidelis caught him. He and Cruentis, first doyen of the third faction, were in a fierce discussion about the prisoner.

"Apologies, Grandmaster," Cruentis said, "but if I bleed him much more, he'll die. And dead men don't make good bait, sorry to say."

"We still have the kid," Grandmaster said. "And you were there this afternoon; she tried to make a connection with him."

"She *did* make a connection with him," Cruentis said. "She overruled your control entirely for several minutes."

"You're looking as if that's a bad thing, Friend Cruentis," Fidelis said. "I see it as confirmation. Aurelia Altenar *is* the Spinner, just as I have theorized for years. And there she was today, in the flesh, so close . . . and now that we have the Spinner's Codex . . ."

The men walked by the cell he was hiding in, and Chydaeus pushed his back against the stone, hoping that the walls between them would keep Fidelis from catching any stray thoughts. When they were gone, Chydaeus slipped out and hurried down the corridor of cells. There were no other guards. The Circle was run so tightly that there was hardly any need for them.

The man's cell was only latched from the outside. Chydaeus opened the door slowly and slipped inside. Valentin was tied to a chair in the center of the room, stripped down to the waist, exposing skin crisscrossed with cuts and abrasions from a whip. When he saw Chydaeus, he wheezed, "Conrad. You shouldn't be here. It's not safe."

"Who are you?" Chydaeus demanded without preamble. "I shouldn't know you, but I do. You helped me during the endurance rite, didn't you? You . . . took me through the mirror."

"You know me, Conrad." Speaking was a struggle; his lips were swollen and bleeding, but he kept on. "Somewhere deep down. I know they made you forget—frostlace, most likely—but some things you know. Think, Conrad. Think."

"My name is Chydaeus," he corrected.

"Your name is Conrad. Conrad Costin Altenar. King of Renalt."

"No," Chydaeus insisted, distress rising.

"You're the son of King Regus and Queen Genevieve of Renalt. You have a sister." His voice fell, becoming almost reverent. "Aurelia."

"The Spinner?" Chydaeus mumbled. That's what he'd just heard Fidelis say. Aurelia was the Spinner.

"Yes."

"You still haven't answered my question," Chydaeus said. "Who are *you*?"

"Nobody," the man replied, and Chydaeus remembered the meaning of his own name. Nothing. No one. Common. Nobody. And yet this man was trying to tell him he was a king.

It was a ridiculous notion. But still . . .

"Fidelis called you Valentin. Is that your name?"

"You shouldn't be here," the man said again, not answering the question. "He'll read your thoughts. He'll find out you spoke to me."

"You said he can't read yours. How?"

"I have . . . a very unusual friend," he said. "She made me immune to high magic. As a gift."

Chydaeus asked, "Could she do it for me?"

The man regarded him carefully through one good eye; the other was nearly swollen shut. "I don't know."

"If I were to get you free, could you take me to her?"

"How, exactly, do you plan on getting me free?"

"During my endurance rite," Chydaeus said, "you used a mirror."

That got his attention.

✦

The first thing Chydaeus had to do was retrieve something from the explosion site. "The chain must have broken when I got knocked backwards in the explosion," Valentin said. "It's a bell, about the size of my hand, shaped like a sombersweet flower."

Should be easy enough to find, Chydaeus thought.

That was before he came to the site of the detonation.

Where the kiln had once stood, a crater was carved out of the dirt. Pieces of the building and the bricks that had been held within it were lodged all across the surrounding circumference; Chydaeus felt sympathy for the Midnighters who'd lived through the first explosion only to be assailed by those deadly missiles falling from the sky.

The area was humming with first- and second-level initiates, who were gathering body parts and bone fragments into wheelbarrows and trundling their macabre loads into a nearby barracks, where third-level initiates were picking through the pieces, laying some out like a gruesome puzzle.

In his initial shock at the scene, Chydaeus forgot to be furtive, and one of the third-levels looked up and saw him. She bowed, hurriedly, and said, "Friend Chydaeus! How honored we are to have you in our presence. Wh-what can we help you with, sir?"

"Why are you doing this?" Chydaeus asked. "Should we not . . . bury the remains? Show some respect for the dead?"

"Grandmaster's orders," the third-level replied. "We're to collect all their medallions and other remnants and return the metal to the armory to be reforged into weapons for the coming battles. He did not tell you, when he sent you out to observe?"

"He did," Chydaeus said. "I was simply testing your knowledge. Congratulations, you passed." It was a feeble lie, but so much of life in the Circle was a test that she did not seem at all surprised; instead, she flushed from the pleasure of praise. "May I see what you have already collected?"

She nodded and led him to a table full of scavenged artifacts: melted medallions, broken shoe buckles, even some gold-filled teeth. Most of those caught in the blast had been unarmed first- and second-levels, so there weren't many weapons among their leftovers. As he hovered over the findings, the lower initiates kept bringing more things in, eyes blank of any emotion despite the fact that the fallen were, certainly, people they knew and worked with daily.

It was in one of these deliveries that Chydaeus spied something incongruent: a gleam of violet-red among the charred bits of other metal. He moved the pieces around it aside, and nearly gasped—it was, indeed, a bell in the shape of a flower, with a dewdrop-like jewel dangling from its center. It shone with its own ethereal light, unblemished by soot or dirt or scratch—though Valentin was right, the chain was broken. It was tangled, too, in another necklace, of a white-stone ring and a strange little charm depicting a carnelian-eyed firebird. He took both.

He gave a stealthy look around, astonished that no one else had noticed these things. So mechanical were these initiates, so automatic in their tasks, that such exquisite objects could be overlooked, and lumped in with other debris as if they were the same thing. The initiates had been ordered to collect metal, and that was what they did. Without question or doubt or any desire for further inquiry.

The bell had a nice weight in his hand, and a comforting warmth. He held it so that it was covered by the long sleeves of his robe until he was away from the tent and out of sight of its facile flock of workers. As he trekked back to the big house, he untangled the chains, bending the hooks back into place so that he could hang them around his neck. They were easier to hide that way, tucked into the loose folds of his robe.

Valentin, when Chydaeus returned, was with Cruentis again. Before he even made it all the way down the dungeon stairs, he could hear the crack of the blood mage's whip. "We're going to use your blood, friend, to send your princess a message. Won't that be nice? Give the girl a pretty red ribbon as a token of your affection? Fidelis said she's very fond of ribbons. He's seen it in her brother's mind, the little game they'd play."

Yellow for up. The thought came to Chydaeus unbidden.

"Go to hell," Valentin said.

"You know, I actually feel bad for you. After your companions left you here all alone, without a second thought." Cruentis clicked his tongue. "Poor thing." Chydaeus could hear him patting Valentin's knee. "Well, not for long. Fidelis has tracked them, you see, using the blood they left behind." He laughed. "The Spinner will be caught, make no mistake."

Valentin's voice changed then, from defiance to obeisance. "Don't hurt them," he begged. "Please."

"We'd never hurt the Spinner," Cruentis replied. "She is destined to join us. It's what is written in the Midnight Papers." He paused at the door, and when Chydaeus peeked around the corner, he could see the long ribbon hanging from his hands, wet with Valentin's fresh blood. "She," the doyen said, "will be our queen. I can't speak to what will happen to the rest of your friends, however." Then he left, smiling to himself.

When Cruentis was out of sight, Chydaeus hurried into Valentin's cell, where the man was so bruised and bloody, he hardly looked human. "You found it?" he asked, his voice coming in whistling gasps. And Chydaeus pulled the chains from his robe and laid them both over Valentin's neck.

"And this one, too," he said, pointing out the one with the ring and the firebird pendant.

"Thank you," Valentin said, "I didn't think I'd ever get these back. Good work." And Chydaeus suddenly felt more pride in this one accomplishment than all of his initiation rites put together.

He hurried to untie the ropes around Valentin's hands. "My room is on the top floor," he said. "Up four flights of stairs. But there's a mirror there—"

"I won't make it that far," Valentin wheezed. "There's no way."

"Then . . ." Chydaeus fumbled for an alternative. "Maybe I can bring the mirror down to you. It's pretty big, though, and heavy . . ." He stopped. There were voices coming down the dungeon stairs. Fidelis, from the sound of it, talking to Cruentis.

"No time for that," Valentin said. "We'll have to make do with what we've got." He groaned as Chydaeus helped him from the chair.

"Maybe someday I'll get to thank that brute for bleeding me so much. This wouldn't be possible otherwise."

"What wouldn't be possible?" Chydaeus asked, fear making his voice shrill.

"We're going to travel through the reflection in the blood," Valentin said. "I've done it once before. Here, bring that lantern. Now hold on to me. Do *not* let go."

The instant that Valentin grabbed Chydaeus, the reflection in the blood changed from their faces to a vortex of whirling clouds.

"See how it changes? It's the bell."

"You want me to go into *that*?" Chydaeus squeaked. The voices were getting closer.

"Don't look," Valentin said. "Don't think. Just trust me. Ready? Now . . . jump."

42

THEN

ZAN

There was a rush of wind, and Zan felt himself falling, falling, falling . . . but when he looked around, he wasn't falling anymore. He still stood on the deck of the *Contessa*, but the scenery around it was changing. It was ocean, and then it was docked in a bay, surrounded by snowy peaks, and then it was drifting a mile or so off a craggy, black stone beach. He knew that beach—it was on the eastern side of Achleva, near the border with Renalt.

Hand still tightly wrapped around the bell, Zan knitted his eyebrows tight together and forced himself to focus on that shore. On those rocks, and the sound the waves would make crashing against the nearby cliffs. When he opened his eyes again, he wasn't on the *Contessa* anymore, but looking out at it from the shore. He was startled enough that he let go of the bell, and the world seemed to move under his feet, solidifying in a single second from the shifting mists of the Gray into fully formed reality. When he grabbed the bell again, nothing happened.

All right, he thought. *I need a reflection to get into the Gray, but only have to let go of the bell to get out of it.*

To test his theory, he trudged along the shore until he found a pool of water cupped in a curve of stone, orphaned by low tide and placidly waiting for its return. It was home to eddying anemone and clusters of mussels, and a tiny pink starfish that curled away from his touch. But when he took hold of the bell again, the tide pool became a window into the Gray.

Stepping into it, he didn't even get wet. He took a moment to get oriented by fixing the location he wanted to go in his mind. The Gray showed him the Quiet Canary, then Aren's tower standing among the ruins of Achlev, and then the lighthouse on Widows' Isle. When he was certain he had the hang of it, he let himself imagine the sanctorium chapel at the Assembly, as the Malefica had shown him.

And then he was there. He kept ahold of the bell, getting slowly to his feet, taking in his surroundings as they came into focus and the floor solidified beneath him. The rich carpets. The high ceilings, the soaring stone columns and painted frescoes. For centuries, this was the place where mages of all varieties were trained in their otherworldly disciplines, where they learned and taught and prayed.

Indeed, some of them had died here, praying, when the Assembly was attacked by Cael all those centuries ago. Zan's eyes slid over the long-dead supplicants, frozen forever in their prostrations, and then he turned toward the head of the sanctorium, and the coffin that rested at its altar.

Zan didn't dare breathe as he approached, afraid that if he moved too fast or closed his eyes, the illusion would break and he'd find himself alone again, drunk in the crypt of the Stella Regina, or asleep with his head on the desk at the Quiet Canary, or tossing feverishly on a cot in the abbey infirmary.

But the vision did not fade as he got close enough to finally see what lay on the other side of the gleaming glass.

Aurelia.

"Beautiful," said a voice from behind him. "Isn't she?"

Zan whirled around, still clutching the bell, and found Isobel Arceneaux there, as if she had been there since their last encounter, just waiting for him to arrive.

"Yes," he said, heart in his throat. "She is."

The Malefica walked her Arceneaux illusion up to the glass coffin. "You know, I never understood beauty before. Not until I lived inside a human skin." She tilted her head, gazing down at Aurelia with something like wistfulness in her onyx eyes. "I used to think it was all balance and order and symmetry. And those things *can* be beautiful." She touched the glass, tracing the outline of Aurelia's face—eyes, nose, lips, chin—with her phantom fingertip. "But the things that are the *most* beautiful are the ones that deviate from that symmetry. That sameness. The things that are different, and flawed, and strange, and memorable. I see it now. I understand."

The Assembly was gone, and he found himself looking down, once

again, upon the Malefica, still shackled by magic to the ground outside of the Stella Regina. For Zan, it had only been a few days since
he'd first seen her, first taken the bell, but she looked as if she had aged
years in that time. Her skin was beginning to sink into the hollows of
her bones; her hair had become wispy and white.

"Release me, boy," she said.

"I can't," Zan replied. "But I can give you this." He knelt beside
her and took from his pocket the hard crust of bread he'd saved from
the *Contessa* and offered it to her.

"I'm sorry it isn't much," he said as she wolfed it down.

"You treat me with kindness," she said. "For that I must also repay
you. First, I gave you the bell. This gift is not tangible—it will be a
spell. Hold out your hand again, that I may grant it upon you."

Zan did not know what to expect, but he did as he was told. She
smiled and then bit him, sliding her teeth across the flesh of his palm.
He yelped, and pulled back, but she said, "Be still, boy. My power
has always come through the shedding of blood, though I have none
of my own to wield it." With his blood on her lips, she pronounced
a word in a language he did not recognize, but it had the lilt of a
blessing. He felt strange and light-headed for a minute, and when
he looked at her again, she was licking her lips, as if the blood had
restored her far more than the bread.

"You are protected now," she said, "from my sister's power. No
high mage will be able to hear your thoughts, nor give you any that
are not your own."

"Thank you," he said, though the statement carried the cadence of a question. When he rose again, the Malefica said, "Do not go back to the Spinner, boy. There is only pain to be had for you there."

But Zan didn't hear; he had fixed the Assembly sanctorium in his mind, and the scene was already changing. The Malefica did not bother with an illusion this time, instead maintaining her true self against the new background—a hunched and wretched wraith on the sanctorium floor.

"Pain can be beautiful, too," Zan said, turning again to the casket.

"I've seen the possibilities, boy." But he was already walking up the aisle. "They shift and change—fickle, they are, until they are lived and become fixed. But in this I am not mistaken! If humanity is to survive—beautiful, horrible, wonderful humanity—the Spinner *must* stand with her consort under the Midwinter sky at midnight in the Ebonwilde. She *must* complete the spell that she began a thousand years ago. She *must* do all these things, or everything will die . . ."

If she said anything else, Zan did not hear, because he'd let go of the bell, and the Assembly had become solid around him, and the Malefica was gone with the Gray. But even though she was not there, her words rang in the rafters.

The Spinner must stand with her consort.

Her consort was Adamus, reborn as Dominic Castillion.

No matter how much Zan loved her, no matter how much he ached for her, her destiny was already laid out. She would save the world, and she would do it without him.

He turned toward the coffin, and prepared himself to say goodbye one last time.

43

NOW

CHYDAEUS

5 DAYS TO MIDWINTER
1621

The fall into the reflection in Valentin's blood was more frightening than anything Chydaeus had ever experienced. It was like being swallowed by a storm or a bottomless pit, or swept away into an ocean of nothingness. Worse still was the fact that Valentin—his only guide —appeared to have lost consciousness in the fall. Terrified, Chydaeus called out into the void, "Help! Help! Is anyone there? Can anyone help us?"

And to his surprise, the mist parted. They were not falling any-more . . . they were lying on the ground of a plaza beneath a white sanctorium. A clock tower loomed overhead, its hands stuck at twelve.

A woman waited there, breathtaking in a white capedress, with a sweet, pink smile and glossy chestnut hair. Her eyes, however, were black—not like the eyes of those recovered from the Bitter Fever, with no differentiation between pupil and iris; these were the color of obsidian from one side to the other.

"Careful not to let go of him, nor to let him relinquish the bell," she said. "He is what is holding you both here, and the Gray can be chaotic if you are lost in it, unanchored. You could go mad."

"Are you Valentin's friend?" Chydaeus ventured. "The one who made it so Fidelis could not read his mind?"

"I am," she replied, bending to grace him with her enchanting smile. "You may call me Lily."

"Lily," he said, testing out the name. It was pretty, like a flower. There weren't many flowers left in the Midnight Zone; they had all been pulled up to make room for battle rings and barracks and ship-yards and smithies. "Will he be all right?"

"I will send him to someone who can help him," she said. "He has been kind to me on more than one occasion. I find that I do not wish to see him die."

"Me either," Chydaeus agreed. "He helped me, too. During the endurance rite. And I think, maybe, sometime before? I have trouble remembering sometimes."

"Yes," Lily said. "I've seen that."

It struck him that perhaps she had seen his entire life. That perhaps, maybe . . . could he be looking at the very Goddess that Fidelis spoke so much about?

"Do you see . . . everything?" he asked. "Are you the Empyrea?"

"No," Lily replied. "I am not her, but I do see a lot, from here in the Gray. Watch," she said. She waved her hand, and they were no longer in front of a sanctorium chapel, but in Grandmaster Fidelis's study. Chydaeus yelped, but she said, "Worry not, little one. He cannot see nor hear you."

The Grandmaster was poring over a book, written in long-faded ink. The Spinner's Codex, Chydaeus guessed, after what he'd heard them speaking about earlier. A man came into the room, and Fidelis looked up. "Did you find him?" he asked.

Cruentis shook his head. "He's vanished, Grandmaster. Seemingly without a trace."

Fidelis tried to hide his anger, forcing it into a simmering calm. "Let him go, then. We don't need him. Not when we have the boy. And the message?"

"Delivered," Cruentis said. "Friend Geminus of the second faction was able to transport long enough to tie it just outside the witch's land. They will see it."

"Good," Fidelis said, leaning backwards. "The time is drawing near, Cruentis. The new day is close at hand. After one thousand years, the Spinner will finally be reunited with her consort."

Chydaeus found himself shivering, though he didn't know why. Grandmaster Fidelis was his friend! He had nurtured him, guided him through all of the initiation rites, propped him up as a leader among the Circle Midnight. Why, then, did he hear these words and tremble?

Lily changed the scene again, bringing them back to the plaza beneath the sanctorium clock tower. "You have two paths ahead of you, little one. Two choices. You can go with Valentin now and leave the Circle behind, or you can return to it, and stay close to its leaders and, when the time comes, be ready to take your final rite."

"Which one would you choose," he asked, "if you were me?"

"I don't know," Lily said, as if surprised. "I've never had the chance to choose. But this I will say: you have earned the easy path of the first, but you are brave enough and strong enough to endure the path of the second. I've seen it."

"Then that is the one I choose," Chydaeus said. "I want to be brave."

Lily nodded. "Then, little one, brave you will be." The shiny, pretty woman faded, and in her stead sat a haggard crone. Her hands were stuck to the ground, black veins wriggling under near-translucent skin. "Hold out your hand."

PART III

THE LONGEST NIGHT

44

NOW

Rosetta cast a summoning spell at the edge of the woods, and four horses answered, one from each compass direction. They were wild and handsome, appearing from between the trees like spirits born of the Ebonwilde itself. Well, all except one.

"Madrona?" I said, stifling a laugh as the crotchety old beast cantered toward us with a sour reluctance, as if she had been disturbed in the middle of her supper. I could tell she had been running free for a while by the unkempt look of her mane and coat, but the freedom seemed to have worked wonders with her temperament. When I saddled her, she only tried to nip at me once.

"You know," Rosetta mused, watching me scold her, "you could transform into a horse yourself, if you wanted. Or an eagle. Or—"

"—a fox?" I asked. Then I said, looking away, "I don't know how, Rosetta."

"It's natural," she said. "The transformation is just . . . something you do. As easy as breathing."

"Or as hard," I said. "Try teaching someone to breathe who doesn't already know how to do it."

"You're the Spinner," she argued. "You should be able to do everything she did. You already know how. You just have to remember."

"Well, maybe Vieve should have picked someone a little smarter to be reincarnated into," I said dourly.

"Maybe," Rosetta said hesitantly, "when you get a little more . . . used . . . to your capabilities, you could use them to . . . undo what was done."

"You want me to make us mortal again?" I asked. "I wouldn't know where to begin."

"But you could at least try," she replied. She cast a quick, reflexive glance at Nathaniel before catching herself and forcing herself to look away.

Before we set out, I helped Rosetta one more time with her healing spells on Nathaniel, though without the urgency of the last life-and-death situation, I fumbled through it so badly she finally dismissed me and finished it up on her own. Nathaniel was already looking better, buoyed as he was by Rosetta's stealthy, magic-weaving fingers and the prospect of seeing his little girl again so very soon.

That love he had for Ella . . . I feared it nearly as much as I envied it.

"Go swiftly," Nathaniel said, giving me a hug goodbye.

"Go safely," I replied, returning the embrace fiercely.

"I've bent the paths," Rosetta said, reining her horse alongside his, "to make them shorter for both of us. Hopefully it will help us save some time."

I nodded. "We'll see you soon, at the fort."

"At the fort," she replied, and she and Nathaniel began their trek on a road veering eastward, while Dominic and I headed straight north. We left the bloodstained ribbon in the tree, and I watched it as we cantered past, wondering whose blood had been spilled to make it, and if the perpetrator who left it there for me was still somewhere close by, waiting for us.

We rode all day on Rosetta's preternaturally shortened track and camped for just a few scant hours, mostly to rest our horses and for Dominic to catch a few hours of sleep while I pretended to do the same, head on my pack, several feet away from him. It was colder that way, but I could not bring myself to get closer to him. I'd shut off my apprehensions and inhibitions to kiss him, but they had not stayed locked away for very long afterward. I was plagued with the sense that I had done wrong, but whether I'd sinned against Dominic, or Zan, or myself . . . I could not be sure.

The next morning, as we were packing our small camp away, Dominic said finally, "You're avoiding me."

"I can't avoid you," I said, with a light, flimsy laugh. "We're the only two out here."

"You know what I mean."

I turned to face him. "I'm sorry," I said. "It's just all been very . . . confusing."

"You don't have to give me an answer until you're ready to," he replied. "I will not ask you for anything you're not ready or willing to give, Aurelia. But please, I beg you, don't freeze me out." He lifted a gloved hand to my cheek. "Let me know your doubts and fears, so that I can have the chance to assuage them."

I mustered a nod. Stars! This would all be so much easier if he were still that man I met on the *Humility*, the one I knew how to hate. When I knew him as a simple villain of black and white, and not this complicated tapestry of damage and determination and dogged commitment to annoyingly virtuous ideals. And I *felt* something for him, I did . . . I just didn't know what, nor how much.

Another half day later, we stopped by a stream to rest and water the horses. I led them to the snow-packed bank while Dominic pored over the map, trying to figure out where our truncated travels had landed us and how far we might still have left to go. The wind had kicked up, and though the sky had been, up until now, a bright and wintry blue, clouds were beginning to gather in dusky swaths that reminded me of the Gray.

"We should hurry," I said. "If we don't want to get caught in a storm."

We remounted the horses and guided them into a gallop, racing under the Ebonwilde's distant canopy. The whistle of the wind and thunder of our horses' hoofbeats were loud, but not so loud that we did not hear the snap and crack of branches up ahead as something hurtled through the air and landed with a heavy thud onto the ground, rolling to a spread-eagle stop in the twilit snow one hundred feet ahead.

"Bleeding stars," Dominic cursed. Then, "Aurelia! No! It could be a trap! It could be dangerous!"

But I had already clambered down from Madrona's back and was trudging against the wind toward the inert body.

Dominic dismounted as well, hurrying after me, trying to get between me and the potential danger, but I shook him off. I could already sense the whispering magic whipping past me on the wind —the sure sign of nearby blood.

"They're injured," I said. "And I might be able to help."

Dominic shouted, "Did you even think, for one moment, that this could be the Midnighter who left that bloody ribbon on the tree for you? Let me go first at least! Aurelia!"

"You forget," I shouted over my shoulder, "nothing can hurt me." But as I said it, my boots snagged on something that made a soft tinkling sound as it moved.

I bent down to see, and pulled two intertwined chains from the snow. From one dangled a bell shaped like a sombersweet blossom, from the other, a firebird pendant and a white-stone ring.

And I remembered, long ago, the vision given to me by a ghostly queen of a boy bleeding in a drift of swirling white petals.

"Blood on the snow," I whispered. Only this time, it was real snow, and there were no miraculous flowers nearby to heal him.

Zan.

I shoved the chains in my pocket and ran the rest of the way to his side, falling to my knees to wrench him up out of the snow, tearing off my cloak so that I could wrap it around his bare shoulders—like it would make much difference. The cold was a secondary concern, as he'd die from his wounds before hypothermia would even have a chance to set in; he was *covered* in slashes and welts and mottled purple-and-yellow bruises. He'd been beaten and tortured and dropped here in a snowbank for us to find.

No. For *me* to find.

"It's him," I said, as Dominic caught up to me. "Zan."

"Aurelia," he said, trying to lift me, "it's too late. Step away. Let me—"

"No!" I cried, pushing him back. "No. It's *not* too late. It's *not*." I cradled Zan's head in my lap. His face was a wreck, swollen and bruised, but I brushed his cheek, saying, "Zan. Zan, can you hear me? Wake up. Please wake up."

The call of the magic in his blood was waning—a better indicator to me of his precarious position than his shallow breath or slowing pulse. I couldn't use his blood to save him; the magic left in what he'd already lost was waning, and letting any more would kill him for sure.

With cold and clumsy fingers, I pulled the vial of blood from beneath my shirt; I had to use my own.

"No, Aurelia," Dominic said, urgent and uneasy, "don't waste your blood on the man who couldn't spare a single thought for you."

"I have to," I said. "It doesn't matter what he's done—I can't let him die. Please, Dominic. Try to understand."

He said nothing more, turning his back while I unstoppered the vial and poured the red liquid into my hands, warm as the day it was freed from my living veins. The familiar music of my own magic began to stir, crooning at the joy of its release from the glass. It had done this before; it knew what to do. Indeed, my mortal body's blood seemed to pull toward Zan's life force, recognizing and acknowledging that which had once been its own.

My blood spoke a truth I could not; I'd died giving him the last of my life beside the altar of the Stella Regina, and I'd do it again and again until I had no more blood left to give.

Placing my hands on his bare chest, just under his clavicle, I gave the magic my command. "Exsarcio," I said. *Mend.* "Restituo." *Repair.* Then I drew a pattern with the blood, a knot like the one I saw Rosetta do for Nathaniel, pulling at the wispy strings of power that, when I blinked, were webbing across everything. I plucked them from the air and rerouted them into the spell, pinning them in points to Zan's skin. *Up, down, around, across, back again, forward again, down.* Over and over. *Bind,* I told the knot. *Heal,* I told the blood.

It was a clumsier undertaking than what we'd done with Nathaniel on Rosetta's kitchen table. It had none of the easy elegance of Rosetta's knot work, but what I lacked in grace I gained in sheer forcefulness; it worked because I willed it to. It worked because I could not stand for what would happen otherwise.

Slowly, slowly, the cuts began to close. The bruises began to fade. The swelling began to diminish, and then Zan's eyes flickered open, his irises alight and gleaming molten gold.

He lifted a hand to my cheek. "I found you," he said in the barest, breathy whisper. "At last."

45

NOW

KELLAN

3 DAYS TO MIDWINTER
1621

Kellan had spent the days since Aurelia's intrusion into his meeting with Castillion and their subsequent absence afterward in a state of heightened anxiety. He carried on, in public, the same way as he had been for months: moving among the ragtag refugees, offering his condolences or encouragement as the situation required, and help with raising a tent or fetching water or fixing a wagon wheel when what a refugee or family needed was physical assistance more than meaningless platitudes. But in private, when each day came to a close, he returned to his own tent outside of Fort Castillion's wooden palisades to nurse his private fears alone.

He had just finished his night's rations when a sound outside the canvas sent alarm bells sounding in his head. His body went taut and he raised his silver arm in preparation to fight, when three figures pulled the flap of the antechamber aside and entered. Two women in capes of gray wool, and a young man dressed in the livery of a Fort Castillion guard.

"Oh, thank all the stars," he burst, going to the young man first and pulling him tight to his chest. "I haven't heard from Zan in days, and without his updates, I was starting to think the worst had happened to you. Did you make the switch?"

"We did," Jessamine said, removing her cape. Beside her, Cecily produced a sheaf of papers, wrapped in leather and tied with a string. "Hopefully the abbess didn't notice the difference before she sold the Codex off to Fidelis."

"She won't," Cecily said. "Aveline only ever saw its value as a commodity, not a text to be read and learned from. In all the years I lived and worked alongside her in the abbey, I never saw her look inside it—not even once." She frowned. "But what's this about Zan? You haven't heard from him at all?" Cecily's brow crinkled with worry. "With the Circle on the move and Midwinter so very close . . ."

Jessamine took her hand and held it, a gesture of comfort. "He'll be fine," she said reassuringly. "He's too bullheaded to fail." But after she said it, she went quiet; no one wanted to know what would happen if they lost their eyes and ears among the Circle Midnight now.

"But we have this," Kellan said, looking at the leather-wrapped sheaf. "We have the real Spinner's Codex."

"Now we just need the Spinner to get back to the fort," Jessamine said, "so we can give it to her."

★

With help from Rosetta's shortened roads, she and Nathaniel first caught sight of the eastern caravan train in less than two days, a long, thin stripe of black against the snowy shoreline, the bleak indigo water of the northern sea stretching endlessly beyond. It was getting on in the evening, and they could see the tiny, winking dots of the cookfires speckling the line. The caravan was stopping for the night, pitching their tents in preparation for coming snow.

Rosetta and Nathaniel pulled their horses alongside the ridge to watch it for a moment. "Are you ready?" she asked him.

"I think I am." Somewhere down there, his daughter was waiting for him, and though Rosetta was coming to realize that he was a man of few words, his expression spoke volumes: it was gentle and wistful and warm, his fever-dark eyes full of emotion.

But as she studied his face, the hopeful smile faded away, replaced by concern. "What is that?" he asked, and she followed the line of his gaze past the wagon train to the ocean where, one by one, black ships were appearing as if from thin air. Flying above them was the flag of the Circle Midnight, with its moon cradled in the center of an eight-pointed star. There were two, then six, then twelve . . . and then, too many to count.

They raced down the mountainside, hearts pounding in time to their horses' hoofbeats. The switchbacks down the mountain were steep, but their Ebonwilde horses were surefooted and stout-hearted, and made what should have been a three-hour descent in less than one—though it felt like an eternity. When they reached the valley floor, the wind had risen to a gale, pinioning them between its furious force and the side of the mountain. They pushed through it, however, spurred by the burgeoning scent of smoke and the haunting sound of distant screaming. It was terrible.

Worse, though, was when the screaming stopped.

In the ensuing silence, ash began to blow into their faces, caught on the wind like a driving swarm of moths. Soon, the smoke was so thick in the air that they began to cough on it, arms up to shield their eyes from the sting of flying cinders.

The caravan was burning.

They had to dismount when their terrified horses would go no further, and walked the last hundred feet to break from the trees. When they did, they were greeted with a nightmarish sight: a sky swallowed by angry clouds, a valley choked with burning carts and wagons.

And all along the train, bloodstained ribbons whipped in the sulfurous wind.

"Merciful Empyrea," Rosetta said, but in the shadow of the scene stretched out before them, the phrase had no meaning; a deity that would allow an atrocity of this scale could never be called merciful.

The bitter smell of smoke mixed with damp earth and dark blood. As Rosetta scanned one edge of the panorama to the other, she saw limbless bodies, bodiless heads, entrails, and the mementos of their upended lives—clothes and baskets, food and tools and trunks, dishes and family heirlooms—were scattered like refuse among the burning coals of their carts. And every once in a while the wind would part the smoke to reveal the black-wood longboats moving across the water to the waiting galleons.

Rosetta touched Nathaniel's arm as he blankly stared at the display, just to remind him that she was there. And he turned to her, his composure crumbling, throwing his arms around her as his knees buckled. She staggered beneath his sudden weight, but held on, clutching his head to her chest as he knelt next to her with his fingers twisted into her cloak like claws, sobbing in great, body-racking heaves as a wet snow began to fall. She held him and held him and did not let go even when they were both shivering and soaked to the bone. While he wrung out his sorrow, she traced tiny spells of comfort into his back and shoulders: spells of warmth and easement of sore muscles and spells to alleviate weary bones. She couldn't alleviate his heartache—and even if she had such an ability, she wouldn't use it on him. The pain was proof that his daughter had lived, and that she had been dearly loved. She'd never take that away from him. She'd never want to take that away from anyone.

When Nathaniel's grief was expended, he quietly got to his feet and said, "Those boats will be headed to Fort Castillion next; we have to get there first."

46

NOW

3 DAYS TO MIDWINTER

We beat the storm to Fort Castillion, arriving the next morning before the sun came up.

Though Zan was no longer in any immediate danger, I could not heal him completely without expending the last few ounces of the precious blood left in my vial. I'd pulled him back from the brink, but his body would have to do the rest of the work on its own. Because he was drifting in and out of consciousness, however, he could not ride upright in a saddle, so we slung his body over Dominic's horse while Dominic walked alongside to keep him from sliding off. I volunteered to be the one to do it—if Zan was to be a burden, he should be mine—but Dominic wouldn't hear of it. So I rode behind them, watching them both warily: the man I was destined to love but didn't

—not quite, not yet—and the one I should not love but didn't know how to stop.

The tent city had grown by a mile since I'd last seen it, but it was quiet as we rode through, save for the workers moving through the fever-marked tents, gathering up the night's dead for the fire. We trudged past the palisade and then across the lower drawbridge, with embers drifting up from the ever-burning moat on either side, whirling like bright orange confetti against the predawn periwinkle.

At the end of the upper gate, the portcullis was raised as we approached, and a line of Castillion soldiers was waiting for us on the other side. They must have observed our arrival from the watchtowers, because they took our horses and offloaded Zan onto a ready litter without waiting for orders.

"Please make sure his wounds are treated," Dominic said as four soldiers lifted the handles of the litter, "and then transfer him into a suitable cell."

I bit my lips together to keep from protesting. Dominic had shown plenty of grace for the situation already, and I could hardly demand a lavish suite to house his political rival—the man who had betrayed me.

"Sir," one of the soldiers said, "we have a full brief ready for you in the main hall."

"Thank you, I'll be right there," he said. Then, to another of his soldiers, "Please escort the princess to my study."

"Wait—" I said as he turned to go. "Do you . . . want me to go with you?"

"Go," he said. "Rest. Relax. I'll have some new clothes sent up for you. At least one of us should get some rest."

I could have argued further, but as much as I wanted to be included in important strategic conversations, I wanted to be left with my tumultuous thoughts more. Finding Zan had sent me into a tailspin, the little stability I'd salvaged for myself since waking gone up in a puff of smoke. So I went quietly, allowing myself to be led away and deposited back into Dominic's study without complaint. When I was finally alone, I brought out the chains I'd retrieved from the snow beside Zan and laid them out side by side on Dominic's desk, puzzling over their meaning. How had Zan ended up exactly where I'd find him? How had he come to have the bell in his possession? Why was he still wearing my firebird charm? And the ring . . .

The ring.

I paced and paced, trying to make sense of it, but to no avail.

I *had* to know what had happened. What it meant. And so, before I could second-guess myself, I snatched up the chains and hurried back down the tower stairs, nearly bowling over a trio of maidservants on the way up with new clothes Dominic had ordered to be delivered to me.

"My lady?" one of them called, but I kept moving, my eyes fixed straight ahead. If I hesitated even a moment, I might lose my nerve.

Nathaniel had given me a vague notion about which direction the dungeon was when we'd made our escape through the Trove, so it was not difficult to find. It was small, and cleaner than most dungeons in my experience, with well-swept stairs and snug cells carved straight from the rock, and set with iron bars and padlocked gates. All of them were empty, too, and for a moment I wondered if I had arrived too soon, and if Zan was still being treated elsewhere in the fort. But at the end of the corridor, in the last cell, I could see the shape of a man silhouetted in the fragile beam of a narrow skylight. He was awake now, leaning with his back to the bars, head drooping down, both arms propped over his knees. He was wearing a prisoner's smock, obscuring the view of his healing wounds.

I stopped in my tracks, hovering at a safe distance, not quite able to cross that last stretch between us.

"I know you're there," he said without turning. "Aurelia." His voice was low and uneven, all the sharp, princely polish weathered into gravel.

I swallowed hard and stepped forward. "It's cold in here," I said. "I'll make sure someone brings you a cloak. Or a blanket."

"How very good of you," he said, keeping his gaze trained upon the wall ahead, his hair falling forward in dark strands, obscuring my view of his eyes like a curtain. It was longer now, reaching almost to his shoulders—which, despite the hostile insouciance of his reply, were stiff. As if he were bracing himself for a blow.

"I'll have them send down something for you to eat, too. And a cot, maybe . . . I'm sure Dominic would not want you to—"

"I'm sure *Dominic*," he said, darkly emphasizing Castillion's first name, "could not care less about the quality of my accommodations."

I felt anger rising in my chest. "And what about me? Should *I* care?"

"I have no interest in how you feel about me."

"None at all? Seems like a strange thing to say to someone who just saved your life . . . again."

"I never asked you to do that."

"Next time I find you half-naked and bleeding all over the snow, I'll be sure to wait for your express permission before I intervene."

"Would be a nice change," he said, "for once."

"You'd prefer I left you for dead?"

"I'd prefer you left me alone."

"I'd love to," I snapped. "I'd love to forget you as easily as you forgot me. Please, teach me how it's done."

He was silent, still staring at the wall.

"Nothing to say now? I counted on you," I said. "I bet my *life* on you. And you—you just—"

"I abandoned you," he said. "Failed you. You can say it out loud, Aurelia."

From the depths of my soul, I asked, *"Why?"*

"You already know why, if you read my letter . . ."

"Don't," I snapped. "Don't give me any more of those horseshit excuses. Turn around, Zan. Look me in the eyes. And then tell me the *truth*."

Gingerly, he pulled himself to his feet, holding on to the bars for support. We were face to face now, separated only by a measly handful of inches and a few thin rods of iron. His eyes flashed gold, like sun through honey amber, but his face was a mask of chiseled stone. "I loved a girl named Aurelia," he said, each word carefully chosen and coldly delivered, "but she died in my arms. I did not go after you because *you* are not *her*."

Without breaking my stare, I lifted my fist to eye level. The chain was laced through my fingers, and I loosened my grip just enough to let his mother's white-stone ring drop and dangle, spinning in the light.

"*Liar,*" I said.

With a sharp intake of breath, his eyes flicked to the necklace and back to me — a split-second slip in his mask that gave me a bewildering glimpse at the torment he'd so carefully hidden underneath.

I took a steadying step backwards, as if the truth was an unexpected weight I hadn't sufficiently prepared myself to carry.

"What aren't you telling me?" I whispered, searching his face.

"Aurelia," he murmured, leaning to press his forehead against the bars. "It's better if . . . I can't just . . ." Then, "Go. Just *go.*"

I wanted to. I wanted to flee. To hide. To find a pillow into which I could bury my face and scream. But before I could make so much as a move, there came the sound of heavy boots upon the dungeon's stone stairs, and Dominic — followed by a trio of Castillion soldiers — appeared at the end of the corridor of cells.

When he saw me, he raised a dark brow — not exactly thrilled to find me there, but certainly not surprised, either. "Bring him out," he said with a wave, and one of the soldiers moved to open Zan's cell, while another stepped inside and began to tie his hands.

"What's going on?" I asked.

"Lord Greythorne wants to meet with us. *All* of us, including you" — Dominic's gaze moved from me to Zan, who was watching him guardedly from behind half-closed lids — "and him. He says it is too important to wait."

The soldier pushed Zan out in front of him, and he stumbled forward, still unsteady on his feet. "Careful!" I said indignantly. "He is injured!"

The soldier shot a questioning look at Dominic, who nodded. "Do as she says."

We fell in step behind them, moving up the stairs and out onto the snowy courtyard and to the heavy oak-and-iron doors of the fort's main keep, where Dominic raised a hand of dismissal. "We can take it from here," he said.

"Sir," the soldier said, saluting.

With the door closed behind us, Dominic removed the ropes from Zan's wrists. "If you try anything, you won't get far." It was a feeble warning; Zan was barely able to stand on his own, let alone make a run for it. But Dominic didn't need to let him go unbound, either; he did it for me, and I was appreciative.

The Great Hall of Fort Castillion was a cavernous space made of cold granite, anchored on the western side of the room by a fireplace so massive I could probably stand inside it without ducking. Light was coming in from tall, slit-like windows that lined the upper story of the rectangular room, beaming down upon an empty banquet table made of dark Ebonwilde timber. Four people were already seated around it: Kellan at the far end, flanked by a youthful soldier wearing a Renaltan fleur-de-lis livery on his right side and a woman I did not recognize on the left. She was dressed in a simple silken, cream-colored caftan that set off her beautiful ebony skin, her hair covered by a matching silk shawl. Beside her, however, was someone I *did* recognize, and I nearly shouted with joy upon seeing her.

"Jessamine!" I said, and she rose from her seat to sweep me into a tight hug.

"It is so good to see you again, my dear, dear friend," she said, leaning back to cup my chin in both of her hands. Then she motioned to the other woman at the table, saying, "Allow me to introduce you to Sister Cecily of Widows' Isle. She's one of the Sisters of the Sacred Torch."

"So pleased to meet you," Cecily said, putting out her hand and smiling warmly.

"And you," I said.

Kellan had also risen, though it wasn't me he went to, but Zan. "Thank the stars," he said, clapping Zan on the shoulder with a camaraderie I'd never have believed if I hadn't seen it myself. "After you stopped communicating, I was beginning to fear the worst. And then when Emilie said she saw Aurelia and Castillion bring you in —"

I froze, dropping Sister Cecily's hand to swivel around and stare at Kellan. "Did you just say . . . Emilie?"

Kellan and Zan exchanged looks, and the young man at the end of the table also stood. He took several steps toward me and then bowed deeply. As he did so, the air around him began to glimmer, and by the time he straightened again, I saw that he was not a Renaltan guard at all, but a young woman about my same age and size, her blond hair tied into a long, thick plait. Her face was instantly recognizable, even marred as it was by a tracery of scars on her neck and cheek; it had been etched into my memory forever. I'd even taken her name for a while, back in Achlev, so that I couldn't forget the girl it had belonged to, or what she'd done for me.

And around her neck hung a pendant, like the one I'd just returned to Zan, in the shape of an emerald dragon.

"Emilie?" I whispered, unable to fully convince myself that she was real. Of all the many strange things that had come to pass in the last hours, this was the most unexpected. The maid who'd switched places with me on the night I left Renalt for Achleva and had been burned at the stake in my stead—she was *alive*. And she was *here*.

She smiled. "Hello again, Princess."

47

NOW

AURELIA

3 DAYS TO MIDWINTER
1621

When the reintroductions were finished, I went to the chair to the right of the head of the table, concluding that Dominic would, of course, take that one. But Cecily cleared her throat and said, "No, my lady. You should sit at the place of highest honor."

Embarrassed, I said, "This is Dominic's holding, his fort. It should be him who—"

"No," Dominic said, "Sister Cecily is correct. You are the Spinner, Aurelia. It's time you claim your rightful place." He pulled out the chair for me and gestured for me to sit down. Everyone else was watching me, waiting to see what I would do, and I—too flustered to come up with a sufficient counterargument—hurried to it, just to make the awkward moment end. Castillion moved to the chair at my right, and with no other choices available to him, Zan gingerly low-ered himself into the one at my left.

"Now," Castillion said, still capable of controlling the conclave from the second chair over, "I think it's time we all put our cards out on the table."

"A gambling metaphor," Jessamine said. "I approve."

"We should start with this," Cecily said, laying a leather-bound sheaf of paper in the center of the table and pulling the strings that bound it. Then, carefully, she laid it open. The pages inside were brit-tle and yellowed with age, the ink faded but still legible.

"What is it?" I asked, trying to decipher why a bundle of old papers would feel familiar. But it did; and when she passed one of the fragile pages to me, I understood why.

It was written in my handwriting.

"Every Sister who has lived on Widows' Isle, since the Order of the Sacred Torch was founded, collects their life's writings into a compi-lation called a codex. At their death, it is bound like this and housed in the abbey archive. This was the first to ever make the collection." Her eyes flicked to mine. "It is the Spinner's Codex."

"These are Vieve's writings?" I asked.

"They are indeed," Cecily replied. "It is a record of her life with the mages who took her, as a young girl, from her father's home and were her mentors and teachers from that point until her death."

"The Verecundai," I said, glancing at Dominic.

"They were not known by that name back then," Cecily said. "They were simply eight scholars and mages who wanted to study in solitude, and so they built the compound that would eventually become the Abbey of the Sisters of the Sacred Torch. It was there that they began matching their high mages' visions with the star patterns foretelling the Spinner's power, and her eventual role as first queen in a world that would be remade following the Empyrea's descension from the heavens. All of this information is included in the Midnight Papers."

"Which are . . . ?" I asked.

Emilie spoke this time. "The Midnight Papers are the manifesto written by the Circle Midnight's founder, Fidelis the First. It begins with Vieve's history, chronicling her discovery, then her scholarship and training by the Verecundai, and her eventual love affair with its youngest member, Adamus. It tells of the Verecundai's plan to use Vieve to call down the Empyrea, under the pretense of beginning a new and better era of the world. But in truth, they wanted to use Vieve to steal the Empyrea's power—which is to say, her immortality. So they brought Vieve to a sacred spot on Midwinter Night and had her begin the spell that they had altered. But the Empyrea's wrath was too great, and they murdered Vieve to end the spell and keep the Empyrea at bay. Adamus, in his grief, used his own blood and dying breath to curse them with the longevity they had craved, but in a state of damnation, until the day when Adamus and Vieve were reborn and reunited, and the Empyrea would descend as foretold, and a new world would begin."

Dominic steepled his fingers. "None of this is new," he said. "What does any of it have to do with the Circle Midnight?"

"Because," Emilie said, "Fidelis of the Circle Midnight believes that *he* is the reincarnation of Adamus. He is orchestrating a plot to ensure that he is the one by Vieve's side when the Empyrea descends. And, indeed, everything that he and the rest of the Circle Midnight have done in the last year has been to reach that goal. Every disaster, every death, every illness . . . all done as described in the Midnight Papers, and done in the Empyrea's name."

"I suppose that would explain this," Castillion said, removing a letter from his own pocket and laying it out on the table next to the Spinner's Codex. "My guards tell me that this came three days ago. It is a confirmation that King Conrad is, in fact, currently in the Circle's possession, and a demand that Aurelia meet with Fidelis at Extremitas Point on the night of Midwinter to exchange her freedom for his." He scratched his chin. "But why Extremitas Point? It has nothing to do with any of this."

"That's an easy one," Jessamine said. "He chose Extremitas Point because *we* told him that's where the descension would take place."

"We knew he would be after the Spinner's Codex held at the abbey on Widows' Isle," Cecily added, "so we forged a copy, changed a few things, and switched it out before he got his hands on it."

"I knew Sad Tom here would make an excellent forger if he put his mind to it," Jessamine said, beaming at Zan. "He did not disappoint."

Kellan added, "Extremitas Point was just a convenient misdirect. A place remote enough to keep Fidelis away from where the real events would be taking place."

I nearly knocked my chair over in my haste to nab the missive. "But how does that help anything? It just means I have to go farther away to exchange myself for Conrad."

"No, Aurelia," Kellan said. "It's not that simple."

"What could be *more* simple?"

This time, it was Zan who spoke. "Because if midnight on Midwinter arrives and you are not standing with Castillion at the Verecundai's glade"—his eyes darkened to a shadowy topaz—"everything we've spent the last year fighting for, sacrificing for . . . it will all be for naught."

The only person seemingly more surprised than me was Dominic. "What does that mean?" he asked, eyes narrowing.

Jessamine decided to play intermediary, gesturing calmly as she explained, "What it means is that you—and the Circle—have been operating with only half of the information necessary to understand what is coming."

"And I suppose you have that 'necessary information'? What source could you have that is more reliable than the Verecundai themselves?" Dominic challenged.

"*Any* source would be more reliable," Zan snapped, only to have Jessamine guilt him back into silence with a pointed glare.

"Our source is someone"—Kellan paused, searching for the right description—"uniquely situated to provide answers." He glanced around the table, as if to ask permission of the others before he continued. They all gave him affirming nods, and he said, "She exists in a place that allows her to see the past and present. And, in certain circumstances, the possibilities that can shape the future."

"You're talking about the Gray, aren't you?" I pulled the Ilithiya's Bell out and laid it on the table in front of me. "Is that where you got this, Zan? You took it from *her*." I tried to tamp down my emotions, but they were already boiling, spilling out hot from under the lid.

"She can't be trusted! She is a *monster!* Only motivated by her own interests . . ."

"Could not the same be said for all of us?" Zan was quiet, unruffled.

"She is the reason that I . . . that we . . ." I was on my feet now, seething. I took a breath and said, "She *killed* me."

"*She* did not kill you," Zan said. "*I* did."

That stunned me into silence. It was true, but only obliquely. He *had* drained the last of my vitality away from me, but it was not his fault. That choice and its consequences belonged solely to me.

"The fact is"—it was Emilie who spoke up this time—"that she —the Malefica, or Arceneaux, or whatever you want to call her—is the only reason we've made it this far."

"She is the one who sent me to you out there on the trail," Zan said. "Were it not for her—and for Conrad—I would be dead in a Circle Midnight cell right now."

"They *did* get you," Jessamine murmured. "How? We've been so careful . . . after all of these months . . ."

"I was in the Midnight Zone," Zan said. "Checking on Conrad. The endurance rite was hard on him, and I'd been keeping a closer watch since then. Fidelis has been parading him around the regiments for several weeks—what better way to prove his power than to make an example of a deposed, indoctrinated king? That's the kind of intimidation that sticks even without thought control—but things went sideways when *someone* decided to infiltrate Fidelis's own high magic with some of her own."

"You were there?" I asked.

"Yes," Zan said. "And I also saw that you were mere seconds away from having a horde of hive-minded Midnighters converge upon you. For months, we've been trying to keep you out of their hands, only to have you waltz right up to their front door and basically offer yourself as a Midwinter present for Fidelis." He shook his head in exasperation. "I had to make a distraction, so I set up one of their kilns to explode."

"The blast," I said, subdued. "That was you?"

"It was," Zan replied, matter-of-factly. "And it worked well enough —you got away. *I* was knocked out by the force of the explosion, and that is how the Circle got me. Let's just say, they weren't kind."

Emilie said, "Knowing how Fidelis operates, I'm shocked that you're still alive."

"It was Conrad's doing," Zan said. "He recognized me from the endurance rite. I think . . . I think there are pieces of his past life that want to resurface. He doesn't know his own name or who he used to be, but despite the effects of the frostlace and Fidelis's hold on his thoughts, the boy we knew is still there. He found the bell for me, and he went with me into the Gray. I'm not certain what happened after that. I can only guess that Arceneaux sent Conrad back to the Circle, and dropped me where she knew I'd be found by someone who could help me."

"Why would she send Conrad back to the Circle?" Jessamine asked.

"Hard to say," Zan said, "but more than likely, it's because she looked at the possibilities and decided the outcomes were better with him there. Indeed, it may tie in directly to Fidelis's ultimatum that

Aurelia meet him at Extremitas Point. If Conrad was not still with him, he would have no leverage to dangle to bring Aurelia to him."

"You just said that I can't go—"

"You can't," Kellan said firmly, "but perhaps, someone else could in your place." He turned to Emilie and said, "If you are up to it, of course . . ."

"It's all right," she said, putting her hand over his silver arm. "I've always known I'd have to face him again someday." She turned to me, and with a quick dance of her fingers, traced a pattern into the air. Before I could react, I realized I was staring into a perfect re-creation of my own visage. With no reflection to work from, I hadn't seen my own face since I went into the coffin on the Day of Shades. I was stunned, for a minute, by the sight of it—long dark hair instead of ashy blond, blue eyes instead of gray, and an expression of cool composure that belied all of the turmoil I felt inside.

Most startling of all, however, was the fact that this girl was . . . not beautiful, exactly. But *striking*. She reminded me of someone else. Someone full of confidence, someone strong and poised and charismatic.

She reminded me of *Arceneaux*.

Emilie's voice came through my lips. "On Midwinter Night, I will go to Fidelis as you, Aurelia, so that you can be where you need to be."

"Emilie," I said, throat tight. "You took my place once before, and you paid an awful price for it. I can't ask you to do it again."

"You're not asking," she said, and my image faded, revealing her own scarred face underneath. "I'm offering. And I won't be alone this time."

She looked at Kellan, who nodded and said, "We will get Conrad back for you, safe and sound."

"Kellan." My heart was too full to say more than just his name.

"I'm a soldier of Renalt," he said, his silver hand morphing into a fist. "I made a vow to its royal family. To its rightful king. I've made some terrible mistakes, but it's time to put those behind me. It's time to honor that vow."

48

NOW

AURELIA

3 DAYS TO MIDWINTER
1621

When the meeting was adjourned, Jessamine came with me to Dominic's study. As soon as the doors closed behind us, she gave a dreamy sigh and sank into one of his overstuffed chairs. "After spending so much time on the road, I cannot begin to tell you what a luxury a chair and a fireplace feel like." Then, "Don't tell Cecily. She thinks austerity is good for the soul."

"*Cecily,*" I said, giving her a wry smile. "Do tell me more about her."

"She's a *nun,*" Jessamine said, rising to inspect the copper basin, turning the valves and giving a pleased laugh when heated water started pouring from the spout. "Isn't that delightful?"

"I thought Delphinia was the one who enjoyed corrupting the saintly."

"Delphinia." Her smile faded.

"Jessamine," I said. "Is Delphinia . . . ?"

"It was the Bitter Fever." She pointed to her eyes. Once hazel, they were now as black as obsidian beads. "I was lucky to recover from it. Delphinia . . ."

I closed my eyes, picturing Delphinia's heart-shaped face, her daffodil hair and joyous smile.

"She died on the road," Jessamine continued. "Zan and I buried her as best we could."

"Zan?" I asked with a start. "Zan was with you?"

Jessamine looked as if she had just divulged a secret she was sworn to keep. "Yes. He was with me." She dipped her hand in the bath and swirled it around. "Water's ready."

I stripped off my soiled clothes and stepped into the basin while Jessamine gathered them up into a bundle for the maids to collect in the morning. "Jessa," I said. "Zan. Please tell me what happened. Tell me *everything*."

She gave me a long look, as if she were balancing the options. Finally, she nodded and pulled a chair next to the basin. "After the Day of Shades, Zan was . . . broken. He wasn't eating, he wasn't sleeping. I honestly thought he might die in that crypt beneath the Stella Regina. The one where we . . ." She stopped, flushing.

"Where you what?"

"Where we buried you, my dear."

I pulled my knees up and balanced my chin on my arms, watching the water separate into little droplets on my skin.

"He was painting a portrait of you," Jessamine continued, "on your tomb. He worked on it day and night—that is, when he wasn't drinking himself into a stupor. Just after Midwinter, he showed up at the Canary—I think he'd probably run out of food. We took him in, tried to help him get his feet back under him. And then, a few weeks later, the Bitter Fever started spreading. Zan, Delphinia, and I were exposed, so we left to keep from infecting the others, and to find help. Delphinia said her favorite sister was a healer, so we set out to find her. She died on the way there. We had to figure out afterward that the 'sister' she was referring to was a nun she knew from her own days in the sisterhood, short-lived though they were."

"Cecily?" I asked, and Jessamine nodded.

"After Delphinia died, we found a boat that was on its way to Castillion that would stop by the Abbey of the Sisters of the Sacred Torch and bought passage, but before we arrived, the captain found out that Castillion was offering a reward for bringing Zan in. We stole one of their longboats just as a storm was coming in and managed to make it the rest of the way to the abbey's island, but by then I'd come down with the sickness myself."

"But you recovered," I said. "Thank the stars."

"Thanks to the Sisters, I did. I don't remember much about those days, honestly, so I can't tell you everything that happened. But when I woke up, Cecily told me that the captain of the ship had returned for Zan, and that Zan had told her to go with me to the Canary. I only found out later that before the captain returned, she and Zan had been tripping on some hallucinogenic incense that had accidentally sent Zan into the Gray." She shook her head disapprovingly.

"You were mad about that?"

"Mad that I wasn't invited," she said, pouting. "I know I was still sick, but come on—they could have waited."

I stifled a small laugh, and she continued, "When I was fully recovered, Cecily and I borrowed one of the Sisters' boats and returned to the mainland and headed back to the Canary. When we arrived, Kellan and Emilie were already there. Shortly thereafter, Zan showed up, too—stepping out of thin air into the middle of the dining room floor. Damnedest thing I ever saw. He had the Ilithiya's Bell with him—Arceneaux had given it to him in the Gray, and after all of the sailors of the boat were dead from fever, he used it to get away. He'd discovered that, when holding it, he could enter the Gray through a reflective surface. To leave it, he just had to tell the Gray where he wanted to be and then when he got there, let go of the bell."

She paused her story to help me lather my hair with some lavender-scented soap, and then rinse it out by filling a cup and pouring it over my head, careful to keep the suds from getting in my eyes. "It was the Malefica, through Zan, who told us who you really were and how survival—not just our own, but that of humanity itself— depended on you and Castillion being reunited, so that you could stand together on Midwinter."

"And so," I said slowly, watching the soap from my hair swirl into a white lace on the surface of the water, "he turned his back on me."

"No," she said. "He let you go, yes. But he never turned his back on you."

"But he did it so easily . . . he sent a letter . . ."

"Nothing about what that boy did was easy," she said sternly. "He did what he thought he had to do. For you."

"For humanity . . ."

"No. Not humanity. He did it for *you*. Because he had learned that your destiny belonged to someone else. And I think, in truth, it didn't surprise him. Because, deep down, he never thought he deserved you. Not really." She set the cup aside and dried her hands on a nearby towel. "Aurelia, I think cutting out his own heart might have been easier than letting you go. And I can't say whether it was the *best* choice to make . . . I can only say that he made it because he believed that he had to. So that you could forget him and be with Castillion —your soul's true mate."

"Zan still loves me?" I murmured, thinking of his face behind the bars of his cell when I showed him his mother's ring.

"My darling girl," she said, tucking a lock of my wet hair behind my ear, "he never stopped."

I did not know, until that moment, whether I could still cry.

Jessamine helped me from the bath and got me dressed, then let me lay my head in her lap while she combed the tangles from my hair, all while tears rolled down my cheeks.

"What do I do now?" I whispered, curled up like a child, letting Jessamine's careful strokes with the comb soothe me.

"What do you *want* to do?" she asked. "Forget prophecies, and destinies, and the fate of the world. Love is simple, even if the circumstances are not. When you strip away every complication, every obstacle, every obligation, what is left? Who do you see?"

I want to wake up every day to the sun. I want to fall asleep with you beside me. I want days of hard work and sore muscles and arguments and nights spent reading together by the fire. I want a life, Aurelia. A real life.

In a trembling voice, I said, "Vieve loved Adamus. I've felt it . . . remembered it. But . . ."

"You are not Vieve," Jessamine said. "Are you?"

I sat up, looked Jessamine in the eyes.

"Can I tell you something?" she asked. "I was not born as you see me now. I felt, in my earliest years, that there had been, perhaps, some sort of mix-up. As if I should have gotten one body and was given another. My grandmother, bless her, recognized this. She was a feral mage, if you remember, and she cast a spell of transformation for me. See?" She held out her wrist, where a spell knot had been embedded into the skin, almost in the shape of a butterfly. It gleamed a faint, silvery white—like a scar, but not quite. "I don't believe that who we are is ever set in stone. We are transitory creatures—every day, we wake up as someone new, changed just a little bit by the experiences of the day before. Who we were is always a part of us, but it doesn't determine who we are, nor who we can still become." She smiled, tilting her head. "You are not the same girl I first met on the gambling floor of the Quiet Canary. If you can change so much in that short time, how can you expect to be the same person you were another lifetime ago?"

I shook my head. I didn't know.

"Choose what is right for the person you are today," she said, brushing a tear from my cheek with the back of her fingers, "and let it shape you into who you'll be tomorrow."

"But . . . what about Midwinter? What about the Circle Midnight, and the Spinner . . . ?"

"I have no fear of Midwinter, or the Circle. I have faith that somehow, you'll get us to the other side."

★

I found Dominic sitting alone at the empty table in the Great Hall. His back was facing the door as he gazed into the enormous fireplace, a bottle of liquor his only company, though his glass sat empty beside it.

"Dominic?" I ventured, wringing my hands nervously.

"I know what you're going to say," he said, standing. "I knew it the moment I saw you with him, out there in the Ebonwilde."

"I'm sorry," I said sincerely. "I do care for you, Dominic. I do. But . . ."

"But you won't marry me."

"No."

He nodded, closing his dark eyes. His hair was haloed by the light from the hearth behind him, turning the ice to fire.

"Whatever happens," I said, "I *will* stand beside you on Midwinter Night. We will end the curse and prevent the razing of the world, and we will do it together."

"But not *together*."

I shook my head. "Vieve loved Adamus. I know that. I've felt it. I remember it, in a way. But the truth is . . . I am not her. Not anymore.

Whatever happened in that former life, it can't erase the life I have now. And in this one . . ."

"You don't love me."

Mutely, I nodded.

He gave a curt, self-deprecating laugh. "And I thought the worst thing you could do to me was let me drown on the *Humility*." I tried to reach for him, but he lifted his hand as a rebuff. "No," he said. "Don't try to comfort me. I'm happy for you. I really am." He uncorked the bottle and filled his cup to the brim. "I will arrange for Valentin's release into your custody."

"Dominic," I said, voice tight. "I'd have never made a good—"

"I respect honesty," he said gruffly. "Don't start lying to me now." He gave me a wounded smile from behind his glass before taking a long drink. "I hope you won't think me a hypocrite if I leave all semblance of sobriety behind, just for tonight."

49

NOW

AURELIA

2 DAYS TO MIDWINTER
1621

The Night Garden was quiet, the air inside the glass walls thick with the scents of pine and evening florals. I waited under the dome facing my casket, my phantom heart thudding heavily in my chest as I listened to Zan's footfalls approach the center cloister. When they came to a stop, I finally turned to face him.

Gone was the prisoner's smock. He was clean and newly shaven, dressed in a high-collared jacket of jet black, embroidered on each shoulder with golden leaves that matched exactly the color of his eyes, which were guarded and wary.

He looked . . . dignified. Self-possessed. *Royal.*

We watched each other for a long while, as if the suspended silence was a sheet of glass, and in breaking it we risked bleeding.

I turned back toward the casket, fingering the ring on the chain, and finally spoke. "You came to me," I said. "At the Assembly. Didn't you?"

There was no use lying to me anymore, so he said simply, "Yes."

"You opened the casket."

"Yes."

"But then you took the ring," I said. "You had decided that I was destined to be with Dominic and you just . . . left me there for him to find."

His voice was almost inaudible, little more than a bare exhalation of breath. "No."

"I don't understand."

"You do," he said. "Frostlace is powerful, but it can't erase memories completely. They're still in there, somewhere."

"Frostlace?" I whispered, glancing at the Night Garden's swelling buds, remembering the open blossoms around the Verecundai's glade, and a purple bottle in the back of Onal's old stillroom, next to the badger milk and the salamander eyes.

Frostlace only has one purpose: to make you forget.

I whirled to face him. "What does that *mean?*"

"We decided together," he said, finally meeting my eyes. "We did it together. I could never have gone through with it on my own."

Slowly, slowly, the pieces began to fall into place. "You woke me up. You . . . you didn't abandon me."

"No," he said.

"But . . . without Castillion . . . without blood magic . . ."

"It was your blood," he said. "And the Malefica's magic."

That image of Zan leaning over me in the glass coffin, lit by a cascade of prismatic colors . . . that was *real*. Not just a dream, not just an imagining . . . a *memory*.

"She did not want to do it. She had seen many versions of the future in the Gray, and the only ones we lived through—that humanity lived through—all showed the same thing: you and Dominic Castillion, hand in hand in the Ebonwilde on the night of Midwinter. To come between you at all, she said, would put the future at risk. But she did as I asked, even so."

Scraps of memory whirled around me like leaves in a blustery wind, too far out of reach to catch and hold, but close enough to convince me that everything he was saying was true.

He continued, "I told you, then, everything I knew. About who you really are, and who Castillion is to you, and what the Malefica said about what was to come. The frostlace was your idea. I had to make you think that I'd abandoned you, so that you could turn to Castillion instead."

"The letter . . ."

"You helped me write it. You chose the words yourself . . . each designed to convince you—this you, the future you—to leave me behind in the past."

"How could you bear it?" I asked.

"You died in my arms, Aurelia," he said, voice breaking. "At least this way, I'd know you were *alive* somewhere in the world. Safe, and loved. For me, that was enough."

For the space of a breath, I was unable to move or think or even *breathe*. I was suspended in a flood of astonishment and relief, immobilized as the last of my doubts ebbed away and all I was left with was brilliant, burgeoning joy.

And then I crossed the cloister floor.

He shuddered a little at the first touch of my lips, his mouth slowly yielding as my gentle, searching kiss deepened into something more determined, more insistent. And when his arms went around me, pulling me tight against the firm length of his body, that insistence morphed again, this time into a dull ache at my core, like a hunger.

"Aurelia . . ." he said, pulling away. "We *can't* . . ."

I whispered, "Why not? Because of some distant history? An obscure bit of prophecy? A prediction of the future that changes minute by minute? Stars, I can't even trust my own *memory* anymore." I lifted my hand to his face, letting myself lightly trace the hard line of his jaw even as it clenched tighter beneath my touch. "But I trust this. I *believe* in this."

He said quietly, "I am so afraid. Of wanting you. Of losing you." His voice dropped even lower. "Of *touching* you."

"You can't hurt me now," I said, my thumb grazing the taut edge of his lower lip. "And you can't change my mind. Everything I have, everything I am—it's already yours. I'm choosing you, Zan. And I will keep choosing you, every day, every hour, every minute, for as long as I live."

With a ragged exhale, he turned his face toward my hand, pressing a kiss into the inside of my palm. We stood like that for a long time, together but still apart, unable to speak even while the steadily increasing quickness of our breath began telling a truth we were not yet able to vocalize to each other, or to ourselves.

And then slowly, slowly, I unclasped the spider pin at my throat and let my red cloak drop.

My shirt was next. I lifted it over my head and let it flutter to the ground beside us, my dark, tumbling hair my only remaining modesty. I could feel the barest touch of Zan's breath across my vulnerable neck as I slid his shirt from his shoulders and surveyed the remaining marks of the Circle's torture. Carefully, I touched my lips to each one in turn, tracing patterns of mending into his skin as I kissed the cuts and bruises away, starting beneath his ear and then moving delicately across his neck and shoulders, wickedly enjoying the hitch in his breath as I made my way down, kissing and teasing and healing.

Each step in this dance was a choice, and I made each choice delicately, deliberately. I took my time. I made him wait. And when his pliant mouth found my parted lips again, it tasted just like the Verecundai's apple: tart and honeyed both at once . . . so wonderfully bitter, so terribly sweet.

"Merciful stars," he murmured against my ear. "I may die of this."

"I forbid it," I said, and drew him close again.

It was a dance, yes, but also a spell—a stitch, a knot, a promise, woven with our bodies and written into our souls, with the starry constellations in the greenhouse dome bearing witness. Everything that had ever separated us, every lie, every loss, every hurt, mistake, and misunderstanding, now became what dragged us back to one another.

We flowed together and broke apart, touching and tasting and kissing and clinging, alone under a canopy of branches and surrounded by moonflower and wisteria and the tender buds of near-Midwinter frostlace.

And when it was over and I lay with him in the hazy afterglow of our joining, sweetly spent and dreamily content, his body curved protectively around mine and the soft in and out of his breath ruffling my hair, I closed my eyes.

And for the first time since emerging from the casket, I slept.

★

When we emerged from the Night Garden at dawn, it was to a roaring commotion in the town below. I caught the arm of a passing soldier and said, "What is going on? What is happening?"

"The Circle is coming," the man said. "We received word during the night that they slaughtered a train of refugees on the eastern track, and that they are headed here next. Commander has ordered everyone inside the palisade. All the people from the tents, even the sick. Everyone."

I gripped Zan's sleeve as the soldier hurried off. "Rosetta and Nathaniel were on their way to that wagon train. He was going to see his daughter—she was with the Canary girls."

"They started with the train," Zan said, "but only until the coast, where Kellan picked them up on the *Contessa.*"

"The ship you were abducted from the isle upon?" I asked. We spent most of the early hours whispering to each other in the semi-darkness, sharing the things we'd missed. I was still trying to put them all together.

"After you went back into the casket," he said, "I returned to the Quiet Canary and convened with the others. I did not—could not —tell them everything, but between my connection with the Malefica, Cecily's knowledge of the Spinner's Codex, and Emilie's history with the Circle, we were able to cobble together a plan of action. I was to use the bell to keep an eye on Conrad while Jessamine and Cecily worked to retrieve the original Spinner's Codex and replace it with our altered version. Kellan threw himself into the task of moving Renaltan refugees to safety as the Circle's borders expanded every day. I happened to know of a ship without owner or crew that he could use." He cringed. "He was really excited about it until I used the bell to take him to it. It required . . . a bit of a cleanup before being put back to use."

"And that's how he became the 'lord protector' of Renalt?"

"It is," Zan said. "He's been sailing that thing up and down the coast ever since. The Canary girls were reluctant to leave their home at first . . . they boarded late, on the last of his excursions before arriving here for the final days before Midwinter."

"Come on," I said. "Nathaniel's going to need to know this."

We found everyone else in the Great Hall. This time, however, Kellan, Jessamine, Cecily, and Emilie were joined by Rosetta and Nathaniel, who were as bedraggled and soot-stained as if they'd been through a battle. Dominic, at the head of the table, stood at the sight of Zan and me together, his expression intense and inscrutable.

"The ships are being cloaked by feral spells," Rosetta was explaining. "There are dozens of them, and all headed this way. What they did to that caravan . . . it was awful. Absolute devastation."

Nathaniel was quiet as she spoke, leaning forward in his chair to look at the ground, his back bent as if he were carrying a heavy, unseen load.

"Kellan," I said without preamble, "the Canary girls . . . they arrived with you on the *Contessa*, days ago. Didn't they?"

"Yes," he said. "I picked them up in Fimbria. Lorelai, Rafaella, and all the children."

"Can you tell me . . . did they have a little girl with them? She'd have been younger than the rest, not even two years old yet."

Nathaniel's head had risen, and he had clapped his fever-black eyes on her.

"Yes," Jessamine interjected, eyebrows lifted quizzically. "They call her Laurel. They'll be with the refugees, coming into the walls of the fort right now . . ."

Nathaniel and Rosetta both leaped up and made for the door. I trailed after them, with Zan only one step behind me. He caught my hand and threaded his fingers into mine—such a simple gesture, but one that made me want to laugh and cry both at once—and we followed Rosetta and Nathaniel across the courtyard and down the upper drawbridge, pushing through the swarm of rushing soldiers. Below, the streets between the Fort Castillion houses and shops were teeming with terrified refugees flooding up from the lower drawbridge to pack together in every spare nook and cranny.

We stopped in the center of the upper drawbridge, and the soldiers swirled past us like a river around stones.

"We'll never find them," Nathaniel said. "Not like this."

"Aurelia," Rosetta said sharply. "Could you locate her with your blood magic?"

"Perhaps," I said, "but I lack the blood—and I would need something of hers—"

"Sorry about this," Rosetta said to Nathaniel as she pulled her bone knife from its place hidden in her bodice, and in a quick, lash-like movement, lifted his left palm and dragged it across the center of it. "I'll patch you up later." Then she held his cupped palm out to me. "Can you use his and cover both needs at once?"

I looked from the tiny puddle in the center of Nathaniel's palm up to his face, trying to ignore the call of the magic until I had his permission. "Do it," he said, urgency lacing his words. "Take whatever you need."

I held out my hands and he turned his fist to drizzle the red liquid into them. I closed my eyes as he did, reaching out for the magic within it. Eagerly, it reached back, and I let the power fill me, like sparkling wine into an empty glass.

When I opened my eyes again, it was to a world covered in those slim, glimmering threads, zigzagging to connect every living thing one to another. I let the blood—Nathaniel's blood *was* Ella's blood—guide me as I reached for the threads, plucking them like a harpist and listening for the right reverberations across the web.

Find her, I commanded. *Show me where she is.*

When I opened my eyes, Rosetta was staring at me, open-mouthed. "A feral spell," she said. "Created on the spot, and using blood. You truly are the Spinner."

"She's there," I said, pointing across the crowd. "See that apothecary's shop, with the crooked pipe chimney on its roof? She's nearby it."

"Let's go," Zan said, retaking my hand without care that it was still sticky with Nathaniel's drying blood.

The throng, when we were in it, was even more tightly packed than it had looked from above, filled to the brim with frightened people. I could not tell, as we pushed through, who among them was Achlevan and who was Renaltan—perhaps because there was no differentiation between us, not really, not now. Perhaps not ever. We were all refugees here, clustered together, made equal by circumstance, all carrying the same sorrow and fear.

I was in front now, letting the hum of the gossamer strings and the call of blood to blood lead us through the molasses-thick multitude.

Zan, beside me, said, "The fever will spread like wildfire through this."

"One thing to worry about at a time," I responded. Then, "Look! The apothecary." I pointed ahead, to where a crooked chimney pipe was visible from the top of a thick-shingled roof.

It was Rafaella I saw first, under the alleyway eaves between the apothecary and the mercantile shop beside it, with several small faces huddled in close to her for warmth and comfort. She looked up as I approached, surprise registering on her face as she put down the hood of her cloak to get a better look at me. "Aurelia?" she asked, disbelieving. "Zan?"

At the sound of our names, the woman beside her turned to look. "Lorelai!" I called to them both. "Rafaella!"

"Merciful heavens!" Lorelai proclaimed, shifting the weight of the child she was holding from one hip to the other as she turned. "Can it be true?"

The child.

Nathaniel skidded to a stop beside me as the little girl in Lorelai's arms, bundled warmly in a fur-lined coat, turned her cherubic face toward us. Her cheeks were round and reddened from the cold, wisps of black curls poking out from under her hood, eyes large and gleaming like a silver wood.

"Dear stars," I breathed. I clutched Nathaniel's arm. "It *is* her."

"You know our Laurel?" Lorelai said, surprised. "We've had her for almost a year. She just appeared on our doorstep one night, sweet lamb."

"Ella," Nathaniel said, his voice ragged with emotion. The little girl wriggled from Lorelai's arms and toddled on chubby legs over to him, unafraid, gazing up at him with her strange, luminous eyes. He went to his knees, overcome, and Ella only waited a moment before touching his face with one tiny hand.

"She knows him," Rafaella said in wonder. "How is that possible? She came to us so young."

"He's her father," I said. "We thought she was dead."

Zan threaded his fingers through mine and we watched as Nathaniel extended his arms and Ella walked right into his embrace. He held his daughter to his chest with all of the same desperate, devoted love he had the first time I laid her, as a newborn infant, into his arms while Kate's ghost had looked on.

Rosetta was standing by quietly a few feet back, and I placed a hand on her folded arms. "Thank you," I said under my breath.

425

"I didn't do anything," Rosetta said, but her voice had a strange cadence to it.

When I looked at her face, I saw that there were tears in her eyes.

Rosetta, quicksilver witch of the Ebonwilde, was *crying*.

✳

The plans were made quickly. "I've sent word to my remaining ships to return to the fort immediately," Dominic said, "but I doubt they'll arrive before the Circle gets here, which means there's certain to be an assault on the fort itself. There are a few defenses already set up in the bay, but I fear they won't make much difference against the Circle's fleet. To mitigate losses, we'll need to bring anyone who can't fight into the Trove," Dominic said. "It's the safest place in the fort." Looking to Nathaniel and Rosetta, he added, "You two will stay with them. Most of the soldiers will be needed for the battle, so it will be up to you both to protect those inside the Trove. Between a feral mage and a swordsman, they will be in good hands, of that I am confident."

Rosetta and Nathaniel nodded their assent, and I shot Dominic a thankful glance. Nathaniel was an able swordsman, and while assigning him to a contingent of women and children in the most secure location of the fort was likely a misuse of his skill, Dominic had done it to ensure that the father would not have to be separated from his daughter so soon after their reunion.

"Cecily and I are going on the *Contessa* with Kellan and Emilie," Jessamine announced. "Cecily has the real Spinner's Codex; it might prove useful in bargaining with Fidelis. Perhaps even convincing him that he is not, in fact, the reborn Adamus . . . which may help him choose to stand down."

"Unlikely," Emilie said flatly. "But you're welcome to come all the same."

"Dominic and I will go together to the Verecundai's glade," I said. "We can go the back way, out of the Trove, after Emilie has taken my form. That way, whatever spies the Circle might have watching us will not see us go."

"I have another idea," Zan said. "And before you say no . . . please, just hear me out. I think that you and Dominic should go to the glade through the Gray."

"But," Rosetta objected, "without the Ilithiya's Bell, Aurelia can't—"

"We have the bell," I said, pulling it out from under my collar, where it rested alongside my blood vial. I turned to Zan. "Though I'm not sure why you'd think it would be a good idea . . ."

"Arceneaux—the Malefica—has helped me more than once. She has acted as a guide, of sorts, and I believe that she will help you if she can, before you face her sister." He dropped his voice. "Besides that, she delivered me to you, and now I stand in her debt. It is my wish, Aurelia," he said beseechingly, "that you might free her from where she remains bound by your blood magic."

"If I do that," I asked slowly, "would she count your debt as paid?"

"I believe she would," Zan said. "If I thought her a danger to you, or anyone else, I would not ask it of you."

I nodded, glancing at Dominic. "I'll follow your lead, Spinner," he said. "But with you and me at the glade and Lord Protector Greythorne meeting Fidelis at Extremitas Point, the fort will be left leaderless in the face of its most desperate battle. Who will head the fight here?"

"I will do it," Zan said quietly. I knew the look on his face—it was the same one I saw when he took the stage on Petitioner's Day, standing against his father in front of an entire city for the first time in his life. His voice was calm and even, and there was a determination in the set of his jaw that made me think that while his eyes were gold, his heart was made of steel. "I will lead them. Half of them are my people, after all."

"Look at that," Dominic said, leaning back in his chair. "The king of Achleva, finally claiming his crown." He said it without mirth or guile, and I wondered if, like putting Nathaniel in charge of the Trove, this was another one of his clever calculations . . . and if everything he'd done in the past had not been in conflict with the Achlevan crown, but in service to it.

Dominic gave me a cunning little half smile, confirming and confounding my hypothesis, both at once.

✦

I hugged Jessamine and Cecily goodbye, and then Emilie. "Be careful," she said. "Our hearts go with you."

"And ours with you," I replied. "The last time we said goodbye, I gave you that dragon charm. I wish I had something to give you now."

"You have given enough," she said. "And I already have everything I could want." She stole a glance at Kellan, who looked up from tending the horses and smiled at her. He was so different now than the guard I knew before. Still driven, yes, still brave . . . but there was a calm inside him now. An assuredness that wasn't there before . . . as if he'd finally learned that he had nothing to prove.

"Take care of him," I said softly.

She nodded. "I will." And then she worked her illusion spell, and I found myself gazing into a replica of my own eyes. "We'll take care of each other."

Kellan helped her up the *Contessa*'s steep gangplank, Jessamine and Cecily already waiting on deck, and then he faced me. "I should have never let Conrad get pulled in by the Circle," he said. "But since I can't undo what was done, I'll make sure to bring him back to you."

"I know you will," I said.

He nodded and gave me a deep bow. When he rose, I caught the glint of an amber-colored jewel just under his heavy woolen cloak; he, too, was wearing the charm I'd given him so long ago, the topaz gryphon. I did not know, then, how apt that choice would turn out to be. Part lion and part eagle, bold and courageous and true.

He was about to board the ship after Emilie when I said, "Wait, Kellan!"

He turned just as I threw myself headlong into his arms and buried my face in his cloak. He hesitated for a minute, stunned, and then returned my embrace with equal force.

"My oldest friend," I said as I pulled away, eyes shining. "My noble knight. Thank you. For everything."

"I'll see you again soon, Princess," he said.

50

NOW

By nightfall, the tent city was empty and all of the refugees had been funneled into the fort, behind the safety of the palisade and the ever-burning moat, and the lower drawbridge had been raised. Those unable to fight—mostly mothers, children, the elderly, and the infirm—were being guided into the Trove, where they occupied every spare inch of free ground on each of the cavern's levels. Nathaniel and Rosetta did most of the shepherding, with Rafaella and Lorelai helping to create some semblance of comfort and calm by distributing food and offering words of hope among the frightened numbers. Nathaniel performed most of his responsibilities with Ella asleep on his shoulder; he would not be parted from her now, not for anything.

Meanwhile, able-bodied men and women capable of holding a

sword or shooting a bow were being gathered in the courtyard, where they were each outfitted with weapons. Because of the Verecundai's guidance, Dominic's armory was far more well equipped than could have been otherwise expected, but even so, many at the end of the lines ended up with hammers and cudgels and dull axes.

"All that work over all those years," Dominic said, "and we are still so ill-prepared."

"You did as much as you could," I said. "Imagine where we'd be without you."

He nodded grimly as one young man went past holding what looked like a sharpened broomstick. "Let us pray that the Circle never makes it past the walls."

The mood, as we toured the edges of our ramshackle troops, was pensive and latent with trepidation. Zan was standing at the upper gate, working in the torchlight to assign the limited number of trained Castillion soldiers to oversee different sectors of the volunteer fighters. Dominic and I lingered on the periphery, listening as he issued directives. Most accepted their assignments without complaint, but others did not.

"You," Zan said, pointing to a large, gruff-looking soldier near the front, "we'll need you to take the half mile of north wall on the lower level, overlooking the bay. Your people will be mostly long-range bowmen, equipped with pitch and braziers to light their arrows. When the Circle ships come into the bay, you'll watch for my signal on the upper level before giving the go-ahead for your men to launch their first volley."

"With all due respect," the soldier replied, his voice laced with derision, "who are you to make these kinds of judgments? Two days ago, I was tossing scraps to you in the dungeon." The soldiers around him grumbled their agreement, and it egged him on. "I obey the commander, and the commander only. No one else has the authority—"

Zan lifted his chin, his eyes narrowed to golden half-moons. "That's where you are wrong," he said, steady and even. "I do have the authority. And when I give you an order, you *will* obey."

"You dare to—" The man made like he was going in for a punch, raising his fist like a mallet.

Zan pulled a blade from the scabbard on his hip and, whip-fast, had it pointed beneath the soldier's jaw.

Zan had been trained by Nathaniel to use a sword, back when he barely had the strength to lift it—I'd forgotten, because I'd never seen him wield anything sharper than his tongue. Both were in play here, it seemed, as Zan stared the taller man down. "Try that again," he said dangerously, "and you will regret it."

Dominic put his hand on my elbow and I fell back beside him, waiting to see what would happen next.

The man lifted his arms in acquiescence, and Zan raised his voice so that they could all hear him. "Who else among you wishes to defy your king?"

A murmur spread across the listening guardsmen. *King? Is it true? Can he be?*

Zan turned toward the gate and moved across the drawbridge. He stopped at the center, a bold figure against the cold night sky, black hair and golden eyes and billowing cape of blue, impossible to ignore as he stood high above the buildings and the uneasy collection of new-minted fighters. When he finally spoke, his voice boomed across the quiescent night like the first crack of thunder in the quiet before a storm. "Hear me, people of Fort Castillion! I am Valentin Alexander de Achlev, rightful king of Achleva. Tonight, I lay claim to the title vacated by my father, Domhnall, two years ago. I do so not to rise above you, but to have the honor of fighting alongside you in the battle that is to come. Tomorrow, we face a common enemy. The Circle Midnight comes not simply to subjugate the last independent territory of the Western Realms, but to strike a blow against humanity itself. And we will stand against them to the bitterest end because we are *survivors*. We have not made it this far, and against so much adversity, to quail in this, our longest night. Our darkest hour. We fight not to win, but to endure. Together, we will fight Midnight and together, we will see the coming dawn."

For a minute, the only sound was the wind-tossed whipping of his cape. I waited, breath locked in my throat, for the silence to break. For the crowd to stir at the poignant strength of his words the way my own heart did.

But then, I felt Dominic slip by me, his boots heavy on the drawbridge planks. Zan looked over his shoulder at him, wary. If he wanted to, the lord commander of Fort Castillion could use this moment as his final public challenge to Zan's rule.

I did not think my body could take any more tension, but watching Dominic march past Zan to stand directly facing him on that high perch, in front of what remained of two nations, I felt as if my chest was locked in an ever-tightening vise.

When Dominic pulled his own sword from its scabbard, the vise wrenched so tight I thought I might crack in half. "No," I said under my breath. "No, Dominic—"

And then, Dominic stuck his sword into the drawbridge wood in front of Zan. I gaped as he went down on one knee, bending his head in deference.

"I, Dominic Castillion, lord commander of Fort Castillion, do hereby pledge my sword, my life, and my loyalty to you, Valentin Alexander de Achlev, rightful king of Achleva."

Merciful stars.

The crowd shattered into applause and cheers, and Zan put out his hand. "I accept your offer. Rise now, Lord Castillion, and stand beside me as an ally and a friend." Zan helped Dominic to his feet, and they stood there together in the winter wind, arms clasped in a show of brotherhood.

They were as opposite as they could be—one with white hair, one with black, one my destiny and the other my decision, one the mate of my soul and the other the choice of my heart—but in that moment, I loved them both. For different reasons and in different ways, but what I felt watching them that night was definitely, undeniably love.

I was, after all, the Two-Faced Queen.

The morning of Midwinter dawned cold and quiet, with all eyes turned toward the bay, watching for the Circle's ships to appear on the arctic horizon.

Dominic and Zan had spent the long hours of the night with the men and women now lined along the edges of the fort's upper and lower walls, never telling them that the lord commander would not, in fact, be fighting alongside them. We had decided it was better that way—better to not add to their worries or fears. Zan was their king, and he would be with them, and that would have to be enough. And I watched them both, wondering what life would look like on the other side of this battle and whatever lay in wait for Dominic and me in the Verecundai's glade.

By late afternoon, a lookout on the top of the keep shouted down to all waiting below, "Ships! Ships! They've come!" And all the people clamored to the edge as the black vessels appeared one by one, as if conjured from the watery mists, flags waving the Circle's eight-pointed star and the sliver of moon suspended inside its center.

With the signal given, the doors of the Trove were shut and bolted, and the archers lined up along the battlements with their longbows poised and ready.

I felt a hand on my elbow. "Time to go, Aurelia," Dominic said, and I could see that it pained him to leave his home like this, with devastation sailing so blithely into port. I nodded, following him across the courtyard to the tower of his study, where Zan was already waiting. We all three went up together, moving quietly through the study to the waiting mirror on the other side.

Zan closed my fingers around the Ilithiya's Bell. "Whatever you do," he said, "don't let go until you're where you need to be."

"And the Malefica?" I asked. "Arceneaux?"

"She will be exactly where you left her," he said. "Though you will find her much altered. The Gray has not been kind to her."

"I'll do what I can for her," I said, "to pay her back for what she did for you." He nodded, and I looked at him with tears in my eyes.

"What does one say when facing the possible end of the world? Good-bye?"

"Not that," Zan said, kissing me. "Never that. Never again."

"Then—how about 'si vivis, tu pugnas'?"

"Better," he said. Then he unclasped the chain from around his neck, letting the white-stone ring slide into his palm. "Aurelia," he said, almost shyly, "this belongs to you." He slipped it onto my left hand.

"I love you, Sad Tom," I said, and he laughed.

"I love you, too, my beautiful witch princess," he replied in a whisper, tangling his fingers in my hair as he bent to give me one last soft, lingering kiss.

Dominic cleared his throat, and Zan stepped aside so that he could join me in front of the mirror. With the bell clasped in my hand, I could not see the study in its reflection anymore; the frame was filled from end to end with the tumultuous, churning smoke of the Gray.

"Are you ready?" Dominic asked. When I nodded, he threaded his fingers through mine and together, we stepped forward through the glass and into the murky depths waiting for us beyond.

51

NOW

MIDWINTER

Fidelis was quiet all the way to the meeting place at Extremitas Point, too preoccupied with his own thoughts to bother with anyone else's. Chydaeus counted this lucky; with no one else around to distract, he was sure the Grandmaster would notice the vacuity where the boy's thoughts used to be, so malleable. So easily extracted. But the older man did not seem to catch the incongruity at all. So confident was he in his manipulations that he never even considered that Chydaeus might have somehow slipped his grasp. But if he did . . .

I chose this path, Chydaeus told himself. *I chose to be brave.*

It was near dusk when a ship came into view.

Chydaeus squinted as four figures exited, making out a man with brown skin and hair plaited into a collection of long black braids leading the way. Behind him were two women, bundled in furs to protect from the cold—one vaguely familiar, the other someone he'd never seen before. And lastly came a girl with long black hair and lake-blue eyes.

Aurelia, he thought. That was her name—Aurelia. The Spinner. Vieve reborn, the one whom Fidelis thought would become his queen in the new world.

My sister.

"Welcome," Fidelis said with a broad smile as they approached. "So good of you to come."

✷

Rosetta did not know, until the doors of the Trove were closed and bolted, how unnerving it would be for a creature so used to the open air of the forest to suddenly be trapped beneath a thousand tons of rock. Worse still, there was no place in the cavern that was not occupied by people—sick people, sad people, hopeless people. Some crying, some praying, all scared of what was going on on the other side of the stone walls.

We're helpless here, she thought. *Trapped. Cornered.*

Nathaniel, somehow, seemed to sense her amplified unease. He shifted the sleeping Ella to his other arm so he could place a calming hand on Rosetta's knee, which was bouncing up and down at the pace of a woodpecker's beak against a hollow tree.

"I'm sorry," she said. "I'm not used to being confined."

"You didn't have to be in here," he said. "I'm sure they could have used you out there."

"No," she said. "I wanted to be here." She looked fondly at the little girl, drooling onto his sleeve. "She's here. And"—she glanced up at him—"you're here."

"For what it's worth," Nathaniel said, smiling, "I'm glad you're here, too."

✦

It was dark when the Circle Midnight's ships finally came close enough to shore to launch the first wave at the fort's defense.

Madrona stamped the ground as if she, too, were impatient to get the battle going. It was Castillion's idea to have Zan ride—easier and faster to move wherever he was needed, and it lent him a greater air of authority. Not that Zan needed it now; the man's display last night was genius—cementing Zan's position as king in a single stroke. Zan wanted to think that Dominic had done it with some underhanded, ulterior motive, but could find none. Dominic Castillion cared for his people, and that meant doing for them what was in their best interests, even if it was not in his own.

It was the same with Aurelia. Whether his affection was the remnants of Adamus's long-ago love for Vieve or something newly forged with Aurelia, it didn't matter; he'd stepped aside for Zan because that was what she wanted, without conditions. Without complaint.

When it came to Dominic Castillion, Zan had felt just about every emotion: hate, fear, anger, envy . . . but the most surprising one of all was trust.

Take care of her for me, he thought. *I'll take care of Fort Castillion for you.*

"Archers!" Zan called across the line. "Light your arrows! Ready. Aim." He took a breath, steadying himself. Then he opened his eyes. "Fire!"

★

It didn't matter how many times I'd entered the Gray, it was impossible not to be overwhelmed by that first step into it, overtaken by a whirlwind of eddying, colorless clouds with no up or down, no beginning or end, no ground below or sky above.

On my left, Dominic lurched against the disorienting tumult, and I squeezed his hand tighter. "Don't let go!" I cried. "Close your eyes if you have to." Then I fixed my mind upon the Stella Regina, re-forming it from my memory until it began to take shape in front of me.

"Bleeding stars," Castillion swore as the mists cleared and we found ourselves standing under the cathedral's familiar clock tower, housed in stately white marble.

"Hello, Aurelia," a voice came from behind us. "It's been a long time."

Isobel Arceneaux was luminescent in her white capedress, sitting on the edge of Saint Urso's fountain with a lovely smile painted across her shining countenance. Dominic gaped as she stood and walked toward us, graceful and gracious.

"I'm surprised to see you here," she said, "at so late an hour."

Though the clock overhead pointed at midnight, I knew that the hour of which she spoke had nothing to do with the telling of time. "Arceneaux," I said.

"Lily," she corrected. "Call me Lily."

"Lily," I said, feeling a wistful pang. It was the name Onal had chosen for the daughter she never got to raise. "You saved Zan's life when you sent him to me," I said. "Before we go to the Verecundai's glade, I came here first to repay his debt."

"And how," she asked, "do you expect to do that?"

"I'm here to set you free," I said.

Her expression changed, losing some of its beaming sublimity to suspicion. "Why?" she asked. "You were the one who trapped me here in the first place."

"I know," I said. "I did so because I was afraid of you. Of what you would do to the world if you were set free within it. You were a goddess, you see. A deity, too far removed from the material world to know its value. I saw you as a danger to those I loved—all human. All mortal."

"And now?"

"And now . . ." I gazed at her. "I think you do see the value now. You've seen kindness, and you've returned it without expectation."

"Humanity is imperfect," she said. "But what is imperfect is also beautiful. You were right to be wary of me. I did not know, then, what I do now. I only wanted what I could not have."

"And what do you want now?" I asked.

"To be free," she said. And with that, the illusion faded. Gone was the unblemished marble cathedral and the manicured hedge and Isobel Arceneaux, the beautiful and powerful magistrate of the Tribunal. They were replaced by a forgotten, soot-stained edifice and a thatch of thorny, overgrown brambles and a haggard crone of black-veined skin and protruding bone, her once-white dress hanging from her feeble frame in filthy, tattered rags. In the year that had passed in the material world, she'd lived a thousand trapped here in the Gray.

"Set me free, Spinner," she said in a voice as frail as a skeletal autumn leaf.

Dominic said under his breath, "Is this the same spell you used on me, aboard the *Humility*?" I nodded and he said, "I didn't realize how lucky it was that you came back for me that night."

I replied, "I didn't realize how cruel it was, leaving her here like this in the Gray."

Gingerly, I hung the Ilithiya's Bell around my neck, careful to never let it lose contact with my skin. When my right hand was free, I moved it to the vial of blood, popping the top and tilting it so that a few of the last precious drops fell into my hand. Even in the Gray, the magic sent a delicious thrill through me, and I took a deep breath to steal a moment of enjoyment from it. After this, there would only be another drop or two of my mortal blood left—enough for one more spell if I was lucky.

✳

Then I exhaled, and let the magic and the blood spill through my fingers, which I placed overtop of hers, splayed out on the ground. "Libera," I said. *Be free.*

With a crow of delight, she lifted her hands from the ground, wrapping her gnarled fingers around mine for support as she stretched creakily to stand.

"We must be soon away to the Verecundai's glade," I told her. "But if you tell us where you want to go, we will take you there first."

"No," she rasped. "Not quite yet. There is something I must show you."

As she said so, the world in front of us seemed to split, and we found ourselves standing beneath an orrery of brass planets in a spacious room full of books and bottles and maps and models of fantastical contraptions. "What is this?" I asked in awe.

"I know this place," Dominic said. "It is one of the things the Verecundai showed me that night when I first came to them as a boy. It is their workshop, on what would become known as Widows' Isle."

"And is that . . . them?" I asked, as seven mages streamed into the room, a woman in step behind them. I knew her immediately now, as well as I would have known my own reflection. Vieve.

"Can they see us?" Dominic asked.

"No," Lily replied. "You're ghosts here. Intangible as long as Aurelia is touching the bell."

The mages spread out around a circle laid in glossy tile on the floor, their long black robes pooling at each point of an eight-pronged star. Thin silver lines of metal wove through the larger image, and I recognized them as the feral knot Rosetta once used to send me into the Gray.

There were words, too, marking each section between the points of the star: *Humilitas, Abnegatio, Fortitudo, Integritas, Iudicium, Oboedientia, Patientia, Fidelitas.* When the Verecundai came to a stop, and Vieve went to stand in the center of them, only one word was left unoccupied: *Fidelitas.*

The missing mage was Adamus.

"You have looked into the future for yourself," one of the mages was saying. "You've seen the truth of what is to come."

"The Empyrea has lied to us," said another. "Everything that we have worked to bring to pass . . . it has all been predicated upon the belief that she is coming down to edify. To uplift. To bring the world into a new phase of enlightenment."

"In truth," another continued, "she does not wish to make you queen—she never did. We were wrong. Misguided. We know that now. Her true intent is to destroy what she did not make, what she could not control."

"I have seen it," Vieve said in a voice untainted by doubt. "I've trod the silver paths to discern the future's possibilities, and know now that there is only one choice left to us: We *must* do as the Empyrea has commanded, and meet in the glade on Midwinter. We *must* work the spell as planned. We will let her begin her descent, believing that we are fulfilling our obligation to her, and exemplifying the obedience she requires."

"And then?" one of the mages asked. "If she comes to earth, she will destroy it."

"And then," Vieve went on with conviction, "we will use the spell to trap her. To make her mortal." She looked at each of the mages' faces in turn. "Because what is mortal can be made to die."

The mages began to murmur among themselves as they absorbed Vieve's proposition. Kill the Empyrea? The Goddess they had dedicated their lives to serving? But what other choice did they have? She wanted to end the world they loved, and all the people in it.

Finally, one of the mages spoke up. "Such a spell would require an immense amount of power. More than we have at our disposal."

Vieve said calmly, "It will. And we do have that much at our disposal, but it will demand—"

"Sacrifice." This was from the mage standing between the old words for *humility* and *abnegation*. "We have enough power to do this, but it will cost us all our lives."

"Yes," Vieve said solemnly.

"Is this why," the mage occupying the space between *obedience* and *endurance* said, "you have convened this meeting without our last member?"

Vieve said, "The spell would require all of our deaths—including mine. Adamus would never agree to it. For this to work, he must be kept from the truth."

"And yet," said the mage standing between *honesty* and *judgment*, "you believe that *you* will have the strength to take his life? To let him die in ignorance?"

"Yes," Vieve said again, softening just a little. "Because if we do not, *all* will die." She straightened her shoulders. "You have trained me to be a queen, and a queen's obligation is first to the people she serves, and to her own heart second." Her eyes glistened as she added, "I have faith that he and I will be reunited in the After."

The mage standing at the edge of *endurance* said, "As the Spinner speaks, so let it be done."

"She knew," I breathed as we watched the meeting adjourn from the edge of the cavernous room. "She knew going into it that she would have to die. That they would *all* have to die."

"But *he* did not," Dominic whispered. "Is this what you wanted us to see?" he asked Lily. "That the spell they began a thousand years ago was left unfinished because they chose to keep it a secret from one of their own?"

"There is more," Lily said, and the next thing we knew, we were in the glade on that long-ago night. The spell had begun, with Vieve at the center, weaving starlight and the connective strings of feral magic with that pulled from their willingly given blood into a web of pulsing power. The Empyrea began to answer her call, descending from the heavens toward the trap they had set for her below.

As Vieve worked, she and the mages on her periphery began to shrink and wither, dying as she dragged more and more of their vitality into her spell. But their eighth member—their last member—cried out in confusion.

"Vieve!" Adamus said, his voice nearly lost in the wailing wind. "What is happening to us? To you?"

And Vieve looked up from her spell and saw her beloved writhing in fear, in agony, and faltered.

The strings of her magic began to snap. The tapestry began to unravel. The Empyrea's descent was in motion, and the Spinner was losing control. The power was too great, and she screamed as it began to consume her, eating away at her from the inside out.

To end the spell and Vieve's agony, the Verecundai lifted their knives and converged upon the woman they had raised from a young girl. The one into whom they had once poured all of their hopes, the one they had aspired to make a beloved queen.

"Please," Dominic said to Lily, voice thick with emotion. "End this. You don't need to show us the rest."

"Not yet," Lily said. "There's still one thing more."

Adamus was with Vieve now, and pronouncing his curse upon the fellows that had killed her. The seven mages shrieked as their bodies disintegrated the rest of the way, leaving them in the wraithlike form they still inhabited. This was where the vision had ended before, when the Verecundai had shown it to me.

"Watch," she said, pointing.

The storm ended.

The Empyrea retreated.

And then, Adamus stood.

He stood and looked around at the devastation one night had brought him—the night he'd thought would be the beginning of a new world.

"He didn't die," I said, trying to make sense of it. "He lived past Midwinter."

The next things we saw rushed past in quick succession—flashes of the aftermath. We watched him bury Vieve in the same place she had fallen, and then plant an apple tree over the spot. We watched him carve the warning sigils in the trees around the glade—a star with seven prongs.

Or a spider with seven legs.

Dominic was watching from just over Adamus's shoulder, wide-eyed. "It can't be," he whispered. "It can't be true."

But the next image Lily showed us removed any remaining doubt.

Adamus was seated at a table in a candlelit room, hunched over a stack of parchment as he furiously worked, filling page after page with spidery scrawling. We watched from the darkness outside his candle's reach, until Dominic bent forward to inspect the top page of the pile.

"These are the Midnight Papers," Dominic said.

"It can't be," I said, but it was true: *Adamus* was the true author of the Circle's prescriptive prophecy—detailing a future filled with floods and sickness and war and death, beginning with the clocks stopping at midnight and ending with the Empyrea's return.

When the volume was done, we watched him sign the last page with a new name, one he'd chosen for himself. A part of his past as a member of the mages who became the Verecundai, and the one we'd come to know as the name of the founder of the Circle Midnight.

Adamus was Fidelis the First.

52

NOW

MIDWINTER

Chydaeus held his breath as the two travelers exited their sleigh and Fidelis leaned over to him and said, "At long last."

The man approached first. "I am Kellan Greythorne, Princess Aurelia's sworn guardian. These are her companions, Lady Jessamine of the Quiet Canary, and Sister Cecily of Widows' Isle."

"One of the Sisters of the Sacred Torch," Fidelis said appreciatively. "Our order has a long history with yours."

"And ours has an even longer one with the Spinner," Cecily replied. "For the grounds we now inhabit were once her home, too."

"Yes," Fidelis said. "Before the mages who built it betrayed her. There was no power left there after they were gone and none but their powerless widows were left. It has, for a millennium, been nothing but an island full of spiders and spinsters."

"Not powerless," Cecily said. "We kept the flame alive. We protected the knowledge that the Spinner left behind. You know this, Friend, because you went there after it." She smiled. "Didn't you?"

"Abbess Aveline was helpful enough, I will admit," he said. "But less than pleasant to work with. It may be that there's another opening for the position if you're interested."

"No, thank you," Cecily said, glancing at Jessamine. "As it happens, I've recently left the sisterhood. But"—she lifted a bundle of papers so he could see it—"I didn't depart without a souvenir."

Fidelis's smile faded.

"Yes, Grandmaster. This is exactly what you think it is," Kellan said. "We have the Spinner *and* her original Codex."

Fidelis's arm came around Chydaeus's shoulders in what might have been a friendly, protective gesture, were it not for the slim knife he had also pressed against his neck. "And *I* have the Spinner's precious little brother."

They were silent.

"Now, friends, let's make a trade."

★

Hours after the doors of the Trove were bolted, Rosetta heard the first *boom*.

The rock rattled, sending dust and bits of loosened gravel raining down upon the huddled people below.

"It's the doors!" someone shouted. "The Circle is here—they're trying to get in!"

"It's not the doors," Nathaniel said, moving to settle Ella in Rosetta's lap. "We're in no danger yet."

"Then what is it?" This came from a man of advanced age, holding a quavering hand to a walking stick. His eyes, like Nathaniel's, were black; he too was a survivor of the Bitter Fever.

"I'm guessing that the Circle's ships are catapulting stones," Nathaniel said. "But the fort's walls were built strong; they will hold. And"—he put a hand on the old man's shoulder—"even if the walls do fall, the mountain will not."

Rosetta wished she had his confidence.

In her arms, Ella fluttered her thick lashes and her eyes opened. She looked up at Rosetta, rubbing sticky sleep from her eyes.

"Hello again," Rosetta said. "Do you remember me?"

Ella did not speak—Lorelai and Rafaella had said that since she'd been with them, she'd never uttered a single word, though they were certain she understood everything they said to her—but she tilted her head half an inch, as if to say yes. Then, she put up her hands to cover her ears.

Two seconds later, a second blast shook the Trove.

Rosetta said, "You knew that was coming, didn't you?"

Ella climbed from Rosetta's lap and tugged her dress, as if she wanted to show Rosetta something, or to have her follow her. Intrigued, Rosetta stood and took a few steps, just before another blast hit and a chunk of rock broke free from the ledge of the second level above their heads and smashed into the spot Rosetta had just been sitting.

"All right," Rosetta said. "Message received."

Nathaniel had seen the close call and hurried back. "Are you all right?" he said, scooping up Ella and pulling Rosetta into his chest protectively. Though they were surrounded by refugees, Rosetta felt like Nathaniel had made a private space for them.

"Well enough," Rosetta said. "Though we should probably get out from under this ledge. I could be smashed by a rock and make it through just fine, but you or Ella . . ."

"You're like Aurelia is now," Nathaniel said. "Made of quicksilver." Another boom, and he looked around, wiping dust from his eyes with the back of his sleeve. "I heard you ask her to try to change you back."

"Unfortunately for me, she wouldn't try."

"Unfortunately?"

"It may seem like a blessing," Rosetta replied honestly, "to go unaging, undying . . . but forever is a long time to be alone."

"Maybe," he said. "But I've lost someone I loved before, and . . ." His voice dropped low. "And knowing that *you* could not be taken like that . . . so quickly, so cruelly . . ." His sentence trailed off, and then he cleared his throat, as if embarrassed. "I can't regret that you are not so vulnerable."

Rosetta met his gaze searchingly. In truth, she felt *more* vulnerable than ever before.

Boom.

✸

Boom!

Screams went up from the lower battlements as another round of incendiary projectiles arced overhead and landed against the fort's upper walls, raining rocks and fiery shrapnel down upon the fighters below.

"Aim for the ballistae!" Zan shouted over the din. Madrona reared up beneath him. "Take out the weapons first!"

The next volley of arrows struck across the sky, trailing thin lines of light as another round of boulder-size fireballs blazed past them and exploded upon impact against the ramparts. Ash and cinder darted like insects around Zan's face and he urged Madrona further down the line. "Stand your ground!" he cried. "Just a little longer!"

That was when the first Circle Midnight ship met the chains that —hidden by the darkness—had been raised on either side of the bay. It shattered into a mess of broken timber, catching on fire as it sank. It was too late for the other ships at the front of the line to slow down or turn around and, within a few short minutes, four others had met the same fate.

"Ha!" Zan said, pumping his fist, but the victory was short-lived. The chains had destroyed five ships, but there were dozens more behind them that would not make the same mistake. Already, those boats had pulled back, and now hundreds of skiffs were being lowered into the water, each densely packed with fully armored Midnighters.

"Come on, come on, come on," Zan muttered under his breath, watching the horizon.

And then he saw them—Castillion ships, coming up behind the Circle's fleet, penning them in. They were not of equal number, but were made to exert far greater might, constructed of metal instead of wood and fueled by coal. All bore names of Castillion's favorite virtues: the *Abnegation*, the *Honesty*, the *Fortitude*, the *Judgment*, and the

Fidelity. The *Humility* had been lost in the fjords of Achleva, sunk by Aurelia herself, and the *Endurance* had met its end in an earlier battle with the Circle. But Castillion had learned from those experiences and improved his tactics—keeping his ships on the move in secret until he called them back to shore.

And now, thank the stars, they'd finally arrived.

We might do this, Zan thought. *We might actually survive this night.*

But there was still so much work to be done.

★

"This is it," Fidelis whispered, pulling the knife back from his throat. "The time has come, Friend Chydaeus."

Chydaeus nodded, feeling the weight of his own blade in his pocket. So far, everything had gone exactly as Fidelis had planned. *Your fidelity rite will take place on Midwinter,* the Grandmaster said before they'd left the fleet of Circle boats and set off alone. *Once it is done, you will be a fully fledged member of our society.*

Fidelis pushed Chydaeus forward, just as Aurelia, holding the leather-wrapped sheaf of paper in her arms, also took a step. *The exchange will be made,* Fidelis said in his memory. *You'll cross from our side to theirs. But as soon as I have the Spinner in my grasp, you will strike.*

I could be a full-fledged member of the Circle, Chydaeus thought. *All I have to do is kill three more people as proof of my fidelity to the Grandmaster and to the Empyrea.*

There was a time, he could recall, when such a prospect would have actually tempted him, but not anymore.

Two steps. Three steps. Four steps. Five. Chydaeus and Aurelia were side by side now, close enough that he could smell the scent of her perfume—like violets.

Violets.

The girl in the alley, dressed in furs. *Who are you?* he'd asked. And the answer: *a friend.*

The girl in the sanctorium at the castle. *Stay away from the Circle. They are dangerous.*

The girl in his room. *If you see my face, he will see my face.*

She had been so scared. Scared of the Circle, scared of Fidelis. And now, she was walking herself right into the hands of the monster she had tried so hard to keep him away from.

He stared at her, now that he remembered who she was. The girl in the furs. The girl who could make illusions. The girl who had tried to warn him, and he had not listened.

As she passed by him, she gave him a tiny nod.

She was not Aurelia after all.

Before he knew it, the guard—Kellan! How could he have ever forgotten Kellan?—had reached out and pulled him the rest of the way, hugging him tightly. "Thank the stars," Kellan said. "We've got you back. We've finally got you back."

The Aurelia-who-was-not-Aurelia was now in Fidelis's grip as well. "Now!" the man yelled. "Chydaeus! It is time to finish your rite! Prove your true fidelity!"

Chydaeus pulled the blade out and turned, looking at the Grandmaster over his shoulder. "My name," he said, "is Conrad." And he tossed the knife into the snow.

Fidelis's face crinkled as he reached out with his mind and found that Conrad's thoughts were no longer there for him to manipulate.

The girl in his grip managed a laugh. "You've failed, Grandmaster. Here you are, on the edge of your finest hour . . . and you've *failed*."

He whirled her around so that she was facing him, his wicked knife at her neck, but his discomfiture seemed to only give her courage.

"Put that down," she said. "We both know you don't know how to wield a weapon yourself. Always made someone else do your dirty work for you."

He lowered the knife, a petulant scowl on his face, as she tossed the papers down at his feet and said, "There's the Codex you were looking for. I know you only wanted it so that you could destroy the last proof that you are not, in fact, the reincarnation of Adamus. So that when the Spinner met an unfortunate, untimely end tonight and the Empyrea did not come as you had promised, none of your followers would ever find out the truth: that you are actually just poor Richard Crocker, the forgotten third son of a penniless tradesman with the high magic ability to read and influence thoughts."

Fidelis's mouth twitched with anger. "Where did you hear that name?" he shouted, feebly waving his knife in the air. "Where? Where?"

"My mother told it to me," she retorted. "She knew you before you ever heard of the Spinner, or joined the dwindling underground organization called the Circle Midnight, before you set yourself up as its new leader, before you transformed it to suit your will."

"Your mother?" Fidelis asked.

"What?" she said. "You don't recognize me?"

The image of Aurelia began to dissipate, and Fidelis's eyes grew as wide as saucers as the girl's true face began to show underneath. "It's me, Father. Emilie. Your daughter."

He stumbled back as if he'd been bitten by a viper. "You are not my daughter," he said. "This is another illusion. My daughter is *dead*."

"Yes," she said. "The daughter you knew is dead. She burned to cinders at the stake, in service to your plan to get close to Aurelia. After, of course, you turned in her mother — your own wife — to the authorities of the Tribunal."

"No," he said. "No."

"Don't you recognize the perfume?" she asked. "Mother taught me how to make it. She loved violets. You remember, don't you?"

Cecily and Jessamine had come up next to Kellan, who was seething, radiating anger like rippling heat from a stove, his silvery hand clenched into a fist. Jessamine put both hands on Conrad's shoulder, gently pulling him back out of range of the brewing fight.

"You've lost," Emilie said. "Tonight, the real Spinner and the real Adamus will face the Empyrea. They will determine the fate of the world. And you — you will die here. And you will be forgotten . . . just like pathetic old Richard Crocker."

And then, it was Fidelis's turn to laugh. "You've underestimated me, daughter. Just as my parents did, and your mother did, and the world did before I brought it to its knees. You think I am beaten?" He gave a grating bark of a laugh. "I'm only just getting started." And then his eyes flooded with black, end to end.

"Jessamine?" Cecily cried out, but it was too late. The Canary girl's eyes had pooled black as well, and all trace of expression disappeared from her face. In her hand was the dagger Conrad had dropped, and before anyone could do anything to stop her, she had lunged at the boy.

Cecily shrieked, and Kellan dove, and the knife missed the boy's neck by an inch, instead plunging into Kellan's side up to the hilt.

✴

The wounded were being pulled back from the battlements and brought into the Great Hall. A man was crawling across the upper courtyard, cradling an arm that had been broken, the bone sticking right through the skin, when he collapsed, his strength gone. Zan dismounted Madrona and helped the man to his feet, draping his good arm over his shoulders.

Dazed, the injured man looked at him with fever-dark eyes and Zan instantly recognized him as the soldier who had challenged his authority the night before. Groggily, he said, "You? Why would you help me?"

Zan said, "We're fighting on the same side, Lieutenant."

Inside the keep, Zan propped him up against the wall where one of the attendant women could come and look him over. "Thank you," the man said, "King Valentin."

"No thanks are needed," Zan said. "What is your name, soldier?"

"My name is . . . my name . . ." But something in the man's face changed. His expression went blank and the black of his iris and pupils began to spread into the whites of his eyes. Zan reared back—was the plague returning to claim him? How could such a thing be?

But this was not the Bitter Fever; the man who had only moments ago been racked with pain and needed Zan to help carry his weight to the Great Hall was now on his feet, sword drawn by the same arm from which white bone protruded. There was no feverish sweat glazing his skin, nor delirious ramblings. He was simply empty, void of his senses, and with one imperative: attack.

Zan kicked the sword from the man's hand, the force wrenching the broken arm backwards with a sickening crunch, where it then dangled from a few stringy bands of flesh and sinew, but the man did not falter or make any cry of pain.

But more sounds of alarm ricocheted around the hall as nurses turned on other nurses and other injured fighters rose up from their repose and, like the soldier Zan had just brought in, began to battle with any living person within their reach. And each of the mindless mob bore the same distinguishing trait: eyes of black, end to end.

Zan drew his sword and swung it at the man's legs as he charged again, then pushed him back behind the Great Hall's doors, throwing his weight against it to pin him there while he shouted, "Don't fight them! Run! Run! Run!"

Those who could flee did, streaming past him in a panicked frenzy. Before the fever-marked could follow them through, however, Zan pulled the doors shut, threading his sword through the handles to secure it.

It did not matter. When Zan, panting, turned around, the courtyard of Fort Castillion was in chaos: any who had been touched by the Bitter Fever and recovered were now moving, like vacant puppets on unseen strings, against their own.

The battle would be over before the Circle Midnight ever set a single foot onto shore.

53

NOW

MIDWINTER

When the Verecundai's glade appeared before us, I let go of the Ilithiya's Bell.

It was a violent reentrance into reality, all three of us bumping and rolling and skidding, dazed by the sudden eruption of sensation after the numbness of the Gray: the biting cold, the blooming pain at the impact of the fall, the sharpness in our chests at the first inhalation of icy air. Dominic was closest to me. He spat snow as I rolled him over.

"Are you all right?" I asked.

He nodded. "I think so. Where is—"

"Lily!"

She was lying faceup under the branches of the gnarled, long-dead apple tree, her brittle bones broken, her near-translucent skin turning blue. My heart sank in concern.

"Lily," I said, hurrying to her side. "I should have held on tighter. I'm sorry. I didn't know it would be so rough—"

"Look," she said reverentially, her onyx eyes reflecting the sky.

I followed her gaze through the misshapen branches, where the aurora was ribboning in phosphorescent green and rosy cerise against the star-studded vault of the midnight firmament.

"Beautiful," she whispered on a gentle, exhaled breath that, when it reached its end, was not followed by another.

After a moment, Dominic moved to close her eyelids, but before he could, a gust of wind whisked a flurry of snow across her fragile body, and when it cleared there was nothing left behind but a few scraps of once-white fabric.

She was gone. Lily . . . Arceneaux . . . the Malefica . . . whoever she was, she had wanted to experience mortality, and for one tiny, fleeting moment, she'd gotten her wish. "Empyrea keep you," I said. It was a ridiculous sentiment for someone about to set a trap to pull that selfsame Goddess down from her throne in the sky, but I had no other words at hand with which to offer a tribute.

It was just Dominic and me now.

I got to my feet. "It must be getting close to midnight," I said, dusting the snow from the knees of my breeches and shaking it from my cloak. "We should probably call the Verecundai soon . . ."

"Aurelia," Dominic said, his dark eyes solemn. "We need to talk about what we saw in the Gray."

"What is there to talk about?" I said.

"Maybe we could start with the fact that I . . ." His voice caught. "I'm to blame for all of this."

"Dominic," I began. "You can't—"

"I can," he said. "I'm not *just* Adamus. I'm Fidelis. I'm the one who wrote the Midnight Papers. *I'm* the one who founded the Circle Midnight. Everything that has happened . . . it is all my fault."

"No." I shook my head vehemently. "You are not to blame for this, Dominic. Two days ago I told you that I was not Vieve, and you believed me. You took my word for it. You must now give yourself the same courtesy. Forget Adamus. Forget Fidelis. You are Dominic Castillion, lord commander of Fort Castillion. You are clever and inventive and"—I cast my eyes to the sky—"*incredibly* exasperating. You're decent at Betwixt and Between—though let's both face it, I am better—and you're brave. And loyal. And . . . magnanimous, or . . . I don't know, pick your favorite of those other horseshit virtues you're always going on about." I moved in closer. "The point is, you are *you*."

Rather than appearing comforted, he looked as if my little speech had only served to cause him further pain.

Disquieted, I put my back to him. "So," I said, trying to make my voice light and flippant. "Let's call up those terrifying friends of yours, shall we?"

"Aurelia." He snagged my hand, and pressed something into it—a dagger, upon the hilt of which had been affixed a jeweled spider with seven legs, spread out like a shape of a star.

My throat went suddenly tight.

"No," I said.

"Ties will break," he replied, his brown eyes solemn as he stepped closer. "Blood will flow." He took my hand, still holding the dagger. "Steel your heart." He placed the point against his chest and whispered, "Strike the blow."

It was what the Verecundai had told me back at the sombersweet meadow. I'd thought he was insensible for that, but he'd heard it. He'd remembered it.

"*No,*" I said again, harsher this time, angry.

"You are not Vieve," he said. "And that's good, because Vieve's love for Adamus caused her to falter. She couldn't let him die, and they all paid the price for it." His hair danced against his cheek. "You will not make the same mistake."

I closed my eyes, letting two tears spill hot from beneath my lids.

He was so calm. "It's all right, my Two-Faced Queen. They told me long ago that you would be the end of me. Go ahead," he said. "Break my heart."

✷

After the first dozen blasts in quick succession, there followed an extended stretch of time that was quiet, and the Trove settled into the lull, listening intently, too rattled to believe that the fighting could be over already, so quickly.

As the silence stretched, so did Rosetta's nerves.

"I'm not sure I can take this much longer," she confided in Nathaniel, pacing in time to her staccato breaths. "I have to get out. I need air."

Ella was lying on her stomach at his feet. He'd given her a rock and showed her how to use it to scratch lines on the Trove floor, and she was busily drawing nonsensical little pictures on the stone.

"Very good," Nathaniel told her before scooping her up into his arms once again. "We'll have to get you some real paper and chalk." To Rosetta, he said, "I know another way out. A tunnel that leads out the other side of the mountain. If you think it will help, I'll show you where."

Rosetta could not hide her relief, and fell in step behind Nathaniel as he wove through the waiting crowd and led her up the stairs to the next level. No one paid much attention; everyone was listless and distressed.

"It's back here," he said. "Aurelia and I went through it once already, to sneak out from under Castillion's nose and head out to the Midnight Zone." He grimaced. "You know how that turned out."

"I do," Rosetta said. She peered into the tunnel and blanched; it was so tight, and so dark. Only the prospect of open air on the other end of it made her even *consider* venturing inside.

Ella made a strange little squawk and began to squirm out of Nathaniel's arms. "Ella," he chastised, kneeling to keep from dropping her. "It's not safe for you to run around up here. Ella!"

The little girl darted past him and into the mouth of the tunnel. "Well, I guess we've got to go through now," Rosetta said. "She seems to have a sense when something is about to . . . Nathaniel?"

Nathaniel's body had suddenly stiffened, his countenance going blank. The centers of his eyes began rapidly enlarging. Beyond the ledge, alarmed shouts started to echo up from the bottom of the Trove. Within moments, the whites of his eyes were entirely gone, and his hand had moved mechanically to the hilt of his sword.

Rosetta spun on her heel and darted toward the tunnel, scooping Ella into her arms as she ran.

"It's all right, I've got you," she said, over and over, as they moved deeper and deeper into the darkness, though she wasn't sure if the words were meant to reassure the two-year-old or herself. She could hear Nathaniel clunking around in the tunnel behind them, his sword clanging from wall to wall as he blindly slashed the space in front of him.

When she got the first whiff of cold, fresh air, she began to feel some hope. She hugged Ella tightly when she saw the opening—a small circular hole. She pushed Ella through first and crawled on her belly after her, only to feel Nathaniel's sharp blade slice into her leg. She kicked backwards as hard as she could, connecting with his face. It stopped him just long enough to allow her to tumble free of the exit, rolling out onto the narrow strip of snowy ledge.

Ella was crying, her back against the mountainside. "I've got you," Rosetta repeated, reaching for the girl, only to let out a curdled scream as Nathaniel's sword swiped heavily against her back. Instinctively, she curled her body around the child as Nathaniel, utterly out of his senses, struck her again and again and again.

"Stop," Rosetta begged. "Nathaniel, wake up. Don't hurt her. You love her. You only just got her back."

But he didn't listen—he couldn't hear her. She could smell the stench of corrupted blood magic on him—sickly and sulfuric—but she could not lift her hands to cast a counterspell of her own without leaving Ella exposed to the swing of her father's sword. "Nathaniel, stop!" she cried one last time, throwing her arms around Ella and whirling together with her away from the punishing edge of the blade. Nathaniel's swing struck empty air, and the momentum sent him stumbling backwards, over the edge and into the blackness below.

✱

Cecily wrestled Jessamine to the ground, straddling her body and pinning her arms as Conrad stared and Emilie screamed, rushing to Kellan's side.

Fidelis laughed as he backed toward his getaway skiff.

The northern lights pulsated in an array of vivid colors, green and violet and pink following specific, precontrived paths that intersected with each other like a spider's web.

"The Bitter Fever was not made *just* to weaken your old, iniquitous kingdoms. Not just to thin your ranks, not just to break your spirit," Fidelis said, triumphant. "It also has the valuable side effect of putting all those that survive it under *my* control. It was made with my blood. I *am* the Bitter Fever."

"The knife!" Cecily barked at Conrad as Jessamine writhed beneath her. "Take her knife!"

Conrad swooped down and pried the blood-slick blade from the Canary girl's clawlike fingers.

Emilie had grabbed Kellan by his cloak and rolled him over, trying desperately and unsuccessfully to stanch the blood pouring from his side with just her hands. It was of no use, however; the puncture was surely fatal.

Conrad sank to his knees beside them. "Kellan?" he said, his voice small and quivering. "Kellan, I'm sorry. If I had been older, and smarter . . . a better king . . ." He tried to gulp down his guilt, but it only bubbled back up in childish little hiccups.

"Chydaeus," Fidelis called in his most soothing voice. "There's still time. You have the blade. You can finish the rite. You don't need them, you never did."

Conrad gritted his teeth and tightened his grip on the knife, then got to his feet, ready to lunge for the man he'd once revered.

But he couldn't move; something was holding him back.

He turned to see that Kellan had reached up with his silver hand and grabbed a fistful of Conrad's Midnighter robe.

"No," Kellan said, wheezing. "You're . . . you *are* a good king. You just needed . . . a better . . . protector."

He let go of Conrad's robe, some of the silver of his arm rippling and remolding, flowing up around his shoulder and over his leather breastplate, pooling into the wound in his torso and filling it.

Slowly Kellan rose to his feet. "I am a knight of the Renaltan realm," he said, repeating the oath he'd taken long ago, when he received his first assignment as Aurelia's bodyguard. "Sworn to protect the crown, and the rightful monarch who bears it."

He lifted his silver hand, and a sword began to form within it, a gleaming blade with a hawthorn branch hilt.

But Fidelis smiled and drew his own. "As it happens," he said to Emilie, who had wrapped her arms around Conrad, pulling him clear of the impending fight, as Cecily continued to hold the writhing Jessamine to the ground, "I am *perfectly* willing to get my hands dirty."

The sound of a swordfight began to ring out as Grandmaster Fidelis and Kellan Greythorne clashed in an arena of ice and empty sky. What Fidelis lacked in training he made up for in mad determination, throwing himself into the fight like a rabid dog. Every time their blades met, a shower of sparks burst from the collision of metal against metal, raining down upon them. Soon, Fidelis's woolen robe was peppered with tiny, smoldering holes.

One more slash and parry, and Kellan had robbed Fidelis of his sword. He pointed his quicksilver blade at Fidelis's chest and said, "Stand down, Fidelis. You can't win."

"Stand down? *Stand down?* Oh no. You'll have to kill me, boy," Fidelis said, grinning through blood streaming from his nose. "Or the fever will never stop."

"Do it!" Cecily said, as Jessamine thrashed blindly beneath her. "Kellan!"

"No," Emilie said, coming up behind him. "This task is mine."

Kellan dropped his sword and stepped aside.

"You wouldn't hurt me," Fidelis said. "I'm your father."

"You had the chance," Emilie said, echoing the words she'd heard him say when he thought she'd been burned at the stake, "and you squandered it." As she spoke she drew a little feral spell into the air —one of warmth, of fire—and the knot wrote itself into his robe, connecting the smoldering dots until they burst fully into flame.

"No," Fidelis began to scream, trying to pat the flames out. "No! No! Emilie!"

But the fire was a spell, and would not be so easily quenched. Soon, he was fully engulfed, a pillar of orange tongues against the northern sky, where a storm of light and color had begun to churn.

"Goodbye, Father," Emilie said.

54

NOW

MIDWINTER

I looked at Dominic through bleary eyes. His face was edged with sadness, but also marked with purpose. He slowly unbuttoned the length of his shirt and pulled it out from under the knife, so that the point was pressed directly into the center of the spider scar on his chest beneath it.

"I can't do it," I said. "I can't."

"You can," he said, touching my cheek with a gentleness I did not deserve. "And you must."

Beneath the knife point, a thin droplet of blood had appeared. And with it came the first quivering call of magic. "Operimentum in nebula," Dominic said. *From clouds, a shroud.*

Welcome, the Verecundai said, their harsh voices sweeping in with the mist. *Welcome, Adamus and Vieve, queen and consort, reborn as was long ago written in our blood and yours.*

The dim, diaphanous forms of the Verecundai sharpened as they each retook their places on the outside ring of the glade, leaving a single space empty near the top for the last missing member of their cadre.

It is time to finish this. It is time to make our wrongs right.

My hands, on the knife, began to tremble uncontrollably.

Steel your heart, strike the blow. I repeated the mantra in my head, over and over. *Steel your heart, strike the blow. Steel your heart, strike the blow.*

And still, I could make no move against him. "Maybe," I said, "maybe it doesn't have to be this way."

"Vieve said that for the spell to make the Empyrea mortal to work, it would require the sacrifice of all eight members of the Verecundai. *Including* Adamus," he said. "Including me. It's all right, Aurelia. I came to this glade expecting to die once already and instead got thirteen more years of life. I accomplished more than I ever dreamed. And I met you." Softer, he said, "I only ever wanted to be remembered, and now I will."

Eyes full of aching tenderness, he wrapped both of his hands around mine, steadying me. Giving me strength. Then, he helped me push it in, inch by inch.

He gasped with the pain but did not let go, until I forced it the rest of the way between his ribs with a wrenching sob, just to end his agony. We sank down to the ground together, and I pulled his silver head into my lap and sobbed, my forehead against his as his lifeblood spilled out across his pale chest and began to soak the snow beneath him.

"I was wrong," I said as the light in his eyes began to dim. "I said I didn't love you, but I was wrong." I pressed a kiss against his lips, tasting magic, and his heart thudded its final beat and went still.

Aurelia.

I looked up from Dominic's mortal body—to find his spirit standing over us, dressed in molten shadow, like the other Verecundai. He gave me a tender smile, and turned to take his place at the highest point of the ring—on a clock, it would be five minutes to midnight.

With the eighth member of the Verecundai returned, the star was whole once again.

Blue-white light pooled beneath me, and I gently moved Dominic's body from my lap and laid his hands across his chest in repose. Then I stood, filling myself with the magic left behind in his cooling blood, and stretched out my hands.

I didn't have to wonder what to do—the knowledge was already there, waiting for me to reach for it, to free it from the deepest parts of my ancient soul.

The Spinner's spell awakened to my call, and I was suddenly surrounded by the incandescent filaments of light and power that had been waiting, inert, for a millennium. In hue, they were the same colors as the northern lights overhead, but they hummed like the strings of a violin with my every minute movement, an intricate web of music and magic, ready for its maestro to complete the last stanzas of her unfinished symphony.

I knew what to do instinctually, as if I'd practiced this same spell a thousand times before. Because I had. Vieve had. With every move —laying one string over another, plucking here and finessing there —the next and the next became more clear. I realized the pattern: I was weaving a tapestry of starlight, a glimmer of celestial magic that was born of, and bound to, the terrestrial sphere. I was creating a star of the earth that could be seen from the sky, equal parts offering and affront to the Goddess of the heavens.

And it did not take long for her to take notice.

She formed herself from the roiling firmament, a creature of liquid light, her stamping hooves beating so hard against the arc of the atmosphere I expected it to crack to pieces beneath her, and shower us with falling shards of sky.

The Empyrea was coming.

★

With Ella in her arms, Rosetta half slid, half stumbled down the back side of the mountain to the place where Nathaniel's body had come to rest, forty feet below the ledge from which he had fallen.

When she reached him, his eyes had cleared of their darkness, and he blinked up at her with irises the color of umber.

He was alive, but only just.

The damage inside him, when Rosetta reached out with an exploratory spell, was catastrophic. Her skill, on its own, was insufficient to save him. He coughed, sputtering blood, and Ella clambered from Rosetta's grasp to burrow in the crook of his arm.

Rosetta, swallowing her own sorrow, removed her cloak—still hanging together, despite being crisscrossed by new slits from the slice of Nathaniel's sword—and tucked it around father and daughter, so that their last moment together would be one of warmth. Then she traced little spells of comfort into his skin, soothing away his pain.

"I can't be sad," he said between labored breaths, repeating what he'd told her in the Trove, "that you're invulnerable."

"I'll take care of her," Rosetta whispered, curling up in the rocky snow beside them. "I'll see her grown." She kissed his forehead, resting her cheek against his hair and cradling them both as his life force flickered and ebbed away. "I promise you. I promise you. Go now to the After, knowing that your little girl will be safe and loved."

"Thank . . . you," he said, and then he turned his gaze to a plane Rosetta could not see, and breathed one final word. *"Kate."*

Overhead, the clouds began to gather, and the northern lights spread across the sky.

✶

Come and find me.

Everything had slowed to a crawl—the ash stinging Zan's cheeks; the billowing smoke; the movement of his hair, wet from snow and sweat; and the swing of his arm as he so desperately blocked and parried, vastly outnumbered by adversaries in a sea of fallen comrades. The inside assault from the fever survivors had wreaked havoc upon their forces, and both the upper and lower levels of Fort Castillion were littered with the bodies of the dead. By the time the fever-madness had unexpectedly dissipated and all traces of the bitter blackness had cleared from their eyes, little more than a third of their fighters were left alive; and now the Midnighters had reached the shore.

Come and find me.

Zan.

Another fiery missile from the Circle's naval ballistae struck just in front of Zan in the fort's courtyard, sending him flying back through the Night Garden's wall, where his body came to a stop in the center cloister, on a bed of glass from the broken dome, surrounded by frost-lace flowers just beginning to unfurl their filigree petals. He stared dazedly through the twisted, metal bones of the glassless greenhouse, where the wind was raging and the sky was boiling. A figure of terrifying majesty had begun to descend, made of smoke and cloud and colored flame.

Zan!

The voice was more urgent now, touched with fear.

Aurelia's voice.

He'd heard her call like that for him once before, the night of Ella's birth and Kate's death, a cry that had sent him tearing through the forest, abandoning his father's hunt, just to get to her side.

Every part of him hurt, but he rolled over in the broken glass and got to his feet by pulling himself up against her cracked and empty casket. *Si vivis, tu pugnas,* he told himself. *If not for yourself, for her.*

Live for her. Fight for her.

Outside the Night Garden, and beneath the descending equine deity, another horse came galloping toward him through the mist. "Madrona," he said through cracked lips, and she bent to allow him to crawl up on her back.

I'm coming, Aurelia.

55

NOW

MIDWINTER

The Empyrea was a black horse now, rearing up on her powerful, half-corporeal legs, screaming with the force of a hurricane. She bore down on me, ready to stamp me into dust, her power more vast and limitless than I could have ever dreamed. And even as my quicksilver body sang with the heady joy of the Spinner's spell, I found my mortal heart full of doubts. Because, even as terrifying and brutal as this descendant, deific creature was, she was also *exquisite*.

Could I do it? Could I take the Empyrea's immortality from her? Could I render her killable, and then take her life?

Could I snuff out all of this dazzling power and light?

But I had to—didn't I? I had to end her, so the rest of humanity could live on. Because humans were imperfect and flawed and beautiful—sparks that flared and broke into new sparks before dying out, turning fallow.

The things that are most beautiful are the ones that are finite and fleeting. A falling star. A flake of snow. A fertile season. A mortal life.

Love.

Everything that was good and wonderful in the world had an end. Living forever with unlimited power had shaped the Empyrea, had divorced her from the pitfalls and perils of humanity. She could not know love, as she had never experienced it. She did not know what it was to be rocked to sleep with a lullaby, or to listen to a delicate heartbeat in a loved one's chest. She did not know the agony of loss, because she had never cherished anything enough to grieve losing it.

I closed my eyes and reached for the magic of mortality. I could feel it everywhere in the Ebonwilde—the crumbling leaves beneath the snow, the scrape of beetle's wings in the loam far below. It was in the turn of each season, and the frostlace buds opening now on the coldest, longest night, into blossoms that would never see the sun. It was in the saplings that might never grow tall enough to scrape out their own piece of open sky, and in the slow grinding of bones into dust over centuries.

I imagined Conrad's shiny hair, and his many-colored ribbons, and his laugh as he discovered the final trick of a puzzle box that opened to a trove of cinnamon candy. I thought of the Canary girls and their tavern full of rowdy children, of Jessamine and her Cecily, of the starlike tears in Rosetta's eyes as she watched Nathaniel and Ella find each other again. I imagined Dominic's wicked grin across the

Betwixt and Between table, and Onal's angry remonstrations when I confused herbs again. I thought of Kellan and Emilie, those who'd suffered grievously at my hand and in my defense and still could find it within them to forgive me. I thought of Kate's warm hearth and yellow kitchen, of a little girl named Begonia who loved dolls. I thought of Vieve and Adamus, the star-crossed pair who'd met their ends in this very spot, whose love caused their own rebirth ten centuries later. And I thought of Zan, the sad and troubled boy with green eyes, now gold, who wanted to buy a horse from me and stole it instead. The prince who'd loved me enough to let me go.

Come and find me.

Zan.

This is what it means to be human, I thought, gathering those memories to me and letting them flow through me the way my blood once did. *This is what the Ilithiya spent the last of her divine light to create. Hundreds and thousands of stories. Heartbreaks and triumphs. Sorrows and joys.* And I found myself sorry, so very sorry, that this being of light, this creature of the stars, would never understand the beauty of it.

Unless she were able to experience it herself.

I remembered Jessamine's words. *I don't believe that who we are is ever set in stone. We are transitory creatures—every day, we wake up as someone new, changed just a little bit by the experiences of the day before. Who we were is always a part of us, but it doesn't determine who we are, nor who we can still become.*

If the Malefica could become Lily, could not her sister also become . . . someone new?

I opened the vial around my neck and emptied the last two drops of my blood into my hands.

When the Empyrea charged at me again, I did not dodge or counterattack. I let her come, and when she got near, I threw my arms around her neck and held her tight as she bucked and screamed. The strings of the Spinner's spell began to dissolve around me, encircling both me and this thrashing Goddess in ribbons of radiant light. I held tight as she changed from horse to dragon to a pillar of fire so hot I wondered how I was not yet ash. She became an ocean, a mountain, a star, and then a void blacker than the deepest edge of night, and still I clung to her, pouring every ounce of my strength—and that of the Verecundai, and of Dominic, and every living thing in the Ebonwilde —into just holding on. And when I reached the bottom of the well of my power, I cried out for the person I knew would hear me, would answer my call.

Zan!

And I heard his reply.

I'm coming, Aurelia.

Filled with new strength, my arms and my power tightened around the Empyrea.

Below, I saw frostlace blossoms unfurl their silvery petals before the light expanded past them, enfolding them into the magic.

Frostlace for forgetting.

I could feel the Empyrea's fight waning as I continued to pour light and love and memory into the link between us.

Sleep, I told her in soft, soothing tones.

Forget.

Hush, now.

I've got you.

Forget.

I won't let go.

Forget.

I'll teach you everything you need to know.

I'll love you.

I promise.

You'll see.

And, slowly, slowly, her struggle against me quieted, slowed. Her light grew malleable in my hands and I did what I imagined the Ilithiya doing all those eons ago, when she first shaped her divine light into the form of a human life. We sank down and down together, tired and weak, coming to rest at the center of the glade.

I removed my cloak and wrapped it around her tiny body. Her skin was pink and new, and I gazed in awe at this creature in my arms. The Empyrea transformed.

Somewhere, far in the distance, I heard the ringing of bells. Midnight had passed. Midwinter was over.

From here on out, each day would grow longer, brighter, warmer.

"Aurelia?"

I looked up to see Zan dismounting Madrona. He was haggard with the effects of his own battles, but his eyes were bright, like discs of summer sun. He started across the quiet glade, first walking gingerly, then breaking into a run. I rose to meet him, stumbling, and he threw his arms around me, kissing away the tears that had begun to flow freely down my cheeks, before burying his face in my hair.

And then, the bundle in my arms began to squall.

"Is this . . . ?" he asked, and I nodded.

Mouth parted, he moved the fabric aside to reveal a tiny face and eyes the color of midnight and flecked with tiny chips of incandescent silver: the glory of the night sky, caught inside a new human body.

"We'll call her Aster," he said, kissing me. "Both flower and star."

PART IV

THE JOURNEY'S END

EPILOGUE

The wedding took place on the first day of spring.

The bride was radiant in a gown of ivory spider silk, the groom dressed in a golden cloak. They both wore charms on chains around their necks: Hers, a dragon. His, a gryphon.

The officiant, too, was similarly adorned. His pendant was made of garnet and carnelian, inlaid into the shape of a firebird. The jewels winked in the light of the twenty-five candles that burned on silver candlesticks at the center of the cloister, one for each year of Dominic Castillion's life. They'd burned now for three months, replaced every day, with the old candles lighting the new ones.

When the bride and groom reached the center of the garden, light was falling in long, golden shafts through the scattered panes of the dome still waiting for new glass. There, they joined hands—hers scarred, his silver—and beamed at each other as they were pronounced husband and wife.

As Kellan and Emilie kissed, Zan met my eyes from over their heads and I smiled gently back at him before turning my attention to the bundle in my arms, which had begun to mewl.

That night, the king of the new, united Western Realms stood at the head of the banquet hall of Fort Castillion to raise a toast to the newlyweds. In the weeks since his tenth birthday, he'd shot up a whole two inches. His hair, too, was beginning to grow out. It had darkened into a sandier shade of blond, but was still just as curly as ever.

"To Kellan and Emilie," Conrad said, lifting his glass. "Lord and lady protector of the new realm." His gaze was solemn—he had gained many of his old memories back, but his time with the Circle Midnight had greatly changed him. "I know it is not an easy thing I've asked you to do—putting all of your own wishes and plans aside to stay here and guide me through the next years of reconstruction. But I do not think I could do it without you. So thank you. Thank you both."

We all drank to that.

Cecily, seated across the table from Zan and me, shuffled a deck of playing cards. "Can I interest any of you in a game of Betwixt and Between?" she asked.

Jessamine came behind her, kissing the top of her head before warning us, "Don't fall for it. She's a shark. You'll leave here naked and shoeless if you go against her, mark my words."

"She's just sour," Cecily said, "because I'm so much better at it than her."

"I never should have taught you," Jessamine said with a glum shake of her head.

"I think we'll pass," Zan said. "I'm rather fond of these shoes."

As the celebration began to wane, I saw Rosetta stand to leave, and so I transferred the bundle of blankets into Zan's arms while I hurried to catch her in the courtyard.

"Rosetta," I called. "Wait!"

She turned to look at me, careful not to disturb the sleeping Ella, who was drooling onto her shoulder.

"Before you go," I said. "That thing you asked me to do . . . back at the homestead . . . I think I can do it. If you want me to try."

Her voice was soft. "Maybe someday I will take you up on the offer," she said. "But for right now . . . I think I'll keep my invulnerability just a little bit longer."

When I returned to the gathering, I overheard Jessamine talking to Zan. "Well, Sad Tom. You did become a king after all—if only for a few short days. Where are you three headed now that you have given up power and fame and untold wealth?"

"Home," he said simply, and I smiled.

The next day, we said goodbye to my brother and our friends and began our own trek into the Ebonwilde. I hummed a little lullaby to Aster as we went—an old folk song my mother once sang to me. Zan, listening, put his arms around me.

Somewhere deep inside that woodland sea, in the ruins of a once-great city, a cottage lined with yellow flowers was waiting for our return.

ACKNOWLEDGMENTS

The first and most profuse of my thanks must go to my editor, Cat Onder, who guided Aurelia's journey—and mine—from beginning to end. I'll be forever grateful for your insight, encouragement, and patience. Huge thanks must also go to Gabby and to the teams at HMH Teen and Clarion Books for all of their hard work on this book and on this series as a whole. Much love and gratitude also to my all-star agent, Pete Knapp, and to the extraordinary people at Park and Fine literary. A hearty thank-you to ultra-talented cover artist Chantal Horeis, map-maker extraordinaire Francesca Baerald, and to ace designer Celeste Knudsen. And to all of the people who've worked tirelessly behind-the-scenes on this book and on the Bloodleaf series.

Thank you to Carolanne for always knowing how to fix it, to Brandon for making it a game, to Carma for the positivity, to Melody for providing the soundtrack, and to Stacy, Katey, and Tiffany for cheering me on. To my Mom and Dad, for the steady support and endless, cheerful generosity. You're always there for us in a pinch and I can't thank you enough.

Thanks to Amy, Paula, Stan, Logan, Beth, and Marcus—if I tried to fully express how much I appreciate everything you do, I'm sure it would end up as a hilarious text chain and we'd all be cry-laughing by the end of it.

To Jamison and Lincoln—I'm so proud to be your mom. Thank you for hanging in there with me when I'm distracted and sleep-deprived and ordering DoorDash for the tenth time in a week. To Keaton, for keeping it (and me) together. Couldn't have done it without you.

And to my readers: thank you for taking this journey with me.